MARY CRAWFORD

Identity OF THE Heart

HIDDEN HEARTS BOOK 1

COPYRIGHT

Published on September 21, 2015 by Diversity Ink Press and Mary Crawford. Publisher may be reached at MaryCrawfordAuthor.com.

ISBN-13: 978-1-945637-29-2

Large print edition: ISBN-13: 978-1-945637-23-0

Cover by Covers Unbound.

HIDDEN BEAUTY SERIES

Until the Stars Fall from the Sky
So the Heart Can Dance
Joy and Tiers
Love Naturally
Love Seasoned
Love Claimed
If You Knew Me (and other silent
musings) (novella)
Jude's Song
The Price of Freedom (novella)
Paths Not Taken
Dreams Change (novella)
Heart Wish (100% charity release)
Tempting Fate
The Letter
The Power of Will

HIDDEN HEARTS SERIES

Identity of the Heart
Sheltered Hearts
Hearts of Jade
Port in the Storm (novella)
Love is More Than Skin Deep
Tough
Rectify
Pieces (a crossover novel)
Hearts Set Free
Freedom (a crossover novel)
The Christmas Message (novella)
Love and Injustice (Protection Unit)
Out of Thin Air (Protection Unit)
Soul Scars (Protection Unit)

OTHER WORKS:
The Power of Dictation
Vision of the Heart
#AmWriting: A Collection of Letters to Benefit The
Wayne Foundation

Dedication

To all the soul mates out there.

Whether you find yours through adoption, online
dating, or the old-fashioned way,

Love them the best you can.

Chapter One

Rogue

"I THOUGHT I TOLD YOU guys not to do this crap!" I protest as I examine the 356 email messages from the BrainsRSexy online dating service. "Where did you guys find that strange picture of me? I don't even recognize that shirt and I swear I haven't had that color of eye shadow since I had braces."

Marcus raises an eyebrow at me, "You sat still long enough for braces?" he asks sarcastically.

Sticking my tongue out through my sparkling white Chiclet teeth like a six-year-old, I ask again, "Funny, but seriously, where'd you get that picture?"

Marcus looks up from where he's sketching a design on the light-box. "I don't know. I wasn't really paying attention. We were all playing pool and online poker on the computer, and someone thought it would be funny to set up a profile for you. Somebody probably had it on their Facebook or Instagram or something."

"First of all, unless you guys are going to pay me

like a reality show and come attached with Ashton Kutcher, you really should leave the punking to the professionals, because this really sucks." I turn the computer screen toward Marcus.

He cringes as he watches a particularly colorful video showing things a girl should never see even for six-seconds.

Ducking his head back toward the light-board, he mumbles an apology in my direction, "Oh man Rogue! I feel like I need to apologize for my entire gender. I swear not everyone's like that. There are some nice people on this site. My brother met his fiancée on this site. He swore there wasn't anything creepy involved."

I'm starting to feel a little bad for Marcus as he rakes his fingers through his spiky blond hair making it stand on end. He looks like he's had an unfortunate accident with a fully charged outlet. He's wearing large gauges in his ears today; so with his hair, piercings and many tattoos, he looks very fierce. In reality, he's about as scary as a golden retriever.

Usually, I'd have a bit of fun at Marcus's expense. Yet, he seems so upset over my displeasure I'm not sure he won't stroke-out at this point.

I sigh as I concede, "Look, you might be right. Some of these guys seem like they could be normal enough."

I narrow my eyes and pin him with my meanest stare. "But, you're not off the hook. You are supposed to be my best friend. That means you watch my back — even if you are slightly buzzed."

Marcus at least has the good sense to look

chagrined as he's suddenly very interested in getting a precision point on the pencil he's sharpening.

"If you ever get another harebrained idea to sign me up for a dating service, just ask me first," I continue. "I might even surprise you and say yes. But, I'd like to have free choice in the matter."

"Done." Marcus readily agrees. "I know this'll sound lame now. But, we didn't do this to hurt you. It's true — we didn't factor in the creepazoids, but my buddies who play pool with us thought you may meet guys who would knock you out of your rut and give you something positive to think about."

I shudder as I remember the more egregious pictures in my mailbox. "Trust me, I have lots to think about now, but not much of it's positive," I reply. I try for straight sarcasm, but I'm not completely successful in keeping my laughter at bay.

Marcus smirks at my joke. "Come on, you know what I mean. I was trying to get your mind off of he-who-shall-not-be-mentioned."

"You mean Lawrence?" I lift a questioning eyebrow in Marcus's direction.

"I'm just saying the guy has a lot of nerve for someone whose last name is Poser," Marcus mutters bitterly.

"Marcus, it's sweet for you to be all ticked off about it. But, he is just the latest in a string of guys to assume that just because I work at a tattoo parlor I must be randomly screwing bikers in the back room."

"Just because he's not the only one, it doesn't give

him a free pass. The guy was supposed to be your boyfriend. He should've known better than to believe the stereotype. Wasn't he also the charmer who said you'd be perfect for giving him 'little tax deductions' because of your wide Hispanic hips?"

Diet Coke surges up the back of my throat and threatens to come out my nose as I choke back a startled laugh. "You can understand why I don't miss him all that much. Still, it was fun to get into all those nightclubs. Well, let me rephrase that; it was fun to get into the ones he didn't own to do opposition research. Lawrence's were lame. You make a great wingman."

Marcus grins brightly as he declares, "I know. If I don't get you to come up for air every once in a while, my social skills will wither up and die."

"You poor baby. You know, I might actually have sympathy for you, but since I don't make your kind of money, I still have to work hard to keep my scholarship. So, that means studying and apprenticing here."

Marcus's bottom lip slides out like a four-year-old who's just been told that he has to take a nap. "Let me guess, you're not going to go out with any of these guys this weekend because you're too busy?"

"I don't know. There's this guy that wants to shoot his antique car collection and wants to use a couple of models. He requested me and I told him I would probably do it if I could get my art history paper done in time."

Marcus's eyebrows shoot up towards his hairline. "Oh really…"

Aggravated, I shoot a rubber band at him. "Oh

shut up! It's not like that. The last time I was there I exchanged recipes for empanadas with his very lovely wife. She insisted that he give me a big enough tip so I could buy two of my textbooks this term."

"Okay, so I was wrong. I worry about you going out on these modeling gigs," Marcus grudgingly admits.

"Says the guy who signed me up for an online dating service without telling me. Hypocritical much?"

"I totally deserve that. I know you're careful and I know I sound like a crazy, possessive overprotective brother—"

I roll my eyes at him. "Yeah, I'm sure that Sadie would be thrilled if you returned to your post in her life. After all, what freshman girl doesn't want her tattooed, menacing big brother lurking in the hall?"

Marcus scowls over the top of his drafting easel. "Darn straight I should be there. Do you have any idea what eighteen-year-old boys think about all day?"

I smirk at him. "Probably the same thing as twenty-five-year-old men."

He moans and buries his head in his hands, "What's so great about UCLA? There are lots of wonderful schools in Florida."

"Relax, Marc. You've been teaching her to scrape off the bottom-feeders since she was about twelve. She is a pro now. You did your job well — just like you've done with me."

Embarrassed by my admission, I walk over to the filing cabinets and start to re-file the stack of reference drawings and portfolio pictures.

Marcus drapes his arm around my shoulder and pulls me towards his side for a hug.

"Don't mention it," he replies, brushing off the compliment. "I'm your most annoying best friend, it's part of my mandatory job duties."

"Just so you don't get a big head or anything, I feel compelled to point out you are virtually my only friend here in the land of sunny beaches and palm trees."

"Those are just details … you have to look at the big picture here."

"Yeah, you're right. Let's analyze this. You miss your sister. So, you obviously need to make a road trip. Is she planning to come home for break?"

"No! Can you believe this? She said she had too much studying to do over break to make it worth the cost to fly home. I don't think she knows how much I make on a custom back piece," he muses, frustration seeping from every pore.

It's a good thing Marcus can't see my face as I smother a grin. I suspect his little sis is spending Thanksgiving at her boyfriend's place. But, there may be certain things my friend just isn't ready to hear.

"She's probably just busy," I answer carefully.

Marcus gasps. "Rogue Betancourt, you did not just use your 'socially acceptable' polite voice on me!"

The spider web in the ceiling fan is becoming more interesting with each beat of my pounding heart. I hate lying to Marcus — even by omission. Yet, when it comes down to it; it's not even my story to tell.

I nod a tight nod.

A pained look crosses his face. "Despite my zaniness, I know I can always count on you not to feed me any crap — even if it's hard. Why are you changing the rules now?"

I sigh as I choose my words with precision, "Marc, you're my best friend too and sometimes I choose not to tell you things because I know they are going to just stress you out. This is one of those times."

Marcus groans in frustration. "Oh great! Now, I have to wait a whole week and wonder what you mean."

I reach up and pat him gently on the cheek. I sigh. "Okay, don't say I didn't try to warn you. I suspect Sadie is spending Thanksgiving with her boyfriend. It's a scary, liberating thing for a woman the first time she spends a holiday away from her family."

"Woman?" Marcus sputters. "She's still a little girl. She just recently got her driver's license."

I massage the tense muscles in his shoulders. "Marc, I know it's hard, but Sadie is nineteen. Still, thanks to you, she's also incredibly savvy and smart when it comes to guys so she'll be just fine."

"Maybe, but now we definitely need to take that road trip to see what's going on. There is a trade show in San Francisco at the end of December. Does that match up with your break from school?"

"That's a nice fantasy Marcus, but I could never afford to go to California," I shrug out of his half embrace.

Marcus catches my arm and spins me around so I have to look at him. "Look, you're here as an apprentice.

Part of the experience is learning about all the new trends and techniques as well as scoping out the equipment and inks. A trade show is a great way to do that. I know it's easy to forget that I'm a part owner in this place because I'm such a dork, but it is my responsibility to make sure you get properly trained. I would pick up the cost of your trip. I'm not doing this because we're friends. I'm doing this because I want to make you a better tattoo artist."

I'm a little surprised by the serious tone in his voice. Although, I'm not sure why — I know that despite all appearances, Marcus is incredibly successful at what he does and dedicated to his craft. There is nothing more devastating to Marcus than someone who is not happy with their tattoo. Yet, despite the fact that he's made a huge name for himself and is starting to get national recognition, he would rather downplay all of his success and live like a college frat boy. He doesn't treat anybody differently now than he did when I met him five years ago when he was just starting out.

Usually, I'm relatively good at keeping my emotions in check, but my elation over the opportunity to go to California with Marcus to an actual trade show and see Sadie again is just too much to hide. I start bouncing on the balls of my feet as I grin widely. "I'll have to check my schedule to see when my last final is over. I'll make sure I don't take any modeling jobs that week."

"Are you sure you don't want to change your mind about getting some ink?" Marcus asks me with a twinkle in his eye. This is an old debate between us. He's been trying to convince me to get a tattoo for years. He thinks it's hysterically funny I'm apprenticing to be a tattoo artist but I don't have any tattoos yet. I have reams of drawings of tattoos I plan to get — someday.

"With your amazing body and stunning face, I bet there will be some famous tattoo artists who would be itching to use your body as a canvas."

"I know that I'm no Sofia Vergara. For now, I make a few extra dollars on the side as a model. It's easier for me to book jobs if they don't have to cover tattoos with makeup. So, for now it's purely a financial decision for me. I don't plan to make a career out of modeling, it's just a means to make it possible for me to go to school."

Marcus takes a good long leering look at me. "Speaking as your friend here, not your employer, I don't know whoever gave you the idea you're not as hot as Sofia Vergara."

I laugh at his expression. "Knock it off, Marcus. I'm so firmly in the friend zone with you, I doubt you even remember I'm a girl. Do I need to remind you that you challenged me to a burping contest last week?"

"Oh, you mean the contest you almost won? If I hadn't been assisted by a liter of Dr. Pepper, you would've won it hands down. Just because you are my best friend doesn't mean I can't appreciate your many assets as a woman," Marcus wiggles his eyebrows suggestively.

"You might not believe this, but having you as my best friend has really built up my self-confidence. Thanks to you, I can tell when a guy is sincerely into me or just feeding me a line. You've given me some valuable information about guys and their go-to-plays. It's really helped me sort out the crap and not take it personally."

"Geez, I feel like I've broken some sacred man

code or something," Marcus mutters under his breath.

"No really! You don't understand how helpful it's been." I pace around the workspace as I become more animated. "You have no idea what it's like to walk down the street and have people comment on my appearance when all I'm trying to do is grab a cup of coffee. Guys make catcalls and suggestive comments as if I'll think it's some sort of aphrodisiac and drop my panties right there. Before I met you, I used to take all this stuff personally — like there was something wrong or defective with me. I thought maybe I was putting out some weird vibe to attract all the creeps. After you've spent all these years explaining 'guy-ness' to me, I realize that it's not me, it's them. Hanging around you has been great for my self-esteem."

Marcus looks befuddled. "I think there's a compliment in there somewhere. I don't want you to think all guys are like those misogynistic jerks who degrade you on the street. There are better classes of men out there. You just need to find them. I promise we exist."

I stop and look at my handsome best friend and wonder again why he's still single. "I know men like you exist. I see how you treat women and you are amazing to the women in your life. Why some great chick hasn't snatched you off the market is beyond me."

"Maybe I have some pretty great women in my life that show me how high the bar should be and my standards are really high," Marcus comments as he does a full body shake. "Enough of this serious talk. We are so going to go to Disneyland and Universal Studios when we go to California. I want to see if it's different from

Disney World. Besides, the little routine you have going on that you call life is entirely too serious. You're not too scared to go on the roller coasters are you?"

"Umm, no —" I reply, laughing. "But I have heard the It's a Small World ride is a little creepy."

CHAPTER TWO

IVY

"Jessica, come here. You remember that guy, Daniel, I was talking to on BrainsRSexy.com? Look at this message he sent me!" I yell across the room in disgust.

"Great bait and switch babe. Thought you said you were an accountant, not some tattoo bimbo."

Jessica gasps as she reads the text message over my shoulder. "Oh my gosh, what a toolbox. I thought you said you had to reschedule your date with this guy because of your exam."

"I did, so I don't know what his deal is. He sounds psycho. I'm going to block him. It's weird though, because I had several conversations with him and I thought he seemed pretty normal. Maybe this online dating thing was a bad idea."

"Oh, come on. You can't write everyone off just because one guy is weird. Didn't you tell me you've had several conversations with cool guys? Scoot over." With one shove, my roommate literally pushes me out of my desk chair and onto my bed.

After a couple minutes, Jessica squeals with excitement, "Oh Ivy! Did you look at this guy, Mitch? He's a business major, but he volunteers for search and rescue and he has his own search dog which he rescued from the shelter. He trained it from a puppy. He sounds perfect for you. He's totally cute too; his muscles go on for days."

With a reluctant sigh, I unfold my long limbs, hop off the bed and peer over her shoulder at my online profile. She's right; the guy has a strong resemblance to Matthew McConaughey in his more rugged days. But, as I examine his profile more closely, I see a couple of problems. "Jessica, this says he likes petite women and redheads. In case you haven't noticed, I'm almost five-foot-nine, with nearly jet-black hair. I'm neither."

"Pshaw. Those are cosmetic things. I'm talking about the match of your souls — you know, the things that make you guys truly tick," Jessica retorts with a grin.

"*Pshaw?* Did you seriously just say that? What are you — eighty?" I tease. "Anyway, have you ever tried to date anyone shorter than you? It's a drag. Guys get all insecure about it and then I feel like I have to slouch all the time to minimize the difference. It literally becomes a pain in my neck."

Jessica laughs. "Yes, I'm well aware I talk funny. It's a side effect of being raised by my grandparents. You know good and well, the odds of me dating someone shorter than me are minuscule since I'm five-foot-one."

"Do you know how lucky you are? You get to be the cute, cuddly girlfriend he can tuck under his arm and protect from all the dangers of the world. He gets to be your hero and reach all the things you can't. You're a pocket-sized ball of cuteness. I, on the other hand, look like an oversized giraffe. Guys never know what to do with me. I'm too tall for them to tuck under their arm. Many times, I'm actually taller than the men I'm dating — especially if they lie about their height to their matchmaking friends — and I look really awkward dancing."

Jessica's eyes widen in surprise as she hears my self-assessment. "Seriously Ivy? Have you even looked in the mirror? You could be a runway model or something. The guys around campus nearly faint when you walk into the room. Do you really not notice this stuff?" she asks with an incredulous tone in her voice.

I shrug as I fend off her questions. "I don't know. I've always hated my hair. My parents have wonderful thick black, wavy curls. I have such boring 'straight, but manageable hair' as my mom likes to call it. I grew up hating it because it underscored how different I am from my parents. It's funny though, because my mom always says she's jealous of my straight locks."

"I hate to break it to you, but I think everyone is slightly jealous of your beautiful long hair. If I had your hair, I wouldn't be wearing mine in a 'stylish little pageboy' as my hairdresser calls my mess of a do," Jessica runs her hands through her hair. "I still think you should reply to this guy; I think he sounds nice."

I lift my shoulder in a casual shrug. "Whatever, go ahead. Why don't you chat with him for a while and see what you think? If he gets your seal of approval, I'll think about going out with him. I've got to study for my Economics exam. Summer classes are such a pain because they try to cram a whole term into a few weeks. I always feel like I'm behind."

"Doesn't Econ bore you to tears?" Jessica asks sympathetically.

I nod with a wistful expression on my face. "Sadly, yes. Unfortunately, every single class in my major puts me to sleep. The only classes I'm enjoying are the electives I have to take to fulfill the arts requirement of my liberal arts education."

Jessica shakes her head in disbelief. "Ivy Love Montclair! You do realize this *is* college and not high school, right? You don't have to take courses you don't like. You can choose to major in something you enjoy. Why are you torturing yourself with classes you hate?"

"I know, *I know.*" I acknowledge, regretfully. "My dad has always dreamed of opening an accounting firm with me — 'Montclair & Montclair'. I think he's probably already got the business cards printed. My parents have made so many sacrifices for me and I don't want to let him down."

Jessica scrunches her nose up at me and rolls her eyes. "Ivy, do you really believe your parents would want you to choose a career you absolutely hate just to make them happy? Your mom is a teacher. I know she would want you to choose something you're passionate about. I know without a shadow of a doubt you are not passionate about accounting."

"But I want to be, shouldn't that count for something?" I whisper.

"Yeah, it shows you love your dad an awful lot. But, it shouldn't be the only criteria for you to choose your career. I think you ought to go to the advising office and talk to somebody."

Just then, the computer beeps. Jessica and I read the message from Mitch with a mixture of confusion and horror.

Hi Ivy,

Is this some kind of weird joke? I was just talking to you two days ago, but I thought you said your name was Rogue. It's too bad because I thought you were kind of cool.

— Mitch

I quickly motion for Jessica to get up and I slide into my desk chair almost tipping it over in my haste.

At this moment, I'm grateful for all the summers I spent working in my dad's office, as I am able to respond to Mitch's text in record time.

Mitch,

There must be some mistake. I saw your profile for the first time today. You couldn't have been talking to me because I didn't contact you until about 30 seconds ago.

~ Ivy

I hit send. Jessica and I wait impatiently for his response. I can't imagine what it'll be. I walk over to the bed and pick up my Economics textbook. After two paragraphs, it's obvious it's an exercise in futility to pretend like I'm going to even try to study when my brain is completely occupied with the drama in front of me.

Finally, a message pops up on my screen.

Ivy,

Are you for real? Seriously, no kidding? Freaking spooky! This other chick, Rogue, looks just like you. Are you an Art major? Do you work at a tattoo place?

— Mitch

Jessica and I look at each other in disbelief. That's twice in one day tattoos have been mentioned. Something bizarre is going on.

Mitch,

Nope. Definitely not me. I'm an accounting major and I've never even set foot in a tattoo parlor. I don't know what the heck is going on. Can you look at my Facebook page and see if she's using any of my profile pictures?

Thank you so much. I'm sorry, I don't mean to bother you with this weird drama.

~ Ivy

I hit send and wait for Mitch's response. In the meantime, my mind is racing a million miles an hour. Of course, I've heard of cat-fishing. You'd have to live under a rock to not be familiar with the concept. What I don't understand is why someone would be interested in pretending to be me. If you looked up the word boring in the dictionary, it would literally have my picture. I lead the most non-exciting life ever.

The only creature who's ever been interested in my life is my cat, and that's only because I feed her. I had to leave her with my parents when I left home to go to college. I was so tired of the snow in Vermont I chose the warmest place I could think of to go to school. Well, actually Florida was my second choice. I didn't get into the school I wanted to in Hawaii. I'm so invisible here I can't imagine anyone would want to assume my identity.

One of the reasons I signed up for BrainsRSexy was to become less isolated. I've fallen into this weird rut of going to class, the library, and my job at the local ice cream parlor and not much else. Jessica threatened to line up all the guys from her classes and start randomly choosing numbers to set me up on blind dates.

My computer pings again and I glance at the screen with a mixture of trepidation and anticipation. Jessica has no such qualms as she's practically shouting in my ear, "Hurry up and open the message!"

Ivy,

Uber-weird. I didn't get the vibe from Rogue she was running a scam. In fact, we were on a Skype call and I was teasing her about her unusual first name and she showed me her driver's license to prove it was her real name. She has a Florida driver's license with the first name Rogue. I've never seen someone who works at a tattoo place who doesn't have tattoos. I thought it was odd. But, she seemed cool. I looked at your Facebook page, and her picture isn't any of the ones you have on Facebook.

— Mitch — curious in the land of Disney

Mitch,

I have no idea where she would get a picture of me if she

didn't get it from Facebook. I'm not on Instagram because my dad is weird about me posting pictures and the last time I had a MySpace page I think I was in junior high so you would've been able to tell the difference. This is creeping me out.

~ Ivy

Almost instantly, my computer beeps in response.

Ivy,

I don't know, maybe it's a coincidence. You know how they say everyone has a double somewhere. Try not to worry.

— Mitch

Mitch,

That's true. But, I wonder why people think we have the same profile?

~ Ivy

Again, my computer beeps right away.

Ivy,

Another excellent question. Unfortunately, I don't have a great answer.

— Mitch

Mitch,

Sadly, I have to study for my economics exam. So, I need

to go.

> *~ Ivy*

My computer beeps almost as quickly as I hit the send button.

:-)

Economics was one of my favorite classes. Good luck with the exam.

— Mitch

I guess my reaction should be quite telling. The fact that he likes economics actually makes him less attractive. I wonder what I should read into that. I'm sure there are thousands of volumes of psychological studies and abstracts on the very topic.

Just then, an idea strikes me and I sprint down the hall to my neighbor's room and bang on the door. A very startled guy in ratty sweatpants comes to the door. "Hey Craig, what's the name of the guy who graduated like three years ago? You know, the one who was going to start his own security firm specializing in identity theft?"

Craig stretches and yawns as he eyes my pajama shorts and my baby doll T-shirt. "Yeah? What's in it for me?" He leers.

I squint my eyes at him and shake my head. "If you ever want class notes for Poetry 250 which meets at 8 AM Monday, Wednesday, and Friday, I'm counting on you to cough up a name and phone number."

Craig belches and he holds up his hands in surrender. "Okay, no need to be mean about it. The dude's name is Tristan Macklin. He's got a business a couple blocks off campus. I've heard he's spooky good. Are you going into hiding or something? Somebody told me he's better than the witness protection program."

I laugh out loud at Craig's vivid imagination. "I'm sorry to disappoint you. But it's nothing quite as dramatic as that. I'll be sure to tell Tristan you said, 'Hi'." I reach forward to shake Craig's hand.

I watch as the color leaches out of Craig's face. "Oh, that's okay you don't have to mention it. I'll do you a solid because we're practically neighbors." He nervously wipes his hands on his pants and shakes my hand.

As I turn to leave the room, I look back. "For the record, I loved the poem you shared the other day in class. You should speak up more often." I don't think I've ever seen anyone blush in quite the shade of red as Craig's face, but he seems pleased by the compliment.

I'm still grinning when I reenter my dorm room. As soon as I hit the threshold, Jessica yells at me, "Where in the heck did you go? I left for one second to fix my contact lens and you were gone. With all this weirdness going on, I had no idea what happened to you. You left without saying a word. I was so scared!" At this point, she's practically beating me with her throw pillow.

"Oh my gosh Jessica, I didn't even think about it. I ran down to Craig and Derek's room to ask Craig a question," I answer, feeling chagrined.

"Oh man, if your answer was designed to make me feel better, it was an epic fail. Craig is seriously creepy." Jessica gives a full body shudder.

"Really? You think he's so bad? He's a little strange. I mean — you don't see very many full-grown men with a full contingent of Star Wars action figures in their dorm rooms, but other than that he seems nice enough to me. He always walks me to my car with an umbrella when it rains."

Jessica shakes her head at me. "I still find it hard to believe you're a couple years older than me. You seem to be missing some basic survival instincts. Did you not learn any street smarts along the way?" She raises a questioning eyebrow in my direction.

I giggle at her line of questioning. "Hello? I'm the daughter of a kindergarten teacher and an accountant from Coventry, Vermont. My idea of street smart is making sure nobody takes our table at Applebee's."

Jessica collapses on her bed in peals of laughter at my description of the perils of the rough side of suburban life. "Geez, no wonder you don't have a lick of common sense when it comes to judging other people. You grew up in Mayberry, USA. The sheriff came to your football games, didn't he?"

"Well, yes. It only makes sense considering his nephew was the star quarterback."

Jessica narrows her eyes as she examines me closely. "Wait … let me guess." She draws out the words and walks around me in a big circle, "Miss Big Hair and perfect body was a high school cheerleader."

I can't help but flush a deep shade of red. Instead of being proud of my accomplishment, it feels more like a scarlet letter of shame. Although I liked the athletic challenge of being a cheerleader, I never liked the petty social politics and the narcissistic class standing endowed because of it. "It wasn't a big deal. Almost everybody who tried out made it on the squad," I stammer.

"Were you on the squad all four years?"

I nod.

"I bet you were a flyer."

I nod again.

"Captain?" Jessica grins triumphantly.

"Co-Captain my junior year; Captain my senior year," I grudgingly admit.

"See, not only were you a cheerleader, you were a stellar cheerleader. Just like you're stellar at everything else. I know you've been trying to fly under the radar here, but it's not happening. You're the type of person who naturally shines regardless of your surroundings."

"That's sweet of you to say, but I'd just as soon be a background player. I'm not comfortable being front and center. It's the not fun part of being an only child. I had no choice but to be the kid on the awards stand whether I wanted to be or not."

"Hey, at least your parents actually know you exist. Mine couldn't care less. Trust me, there are worse things in life than parents who care too much. So, what can we do about this weird computer thing? If your parents found out about it, they would have an apoplexy and pull you out of school. They give the phrase over-protective new meaning."

"Well, they certainly would try, but I think I've reached an age where they no longer have the right to make decisions for me. Now, I'm not saying they wouldn't be able to guilt me into it, but the school isn't going to give them any right to make decisions for me," I declare with a degree of certainty.

"You know this how?"

"Technically, the law is on my side," I argue.

Jessica rolls her eyes at me and gives me a look of pity. "Well, you can have technicalities until the cows come home, but it won't matter a hill's worth of beans if your daddy thinks you're in danger. He'll march right down here from Vermont and haul your pretty little butt all the way home and lock you in your suburban paradise back in Coventry until he thinks it's safe."

I want to respond with a winning argument, but I don't have one. She's spot on when it comes to my dad. When I was born, I had a blood clot in my lungs. Fortunately, the doctors caught it and were able to remove most of it before it traveled anywhere dangerous. But, because I had to be on blood thinners as an infant and spent many months in the hospital, my parents have a tendency to view me as fragile and they lean toward the over-protective side. It took several campus visits and a meeting with the Dean of Students at the University of South Florida to convince them to allow me to attend school out-of-state. They even insisted on meeting Jessica and her grandparents before we became roommates. Fortunately for me, they found it amusing and not a sign of sociopathic behavior.

"You're right, Jess. That's why I have to head this off at the pass." I put my hair up in a scrunchie. "I think I know someone who can figure this out for me. There has to be some sort of explanation. I think somebody might be pretending to be me. Although, for the life of me, I can't figure out why. But this guy, Tristan, figures this stuff out for a living. Maybe he can come up with an answer."

The expression on Jessica's face is hysterical. "You're going to pay somebody to figure this out?"

Shrugging, I nod slightly. "Well, it's not like I have the expertise to figure it out. Besides, I've got finals coming up. I don't have time to deal with this and I need to keep my grades up to keep my scholarships. My classes this term are sucking out all the joy I ever had toward learning. I'll be lucky if I don't flunk all my classes."

Jessica's mouth is still moving like a guppy out of water. "But how in the world are you going to pay for it? If you ask your dad for money, he'll know something's up."

"Well, you know the pottery workshop I was hoping to go to? I guess there's always next year."

"No way! You've been saving for it for a year and a half. You even gave up lattes for it."

"I did, but, this is more important. I don't want to freak my parents out and I don't want to leave Tampa even though I don't like accounting."

Chapter Three

Tristan

I HAVE TO FIGHT TO contain the stream of cuss words which threaten to come flying out of my mouth when the bell over the front door chimes. Normally, this is a good thing, but not when I've spent the last three and a half hours chasing down code on a nasty computer virus which allows perverts to turn on people's laptop cameras remotely. The sound caused a momentary lapse in my concentration and I missed the anomaly I've been searching for.

I try to take a few calming breaths before I turn around and face my potential customer. I plaster what I think is a semblance of a smile on my face and turn to confront her. "Welcome to Identity Bank. How can I help you?"

When a customer comes into my shop, I usually play a little mental game with myself and try to guess what they might need. Although this beauty seems somewhat nervous, she doesn't have the look of an abused girlfriend or spouse. She is stunningly gorgeous, but she doesn't look high maintenance enough to be on the run from the IRS or anything underground. Quite frankly, she doesn't fit any of my stereotypical clients. It'll be interesting to hear her story. I'm surprised when I hear her softly address me by name.

"Tristan? Are you Tristan Macklin?"

I nod curtly. "Yes, ma'am, and you are?" I hold out my hand.

She grasps my hand and shakes it. I notice she's not afraid to make eye contact. She's not much shorter than my six-foot one.

"Oh, I'm sorry, my name is Ivy Love Montclair. I go by Ivy. You were recommended by a fellow student."

"What's her name? I can give her a referral discount."

"That's really nice of you, but my friend gave the impression he'd rather decline," Ivy answers diplomatically.

I chuckle at her careful answer. "I suspect your friend may have an issue with me."

Ivy grins at me. "It's entirely possible. It's also not my business, so I just thanked him for his referral and moved on."

I appreciate clients with a sense of discretion. Consequently, her willingness to move on without gossiping earns major points with me.

"What can I help you with today?" I balance a yellow legal pad on my knee.

For the first time since she walked into the shop, I notice real tension and stress in her demeanor.

She starts to nervously fiddle with the cuffs of

her sweatshirt as she haltingly explains, "Look, I've probably made a huge mistake coming here. This likely isn't even worth the time it'll take me to explain what's going on. You'll probably think this is the most idiotic thing you've ever heard."

"Ivy, one of the earliest lessons I learned in this business is to never underestimate the instincts of a woman. If they encounter something which makes the hair on the back of their neck stand up, it's something worth looking into."

"Do you really think so?"

I nod encouragingly. "Why don't you start at the beginning and tell me your story?"

"Okay, it started with this stupid challenge from my roommate. She wanted me to expand my horizons, so she dared me to create a profile on BrainsRSexy.com. Apparently, several people who she knew from high school have met their 'perfect soul mates' on the site, so she thought it was worth our while to create profiles. It was going well for a few days. I mean, I got a few lewd pictures, but I guess it's to be expected on this kind of site. I reported them to the site administrator and shrugged it off. I was corresponding with a few guys I thought sounded cool. But, I got feedback from a couple of them who claimed I changed personalities on them during our live date. There's just one problem: I never scheduled dates with any of these guys. I'm in the middle of studying for exams and I don't have time to go out right now. So far, two guys have come forward and said they talked to me when I know there is no possible way I could have been out on a date. This would all be funny except stuff on the internet lives forever. Not to mention I would never lie about who I am. If this is as serious as I think it might be, it could have severe negative career ramifications."

"You're right, it does sound serious." "But what if I'm wrong and it's nothing?" she asks, panic setting into her voice.

"Or, what if you're right and it turns into a big deal and you're the voice of reason who stops this person before they do irreparable damage to someone?"

I watch as Ivy wilts in front of me. She trembles for a few seconds before she pulls herself together. "I don't have a lot of money for a deposit, but I could make small monthly payments. Hopefully it won't take you too long. I already have a first name for you and I might even be able to run down a last name. She supposedly even has a Florida driver's license using the first name Rogue."

"I don't want you to stress too much about the fee. I have a feeling this case may overlap with another case I'm working on, so we'll discuss the nitty-gritty of the fee later. For now, give me twenty bucks so I'm officially on the case."

Ivy rewards me with a misty-eyed grin. The expression changes her from stunning to beyond breathtaking.

"Sure! I can definitely do that," she digs through the small purse she has securely placed across her chest. From the way she's defensively carrying it, I wonder if she's had self-defense training. When I see her remove a small bottle of mace from her purse so she can better reach her wallet, my suspicions are confirmed. She removes a twenty-dollar bill and hands it to me with a grateful smile.

"So, do you have a physical description of this Rogue?" I ask as I pick up my pen and paper, ready to take a detailed physical description.

Much to my surprise, my question elicits a snort and a smirk from Ivy. "Well, I haven't seen her personally, but I'm told she looks identical to me," Ivy answers. Her eyes are so filled with mirth that I'm not exactly sure if she's pulling my leg.

"Seriously?" I blurt, kicking myself for the question. Way to sound like a professional, Macklin.

"Yes, I'm dead serious. The people who have seen both profile pictures thought we were the same person. I've had a couple of long conversations with Mitch — he's one of the guys looking for dates on the dating website. He went on my Facebook page to see if this Rogue woman was using my Facebook pictures for her profile page and he said it was a different picture. I'm a little creeped out because I don't know where the picture came from. I don't know why anyone would even almost want to cat-fish my life. My life is exceedingly tedious. I bore myself most days. Why would someone want to pretend to be me? It makes no sense," her explanation trails off as she runs out of steam.

"The motives of criminals are rarely logical. You'll drive yourself crazy trying to figure out how they think. You can't apply logic to the illogical. But, before we decide if it's something criminal, we need to rule out an honest mistake."

Ivy perks up. "It really could all just be a fluke,

right?”

“It’s unlikely, but there is an outside chance that there’s a simple, non-nefarious explanation for everything,” I explain, trying to let her down as easy as possible without giving her false hope.

“Can I have your login information for BrainsRSexy.com? I’ll try to see what’s going on at a programming level to see if I can view both profiles. I’ll also sign up as a ‘client’ to see if I’m matched up with one or the other of you or both of you.”

“Sure, my sign-on is IDreamInColor and my password is TrustbutVerify911,” she replies.

I smirk at her sense of humor. It’s too bad she’s a client.

“Does anyone else use this login?” I inquire.

She shakes her head. “No, only me. My dad is paranoid. He bought me a new laptop when I came to college and he made sure it had biometric security features on it to ensure other people weren’t plagiarizing my work in the dorms. If he knew how poorly I’m doing in my accounting classes right now, he’d know there’s no danger of anyone else working off my papers. I hate that class.”

“This might be a dumb question and none of my business, but if you don’t enjoy working as an accountant, why are you majoring in accounting?” I ask, genuinely curious. It’s not about judgment; I’m just fascinated about how she got here.

“Well, interestingly, that seems to be the sixty-four thousand dollar question this week. The short answer is, I don't know. I guess it's like being with a guy who doesn't care if you're a good parent or a good wife. It's easy to go through life on autopilot trying to make other people happy," she replies with a small frown.

"What about what makes you happy? Isn't that the most important thing? Doesn't every other decision you make in your life flow from your joy? If you're not happy, you can't have a happy relationship with anyone else."

"You know, for a guy, you give pretty solid relationship advice. You're right, I need to decide what I want to do for me instead of trying to make everyone else happy," Ivy concedes.

An alarm goes off on Ivy's phone. She glances down at it and gasps as she looks at the time. "Oh crap! I've got to go. I have a test in a few minutes," she declares as she picks up her backpack and snaps the closure on her purse.

I touch her on the shoulder as she's headed out the door. She pauses for a moment. "Ivy, don't worry about this. I've got it covered. I'll figure this out. It's as good as done."

Ivy gives me a small tight smile. "Yes, I know. We women have an intuitive sense about these things."

I scrub the sleep out of my eyes and try to rub the impressions of the keyboard from my cheek. If there is anything predictable about this case, it's that nothing, I mean nothing, has followed the normal script. Just when I think I've run down a lead and followed it to a conclusion, something else pops up.

I'm going to meet Rogue Medea Cisneros Betancourt face-to-face and see if I can get a better feel of the threat level. If she is trying to cover her identity, she's done a really crappy job of it. It's all out there for the world to see. Ms. Betancourt has a habit of being chronically late with her rent, but somehow manages to not get evicted. She seems to patch her income together from several sources, including a scholarship.

I watch her enter the coffee shop and tuck herself into an isolated booth. She removes a large textbook and yellow highlighter from her backpack. On the surface, she looks nearly identical to Ivy. But that's where the similarity ends. This woman is much more self-aware and wary. Her eyes are watchful and openly suspicious as I approach her table with a steaming cup of coffee. "Would you like some coffee?" I hand her a cup. "I had the barista sign and date the lid around the rim so you would know I didn't tamper with your drink or anything."

"Oh, okay —" She looks confused.

"Hi, I'm Tristan," I grab a table near hers.

"Tristan, if you're good enough to buy me coffee at o'dark thirty on a Sunday morning, you've earned a spot at my table. Not that I'm in a great mood for company —" Rogue gestures for me to have a seat.

I move my book bag over to her booth. "Thanks, I didn't think anyone would be here to keep me company this early on a Sunday morning,"

Rogue is taking great care to scrutinize me from head to toe. I force myself to relax and breathe normally.

"How about you tell me why you're really here,

Tristan? I have homework to do — otherwise, I might enjoy a little game of cat and mouse. I'm just going to put it out there. I have serious doubts. You're not some college student out bright and early on a Sunday morning trying to pick me up," she challenges, her body language screams closed off, if not totally hostile.

I can't help but smile at her uncannily accurate reading of the situation. I nod my head in acknowledgment.

"Please allow me to more formally introduce myself Ms. Betancourt, my name is Tristan Macklin. I run a security company called Identity Bank and your name has come up in connection with a case. I have some questions. It'll just take a few moments of your time, if you don't mind."

I watch as her eyes widen with alarm. "Security Company? Is my mom okay?" she demands, her voice growing husky with emotion.

Once again, this case is not following the typical script. That's not even close to the reaction I expected to receive. "Yes ma'am, as far as I know, the case I'm working on has nothing to do with your mother. I'm sorry, I didn't mean to alarm you."

"Does this have to do with my so-called-father? Do you know he ditched my mom when he found out she was pregnant? He was even a no-show in the delivery room even though he promised to drive her and stay by her side."

"Unfortunately, I don't have any information about him either. Although it would be tempting to try to find him so your mom can get what she's owed."

Rogue slashes her fingers through her hair and it settles around her shoulders in an intoxicating puddle of wild beauty. For a second, I am completely mesmerized. "I don't understand. Why are you here?"

For the first time in a long while, I don't want to have to do my job. Usually, there are clear-cut good guys and bad guys. In this case, it's not clear. In fact, I'm not even sure there are any bad guys at all. Well, except for Rogue's dad. I owe Rogue at least some sort of explanation, and I owe Ivy a satisfactory resolution to this case. I won't get any resolution unless I figure out what role Rogue plays in this drama. I have a theory that is growing increasingly likely with every second I interact with Rogue, but if it's true, it'll rock the world of both women.

I hear a snap in front of my face. "Tristan? Did you hear a word I said?" Rogue asks with a look of exasperation on her face.

"I'm sorry, I was gathering my thoughts and I missed that."

Rogue's shoulders slump in defeat. "Oh my gosh! You must have to tell me something really f-ed up. Do I need to have somebody here with me?"

"What? No ... well not unless you want to," I stammer. *Geez, I must've left my professional demeanor in my other pants pocket this morning.* "I don't necessarily have bad news for you. It's just an extremely complicated situation I'm trying to puzzle out. I'm still not sure how it'll resolve itself. A lot of it depends on the information you provide." I hate how disjointed I sound.

Rogue relaxes a bit and sits back into the booth.

"Please go on with your explanation, because you're starting to freak me out."

The tension is thick in the room as I pull an eight by ten glossy image of Ivy out of my folder and place it in front of Rogue. Thank Goodness, I obtained Ivy's permission to disclose the details of this case as I deem necessary, because this is not playing out at all how I originally thought it would.

Rogue picks up the picture and immediately drops it as if it is on fire. "Holy crap! Who in the heck is this? She looks just like me, but she's not me." Rogue looks at me, her eyes pleading for answers. The myriad of emotions crossing her face reminds me of the viewfinder toy I had as a kid. One second, she looks angry, the next hopeful, the next scared, the next excited. Finally, she turns very pale and still.

"Does this mean what I think it means?" Rogue asks in a voice barely above a whisper.

I reach out and grasp her hand, which is ice cold. "Rogue, I wish I had some answers for you, but I don't. The pieces of the puzzle aren't coming together neatly."

A single tear slides down Rogue's face. "Tell me what you know."

I start to tell her the whole saga, "My client, Ivy Love Montclair, came to me because she suspected someone had stolen her identity. She encountered some unusual activities —"

Rogue interrupts me. "Don't tell me .. she signed up for BrainsRSexy.com. I knew I didn't recognize that picture!"

"How could you post a profile with a picture which isn't yours?" I try to understand the situation.

"Funny you should ask because I just happen to have an awkward story to tell you," Rogue says with a self-deprecating grin. "My best friend is this guy named Marcus Brolen. Marcus thinks he's a regular stand-up comedian. One day he and a bunch of his buddies got a little buzzed. They decided it would be a spectacular idea to sign me up for this ridiculous matchmaking website to alleviate my chronic singleness. Unfortunately, they didn't warn me ahead of time they were going to do it. Since I work for Marcus at Ink'd Deep, he knows all of my email addresses and passwords. We've been friends for over five years, so whatever biographical information he didn't know about me, he embellished. Even he can't figure out where the picture came from. He thought maybe one of the other guys had it on their phone, but we went back and checked. No one's ever seen that picture before, so it must belong to Ivy. Yet, I'm not sure how it got on my profile. I didn't put it there."

I think about her question for a minute and use my background in computer science as I try to figure out what might've gone on behind the scenes. It's extremely far-fetched but I guess it's theoretically possible. "Okay, I have an idea, but it's a total long-shot. It presupposes a lot of things we haven't even begun to prove."

"First, I have a hunch you and Ivy are actually twins," I announce, trying to be gentle with my earth-shattering news.

"I don't even know how to respond." Rogue takes a large gulp of coffee. "I mean, on one hand, I have the picture right in front of me. It's hard to argue with that kind of proof. You've actually seen Ivy, does she really look this much like me?" she asks, the question looming over us like a large thundercloud.

"Rogue, I don't know which answer you're hoping to hear, but unequivocally, she is the mirror image of you physically," I confirm. "Beyond that, your voices and laughter even sound the same. Her Vermont accent is a bit stronger, but her tone sounds very much like yours."

Abruptly the atmosphere in the restaurant changes again. I'm not quite sure what I said to trigger the change. Rogue is looking almost faint. in a low, strained whisper, "Did you say Vermont?"

I consult my notes to make sure I'm not making a mistake, "Yes, some place in upstate Vermont ... Oh here it is—Newport," I confirm.

This time, Rogue visibly sways. I yell at the barista, "Grab me an orange juice and a chocolate chip cookie."

The barista quickly brings them over. "Don't worry about it, they're on the house."

I nod at her. "Thanks."

I stick a straw in the juice and unwrap the cookie. "Rogue, you'll feel better if you take a sip."

Trembling, she grasps the straw and takes a long sip and then eats a small bite of cookie. "I don't even know how this is possible. I'm not adopted. How can I have a twin? But I know I was born in Newport. I've seen my birth certificate. My birth certificate doesn't list me as a twin. None of this makes any sense.

Remember when I said there were pieces of the puzzle which don't fit? This is what I meant. For example, Ivy has a completely different birthday than you. I want to go back to the mystery of the dating profile for a minute. Bear with me as I work through a very strange theory. It might be nothing or it might be the key to what happened. I'm kind of a science and genetics nut. I've studied a bit about the genetic bond between twins, and I wonder if it might apply to you and Ivy."

Rogue glances at me sharply. "How could it? I didn't even know she existed."

"But, what if your brains process information in the same way? Look, my theory could be totally whacked, but I think maybe you and Ivy have exactly the same user name and password at BrainsRSexy.com, and somehow your profiles merged. I think there is a glitch in their database."

For the first time in about twenty minutes, Rogue smiles. She's pretty enough to stop traffic with any expression on her face, but when she smiles, she takes gorgeous to a whole new level. She chuckles in a deep husky tone that reminds me of hot buttered rum, "Oh man, that would be wild, wouldn't it? They could write scholarly papers on it or something," she says laughing. "Do you promise not to laugh at my stupid user name and password Mr. Security person?"

"As long as your password isn't 'password' or 1234," I tease.

"Do people really do that?" she asks, shock evident in her voice.

"With frightening regularity."

"Whew, I guess I'm safe then. Mine is a little more complicated. My username is IDreamInColor and my password is TrustbutVerify911."

I draw in a sharp breath as I realize the implications of what happened. It's one thing to have a scientific curiosity about how the whole twin connection works; it's a whole different thing to see the real human ramifications play out in front of your eyes. I shut my eyes briefly as I try to collect my thoughts and determine the best way to frame the discussion.

When I open my eyes, it's clear Rogue has already drawn her own conclusions based on my facial expressions and body language.

She looks at me with misty eyes. "We did the impossible, didn't we?"

I nod slowly. "You sure did."

"What do you think the odds are we could have done it without being twins?"

"I'm no math major, but between your username and password, there are about 30 digits. I remember from my statistics class that the odds of guessing an eight-digit number is about three trillion to one. It goes up exponentially for every digit thereafter. For thirty digits, you might as well figure it's incalculable. Additionally, your password is broken into two distinct units and contains both upper and lowercase characters which makes it more difficult to guess."

Rogue shakes her head like she's trying to clear an image. "I thought you might say that." She wipes her eyes with the cocktail napkins the barista provided.

I reach out and remove the crumpled napkins from her hands and warm her hands between my own. "Rogue, I don't know how to tell you this, but the chances this was just random are pretty much nil." I reach up and brush a tear off her cheek. She leans her face into my palm and takes a deep breath.

"I think I knew from the moment I first saw Ivy's picture. Actually, I think part of me has had a sense of it for an extraordinarily long time. I've always been a bit of a nomad looking for something or someone I couldn't find. There were times when I was young when I would collapse from pain and no one could determine the cause. Now I wonder if I was having those phantom twin pains. If I had to guess based on my childhood, I suspect Ivy has asthma or something like that wrong with her lungs. She must've completely trashed her ankle somewhere around the tenth grade. That sucker hurt for almost an entire year."

I'm blown away by Rogue's composure. If I were in her shoes, I'm pretty sure I would be completely freaking out. "I'm impressed that this doesn't seem to be fazing you much. I think if it were me, I'd be a blubbering idiot."

When Rogue hears my voice, she blinks as if she just remembered I was in the room. "What? Oh! Trust me, I'm having a multilayered response. Part of me is relieved. I'm just happy I haven't been crazy my whole life. Depending on which specific second you ask me, I'm either totally jazzed or completely terrified to meet Ivy." She digs her cell phone out of her backpack.

"I should really call Marcus. Oh Geez, how do I explain all this to him?" She turns and spins on one foot like someone who's had many years of dance lessons. "Wait! Is any of this confidential? Should I wait to tell folks?"

I can almost watch the questions tumble around in her brain like bingo balls at a retirement home. "Ivy gave me permission to share her story, so I doubt she would mind."

"Does Ivy even know she was adopted? Why hasn't my mama said anything during all these years? Even when I went to the doctor with my mysterious pain, she never said a word. I'm so confused." Rogue grabs her cell phone and gets up to walk outside.

I pause for a moment, uncertain what to do. I want to respect her privacy, but she's still shaky and I'm worried about leaving her alone.

When Rogue notices I still haven't moved, she turns around and motions for me to follow her. "Are you coming? I want you there. I'm not ready to be alone right now."

I'm not sure why I have such an inordinate sense of male pride and empowerment from her simple words of trust, but I do. I'm also aware this is a completely inappropriate time to be thinking about how attractive she is. Yet for some reason, I can't seem to stop my brain from going down that path. It's kind of bizarre for me since I've met both sisters. I thought Ivy was pretty in a generic sense of the word pretty and I appreciated her sense of humor, but I wasn't extraordinarily attracted to her.

Even though on the surface, Ivy and Rogue look alike, from the moment I started surveillance on Rogue, her energy attracted me. She has an external toughness which hides a real tender side.

By the time I grab our drinks and book bags and finally catch up with Rogue, she's already on the phone with someone. I'm not purposely trying to eavesdrop, but I hear her becoming more agitated. "… No … listen … Marc! I can't explain this on the phone. Can you meet me at the coffee shop? Let's see … on the scale of importance … this is like a hundred. Remember when that waitress tried to pretend she was pregnant with your baby? That was like a three. This is like a 27… Oh shut up! I am not pregnant! I would actually have to have sex before I can get pregnant. You of all people should know I don't even have time to breathe, let alone have sex. I'll see you in ten minutes, you big, stupid jerk."

Rogue hangs up her phone and stuffs it in her back pocket. She surreptitiously wipes tears from her eyes with the hem of her oversized Miami Heat T-shirt.

I clear my throat to alert her to my presence. She spins around and her eyes widen when she sees me. Her hand covers her mouth in horror and she gasps. "Please tell me you didn't hear my conversation."

I shrug nonchalantly. "Okay, I'll tell you I didn't hear your conversation."

"For my own sanity, I'm going to choose to believe you. That was my friend, Marcus. He'll be here in a few minutes."

"He's your best friend, right?"

Rogue nods. "Yeah, he's like a big brother, only

way cooler. I don't know how I would've made it the last five years without him." Her affection is clearly evident.

"Have you decided what you're going to tell him?"

"Not precisely, but I'm guessing it'll be something along the lines of my entire life is about to change."

The conversation seems lighthearted enough, yet as soon as she utters those words out loud, she starts trembling uncontrollably again. I lead her over to a little bench in a secluded corner of the patio. I motion for her to sit down as I remove my jacket and hang it around her shoulders.

I snag our drinks and place them on the side table next to the patio bench. I silently sit next to her and place my arm around her shoulders. As corny as it sounds, I simply sit there quietly and wick away some of her pain. I can't think of anything more useful I could be doing at the moment. We sit there for about five minutes, the sound of silence so deafening I'm sure she can hear every beat of my racing heart.

"Tristan," Rogue says in a small voice. "It's true you know."

"What's true?" I ask, having lost complete track of the conversation.

"That everything is going to change in my life. I'm so scared. I was barely juggling everything as it was. Now I have a bunch of new complications. I don't know how I'll cope. What if Ivy hates me because Mama decided to keep me and not her? What if Mama hates me because I found out her secret? What if they hate each other and I'm stuck in the middle? What if Ivy's disappointed in me and doesn't want anything to do with me?"

I reach up and brush Rogue's hair out of her face as I try to calm her fears, "First, I can't imagine anyone being disappointed in you. You are bright, funny and obviously a hard worker. Second, I've met Ivy. She's also charming and sweet. Chances are she's also felt like something has been missing all of these years and she'll probably be just as anxious to meet you."

Rogue gives me a watery smile. "Thanks, you're probably right. I wonder who should tell everybody? I feel like I've been dropped into the middle of a Lifetime movie without a script."

"Isn't life best done as an improv anyway?" I quip. "Seriously though, I'm here as long as you need me. Let me play facilitator, mediator, or sandwich boy. I'm fine with whatever works for you. Just let me know what I can do to help," I offer.

"Don't you have a business to run?" Rogue asks pointedly.

I laugh at the sass in her tone. "Yes, as a matter of fact, I do. One of the perks I like best about being the boss is I get to decide what my priorities are. You, Ivy and your mom have just moved to the top of my list."

"What about your other clients?"

I shrug. "With the exception of the assignment that I'm literally writing code for right now, every other client can be reassigned to employees."

"You have employees?" she asks, startled. "I was under the impression you were a one-man shop."

I lift my shoulder in a one-sided shrug as I respond, "I am if I choose to be, but I also have the flexibility to bring in as much staff as I need to if I have a large project."

"Wow! It must be nice to be the head honcho. I can only dream of the luxury of setting my own hours. Actually, just cutting down to two part-time jobs instead of three would be nice."

I squeeze her shoulders lightly as I respond, "I remember those days. When I was in college, I had a work-study job in the computer lab, I was coding on the side, I proofread papers to make extra money and I delivered pizzas. The thing I don't remember doing is sleeping. I got really lucky and I got in early on the phone app craze. I was able to develop an app which detects whether your iPhone or Android has a keystroke logger installed."

Unlike most people I tell this story to, Rogue's eyes aren't completely glazed over with boredom, nor does she look like she's mentally trying to calculate my net worth. Instead, she seems to be merely listening. What a refreshing change of pace. I feel oddly energized.

"Initially, I marketed it as a standalone and it did well. Then I was approached by all three of the big virus protection companies. I did something that at the time was relatively unheard of, and I made a deal with all three companies to incorporate my technology into their existing software packages. Consequently, I found myself in a position where I didn't have to cobble jobs together anymore. In fact, realistically I probably don't have to work another day in my life, but it's just not the way I'm wired. For the most part, unless I have a charity project I'm working on, I completely ignore my bank balance and let the accountants and lawyers worry about all that stuff. I live my life the way I always have with slightly upgraded housing and transportation options."

Before I can figure out what's going on, I feel a stinging sensation in my thigh. I can't believe the little minx pinched me!

"Ouch! What was that for?" I rub the sting out of my thigh.

"I'm just checking to see if you're a figment of my imagination." Rogue shakes her head in disbelief. "I don't know any sane person on the planet who would haul their butt out of bed on a Monday morning to go to work if they don't need to. You must be bonkers!"

"Well, I might go into the office a little later on Monday mornings."

"Still, it's bizarre. You have tons of money and you're still working all these crazy hours to do what exactly? Earn more money? I guess if it were me, I'd have a little fun celebrating my success," she comments wistfully.

"Really? What would you do if I gave you an unlimited account at a travel agency?"

Rogue's eyes widen for a split second before a shrewd look crosses her face. "Well, the first thing I would do would be to clarify your definition of unlimited. Does it apply to only me? Is it for a specified period of time? Can it be applied to a group? Can the group be amorphous? There are a lot of things to consider."

"I could've sworn you were an art major, not prelaw. But, just for the sake of this hypothetical, let's say I'm all in. Now what?" I ask, curious about where she's going to take this.

"In that case, there are so many choices — it's mind-boggling." She becomes animated. "I'd be tempted to head down to a homeless shelter and ask if anyone would like to go home and be reunited with their families. It would also be great to go to all the foster programs and treat all the kids to vacations at any theme park they wanted, with all the junk food they could possibly eat. Maybe I'd meet with military family support groups and offer to reunite the families for a surprise visit with their loved ones for Christmas. If I had no restrictions on travel, I could work with some nursing homes and bring some out-of-town relatives to visit their patients who are always alone. See, you might be sorry you let me get started; you might've created a monster."

I'm absolutely humbled by Rogue's choices. I have a whole team of people in charge of my money, yet none of them have come up with as many great ideas as she's rattled off in the last twenty-seconds. Even more telling to me is that not one of those requests benefits her personally. As if I needed one more reason to find her irresistible, she's given me about half a dozen.

"Monster? I don't see a monster. I see the most generous person I've seen in a while. Yet, I can't help but notice you conspicuously left yourself off the list."

Rogue blushes. "Well, it's okay. Between my work and school commitments, I don't really have time to travel anyway, so it's better not to even think about it."

"Hey now, this is pie-in-the-sky hypothetical fantasy stuff. You're not allowed to let real-world problems drag you down in hypothetical land. It's a violation of the rules. Everything is happy in hypothetical land. Consider it an open-ended ticket."

"Okay, I'll tell you, but you'll probably think I'm a total nerd," she confesses, sheepishly.

A loud bark of laughter escapes before I have a chance to self-sensor. "Rogue, I write computer code and I have a chess game set up in my living room — not a decorative one, a run-of-the-mill chess set—one that gets regular use. Does it seem like I would be in a position to judge?"

A grin tugs at her lips. "Well, when you put it like that, perhaps mine doesn't look so silly by comparison. I've always wanted to go to the Louvre and see all the famous artwork. I've also never flown first class. I'd never make a habit of it, but it seems like something you'd want to check off your bucket list. I just want to see what it's like to be treated like you're the most important person in the room," she admits.

I chuckle. "Trust me, flying first class on an international flight is entirely worthwhile. It's one of those luxuries you might not want to forgo once you've had a taste."

"Oh, I don't think I'll ever have to worry about that. If I ever got to go anywhere like the Louvre, it would be a once-in-a-lifetime trip for me. It would mean I won the lottery or I was going on my honeymoon," Rogue explains. "A normal person doesn't just take those trips on a whim. Those are the kind of trips you take to celebrate a momentous occasion. That's why my trip to the Louvre is staying firmly in fantasyland, because in reality it's never really going to happen."

"I don't know. Going to Paris on a random Tuesday is a seriously underrated little nugget of happiness. You can never stop dreaming big because one thing can change your whole life."

Rogue smirks. "Well yeah, if you're some brainiac computer whiz who invents some amazing computer program. But I'm studying art at Santa Fe College so I can be a tattoo artist. In case you haven't noticed, there's a tattoo shop on every corner. People are even ordering tattoo gear off of Amazon and holding their own tattoo parties. Everybody thinks they can do it now. There's a long road between me and greatness."

"Something tells me you're pretty stubborn —" I tease.

Rogue does something that catches me completely off guard. She makes a funny face and sticks her tongue out at me. It shouldn't be sexy, but in an odd way it is. All I can think of is kissing those amazing lips.

"So mature too," I add in response to her gesture. "I didn't mean it as an insult. I meant you seem tenacious enough to reach your goals. You're very compassionate, so I bet you're an amazing artist."

Rogue's eyes tear up and she buries her head in my chest. "Tristan, that's the sweetest thing anyone has said in a long time. Not everybody gets me."

Just then, a loud voice bellows across the patio, "What in the heck did you do to her?"

Rogue jumps out of my arms and stands up quickly. She places her hands on her hips and barks an order at the guy marching toward me.

Instinctively I shoot to my feet and step in front of her to protect her from the guy with fire in his eyes. But, she is having none of it. She brushes me aside and pokes him right in the chest.

"Marcus Taylor Brolen, back up! Tristan was not hurting me. Not that it's any of your business, but Tristan actually said something really nice to me."

Marcus gives me the evil eye. "If he wasn't hurting you, why do you have raccoon eyes?"

Rogue gasps as she licks her thumbs and starts wiping under her eyes.

I lean over and murmur in her ear, "Relax, he's exaggerating. Until he pointed it out, I didn't even notice. You still look beautiful."

Rogue looks up at me and smiles. She mouths the word "Thank you," before she turns to Marcus.

Rogue walks up to him and pokes him in the chest. "I've been crying. Women do that. Last I checked, it's a free country and I have the right to be emotional. If you'd had the day I've been having, you'd be emotional too, so stop being a jerk."

Obviously I missed something. Maybe it had to do with their earlier conversation, but all things considered, I didn't think his reaction was so out of bounds. After all, he did find his best friend in the arms of a total stranger and she does look a little worse for wear.

I walk over to Marcus and stick out my hand. "Hey, I'm Tristan."

Grudgingly, he nods and shakes my hand. He glances back and forth between Rogue and me. "Does someone want to tell me what's going on here?"

I look around at the patio which is starting to get crowded with Sunday morning breakfast patrons. "Let's go grab one of the booths in the back so we've got some privacy."

"I'll go talk to the manager. I come here so often I've got a table in the back corner which practically has my name engraved on it. How do you take your coffee, Tristan?" she asks over her shoulder as she walks away.

"Black, as strong as it comes," I answer.

I watch as Rogue has a visceral response to my answer. I can see her full body shudder.

She shakes her head in disgust, "I don't know how you can drink that stuff. In my opinion, it should be used to strip paint."

I laugh at the sour expression on her face. "Remember how I told you I never slept in college? I never said I didn't have help from industrial-strength caffeine."

Rogue turns back toward Marcus and asks, "The usual?"

He responds, "Make it a double."

Rogue's eyes widen in surprise. "Marc, don't you have Nicola's back piece this afternoon?"

"Why do you think I asked for a double?" he answers. "Somebody I know got me out of bed before my alarm clock went off."

Rogue looks concerned but eventually shrugs. "Well, double fisting Red Bull wouldn't be my choice before a back piece, but I'm not you."

As she walks away, Marcus looks over at me. "Women can be such nags."

If you were to look up the definition of a no-win situation, this would be it. I could have a male bonding moment with him and agree. But, I also know he is Rogue's best friend and any disloyalty to her will reflect badly on me. There is no good option here. I elect to do what any prudent person would do under the circumstances. I look down at my phone and I check my text messages. I hold up my index finger. "Just a sec, this might be important."

I can't help but smile as I read the incoming text from Kelly. It looks like our budding remote videographer was in a bit of panic to leave his latest victim and left some coding strings behind. Since every programmer tends to code slightly differently, this could potentially be a big break.

I look up and notice Marcus studying me intently. He raises an eyebrow at me. "Good news?"

I nod. "Extremely. I'm closing in on a pedophile who's terrorizing high school and college women in three states. If all goes well, he's about two hours from being caught."

For the first time, I actually get a friendly smile from Marcus. "That's epic. Congratulations. What's going on with Rogue? She doesn't usually trust anyone. I knew her four months before she let me close enough to hug her. I don't even know you and I find her in your arms?"

I try to contain my sigh. I wonder if Rogue knows her best friend is more than a little in love with her. "Look, I know where you're coming from. It's not my story to tell. Today's been a rough day and I think I was just a person for her to lean on in a time of crisis. I don't know if there's anything more to it," I reply trying to avoid an awkward turf war with her best friend.

"But, you think she's hot, right?" Marcus probes.

Now, I'm thoroughly confused. I decide to roll with it and answer honestly, "I've got eyes. It's hard not to appreciate what's in front of me, but today isn't for that kind of stuff."

"Under different circumstances would Rogue be your type?"

"In a New York minute. But these aren't different circumstances and I have to deal with the ones I'm dealt."

Marcus nods. "Still, your circumstances are only temporary."

Scrubbing my hand over my face, I reply, "It's complicated. I don't know how long our lives will be enmeshed. I know it's not my business, but it's pretty obvious you love her, why isn't she your girlfriend?"

Marcus chuckles. "I like you, man. You don't play games. You're right, I fiercely love Rogue. I would go to hell and back for her. The only problem is I'm not 'in love' with her. She's like my sister and my buddy rolled into one package. Would I like to find somebody just like her that I had romantic feelings for? Absolutely! Sadly, Rogue and I simply aren't couple material."

Just when I think this case or this day can't get any weirder, it does. Of all the things I expected him to do and say, backing off and encouraging me to take a run at Rogue was not one of them. It's kind of like when I was a kid and my brother and I used to play opposite day.

I'm still trying to wrap my head around it all when Rogue comes back to the table carrying drinks. I immediately stand up. It's a force of habit. My dad drilled it into us when we were kids. When a lady enters the room, a gentleman always stands. Everyone my age thinks it's bizarre, but I can't seem to un-train myself. Rogue seems to notice the gesture. She winks at me and playfully slaps Marcus on the shoulder after she puts two cans of Red Bull in front of him.

"Marcus, are you paying attention? It's those kind of manners which attract a woman of substance," she instructs.

"What? The dude stood up. Maybe he had a muscle cramp," Marcus argues.

Rogue rolls her eyes. "Geez, Marcus do you pay attention at all? Let me walk you through this from a woman's point of view. Here's what Tristan's gesture said to me. First, it indicated he cared whether I came back. Second, it showed he was anticipating my return. Third, it showed he was watching out for me. Fourth, it showed he was being respectful. Fifth, for bonus points, Tristan's eyes lit up and he smiled the minute he saw me enter the room even though he didn't know I had seen him yet. Do you know what that kind of attention does to a girl's ego? It's a thousand times better than a 'Hey baby, I think you're sexy. Let me buy you a drink.'"

When I go home for a visit, I'm going to take my dad out for his favorite pizza just to thank him for his stellar dating advice.

Marcus looks completely gobsmacked. "Seriously? All of that because he stood up? What does he get if he helps you put on your coat?" he asks, somewhat sarcastically.

Rogue doesn't take the bait; she continues answering the question in the same even tone, "Well, it depends. If he's only doing it to get brownie points, probably not much. If he helps me get my coat on because he's truly being a gentleman, who knows? We tend to notice the little things, and they add up over time. For example, today without being asked to when I was feeling ill, Tristan made sure I had some juice to drink and a cookie. When he thought I was cold, he took off his jacket and put it around my shoulders. Just as importantly, he didn't pair all his good deeds with some cheesy pickup line. He was nice with no strings attached."

It is totally bizarre to hear my behavior analyzed from the female perspective — helpful, but bizarre. It also makes me really glad I'm operating under the constraints of professional behavior. Had I been left to my own devices, I probably would've laid it on a little thicker and I might have blown my chances. I'm glad I chose to show some decorum today.

Marcus tries to high-five me. "I think she likes you, dude."

I don't usually leave someone hanging on a high five, but I had to let him fly solo on this one. I couldn't embarrass Rogue like that.

Rogue gasps and hides her face when she hears his comment. "Oh my gosh, I'm so sorry. This one has absolutely no filter. I can't take him anywhere. It's like traveling with the ten-year-old class clown."

"Rogue, it's fine, really. I won't hold you responsible for the antics of your friend," I assure her. "But, for the record, it would be totally cool with me if you did like me."

"Ooh the boy's got game!" Marcus teases.

Simultaneously, Rogue and I hiss, "Shut up!"

Marcus looks hurt. "Dude, I'm trying to help you out."

I try to hide my grin. "Oh, was that what it was? I appreciate your efforts, but I think I'm doing all right."

Before I can say anything else, Marcus interrupts me again. "You know what, I'm already in the doghouse so I might as well go for broke … Hey Ro … Guess what? Tristan really likes you too."

I hear a low growl before I see Rogue get about two inches from his nose. "Marcus Taylor Brolen! This might be a good time for me to remind you that you are a grown man and not a third grader. Did someone hit you with a stupid stick this morning? I don't care if you are my boss. You don't get to embarrass me. The next time you pull a stunt like that, I'm gonna call your mama and tell her I'm concerned about all the caffeine you drink and how it might be affecting your arrhythmia," Rogue threatens.

Marcus blanches as he processes her words. "You wouldn't," he stammers.

"Just try me." She glares at him with her arms crossed defensively across her waist.

Slumping down in his seat, Marcus takes a long sip of his Red Bull. He starts to mess around with his cell phone. Rogue is shredding a napkin into a small pile of confetti in front of her as she's making a concerted effort not to have any eye contact with Marcus.

I watch as Marcus's eyes fill with pain. "Rogue, please look at me," he pleads. As she raises her eyes to meet his, he continues. "I never meant to hurt you. I was only teasing. The only thing I've ever wanted for you is for you to be happy. I didn't want you to miss the fact that this guy could be good for you."

Rogue's expression softens and she reaches out to ruffle his hair. "I know you didn't mean anything by it, Marc. But, good Lord, could you take half a second to think about what comes flying out of your mouth? It's frightening sometimes. One of these days, you're going to get yourself into some real trouble. How many times have I told you that you're not responsible for my happiness? I'll figure it out — eventually. Until then, I've got bigger issues going on and I need you as my best friend, so don't screw it up." Rogue leans in and kisses Marcus on the cheek. "By the way, I accept your non-apology, apology."

"Hey, I said I was sorry!" Marcus protests.

I catch his eye and shake my head slightly. He glances at me and whispers, "I didn't?" I shake my head again. "Oh geez! No wonder she's ticked at me."

Marcus clears his throat. "I'm sorry I've been talking much more than I've been listening today, and I'm sorry I embarrassed you. You called me for help and I haven't really been there for you today. What do you need from me?"

Rogue's eyes fill up with tears. "That's all I wanted Marcus. I just needed to know you really heard me, because the little drama we just went through is nothing compared to what I'm about to tell you, so I need to know if you're going to be a grown-up about this. I need the Marcus I can count on to be my rock, not the one who can burp the alphabet."

Not for the first time in this conversation, I begin to wonder if my presence is intrusive and wrong. I'm feeling very much like a third wheel. I softly clear my throat because they seem to have forgotten I'm even here. "I have some business I could do in my car if it would make you feel more comfortable," I offer.

Rogue looks panicked. "No, Tristan, please don't leave. I want you to be here when I explain the situation to Marcus. He'll probably have questions I don't know the answer to." She grabs my hand and holds on tightly. "Please stay."

"I don't want to intrude on your private conversations," I explain glancing back and forth between Marcus and Rogue.

"I suspect there'll be very little that's private between us over the next few months. I think we'll be living out of each other's pockets. I believe after today none of our lives are ever going to be the same. You may both regret the day you met me," Rogue responds frankly.

I look directly at Marcus, "How do you feel about me being all up in your business?"

Marcus shrugs. "If Rogue is cool with it, I'm down with it too. You seem like a straight shooter. I know this goes without saying, but I'll say it anyway. If you hurt Rogue in any way, you'll have to deal with me."

"Understood," I state. "I would never intentionally hurt her, but she's going to be thrust into the middle of a very emotionally charged situation. Things could get dicey and communication may break down. It'll be tough on everyone. We'll all have to work hard to pull together instead of apart."

Marcus looks back and forth between us and lets out an exasperated sigh. "Will you two stop talking in code and just tell me what's going on?"

I lean over and murmur into Rogue's ear, "Relax, you can do this. I'm right here if you need some help. Remember, Marcus is a friendly audience."

Rogue squeezes my hand and takes a shaky breath. "Remember the strange picture of me on BrainsRSexy.com?" She slides a picture across the table toward Marcus.

Marcus nods. "I don't know why you object to that picture so much. I think you look amazing in it."

"Oh, I agree. I think both the dress and the makeup are phenomenal. But it's not me."

Marcus squints at the picture. "I don't get it. You go on lots of modeling gigs where you wear other people's clothes. I've never seen you act this way before. What's the big deal?"

"No, I don't mean I don't like the style. I mean it literally is not me," Rogue clarifies.

Marcus picks up the picture and studies it more closely. After a couple of minutes he carefully sets the picture down. I notice his hands are trembling.

Marcus is watching us with the scrutiny he would give a street magician in Vegas. His narrowed gaze travels back and forth between us like he's hoping for an early arrival of April Fools' Day. He performs a cursory search of the room for cameras as he demands, "Are you guys punkin' me?"

Rogue is squeezing my hand so tight my fingers are numb. I'm a little awestruck by this small act of trust.

We both vigorously shake our heads no.

Marcus stands up aggressively and grabs the front of my shirt. "Just what kind of scam are you trying to pull here? I thought you were going to look out for Rogue."

Rogue looks shell-shocked at his outburst, yet I'm not. I'd be suspicious as heck too. In this day and age, it is remarkably easy to doctor photographs.

"Marcus Taylor Brolen! Apologize right now!" Rogue demands.

"Rogue, there's no reason for him to apologize. He's just worried about you. He doesn't know me from Adam. For all he knows, I could be a world-class scammer. I'm not, but he doesn't know that. He doesn't know I routinely work on projects with the Department of Homeland Security and the Secret Service, or that I have the highest level of security clearance in existence other than the President's detail. I wouldn't jeopardize my business just to mess with all of you."

"Well, La-Dee-Da, Mr. Super-Secret-Spy-Guy," Marcus snarls. "What are you doing with the likes of us?"

"I'm trying to help solve a mystery," I respond quietly.

"Why would you take on a case like Rogue? She's got no money for you to drain."

The corner of my mouth quirks up at the audaciousness of his suggestion. This statement even earns a strangled giggle from Rogue. She sighs. "Seriously, Marc. Just stop. You're digging yourself a really big hole here. Tristan is on our side. Please try to listen without marking me up like a fire hydrant."

Marcus makes a sour face. "That's disgusting Ro."

"Yeah? Then I suggest you sit your butt down and hear us out, Macho Boy," she commands as she scowls and points to a chair.

Reluctantly, Marcus lets go of my shirt and sits back down in his chair. He takes a long drink of his Red Bull before setting it back on the table and scooting it away. He picks up the picture and studies it again. "You're right. Whoever this is, it isn't Rogue. This person has a scar over her left eyebrow."

I'm impressed. I looked at those pictures for almost three weeks and didn't notice the tiny discrepancy.

"So, who is this mystery woman?" Marcus asks impatiently.

"We think she's probably my twin," Rogue announces with more clarity than I expected.

Marcus looks at me with skepticism as he probes, "You think or you know? Because as far as I know, Rogue isn't even adopted. This could all be some elaborate identity theft."

I can't help but smile at the irony of his accusation. It seems as if we've now come full circle. "Funny you should say that, because that's exactly the puzzle Ivy asked me to figure out. She was trying to determine whether Rogue was trying to steal her identity."

Marcus's eyebrows shoot to his hairline and his jaw drops to the floor. "What? That's insane! Rogue is the most honest person I know. She would never do anything like that."

"I don't believe Ivy Montclair would either. We think they were victims of a weird twin telepathic phenomenon which resulted in a computer glitch. This caused their dating profiles to merge online. If it weren't for that bizarre coincidence, they might not have ever found out about the existence of the other," I clarify.

"So, does this Ivy know about Rogue?" Marcus asks.

"Rogue and I just put those pieces of the puzzle together a few minutes ago based on additional information she gave me. I haven't had a chance to tell Ivy. I think it's something I should do in person," I straighten the papers in the file.

"I think I should be there … in case she wants to meet me," Rogue suggests as she squeezes my hand.

"I don't know if that's such a great idea," I caution. "This news might come as a huge shock and she may not be ready to meet with you yet. I don't want you to be disappointed. I do a fair amount of skip tracing and adoption reunions, and the one thing I can predict is they're always unpredictable. They are often emotionally charged and volatile—especially if she's not expecting you to be there."

Rogue turns in her chair so she's completely facing me. She grabs my other hand and looks directly at me as she pleads, "I don't know how to explain this, but, I have to be there when you tell her. I'll bring Marcus for emotional support so you can focus on taking care of Ivy. Now that I know she's out there, I can't ignore her existence. I've got to see tangible proof of our connection. I know you don't understand. Right now, I can't adequately explain myself. It's just something I've always felt."

I've got my own reasons for completely understanding where she's coming from, so I merely nod. "Does Saturday work for you?"

CHAPTER FOUR

IVY

THE TEXT FROM TRISTAN COMES in right as I'm leaving my Accounting exam. For a brief second, I debate if I should just ignore it. I'm having major regrets about whether I should've contacted him. After I thought about it for a while, I decided I'd probably been pranked. It's likely somebody from high school who still holds a grudge against me for something related to cheerleading or soccer.

Team related activities can be so cutthroat. During my sophomore year, one of my teammates who wished to be on the varsity team wanted my position, so she purposefully stomped on my ankle with her cleats and broke it in two spots. I had to have a stupid pin put in my ankle and the doctor said I would never play soccer again. Fortunately, my cheerleading coach let me stay on as choreographer so I could letter in cheerleading at least.

As I reread the text, it becomes clear that there's been some sort of important development in the case and Tristan wants to meet face-to-face. My heart starts to race and my palms grow sweaty. I'm suddenly terrified about what he might have found. What if this person wants to do me harm?

Crap! He's not available until Saturday. Then I remember he told me he would be presenting at an out-of-town cyber-security conference all week. Glancing at the clock I realize it's only eight-thirty California time, so I take a gamble and give him a call.

I'm relieved when he picks up on the second ring.

"Identity Bank, this is Tristan," he answers in a professional tone.

"Hi Tristan, this is Ivy."

"Hello Ivy, what can I do for you?"

"I just got your text and I'm freaking out a little."

"Sorry," he says apologetically, "that was not my intent."

"Does this text mean I'm in any danger?" I ask, voicing my fears.

"Certainly not. I'm sorry if I gave you that impression. The update on your case is a bit complex and I'd rather tell you about it in person in case you have any questions."

"You don't think I have any reason to be worried?" I ask anxiously.

"No, I don't have any reason to think you're in any danger. Does Saturday work for you? It's the first day I'll be back in town."

"Yes, Saturday will be fine. Is it all right if I bring my roommate to the meeting? She might think of questions that I forget," I say, repeating Jessica's suggestion. It was the perfect solution because when I'm stressed out, I tend to forget things. It'll be good for her to be there to take notes. I'm so worried about what Tristan might have found, I'll probably completely space out everything he says at the meeting.

"Of course she can accompany you. Is it all right if I bring some people too as long as they sign confidentiality agreements?"

For a moment his request stuns me, but then I remember the location's proximity to the university. He probably has interns working in his office.

"I guess as long as things stay confidential, it wouldn't bother me to have other people observe our conversation."

"If at any time you change your mind, let me know and I'll have them leave," he states firmly.

"Where should we meet?"

"Text me your favorite restaurant and what time works for you and it'll be my treat."

"It's a deal. I'll see you on Saturday. Have a good week." I hang up the phone and bellow for Jessica. Less than a week is not long to prep for a simulated date like this. I know it's a business meeting, but it's the closest thing I've had to a date in what seems like forever.

I fidget in my sundress. It's unseasonably warm for August, even for Florida. This dress seems overly revealing for a business meeting but Jessica says the vintage style is perfectly appropriate. I guess I'm still used to the more conservative styles in Vermont.

"Jessica, what time is it?" I check my cell phone.

Jessica rolls her eyes at me as she sarcastically responds, "About two minutes after the last time you asked me and exactly the same time it says on your phone."

"I wonder why they're late?" I fret.

"Ivy, will you chill? Technically, if they arrived this very second, they would still be four minutes early." Abruptly, she swings her head around to watch something through the window. "Did you say that Tristan is about six foot with wavy hair and piercing blue eyes?"

"Yeah, I don't remember telling you, but that's him," I say in a hushed voice.

"Well, don't have an apoplexy but he's headed this way, and I don't know if that cute guy is with him, but I kind of hope he is," Jessica comments like a play-by-play announcer.

"Oh Lord! What did I get myself in to?"

"Ivy, put your big girl panties on. It's too late to fall apart now. You can do that later. For now, you've got to be strong."

"I knew there was a reason you're my best friend. You're right; it's better to know than to wonder about it. It can't be worse than all the scenarios running through my head. Did I tell you last night I dreamt there was a serial killer stalking me? It can't be worse than that, right?"

"Do you have any revengeful exes I need to be

aware of?"

"My only serious high school boyfriend was killed in a drunk driving accident during his freshman year of college," I admit.

"Oh wow! That explains why you're so anal about everyone having designated drivers. I'm sorry for your loss."

"Thank you. His death was tragic because he was a good guy, but we broke up several months before the accident. The planet is a little less shiny without him on it."

Just then, I feel Tristan's presence over my shoulder. "Good afternoon ladies, may I join you?" he greets us politely.

Jessica smiles widely. "Please do before Ivy blows a gasket."

I nudge her with my elbow. "Geez Jessica, way to throw me under the bus."

Jessica winks at me as she shrugs. "Well, that's what you get for pestering me for the last half an hour," she retorts with absolutely no remorse.

Tristan chuckles. "That's okay, I've been pretty antsy about our meeting too. I'm sorry I had to delay it for so long."

My stomach sinks to my toes as I watch him pull out a thick folder with several parts.

"You're sure this isn't bad news?" I swallow hard.

"Actually, I can't promise that." Tristan opens the file and pulls a legal pad out of his briefcase. "I don't think you're in danger, if that's what you're asking. You might even construe it as good news. At any rate, I'm pretty sure what I'm about to share will be life-changing news."

I suck in a deep breath at his somber tone. I'm not sure I want to hear this, but if I don't — I'll always have the mystery hanging out there and I'm not sure what would be worse. I'm still lost in my head and weighing the options when Jessica jerks me out of my thoughts with her excited chatter, "Girl! What are you waiting for? This is like one of those detective shows on steroids! If it were me I'd be ripping the file out of his hands. Aren't you even curious? This stuff only happens on TV —"

"Jessica! Put a lid on it. I'm just trying to wrap my brain around the fact he said my whole life will change. I kind of like my life the way it is. I'm not sure I want everything to change."

Jessica narrows her eyes at me and tilts her head. "With all due respect, I don't think you really like your life so much now, 'Miss-I-hate-every-business-class-I've-ever-taken'."

"Touché." I give her a mock salute. "You're right, I need to talk to my dad. I don't want to break his heart."

Jessica softens her tone. "Honey, I don't think you're giving your dad enough credit. I think he would be more heartbroken if you chose a career that made you unhappy just to please him."

Tristan clears his throat softly as he interjects, "I'm sorry, I don't mean to butt in here, but I think your friend is right. When I was growing up, my dad owned a construction business. He was very old school about it. He didn't know a thing about computers. He used to call them expensive paperweights. He thought I was crazy spending all those hours in my room programming them. He always dreamed I would go into the business with him. One of the most difficult conversations I ever had with him was when I told him I wasn't going to go to trade school to become an electrician. After I told him why my dreams were so important to me, he became one of my biggest supporters."

My nerves get the best of me and I start tearing the napkin in front of me up into small pieces of confetti. As the pile in front of me grows, out of the corner of my eye, I catch the expression of a cute guy with messy hair and dimples. At first he looks surprised. I watch as his expression turns to fascination, and then to amusement. He's clearly studying me, so I'm not sure what I could possibly be doing to elicit all of those emotions.

Jessica notices my sudden distraction. "Earth to Ivy, did you suddenly leave our conversation? What in the world are you watching?" She follows my gaze. As she spots my target, she comments, "Ooh yummy! Never mind. I'd be watching that too. But can we please get back to the reason Tristan is here? My curiosity is about to kill me." She sighs dramatically and taps her toe.

I take a moment to work out the kinks in my neck and shoulders and lift my heavy hair off my neck. Finally, I decide to trust my gut. I wouldn't have decided to bring Tristan in on the case if I didn't want to get to the bottom of what was happening. Anyway, it wouldn't be fair to ask Tristan to drop his case in the middle since he has already done so much work. I owe it to him to hear him out even if I'm scared of the outcome.

I swallow hard. "I guess I'm as ready as I'll ever be. I hope I don't regret this."

Tristan smiles kindly at me. "For what it's worth, I don't think you will. I think the upside will far outweigh any turmoil this might cause. There's no easy way to start this conversation, so I'll start explaining to you what I found, if that's all right."

I nod in agreement. "Yes, I want you to tell me the truth. Don't sugarcoat stuff for me because you don't think I can handle it. I'm tougher than I look."

"I'll be as straightforward as I can," Tristan assures me. "If I know something, I'll tell you. If I don't know something, I'll tell you that too."

I breathe a small sigh of relief. I'm so used to people trying to over-protect me that it's refreshing to have someone not treat me with kid gloves.

"Great! Now that we've established the ground rules, what did you actually find?" I feel impatient now that I've finally made the decision to move forward.

Tristan pulls a picture out of the file. Before he hands it to me he states, "I can say with almost one hundred percent certainty — this is not a case of cat-fishing."

A wave of relief washes over me. I've just seen so many stories on the news recently. The whole idea of it completely creeps me out. "What a major relief."

"I actually don't think there's any identity fraud involved at all. I think it's due to a computer glitch at BrainsRSexy.com," Tristan explains.

"They accidentally created two profiles for me?"

I ask, confused. "But how did they come up with this Rogue person?"

Tristan rakes his fingers through his short cropped wavy hair as he says in a halting voice, "I apologize, Ivy, I'm doing a really bad job of explaining this. Let me back up."

Tristan hands me a glossy picture. With the exception that her clothes, which are edgier than what I typically wear, it's like looking in a mirror. I pull the picture closer and focus in on her face. For some reason, I still feel the need to rule out a bizarre Photoshopped image of me, yet the small scar I received in youth soccer camp in the sixth grade is not there. Most people don't even know where to look for it. It's not an obvious scar. It makes my eyebrows grow in a slightly different pattern. As my brain processes this new information, my hands shake and I start to hyperventilate.

The guy sitting at the next table jumps up and grabs a bag of prepackaged croissants. He dumps them out on his table and folds the top down a couple of turns. He gently holds it to my face. "That's it, Sugar. Take a deep breath in through your nose and blow it out. You can do it," he urges.

Wow. I could listen to his voice all day. It's deep, rough, and wildly hypnotic. "Okay," I wheeze.

"Slower," he softly commands as he demonstrates how he wants me to breathe. As I subconsciously follow his lead, his lips curl up in a sexy smile. "Much better. How are you feeling?"

I perform a brief self-inventory. I'm not feeling as lightheaded and my lips are no longer numb. I blush when I realize other people in the restaurant are watching our table with rapt attention. The cute rock-star dude looks around to see why I'm blushing. "Oh, don't worry about them. It's a slow news day on Twitter. I'm more worried about you."

I laugh at his attempt to get my mind off my situation. I appreciate him trying to make it less awkward for me. "I'm feeling better, thanks to you."

He gives a self-deprecating shrug and says, "I'm just glad I could help. Have a nice day."

I watch wistfully as he walks away, his tight jeans showcasing a very fine backside.

Jessica kicks me under the table. "Are you going to let him walk away?"

I shrug and roll my eyes. "Well, yeah. What am I supposed to say? 'Hey Dude! Thanks for saving my life. Oh by the way, I think you're cute. Here are my digits in case you need 'em.' Besides, I've got bigger issues to deal with right now."

Jessica shakes her head in disbelief. "No wonder you're still single. You've literally got cute guys falling out of the sky into your lap and you keep throwing them away. Can I have your leftovers?"

"Whatever!" I scoff. "Knock yourself out. Of course for that to work I'd actually have to have leftovers —"

Tristan shuffles some papers and I remember the real reason we're here. The five-thousand pound elephant in the room. Who in the world is Rogue? I look at Tristan and hand him the picture. "This isn't me."

Tristan maintains my gaze. "I know. That's what my investigation uncovered. The person in the picture is a woman named Rogue Medea Cisneros Betancourt. She's a part-time college student here in Florida and she's an apprentice at a tattoo shop where she's learning to become a tattoo artist. We have every reason to believe she might actually be your twin."

"My what?" I sputter. "How is that possible? I was in the hospital for months when I was born. There wasn't another baby there; they would've told my mom."

"I don't know how it happened exactly. There are some details which don't quite match up. For instance, your birthdate doesn't match Rogue's. I don't know if the discrepancy is a record-keeping snafu or what, but there are other coincidences which are too overwhelming to overlook."

I'm completely blown away. I've always wanted a sister. I used to spend hours pretending I was talking to her — even years after it was cool or socially acceptable for me to continue. It got to the point where my mom considered getting me professional help, so I stopped telling her about it. I just internalized the conversations in my head. I accepted that maybe I was a little shy of crazy. Sometimes I would experience unexplained feelings of loneliness or fear even when I was with a group of friends, doing things I liked to do. When I got old enough to go to the library on my own, I did research and figured I was having premonitions. Like all kids who are adopted, I used to dream I had another family out there somewhere. I even went as far as naming them. But never in a million years did I even imagine I might have a twin. If it's true, it would explain so much.

Still, I'm afraid to hope just yet. "Could she merely be somebody who looks like me?" I'm desperate to remove any doubt. "You know how they say everybody has a doppelgänger?"

"There's an outside possibility, I suppose," Tristan admits. "But in your case, there are too many other collateral things which match up. For example, Rogue independently, before ever meeting you, chose the same user name and password as you did to sign up for the dating site. That's what caused your dating profiles to be merged. This is a weird glitch in the dating site's software which they need to address, but that's not your problem."

Jessica and I suck in our breaths as the information sinks in.

"There are other similarities as well. You both listed the same hometown and hospital as your place of birth. That's why the different birthdates threw me off. Don't ask me how, but Rogue seems to empathically know about all your struggles with your lungs as a child. It's almost as if she felt them herself. I never breathed a word."

I bury my face in my hands as I cry. This is what I've always dreamed of but never thought I could have. I wonder what Lenore will think of this. When I can collect myself I whisper to Tristan, "Does she want to meet me?"

I grip the edge of the table and close my eyes as I steel myself against rejection. What if she has no intention of ever meeting me? Maybe she doesn't want to have a sister. I wonder if she was adopted too. This whole scenario is so surreal. People write soap operas about this kind of stuff — and now it's my life.

Tristan touches my hand. "I don't know if you're ready for this today, but Rogue is here if you'd like to meet her."

I look around the restaurant. Hot Rock Dude Guy is studying me intently with a worried look on his face, but I don't see Rogue anywhere. I glance back at Tristan with a confused expression on my face. "Here? ... Today? ... Now?" I wheeze as my ability to speak seems to have abandoned me.

Tristan nods. "Yes, she's been waiting in my rig. Marcus can go get her. She's probably as tied up in knots as you are right now."

I'm completely befuddled. My brain feels like it's made from Jell-O. I've got thoughts attacking me from every angle, so I decide to work backwards. "Who's Marcus? Why has Rogue been sitting in the car this whole time? It's like a thousand degrees outside. Do you know what weather like this does to our hair when we're all sweaty?" I ask, immediately regretting my stupid observation.

Over at the next table, the guy who helped me with my meltdown earlier lets out a bark of laughter. "If I had any doubt before, I don't now. You are so Rogue's sister. I would bet you that Ro's in the car griping about the same thing. She hates her hair with a passion."

I arch an eyebrow at him. "I'm sorry but I don't think we've officially met. I'm Ivy Montclair."

Hot Rock Star Dude grasps my hand and shakes it. "It's nice to meet you. I'm Marcus Brolen. I'm the BFF.

I'm also technically Rogue's boss, but mostly I'm her best friend."

I'm surprised at how disappointed I am to find out Rogue has already staked a claim on Marcus. I was feeling mad chemistry with him which is unusual for me. My aloofness with guys was the impetus for the misadventure which started this whole thing, but I don't poach anyone else's guy.

I politely shake his hand. "I look forward to getting to know both you and Rogue better."

"Awesome! Let me go get her before she goes any more stir-crazy waiting," Marcus winks at me.

That's really odd. Why would he be flirting with me when his girlfriend is sitting out in the car? Men are so weird.

As I watch him leave, Tristan asks me how I feel about all this.

Since his question is so off-the-cuff, I don't really take the time to filter my thoughts and I say the first thing that enters my mind, "I guess it explains a lot of stuff about my childhood. I'm relieved to find out I'm not as crazy as I thought I was."

Tristan is watching me carefully like he's afraid I'll have another episode.

"I'm not sure how much my mom knew about all this, but it might explain why she never encouraged me to look for my birth parents. I always felt like there should've been somebody by my side and there wasn't. I always had a profound sense of loneliness. My mom said it was because I was an only child, but I had other friends who were only children and they didn't seem to feel the same sense of loss as me, so I decided I must be nuts. I guess what I feel is a mixture of fear and relief."

Tristan's smile grows wider the longer I continue to talk. When I finish, he comments, "Would it make you feel any better if I told you Rogue said almost the exact same thing?"

In a strange way, it does make me feel better. Conversely, it also makes me feel worse because I remember those feelings of isolation like it was yesterday. I hope Rogue had a supportive family around her to help her through the rough years.

Through the window, I catch a glimpse of Rogue coming into the restaurant. Marcus has his arm around her in a protective gesture. A feeling of envy hits me like a sledgehammer. I'd like to be sheltered in his arms. I mentally shake myself. What a ludicrous thought! I barely know the man. I watch in total fascination as another version of me walks into the restaurant and up to the table.

It's the singularly most bizarre thing I've experienced in my entire life. Rogue is like a shinier, new and improved version of me. Her hair is bouncier, her complexion is clearer, and her smile is brighter. She moves with confidence and her fashion sense is impeccable. I am beyond intimidated.

It's like watching a mythical character. When she gets close to our table, Tristan reaches out his hands. Rogue grasps both of them with hers. Tristan kisses her knuckles and whispers, "Are you ready for this?"

Rogue nods as she murmurs, "I hope so. I feel

like I've been waiting for this my whole life."

Tristan squeezes her hands. "Just remember, I'm here if you need me."

Marcus exhales loudly. "Is it just me, or do these two need to get a room or something?"

Tristan playfully cuffs Marcus upside the head as he chides him, "I thought we already established that I do not need your help. I've got this. Go find your own girl."

Jessica and I look at each other. At least she's as confused as I am. It's kind of like watching a weird sporting event at the Olympics where you think you know the rules but they turn out to be something else entirely.

Rogue turns her attention to me.

"Wow! This is totally freaky. It's like meeting the classy, refined version of me," she gushes. "You're everything I wish I could be. You're like the new and improved version of me. How spooky is that?"

I snort as I break out into peals of laughter. "Are you kidding me? I was thinking how much prettier you are than me. You're everything I'm not. You're bold, sassy and confident with a sense of style."

Marcus turns to Tristan and comments dryly, "Well, these two will be fun on a double date; they even laugh the same. I wonder if Ivy can sing as well as Rogue. Rogue likes to pretend she can't sing, but secretly she's got mad skills."

At that moment, Jessica chooses to pipe up, "Oh my gosh! So does Ivy, but she won't sing in front of anybody. She does this amazing Pink song."

"I don't know but the researchers will have fun studying it and everything else," Tristan remarks.

Jessica and Marcus don't seem to notice his offhand comment as they yell, "Karaoke night!" in unison.

I look over at Rogue. "Are your friends as disloyal as mine? This one seems to have made a sport out of throwing me under the bus." I point to Jessica.

"Hey is it my fault that someone has to tell the truth in your life? I just happen to be your person. Don't kill the messenger because you don't like the message. Besides, karaoke night sounds like a blast, except who would I go with since everyone here is paired off?"

"Excuse me? Exactly who am I paired off with? Did I miss something?" I protest.

Jessica rolls her eyes at me. "Remember the whole discussion about hot guys falling in your lap? Marcus is exhibit A. He's been drooling over you since he walked in the room. How do you not notice this stuff?" Jessica turns her attention to the other people at the table. "Would you believe that she's a near genius in some areas of her brain? But for some reason, she can't seem to read the signals which are abundantly clear to others."

I'm starting to feel really embarrassed and defensive as I argue, "I don't know if it's all that obvious. Marcus shouldn't be trying to date me if he's already dating Rogue."

Marcus touches my shoulder. "Ivy, I thought I made it clear when I introduced myself that I'm Rogue's best friend and her boss. We are nothing more. We haven't ever been anything more and don't plan to be anything more. We just don't have that kind of relationship."

I look to Rogue for confirmation. She shrugs. "It's true. He is a great guy and totally hot, but it would be like sleeping with my brother."

I try to process this new piece of information. "Wow … umm … okay …" I stammer. "That wasn't what I was expecting to hear. You'll have to give me a minute to absorb it."

Jessica interrupts my thought process. "While you're thinking on that, who should I take to this little shindig?"

Rogue and I look at each other and immediately say, "Mitch."

Tristan and Marcus look very confused.

"Mitch is the business major who does search and rescue on the side," I explain to the guys.

Rogue turns to Jessica and starts to dish more details, "I have to tell you, I was on a Skype chat with this guy. His profile pictures don't do him justice. The man has muscles on his muscles—but only in the best way. You can tell he got them by working hard every day. His dog is amazing and he trained her from the time he rescued her as a puppy from the shelter. I think you guys will probably hit it off."

Jessica grins. "Shoot, I saw the man's profile pictures. If he's better in real life, I might turn into a charcoal briquette when I see him in person. But if you guys are willing to risk that, I'm game."

Tristan claps his hands. "Wonderful, now that

we've got everybody's dating life straight, I think Ivy and Rogue should talk. Maybe the rest of us can grab a bite to eat and make ourselves scarce."

"I appreciate the offer Tristan, but you don't have to leave on my account. My life is so boring that no one will be interested in the dark, gory details," I answer with a chuckle.

Rogue abruptly says, "Show me your left ankle."

I shrug in confusion but comply. My sundress is pretty long so I pull it up a little to give her a clear view of my ankle.

Marcus notices my thin sandal straps cross my ankle twice. He gestures toward my foot. "Do you mind?"

Mutely I shake my head, suddenly powerless to speak. What is it about this man that I find so arresting?

Marcus kneels down to unbuckle my shoe. When he sees my toenails, he voices his approval, "Very nice — sexy and classy all at once." I had completely forgotten that I'm wearing bright red toenail polish with a crystal embellishment on each big toe.

"Thanks." I blush as bright as my nail polish.

I freeze in place when his fingers brush my ankle as he carefully unbuckles the dainty straps. An unexpected tingle surges up my leg when he touches me. I wonder if it's merely a fanciful figment of my imagination until I muster up the nerve to glance at Marcus.

He looks as stunned as I feel. I watch with fascination as his Adam's apple bobs up and down in seemingly slow motion. I notice that his hands have started to tremble. But, the moment is over quite literally in the blink of an eye. As Marcus takes a deep breath and blinks, his whole expression changes. He turns to Rogue. "Hey, I wonder if Ivy is as ticklish as you are?"

"You wouldn't dare," I hiss as I instinctively pull my foot out of his hand leaving my sandal dangling from his finger like Cinderella's forgotten slipper at the ball.

Marcus's eyes light up with glee as he chuckles. "Sugar, I'm like a lethal assassin, I just take knowledge and tuck it away in my steel trap of a brain for use when you least expect it."

"Oh wonderful," I reply sarcastically. "How is it that you already know two of my Achilles heels and I know next to nothing about you?"

Marcus stands up and murmurs in my ear, "Ivy, I don't know if you noticed, but if you packed any more of a punch, I'd be breathing into a brown paper bag."

With my olive complexion I'm not typically prone to blushing, but I seem to be making a habit of it around Marcus.

Rogue snickers as she volunteers, "Don't worry Sis, I've got you covered. I know more dirty secrets about Marc than you'd ever want to know."

Marcus turns to Tristan. "Dude, I owe you an apology. I totally understand what you mean now about 'help' not always being helpful."

Rogue grins at me. "See, that's a perfect example right there. You'd never guess Marcus actually has a college degree in Marketing and Graphic Arts because he insists on talking like a high school surfer dude."

"Ro, you're going to mess with my bad boy image," Marcus protests. "I only did it to be a good example for my little sister. Well, that and it helps with the marketing of Ink'd Deep Inc."

This conversation is so ludicrous. A bubble of laughter erupts from me even though I'm trying to be polite. My mom is always telling me that my sense of humor is going to get me in trouble someday.

Marcus shoots me a quizzical look.

When I stop giggling, I attempt to explain, "This conversation is too surreal. I'm sorry to burst your bubble Marcus, but whoever gave you the impression that you were somehow a bad boy was serving you a load of rainbow-colored unicorn poop."

Marcus chokes on the Pepsi he's drinking, "Excuse me?" he asks, sounding slightly indignant.

"You heard me. I have a feeling that you're a total pretender. You're a nice guy who pretends to be shallow so nobody will figure out you actually give a crap about life."

"But I own a tattoo parlor and I ride a motorcycle," He crosses his arms so his biceps bulge. His flint-gray eyes are intensely focused on me.

I shrug nonchalantly. "When done correctly, tattoos can be amazing," I reply in an even voice. "I bet your shop is immaculate and every person who works for you has the proper safety training and certification, right?"

Marcus nods at me, the muscle in his jaw still a

tight knot. "Darn straight! I've got the best shop in Gainesville. My philosophy is simple: 'If you're not going to do it right, don't bother to do it.'"

I nod sagely as I question him further, "… and your motorcycle? I'd be willing to bet you took a safety course when you got it. Although I suspect you like to tell the women that you're a wild and crazy party animal on your Harley. Yet, I'd bet you don't so much as have a speeding ticket."

Marcus uncrosses his arms and pops a couple of oyster crackers in his mouth before arching an eyebrow at me. "How did you know I have a Harley?"

I let loose with another giggle, "Really? I give you all that, and that's your question?" I retort sardonically. "That was the easy one. After all, don't all bad boys ride a Harley? It's a stereotypical rite of passage."

Marcus's lips turn up in a sexy smile at my cheeky comment. "Well, I don't know if I know you well enough to confirm or deny the accuracy of your statements, but maybe you should try this game from the other side of the table just to see how it feels." His gray eyes are twinkling with anticipation as he waits for my response.

Maybe it's the former athlete in me or maybe it's my tendency to be a perfectionist, but I find it nearly impossible to back away from a challenge even when I know better. Something in Marcus's slightly smug expression tells me he has a sense of that too. Despite my better judgment, even I'm slightly shocked when I hear the following words come flying out of my mouth, "Okay Marcus, tell me what you know about me."

"Oh heck no!" mutters Rogue under her breath.

"So help me, Marc, if you make my sister cry I'll hide your Twinkies and Ho Ho's for a month."

I look at Rogue in shock as I blurt, "How in the world does he eat those and look like that?" I vaguely gesture toward his long lanky body which is presently casually draped in the chair in a way that only guys can sit. He's wearing a vintage Bruce Springsteen T-shirt that's so threadbare, you can see the outline of his abdominal muscles so clearly they might as well have been highlighted. Earlier, he was wearing a beat-up denim jacket with a patch sewn on the back which said, 'If you don't like my opinion, form your own.' His jeans are tight in all the right places, but not obscenely so. Overall, he's about as irresistible as catnip to a cat. There's only one problem — he's cute and he knows it. Generally, guys like that have no interest in girls like me.

Rogue grins at me. "I know, right? He's like a freak of nature. If I ate like he did, I'd weigh three-hundred pounds, but instead, he's so hot girls fall all over themselves to get his phone number."

Marcus has the good graces to blush. "Rogue, I don't think you're helping me here."

"Since Ivy was pointing out your hot bod, you may not need much help," Rogue teases as she winks at me.

For the first time, Marcus appears to be truly uncomfortable. "Enough about me, it's Ivy's turn now," he declares, sitting up straight and studying me intently. If I thought Marcus was intense when he was being lackadaisical, focused Marcus is a whole different experience.

I feel like he's de-coding my soul with his gaze. It is equally terrifying and arousing.

Under his thorough scrutiny, my heart races and my palms start to sweat. I sink my teeth into my bottom lip to stop myself from blurting out random comments. I have this ridiculously bad habit of spilling completely inane, bizarre comments when I'm nervous. The higher my stress level, the more unintelligible my thought process becomes. Unfortunately, this can result in some painfully honest confessions.

Marcus's eyes darken as his eyes zero in on my mouth. He lightly clears his throat as he shakes his body out like a track athlete getting ready to run a race.

"Let's see here," he speaks in a serious voice. "Before me I have Exhibit One, otherwise known as Ivy Montclair. Ivy is well known to the outside world as the model child. She is perfect in every way. She is a model student who gets nearly perfect grades and the scholarships to match. She is a gifted athlete and one of the popular crowd, yet she's likable enough even the unpopular kids at school feel she's one of them. What no one knows is that Ivy doesn't feel like she fits in her own skin. Because under her calm, cool, sophisticated exterior lies the heart of a fierce bohemian artist waiting to emerge. I get the feeling she's been waiting many years for the world to figure out the Ivy she chooses to show the world isn't who she is on the inside."

I gasp. No one on this planet knows the true me — Not my parents, not Jessica, no one. I don't know how he did that. Maybe it's because he knows Rogue so well.

"So, how did I do?" Marcus asks eagerly.

I'm still sitting in stunned silence, stripped raw by his words.

Rogue whirls on Marcus as she hisses, "Shut up! You're hurting her."

Marcus looks baffled, "How?" he asks.

Throwing her hands up in the air, Rogue confesses "I don't know how I know, I just do. Her chest hurts and she's having trouble breathing."

Rogue turns to me and runs her hand down my cheek. "Ivy, talk to me. Are you okay? You're scaring me. What's going on? I can feel that you're not okay."

"Please get my purse," I wheeze, the feeling of suffocation is starting to make my vision grey around the edges.

Tristan reaches under my chair, grabs my purse and dumps the contents on the table. "She must be asthmatic. Here's her inhaler," he says as he tosses it to Marcus. "You had pretty good luck keeping her calm earlier. Give her a puff of this. Do you know how to do it?"

Marcus nods, "My grandma had emphysema and asthma from smoking two packs a day. I used to help her."

Marcus carefully holds my inhaler in front of my mouth. "Sugar, you have to take a deep breath on three," he instructs. "Ready? One … Two … Three … Breathe!" he commands as he presses the button to release an aerosolized cloud of albuterol. As I breathe in the bitter haze of medication, I feel a sense of relief as it begins to kick in.

"I'm supposed to take two doses," I croak, my voice still rough from the wheezing.

The look of concern on Rogue and Marcus's faces are almost too much to bear. "Do you want help with this one?"

A wave of mortification washes over me. I don't want him to have to rescue me a third time tonight. "That's okay, I think I've got it," I say, my voice barely above a whisper.

"Are you sure? I really don't mind helping a damsel in distress. In fact, it kind of makes me feel heroic. An average Joe like me doesn't get to be the hero very often."

I flash him a weak smile, "Really? You could've fooled me. I think you've come to my rescue about three or four times today."

I try to hold the inhaler up to my mouth, but my hands are shaking so badly I can't even push the button.

Marcus folds his hands around mine to steady them. "Count me down and I'll push the button for you," he offers.

I think I shake my head yes, but I can't really tell because I'm so discombobulated by his touch. "Three … Two … One … Now!" I whisper as I try to coordinate my breath with the puff of medication coming out of the inhaler.

After the second dose of medicine has settled into my system, I notice Rogue standing off to the side, quietly watching the drama unfold.

"Rogue?" I call.

She pokes her head around the corner. "How are you feeling?"

"I'm feeling better," I reply. "How did you know I was in pain and not simply upset by what Marcus was saying?"

Rogue shrugs. "It's hard to explain. We got a little side-tracked by real life earlier. Remember the study Tristan mentioned? They're interested in us because we are twins who are identical who had never met."

"I don't understand. Why would they want to talk to us? We just met," I state the obvious as I try to follow what she's saying.

Rogue is undaunted by my confusion, "I want to ask you about the scarring on your left ankle. I want to see if it's as bad as I remember the pain being. I remember waking up with excruciating leg pain. It was worse than anything I've ever experienced in my whole life. What in the heck were you doing at 6:30 in the morning on a Saturday to cause so much pain?"

I feel the blood drain out of my face. The only people who know what happened that day were my teammates and the people at the hospital. Through a terrible miscommunication, my parents didn't even get notified until after I was through with surgery. I know there is no way Rogue could have known anything about that day except through some mysterious twin connection.

"I was playing soccer," I stammer, still unable to believe we're having this conversation.

Rogue smiles happily, "Were you any good?"

"I was until a jealous witch decided she wanted my spot on the team and conspired with a couple of other players to take me out."

"Well, you've got me now. We can go get retribution," Rogue nobly offers.

I chuckle. "No need to. Karma already did a number on her. She turned to anabolic steroids to be a stronger athlete during her junior year, and by senior prom she could grow her own beard."

Rogue laughs as she agrees, "Eventually your own stupidity will slap you in the face."

"Well, that's one way to put it, but it definitely fits. I can't say I'm particularly sorry," I admit.

"So, what's the thing with your lungs?" Rogue asks abruptly. "It was a lot worse when you were a kid, right? Because there were times I could barely breathe and there wasn't any explanation for my symptoms. My mom thought I was crazy."

"My mom thought it a bit nuts too because I would have long conversations with you even though I didn't know who you were. From a really early age I was convinced there should be somebody beside me. I didn't just have a generic invisible friend, my invisible friend was always my sister. Finally, I stopped admitting to people I even thought about you."

"Your lungs?" Rogue prompts.

"Oh yeah, I was born with a blood clot in my lung and I didn't have enough surfactant," I explain. "They were able to remove the blood clot before it traveled to my heart or to my brain, but it caused some tissue damage to my lungs. I had to be hospitalized for a long time after I was born to allow for my lungs to heal and mature. To hear my mom tell it, I guess they weren't even sure if I would make it for a while."

"Wow!" Rogue murmurs, "I almost lost you before I ever knew you."

"I suppose so. It's weird how fate works out," I agree. "So after I survived the touch-and-go phase, I guess the family folklore goes that as long as my parents were changing everything else about me, they took advantage of an error in the hospital records which listed the day the doctors took me off the ventilator as my birthday. My parents never changed it when they filed for adoption."

Rogue turns to Tristan. "I think that clears up the last big mystery. That explains why we have two different birthdays."

A million questions fly into my brain all at once. I guess I knew from the moment I walked into Tristan's office that day something like this was a possibility. The fact that I was adopted was never hidden from me. It would have been silly for my parents to try to disguise that I'm adopted since my skin tone is completely different. My parents have much lighter skin. My mom's hair is beautifully wavy, with a mahogany hue and mine is stick straight. As a child, I used to scour the crowds at the state fairs or other large events trying to find other people who looked like me.

"When is your birthday, or I guess I should say when is my real birthday? Or put even more precisely, when is our birthday?" I ask, excited to know more details.

"Wow, I didn't realize adoptions are still so closed now," Rogue comments. "I figured your adoptive mom would tell you. Anyway, our birthday is on February fourteenth."

"You're kidding! My birthday isn't until April fifteenth. Do you think I was really in the ICU that long? That's scary! How long did you have to stay in the hospital? Were you adopted too?" I continue peppering her with questions.

"I guess I must've hogged all the nutrients and the surfactant because I don't think I had to stay in the hospital more than the normal amount of days," Rogue responds. "I'll have to ask my mom to be sure though. Everyone calls her Mama Rosa, by the way."

"So, you weren't adopted?" I clarify.

Rogue shakes her head, "No, I was raised by our mom."

That piece of news hits me hard. After a lifetime of being the player always left on the bench and the last person chosen to be on every team, her decision to leave me behind at the hospital is devastating.

Marcus immediately notices my crestfallen expression. He kneels down in front of me and puts his hands on my shoulders. Speaking in his low, soothing voice, he directs, "Ivy, look at me." Slowly, I raise my eyes to meet his steady gaze. "Sugar, I've met Mama Rosa personally. There is no way she would have abandoned you unless she had no other choice. That's just not the way she operates. So please, get those thoughts out of your head."

A look of horror crosses Rogue's face as she processes our conversation. "Oh my Gosh! You think she chose me over you? If you knew my mama, you would know she would never do that. She spent her life being a teacher's aide in a kindergarten class. She absolutely loves kids. Something really weird must have happened for her not to take you too," she explains emphatically.

A tear leaks out of the corner of my eye as I ask in a small voice, "Did she ever mention me?"

Rogue pops up from her chair and hugs me from behind. "Oh *Manita*, I'm so sorry, but no."

I hold her cheek next to mine and sob. Marcus rests his forehead against mine and we collapse into an odd group hug right in the middle of the restaurant.

After a few moments we break apart. Rogue and I take one look at each other and start to laugh. Our makeup is completely destroyed. Tristan, per his usual, is totally prepared and hands us napkins with one edge pre-moistened with water. As if we had done this a thousand times, we simultaneously begin repairing each other's face. It is freaky seeing and touching my mirror image. It's like having a life-size doll come to life.

Something in my expression must have given my thoughts away because Rogue giggles. "Don't worry, this is just as bizarre for me, if not more so. At least you were aware you were adopted so you knew there might be siblings out there somewhere. I was completely blindsided."

A knot forms in my stomach and I can't stop myself from asking, "Rogue, are you sorry I found you?"

"*Manita*," she exclaims softly, "I will never be sorry you found me."

"*Man-nee-ta?*" I repeat, trying to mimic her melodic accent. "What does that mean?" I ask.

"It means you are my dear sister," she translates. "Whatever happens with our mom, you will always be my *manita.*"

CHAPTER FIVE

MARCUS

I JUMP ABOUT A MILE high when Rogue taps me on the shoulder. I pull my earbuds out of my ears as I see her lips moving.

"What?" I point to the headphones.

Rogue rolls her eyes at me as she regards the display on my workstation. "Marcus, isn't that the third time you've torn your machine apart today?"

I look down at my disassembled tattoo machine. It's almost as if I had an out-of-body experience when I took it apart. I barely remember any of the process. I hope this run lasts longer since I need the routine to burn off some mental energy. I feel like a kid who's been caught with his fingers in the cookie jar. Normally, I can keep my unusual behaviors under wraps, but my brain is too unfocused to worry about it at the moment.

"You know what a stickler I am over clean equipment."

"Uh-huh. I do know the difference between clean

equipment and dirty equipment because you taught me quite thoroughly. Even making allowances for your fastidiously high standards, you passed anyone's definition of clean last Thursday. The floor at Ink'd is so clean they could perform brain surgery on it. What's going on with you?"

I remove my non-latex gloves and wipe my hands down the sides of my jeans, then walk over and straddle the chair at the station Rogue has been using. She's been mixing some custom colors for an autumn-themed tattoo for one of her classmates. I scope out the beautiful array of colors she has mixed on her tray. Her grasp of color intensity and balance is impressive. I whip off my shirt. "Are you ready to practice on me?"

"Not on your life!" Rogue declares. "You've got big plans for this piece and you don't need a newbie like me messing it up."

"Rogue, I totally trust you. You know that, right? You are an amazing artist. I would be honored to have your work on my body. Your practice stuff is better than some of the professional work I've had done. I know you don't believe me, but it's true."

"Marcus, you're either being nice or you're delusional. I work hard and I practice a lot, but my skills are not nearly as developed as the people who have worked on you before. In comparison, it would look like some kindergartner scribbled on you with crayons. It would be irresponsible of me to try to work on your piece."

I shake my head at her stubbornness. When Rogue gets an idea, there's no talking her out of it. I try a different tactic. "Okay, if you won't do new art on me, will you please help me do some fill-in work? The guy who did my upper bicep was killed in a motorcycle accident and the ink is faded. Your color blending skills are phenomenal whether you want to admit it or not. Please, one friend to another, will you do some touch-up work on it?"

She looks over at me and raises an eyebrow. "You're awfully jumpy today. If I start this, will you be able to hold still long enough for me to get anything done?"

I chuckle at her observation because it's totally true. I'm bouncing around the shop like a Chihuahua who ate coffee beans for breakfast.

"Believe it or not, getting ink actually calms me down. I'll be totally mellow, I promise." I finish stripping off my shirt and lay face down on a table which resembles a fancy massage table and stretch my arm out. Rogue examines my tattoo. "Marc, this is super faded. How long ago did you get this? I'm not even sure we use these blues anymore."

"I can see I taught you well. Let's just say I got this tattoo a long time before I should have, in an environment where it wasn't exactly safe or legal. On the upside, it got me interested in an actual career path."

"Marcus, I'm not sure there's enough here for me to accurately fill in," Rogue protests nervously.

"Rogue, I wasn't kidding when I said I totally trust you. If a cover piece is more appropriate, then go for it. That tat was from a really dark, tumultuous time in my life. I'm not there anymore, so if the piece needs to go, I'm totally down with that."

"I'm not sure I'm okay with your plan," Rogue argues. "Are you sure you're okay with me covering your friend's work, especially since he's passed away? Are you sure you don't want to keep this as a tribute piece?"

I snicker as I reminisce about the time in my life when I got this tattoo. "I was young, dumb, and trying to be something I wasn't. I was twelve years old and trying to prove I was as tough and street smart as my older brother, Tomás. Some of his friends were into street racing and motorcycles. They took me to an old abandoned garage and dared me to get drunk to prove I was tough. Then my brother and I got these back-alley tattoos to prove our loyalty to the group."

Rogue gasps. "Your brother allowed them to do this to you when you were only twelve?"

I turn my head to watch her response to my unconventional tattoo story. I shrug slightly. "Yeah. I didn't know it at the time, but Tomás was already hooked on drugs. It took him years and a couple of treatment programs to kick the habit."

"Wow! No wonder you don't care if I cover it up. I'd want something like that covered too. What did your parents say when they saw it?"

"Well, it happened at the beginning of the school year, so I covered it with long sleeves for months. When my mom did discover it, you can imagine she wanted to go headhunting in the neighborhood. But Tomás and I wouldn't tell her who did it because we were afraid she might start a gang war."

"I've met Anna Lucille. I can imagine she would

stir up your whole neighborhood trying to find answers. How did you talk her into backing off?"

"We told her it was a couple of bullies from out of town and we heard they moved away. I had to promise her I would never get another tattoo without fully thinking it through first."

Rogue raises her eyebrow at me. "What do you think you are doing now *mi amigo?*"

"Oh, I've been wanting you to do this for months, you just don't think you're ready. I know you are. Consider me a client who walked in off the street."

Rogue walks over to an empty station she was using as a work area and grabs some colors she mixed earlier. She swallows hard as she washes her hands and puts on gloves. She loads the paint into metal tubes. She's old school like me and likes heavy machines. Less bounce. Her touch is light and professional as she unwraps a new disposable razor and carefully shaves the area. "Marc, how would you explain the difference between the person you are now and the kid you were then?" she asks softly as she wipes my arm down with antiseptic cleaner.

I take a minute to think about it as I look around the shop. "I guess you could say, I'm learning to find balance. I still go in six different directions at once, but I'm less scattered and more mature about it now. I don't have it all figured out, but I'm trying."

Rogue's brow creases as she focuses on my words, but finally she nods. "To do this design proper justice, I need a little time. Do you want to grab some lunch, or do you want to lay here and take a nap?"

I snort. "How long have I been your friend? What

do you think my answer will be? Have you ever known me to turn down anything which even remotely resembles food in the entire time we've known each other?"

Rogue laughs out loud. "Good point. Go get food Marc. I'll draw this up on the light board while you're out. Can you spot me lunch? My financial aid check is slow this term."

"No problem, I'll add it to the substantial tip I know you'll be earning."

"Oh shut up! You could hate it for all I know. Bring me an iced chai tea please."

"No Red Bull?"

"No, thank you. I'd actually like to be calm enough to draw a solid line on you, if you don't mind. I consider it central to the art of tattooing."

I sit up and roll my eyes at her. "Oh fine, be all safe, responsible and reasonable when you're going to mark me for life, see if I care."

"Go! I'm hungry! I want a Cuban."

"How did you know I was going to get Cubans?"

This time, she rolls her eyes at me. "It's Thursday. You always get Cubans on Thursdays, Mr. I-live-my-life-on-the-wild-side."

"Oh Geez, Ivy hit the nail on the head. There isn't a bad-to the-bone thing in my body. I'm just a senior citizen in disguise waiting for the daily lunch special."

Rogue pats me on the shoulder after I pull my vintage Robert Plant T-shirt over my head. "Relax, Marc. In the real world, women find stable remarkably sexy."

"But what about my reputation as a bad-boy?" I practically pout.

"Who cares? You're not in high school anymore. Besides, anyone who knows you for more than a couple of hours knows better anyway. You volunteer for Habitat for Humanity and Big Brother/Big Sister. You're hardly the picture of a hoodlum."

"Well, I have my reasons. Those programs mean a lot to me," I reply with an embarrassed shrug. It's easy to forget I have no secrets from Rogue.

"Go get some food Mr. Dependable, before I wise up and remember I'm not a real tattoo artist and totally freak out about what I plan to do to your aforementioned perfect body."

"Do I get design approval?"

"Of course! What kind of tattoo artist would I be if I didn't give you design and placement approval before I so much as touch a needle to your skin?" Rogue scolds mildly.

"Well, I'm going to make you trust your instincts on this one. I don't want to see any part of it until the final reveal."

Rogue tightens her lips in a thin line of disapproval. "Are you sure, Marc? What if you hate it?"

"Yes, I'm sure. I've seen you sketch hundreds of tattoos over the last year, and you know me better than anyone on the planet. You haven't done a single one I wouldn't wear with pride. You know me better than my own mama. If you can't nail this, no one can, Ro."

Rogue smirks at me. "Really Marc? You would've

worn one of the Powerpuff Girls with pride? Even the pink one?"

I pause to think for a moment, shrugging. "I'd catch plenty of grief for it, but if you did the ink, I would totally get the Powerpuff Girls. Your caricatures are completely dead on."

Rogue giggles. "Come to think of it, you're just crazy enough that you probably would. Go on and get out of here. I need do some serious artwork so you don't end up with the Powerpuff Girls. While you're at it, can you stop by the garage and see what's taking them so long to finish my car? All I asked them to fix was the timing belt. It shouldn't be taking them a week and a half."

"Didn't Super-Secret-Spy-Guy help you drop it off the last time he was in town?"

"Last I checked, he still went by Tristan," Rogue replies dryly. "But yes, he did help me drop it off because you were busy with Anthony. You guys were at the skate park or something. I know better than to bug you when you're on a Big Brother outing."

"If I had to guess, I suspect that explains why they still have your car."

"What in the heck are you talking about?" Rogue asks impatiently.

"Again, and I'm just speculating here, mostly because you guys told me to butt out, but it seems to me Tristan considers himself to be 'the guy' in your life right now. As 'the guy', it would be irresponsible for him to allow you to drive a car around held together with dental floss and Band-Aids. So, considering he probably has about as much money as Bill Gates, he probably told the garage to fix everything which could possibly be wrong with your car and upgrade everything else while they were at it."

Rogue's expression is like a cartoon. If her jaw could come unhinged, it would be on the floor. "No flippin' way! I simply asked him for a ride home after I took my car to the garage. I didn't ask him for anything else, I swear. Do you think he thinks I asked him for something else? We haven't even officially been on a date yet. Oh my gosh! I can't afford to pay him back. That's why I didn't get the car fixed to begin with. What the heck am I going to do now?"

I'm trying hard to smother my grin because it's a talent almost unique to Rogue to freak out more over good news than bad. If you give her unsettling news like her rent is being raised, or she's being evicted because her place is being overrun by bedbugs, she shrugs it off like she expects that kind of thing to happen to her. However, if you tell her she's won a scholarship, deserves a raise, or has earned a huge tip, she acts like the sky is going to fall at any moment. It's the most bizarre thing. She has the opposite reaction of most people. "Maybe it's a good thing. Your car wasn't exactly safe —" I venture carefully, trying not to hurt her feelings.

"I know, but I still hope you're wrong." Rogue sinks down into a low tattooing chair designed for doing back pieces next to where I was sitting. "I swear, I didn't ask for any of this, but he's definitely the type of person to fix everything."

"I kind of got that vibe from him too, but he doesn't seem like the kind who would brag about all the things he does with his money either. If you hadn't told me he was some sort of kajillionaire, I would've thought he was a grad student studying English or something. He looks like a total bookworm."

"English, really? I would've thought Economics or something like that … he looks too straight-and-narrow for English," Rogue smirks.

"If he's so straight-and-narrow, how come he makes your heart go pitter-patter?" I tease.

Rogue sighs as she twists her long hair between her fingers. "I have no earthly idea. All I know is he feels like a calm, centered space for me. I've never felt that with another person before. Not even with you — and you're my best friend. I feel comfortable with you, but you don't quiet my soul."

"Wow, Ro. That's deep. Are you sure? You haven't known this guy very long."

"I can turn the tables on you, Romeo. You haven't known my sister any longer than Tristan and I have known each other, but you seem to have some sort of cosmic connection with her that you don't have with me. Are you going to dismiss your experience and say it's not possible because you just met?"

Her words are like a punch in the gut. She's right, of course. Even though on the surface Rogue and Ivy seem identical, it doesn't take any time at all to determine they really aren't. Their personalities and outlook on life are radically different.

Initially, it might be tempting to say Ivy is more fragile, but I think Rogue just hides her fragility better under an armor of hard-earned street savvy. When Mama

Rosa remarried a guy Rogue wasn't sure she trusted, she left Vermont on a Greyhound bus before she turned seventeen. She'd doubled up on her classes enough in high school that it was a breeze for her to get her GED and take the ACT to get into college, although because of her nonstandard transcripts she was bumped down to a nontraditional admit status, which I thought was incredibly unfair given her stellar grades and test scores. If they had known that through most of her junior high and high school years she worked an outside job as a housekeeper to help her mom pay the bills, they would've had much more respect for her ability to maintain a 3.8 GPA. But, true to form, Rogue never breathes a word about her struggles to anyone. I only found out about it when my refrigerator came unplugged over a weekend when I was out of town and I had to figure out how to clean up a freezer full of melted and rotten food.

Both women could stand a little buffering from pain. Ivy seems, at least on the surface, to be much more fragile than Rogue. But something tells me that despite her openness and obvious naivety, she has an inner tensile strength few people recognize or acknowledge. Ivy strikes me as a very quiet leader.

Ivy and I have had several entertaining phone calls which have gone really late. We've also been playing this silly computer game where we challenge each other to solve puzzles on our iPads. It's kind of like Pictionary using a stylus. For someone who claims she doesn't have much innate artistic talent, she's remarkably gifted. Every time she complains about one of her business classes, I threaten to swoop in and hire her away to work at the tattoo shop. She laughs like I'm kidding, but what she doesn't realize is she actually has more innate artistic talent than the last guy I hired. For some reason, Venom Q. can't seem to get perspective down, so all of his drawings are a bit skewed. He did a portrait so poorly the other day that I'll have to offer a free cover up. I could tell by looking, the problem started with a bad drawing.

I don't want to fire him, but I think I have to, even though he was recommended by a buddy of mine. I hate this part of the job. Management is not my thing. If I could just focus on the artistic side of owning the business, I would be totally copacetic with it all, but the day-to-day grind of running the shop wears on me. Being a hard-nosed supervisor does not come naturally. For many years, I was just one of the guys as we all learned our craft together. But for some reason, I seemed to have more natural talent than some other guys, so I learned faster and got bigger, better jobs with higher profile clients. Therefore, I got more name recognition and more respect. More respect in the tattooing world equals more responsibility and higher visibility. In my case, the higher responsibility includes co-owning the shop. It definitely has some perks, like being able to mentor younger apprentices like Rogue.

Rogue will soon be an absolute star in her own right. It won't be very many months before she'll be totally out-tattooing me. She'll have her own list of clientele which will far exceed mine. I'm a decent artist and I take pride in my work, but I don't have a fraction of the talent of Rogue. The breadth of her skill is amazing. She can do everything from portraits to pop art, to vintage pinup girls, intricate scrollwork, and old-school tattoos. I haven't seen her run across much she can't handle. Her only problem right now is her overwhelming lack of confidence in her own skills. If she had as much confidence as she has raw talent, she would be meteoric, even right now. She would have clients lining up around the building even though she hasn't completely finished her training. She's just that good.

"You didn't fall asleep, did you? I thought you were getting us lunch?" Rogue asks as she pokes me with the end of the pencil she's using to make the stencil for my tattoo.

I grab the pencil from her and instinctively start to sharpen it. I have this weird thing about pencil sharpeners. I always have, even as a child.

Rogue slaps my hand away and chides, "Knock it off, I just got those to where I like them. What's up with you? You're staring off into space again."

"Sorry, I was thinking about what you said. I was trying to figure out what makes you and Ivy so different, and why she didn't fall into my friend zone."

Rogue snickers at me. "You can say that again! The pheromones spilling off the two of you was something to behold. It was like watching an exotic mating dance or something."

"Well, as my favorite teacher once put it, I definitely have the warm fuzzies when I'm around her."

"I'm still trying to wrap my brain around the fact I even have a sister. Now you're well on your way to falling head over heels in love with her when she looks exactly like me — it's a bit too much of a mind bender for me. Part of me wants to stand up and cheer because you finally found someone whose IQ is higher than her bra size, but the other part of me wonders, if you fell so hard for someone who looks just like me — why you didn't fall for me?"

I rake my hand violently through my hair causing it to stick up even more. "Rogue, I've thought about it a lot. In one way it's weird because you guys do look almost identical, but once you get deeper than the surface, you're not so much alike. You're both funny, but in completely different ways. The same is true about your toughness and your beauty. It's almost as if you are two sides of the same coin."

"I know this sounds stupid, but you've been my friend for so long, I just hope she's not a new and improved version of me and you don't throw our friendship away."

I stand up and hug her as I head toward the door. "No matter what happens between me and Ivy, you will always be my best friend and I'll always love you. Nothing will ever change that. Now, I'm going to go get something to eat because obviously hunger is starting to affect your judgment."

CHAPTER SIX

ROGUE

My hands are shaking as I tape the stencil to Marcus's arm. I'm trying to pretend like he's any other client. This is definitely not my first tattoo. I've been tattooing on real-live people for about eight months now, however most of my tattoos have been small pieces like butterflies, stars, anchors, dice and alligators. I'm always surprised at how many people in Florida want alligator and shark tattoos. It must be a cultural thing here. I was so glad to graduate from tattooing on pork butts to real people, but I still get terrifyingly nervous. If I'd had time to think about this too far in advance, I probably would have completely psyched myself out. Some of Marcus's tats have been done by really famous people, like the ones who have their own reality TV shows on cable.

I clear my throat nervously. "This is your last chance; are you sure you don't want to look? I could be putting the Care Bears on you or something."

Marcus shrugs and winks at me. "I guess there could be worse things. I kinda liked the little green guy with the shamrock on his chest."

Despite my best attempt to be professional, Marcus cracks me up as usual. "You're crazy, you know that?"

"I'm not crazy, I just know you'll do a great job. Now, relax and breathe, you've got this."

I methodically line up my tools as Marcus walks over to the stereo and turns it on to Bruce Hornsby. I turn around with a questioning glance. "That's not really your kind of music Marc. What are you doing?"

He grins at me. "Well, I'm not the one who needs to be relaxed here, am I? I know this stuff puts you into some sort of mental zone where you're all chilled out. Chilled is probably a good state for you to be."

I take a deep breath as I smile at his generosity. "Thanks Marc, I appreciate it. I don't think I could've tattooed to Led Zeppelin."

After Marc lays down, I start to work on the delicate outline of my design. As he predicted, as soon as the needle starts rhythmically piercing his skin, he drifts off into a light sleep. After about an hour and a half, Ivy and Tristan come through the front door. Marcus is so out of it he doesn't even hear the chime. I pantomime my desire for them to be quiet until I finish the color I'm currently working on. When it's time to change colors, I set the tattoo machine down and rush over to the seats to talk to them.

"Hi guys! Do you mind if I work for a few more minutes? I'm almost finished and as you can see, Marcus is in a pretty good headspace right now so what I'm doing isn't bothering him. If I could, I'd like to finish up rather than start over on another day."

Ivy takes a look at Marcus sleeping on the tattoo chair and comments as she fans herself, "No, I don't think it will be hard for me at all to watch him for a few more minutes. I've always wanted to see what this is like. I have a few ideas for a tattoo. I brought my drawing pad with me. Maybe you can tell me if my ideas are any good after you're done with Marcus. I've never even been in a tattoo parlor before today. I don't know if I'll be brave enough to do this, but I've always wanted to. It might be educational for me to see how it really works."

Tristan shrugs. "I'm on whatever schedule you guys are on. This is a vacation for me. I might look around and see about ideas for adding to my own ink."

"You have ink?" Ivy and I ask simultaneously as I load new ink and resume working on Marcus's tattoo.

"Yes," Tristan answers with his eyebrow raised. "Did I ever give the impression I was anti-tattoo?"

"Where is your tattoo?" Astonishment crosses Ivy's face.

"I don't know if I should reveal such a private thing to my client," Tristan answers.

"Oh, I'm sorry. I didn't mean to be rude — I didn't realize it was so personal —" Ivy stammers.

Obviously, Ivy missed the teasing glint in Tristan's eyes. I turn to Tristan. "She thought you were serious, you know. You should probably let her off the hook."

Tristan unfastens a couple of buttons and I have to remind myself I'm in the middle of a tattoo. It doesn't escape my notice that for a computer geek, Tristan has a nice set of muscles. As he pulls his shirt aside, I notice on his pectoral muscle he has a series of zeroes and ones.

"I know that it's computer code for something, but I have no idea what it means," I admit.

Tristan shoots me an admiring smile. "Very good, most people don't even recognize binary code. You wouldn't believe how many people try to guess what language this is written in and try to decipher it as if they're letters of the alphabet. You score major bonus points with me. The answer to your question is it spells out the phrase, 'Be You.' I was only able to be successful in life when I made my own path and started coloring way outside the lines."

Ivy sighs longingly. "I wish I had the guts to do that more often."

"Something tells me if you hang around Marcus much you'll quickly become an expert. He considers coloring outside the lines to be his own personal mission in life. He likes to recruit followers to the cause. Be careful. He may push you clear over the edge. He's convinced me to do some pretty zany stuff over the years."

"What's the craziest thing he's ever conned you into doing?"

"You mean besides keeping the BrainsRSexy account?" I ask, my tongue firmly in cheek. "Honestly, it would have to be what I'm doing right now. This is kind of like me pulling up a ladder and a can of spray paint from Home Depot and painting over the Sistine Chapel."

Ivy walks over to get a closer look at what I'm doing. I move the piece of gauze covering the work I've already done so she can see it. When she does, she jumps back and gasps. It's a good thing I didn't have the needle on Marcus's skin at the moment because I could have done some serious damage. I'm not sure what I expected her reaction to be, but this was not it.

"Is it really so terrible?" I ask feeling completely desolate. When I saw the tattoo in my mind, I thought it would look pretty spectacular. I didn't think my execution was bad, in fact before I saw Ivy's reaction, I thought I was doing some of the best work I've ever done. However, now I'm beginning to second-guess myself. I draw some calming breaths so I don't cry.

Ivy looks at me and notices my reaction. "What's wrong Rogue?" she asks, panic making her voice sharp.

"I honestly didn't think you'd hate it. What if Marcus hates it too?"

"Oh my gosh! I can't believe you think I hate it. I reacted that way because we had another twin moment, you just don't know it yet. Let me show you."

"What are you two talking about?" Marcus asks sleepily as he wakes from his impromptu nap.

"Nothing!" Ivy and I respond in unison. "Go back to sleep."

Ivy pulls a tablet from her purse and shows it to me, hiding it from Marcus. On the tablet is an intricate sketch of a dragonfly breaking free from a ledger with numbers flying toward an artist's palette.

I take the tablet from her and sink down into the chair next to Marcus. "When did you draw this?" I demand in a stunned whisper.

"On the way here in the car," Ivy answers with tears in her eyes. "I tried to think about where I am in my life right now and what I would like to say about myself if I was brave enough to get a tattoo. You don't have to use my drawing or anything, it's just an idea."

"I think it's an amazing sketch. I just think it's interesting that Marcus suddenly wanted to change his tattoo because it didn't fit where he was currently in his life either, so I designed this tattoo to reflect where he is now. Maybe this is some cosmic sign you two are headed in the same direction."

I clean off the excess ink and blood from Marcus's tattoo and apply some antibiotic skin conditioning treatment. "Marc, do me a favor and don't look at this until you get to the mirror. I want you to get the full effect."

Tristan's eyes widen as he sees the tattoo for the first time. Obviously Ivy showed him her sketches. "Wow! I study this stuff for fun but seeing it play out in front of me is too weird. Marcus man, I've got to tell you my girlfriend is one talented chick!"

Tristan's choice of words makes me laugh. "Excuse me Tristan, the 1980s called and they want their jargon back."

Tristan looks surprised. "What? You object to being called my girlfriend?"

"No, girlfriend is not so weird, although it is a little strange since we just met. It was the chick part that seemed a bit obscure."

"What am I supposed to call you?"

"I don't know. I'm not used to being coupled up with anybody so I don't know what the current terms are these days, but I can almost guarantee you chick is not one of them."

"Hey, if the grammar lesson is over, can we look at my tattoo now?" pouts Marcus stretching his back out.

Ivy walks Marcus over to the mirror and whispers in his ear loud enough for the rest of us to hear, "It's perfect for you. Rogue is amazing. It's clear she loves you very much."

I hold my breath waiting for Marcus's response. This is worse than waiting for my papers to be graded at school.

Instinctually, I grab Ivy's hand. Even though she's not actually talking to me, a sense of calm overtakes me and I hear her voice in my head telling me it'll be fine. It's really spooky. I guess I shouldn't be surprised. If I could feel her broken ankle for a whole year, being able to sense her thoughts when she's a few feet away shouldn't be a big deal.

Marcus turns around to look at me directly after staring at his tattoo for several minutes in the mirror. I guess it's time for me to face the music. This is like facing a final exam of epic proportion because there are no retakes in tattoos — especially of the design I gave Marcus. Because of its intricacy and heavy use of black lines. It would be incredibly difficult, if not impossible to cover, not to mention I used virtually every color on the spectrum. I chose the design purposefully because Marcus is, if nothing else, multidimensional and colorful in every sense of the word. A nice sedate pastel or muted gray tone tattoo just would not have done him justice.

I don't even realize I'm holding my breath until Tristan walks up on the other side of me and puts his arm around my waist. "Rogue, take a deep breath and look at the expression on his face. That's one happy man. You could put what I know about tattoos on a computer key from a broken keyboard, but I would say you hit this one out of the ballpark. So, relax and take in the good news."

Marcus smirks at my expression. "I don't know what you were worried about, Ro. I've been telling you all along — you're one of the best apprentices I've ever had. I meant it then and I mean it now. This piece is flat-out amazing. You took my gibberish and turned it into an amazing coherent piece of artwork. The fact that you combined the concepts of yin and yang together with dragonflies is pure brilliance. The symbolism is so deep. I'm so totally stoked about this tattoo. Out of all of my tattoos, this one is my absolute favorite."

"That's nice of you to say, but I'm sure you don't mean it. You've got some nice, expensive pieces of work by some really famous people."

"You're right, I do." Marcus answers with a shrug. "But, even though those pieces are nice, those artists simply used me as a canvas because I have a nice body, not because they really knew who I was or what made me tick."

"Yeah, but —" I start to interrupt.

Marcus holds up his hand to stop me. "Yeah, but nothing; you designed this piece for me personally, because you know me and you listened to what was important to me about balance and maturity and my inability to stay in one spot and focused on one thing for very long and you incorporated all of those concepts into this completely radical, awesome design. I've been doing tattoos for a long time and designing them on paper for even longer and I would not have been able to pull together this tat. I can't even tell you how artistically perfect it is. You were able to listen to all of my incoherent ramblings and pull all this together in the space of half a day. It's absolutely mind-boggling."

"Breathe," Tristan commands softly in my ear as he kisses my temple. "You did it. You were phenomenal. You did everything you hoped to do and exceeded everyone's expectations."

"Super-Secret-Spy-Guy is right. You should listen to him. I had high expectations for you, but you blew them out of the water. I only have one small critique of the entire tattoo. The very first line you put down was tentative and shaky. But after you got into the groove of things, you completely rocked it and it's as solid as anybody who's been doing this for years — or in some cases better — because your sense of color is spot on. I hate to cover this up. But, I know the routine. So, bandage me up and let's get this show on the road. We've got places to go and people to see."

Ridiculously, my hands are shaking just as bad as I'm taping the bandage on to cover his tattoo as they were when I was taping on the stencil. This time, it's simply an adrenaline crash. I have a tendency to build things up way too much in my head in advance before they happen and give them far too much importance. Until it was over, I hadn't really allowed myself to acknowledge the make-or-break nature of this tattoo. In my heart of hearts, I knew

Marcus would not set me up with an ultimatum. I felt everything was riding on this one tattoo. Yet, now that it's over. I feel much more secure about being able to go to the Los Angeles conference with Marcus. Now, I feel more like a 'legit' tattoo artist instead of a glorified file clerk who happens to work in a tattoo studio.

When I'm finished, Marcus grabs his shirt, watch and phone, then he disappears into the back room.

I turn to Ivy and comment, "Are you ready for this? It's a strange way to spend Thanksgiving. Is your adoptive mom okay with this or will she feel like you deserted your adoptive family for your 'real mom'?"

"I don't really know what they think of it all. I dodged the question completely. I told them I met this girl in the college coffee shop who needs my help straightening out a banking problem. I hope it buys me some time to figure all this out. My dad is so proud of me. I don't want to hurt his feelings. I'm afraid this might crush him."

"I know what you're saying. Then again, we didn't ask for any of this to happen to us, it just did. Maybe, we'll know more after we talk to Mama Rosa."

Ivy rolls her neck and pinches the bridge of her nose. "I'm not sure it'll resolve anything for me since I don't even know what to call your mom. She might hate me on the spot for all I know. This visit may generate more questions than it answers."

Chapter Seven

Tristan

The tension in my Escalade is so thick you can cut it with the proverbial knife. Catching Marcus's eye in the rearview mirror, I shrug helplessly. The women don't seem angry with each other exactly. But, there's some sort of discussion going on between them which is just out of our reach. We can't intercede and make things better for them. It's so frustrating.

Finally, Rogue's distress unnerves me enough that I have to say something, "Why don't you lay the seat back and take a rest. This is a long trip and there's no sense in all of us staying awake. You might as well sleep until it's your turn to drive. After what you accomplished today on Marcus's arm, you not only deserve a catnap, you deserve a deluxe treatment at the spa. You were phenomenal."

Rogue snorts. "As if I could afford something as luxurious as even a half-day at the spa. Are you out of your mind? Do you know how many boxes of macaroni and cheese that kind of money could buy?"

I can't keep my visceral reaction to myself as I give a full-bodied shudder. "Unfortunately, I've eaten copious amounts of all that stuff. I'll never forget what it tastes like as long as I live. While I was developing and testing my software program, I put every dime of extra money I had into equipment and paying an independent testing company. So, I subsisted on beans, rice, leftover pizza from my delivery job, macaroni and cheese and Top Ramen for longer than I care to admit. Actually, it wasn't so long ago."

"I know; it's so weird to think you're not much older than I am. Your life is so removed from my reality that you seem like you're from a different generation."

"Way to make me feel like a lecherous old man. Thanks," I joke as I interlace my fingers with Rogue's.

"Right! Like you've got anything to worry about. It's not like you're Hugh Hefner or anything. What are you — like twenty-eight?"

"Almost, but not quite; I'll be twenty-seven in June."

"Then what are you worried about? Ivy and I will be twenty-two in February."

Rogue turns around in her seat to watch Ivy's reaction to her off-hand statement.

Marcus sweeps some stray hair out of Ivy's eyes. "What do you say? Are we going to have one big birthday blow-out on Valentine's Day, or do I get to spoil you guys twice?"

I watch through the rearview mirror as she reaches up with a shaky hand and takes Marcus's in her own. "I guess it'll be tricky, won't it? Figuring out where Ivy Love ends and *manita* begins. But, what we have is so far beyond that. What's the Spanish word for twin?"

Rogue flashes a grin. "Face it, you're stuck with me, because you're my *hermana gemela*."

"Listen to you! You make it sound like poetry. I, on the other hand, sound like I barely passed ninth grade Spanish."

"It's okay Ivy. It'll only take a couple hours around Mama Rosa and you'll sound just like Rogue here. Her accent is contagious," Marcus says.

"Does anybody else think it's completely bizarre I'm just now meeting my mom when Rogue and I are identical twins? I'm so nervous I haven't slept in three days. I'm not even sure what to call her. My mom doesn't know anything about this — or, maybe she does — I don't really know. Maybe all of this was supposed to be an open adoption and something went wrong. Or maybe it was something even worse like I was stolen from Rosa or Rosa abandoned me and moved away. The scenarios keep spinning around in my brain like some deranged inertia toy which won't stop."

Rogue turns around in the seat and grabs Ivy's hand. "*Manita,* I know it's hard, but you have to stop. You're just hurting your heart. We won't know anything for sure until we talk to our parents. Torturing ourselves with thoughts about wild conspiracy theories won't give us any answers any quicker and it'll only cause us more pain."

"What if she truly didn't want me in her life? What if this is a colossal mistake and I should have stayed away forever?" Ivy asks in a voice barely above a whisper.

"In the off chance it all boils over, you'll always have me. But, I know there has to be some sort of explanation. My mama doesn't throw away people — any people. She would never throw away her own daughter. There must've been some sort of extenuating circumstances which prevented her from keeping you. We'll have to wait and see what the explanation is before we decide how to go from here."

"What am I going to do about my mom?" Ivy implores, her voice full of emotion.

Rogue looks positively destroyed. I can tell she's not only feeling her own personal pain but she's taking on Ivy's pain as well. She looks like she's gone about twelve rounds with a professional boxer.

"If I know anything about moms, generally speaking, their ability to love is pretty much infinite. I'd say the odds are great both of you will end up with two moms out of this situation," I interject.

Her hand is trembling as she somberly turns back around and looks out the window. For a while, the only sounds are the soft murmuring of conversation from the back seat as Marcus tries to comfort Ivy and calm her down and the rhythmic beat of the tires on the pavement. Eventually, I hear Rogue's raw admission over the ambient sound. "Actually, I think I may have the most to lose here. Mama Rosa may be furious that I exposed her secret and if I were to guess, I think Ivy's mom will probably be less than thrilled to learn I work at a tattoo parlor and take classes at Santa Fe Community College. Ivy's parents probably expect me to be almost finished at the University of Florida by now."

I reach out to stroke the back of Rogue's hand. "I didn't get that sense of the family at all. They seem solidly middle-class, but they worked their way there. I don't think they're going to judge you for your position in life. They've both been students once in their lives too. Mrs. Montclair is a teacher herself. I would venture to guess she'll be supportive of your education."

"Still ... look how worried Ivy is about disappointing them," Rogue argues.

I grin. "Something tells me that it might have more to do with being an only child than any harshness on the part of her parents. I was the only kid for a long time, and I know the pressure is immense."

"So, what happened to alleviate your pressure?" Rogue asks with a curious expression on her face.

I grip the steering wheel a little tighter and try to organize my thoughts. There really isn't a good way to explain the situation especially in light of what's going on. So, I go for what I hope is a simplified version of the truth. "She adopted her grandson."

Rogue's eyes go wide with shock, but before she can say anything, two voices from the backseat exclaim in unison, "What?"

Rogue regains her power of speech and stammers, "Not that I mind, but don't you think you should've mentioned you have a kid?"

I shake my head and try to keep the SUV on the road as I attempt to concentrate on driving while I explain the soap opera which is my home life. "Oh, I'm sorry. I didn't mean to imply Elliott is my son. When my mom was a young college student, she was attending a very strict Christian college and she suddenly found herself pregnant. Consequently, she gave up her daughter for adoption. One of the first things I did when I started Identity Bank was to look for my half-sister. It wasn't hard to find Francine. Unfortunately, she and my mom didn't have a chance to meet in person before she went in for dental surgery and had a lethal reaction to anesthesia. The courts couldn't find Elliott's birth father and Francine's adoptive parents were not in good enough health to take him in. But, Francine had left behind tons of letters she and my mom had written back and forth to each other and she had recorded their Skype calls for Elliott. So the court awarded Elliott to my mom."

"Oh wow! That's so sad. You mean they never even met?" Rogue asks on the verge of tears.

"No, unfortunately my mom was having some trouble with headaches and the doctor told her it was probably better for her not to fly until she had them better controlled."

"Man, that sucks," Marcus comments.

"The really stupid irony of it all is she ended up flying all the way to Wyoming to go to the funeral and pick up Elliott anyway."

"How did you react?" Rogue asks softly as she squeezes my hand in support.

I shrug slightly. "Honestly, it probably helped turn me into the person I am today. Since I didn't know how to deal with all the drama going on in the house and the grief my mom was feeling, I turned to computers even more often for escape. They became my friends and confidants, as pathetic as it sounds. It was a safe world for me because everything is predictable in the world of computers. Computers don't burst out crying for no apparent reason, and they don't lash out with unexpected emotion. Of course, as an adult, I understand a bit more about what my mom was going through. Back then I wasn't quite equipped to comprehend it all. Unfortunately, it kicked my parents' fighting up to a whole new level."

"Wait a second," Rogue interrupts. "I thought you said you tracked down your sister as part of your business."

I feel my face turn red, like it does every time I have to talk about my extreme nerdiness. "I guess I probably should've mentioned that I first started helping bounty hunters track people down when I was thirteen — unofficially of course. The second I turned fifteen and could get a work permit, I opened an early version of Identity Bank. It was literally based out of my parents' basement."

Marcus whistles between his teeth. "Wow, I was busy trying to stay out of jail and having a competition with my sister about how many spit wads we could stick to the ceiling before our mom would notice. I feel so under accomplished."

"Before you guys start throwing too big a pity party for Marc, he wasn't too much older than Tristan when he became the newest rock star of the tattoo world. It seems I'm the only one who is a late bloomer," Rogue declares.

Marcus scoffs. "Yeah right. Try again, Ro. I've seen your college transcripts, remember? If you're honest with yourself, you could probably give Super-Secret-Spy-Guy a run for his money in the brains department."

I look at Rogue and quirk my eyebrow with curiosity. She looks down and then shyly admits, "I did okay on my entrance exam, but it doesn't mean I'm in the same league as you."

"Mmm-hmm, it doesn't mean you aren't either. Just because I have a completely unhealthy obsession with computer programming, logical reasoning and spatial relationships, doesn't necessarily mean I'm smart in other areas."

"Is your brother like you?" Ivy asks, bringing the conversation back to where we started.

"Surprisingly, not really. In fact, I think he's pretty much the opposite. He's a senior in high school now and the quarterback on the football team. I don't think he's ever met a stranger. Everybody loves him. He is the quintessential Mr. Popularity — right down to being Prom King. However, school doesn't interest him in the slightest. He does the bare minimum to stay on the team and to get recruited by the college team he wants to play for. Other than sports, he couldn't care less about school."

Marcus catches my eye in the rearview mirror and flashes me a crooked smile as he comments, "I'm guessing that wasn't your high school experience?"

Something about Marcus's deadpan delivery cracks me up. When I finally stop laughing, I reply, "No, it's safe to say that if my brother and I had been in school at the same time, he would've been the one stuffing me in my locker, upside down."

Rogue's body tenses. "I thought that stuff only happened to me because I was poor."

A beat or two later she says, "No, you're right. I guess it happened to you too and from what I gather, you guys weren't exactly destitute."

Marcus's gaze collides with mine in the rearview mirror as we both ask, "What did you say?"

Rogue sighs. "I was just telling Ivy she had a good point."

It's probably rude of me, but I can't stop the startled burst of laughter erupting from about belly-level. "It gets more amazing every time it happens —"

"Mr. Macklin if you keep laughing at me, I'm going to take away all those bonus points I gave you for good manners. What the heck is so funny?"

Ivy pipes up from the back seat. "I'm sorry Rogue, I have to side with Tristan on this one. It is pretty funny."

Rogue looks at us all with confusion and frustration as she demands, "What's so amusing? Somehow I missed the joke. I'm not usually so slow on the uptake."

"Manita, I didn't actually say anything out loud. You heard me in your head and answered me out loud. We totally had a twin moment worthy of a Lifetime Movie," Ivy explains with a grin.

"… or the Discovery Health Channel," quips Marcus, half under his breath.

Rogue sticks her tongue out at Marcus. "Hey! I do not have eleven toes on each foot and eat car parts for lunch! We're not quite that weird. If we were the only twins who could communicate this way, it wouldn't be considered a phenomenon, would it?"

I try to play peacemaker between the two best friends before the spat gets out of control. "Don't get me wrong, I'm not criticizing. I think it's totally cool. I wish I could communicate with somebody that way. In case you haven't noticed, I seem to lack the basic ability to communicate smoothly in regular conversation let alone telepathically."

Rogue gives me a surprised glance. "I don't know… aside from your propensity to laugh at me at inappropriate times, I think you do a good job of communicating. Most times, I understand your intent just fine."

While I'm left to ponder whether she means anything deeper than the surface value of her words, Marcus's stomach lets out a huge audible growl so loud it's distinguishable above the road noise.

"I'm going to take that as a sign it's time to pull over and get something to eat. I need to stretch my legs anyway." I pull off the freeway and I'm shocked to find we've been driving for five hours. This is the most patient group of people I've ever ridden with. Usually with a group this large, you end up stopping every twenty minutes.

Marcus is the first one back to the car. "You trust me?" he asks as he holds his hand out for the key.

"Do you have any experience driving anything

which has more than two wheels?"

"I drove a FedEx truck one summer during college."

"I guess if you can drive one of those, you can handle this."

When Rogue comes out of the restroom, I nod toward the back seat and hold the door open for her. "I guess we're playing musical chairs."

Rogue shrugs, but then cautions, "He'll insist he doesn't need directions, but you might want to pay attention to where he's going, because he tends to be a little directionally challenged."

"Geez, thanks Ro, way to throw a guy under the bus."

"That's okay Marcus, I'll be your navigator. I'm pretty good with mental maps," Ivy offers.

I chuckle softly at the flirty interplay between everyone. "Well, there you go. It seems like everyone is well matched."

After the women climb into the SUV, Marcus expertly navigates us through traffic until he pulls up to a nondescript building. It has faded turquoise and rust stucco on the outside with terra-cotta tiles on the roof. The rest of us look at each other in confusion trying to figure why out of all the restaurants Marcus could have chosen, he would choose such a nondescript yet kitschy hole-in-the-wall.

"Come on guys!" Marcus urges as he tumbles out of the car. "This place has the best wings and potato skins."

"Wings?" I ask, my eyebrows drawn together in confusion. "Are you sure you don't mean Mexican food?"

"I'm positive," he asserts. "Hurry up. All the tables with a good view will be gone."

I guess his odd phrasing should have been my first clue. Unfortunately, I let it fly right over my head; I was blindsided when we walked through the big heavy wooden door and were presented with a 50s-themed karaoke bar.

I notice Ivy pulls her hand away from Marcus. "I can't believe you tricked me into coming to a karaoke bar. If I wasn't so weak from hunger, I'd smack you upside the head with my purse. But, lucky for you, I'm too tired to fight. So, I'm going to roll with it. But, I'm not responsible for any permanent damage done to your hearing as a result of this epic experiment."

"Sugar, there isn't any possible way you sing worse than I do. So, we won't make this a contest about who's better or worse. This is all about being free and creating your own fun. In case you're completely identical to Rogue and you don't recognize this behavior, it's called hanging out and having fun."

"Very funny!" the women respond in unison. They look at each other and say, "Jinx!"

When I see the kitschy stage filled with pictures of Elvis Presley, Sammy Davis Jr. Lucille Ball, Desi Arnaz and Marilyn Monroe, my heart sinks to my toes and is trying to dig a hole through the floor to hide. This is my worst nightmare come to life.

To say I'm shy and awkward is radically understating the situation. You know the kid in the back of your classroom? You know him, the one you know was there but you don't quite know his name — the smart one you sometimes copied from in class, but before you did, you had to look at your yearbook to figure out who he was? That's me. No one ever noticed me until they needed me for something. I was quite happy being that person. I didn't have any social aspirations to be a popular kid or venture out of my shell. Although I'm sometimes called upon to do lectures on cyber security and Internet safety, not much has changed since junior high school when I wanted to disappear into the pale green walls of the classroom.

Rogue notices my discomfort. She slips her arm around my waist and whispers into my neck, "Will you be all right? You don't look so hot. I guess it's my turn to tell you to breathe."

"I suppose it's too late to turn around and go back home?" I ask, only half joking.

Rogue chuckles. "Oh, I wouldn't worry too much about Marc. He's only burning off some nervous energy."

"Well, does he have to do it so publicly?"

"Look on the bright side, nobody here knows us from Adam. So, it makes no difference how badly we suck, we'll live to sing another day."

I groan. "Actually, that's what I'm afraid of. It seems like Marcus makes a habit of public spectacles."

"Don't worry, you get used to it … after two or three years," Rogue deadpans.

Before I can even blink, Marcus scoops up a twin on each arm and escorts them to the stage over a heated protest coming from Ivy. Finally, she acquiesces after she's allowed to pick the song. As they punch the song into the karaoke machine and arrange themselves on stage, I have to admit Marcus looks like a seasoned rock star and the twins look like his professional backup singers. I don't know if they intended to, but they even dressed similarly today, although Ivy's outfit is a little more conservative than Rogue's.

I decide to film the song with my cell phone because I figured they would want this as a memento of their first big road trip. I guess it really shouldn't surprise me that the trio is actually quite talented. It isn't long before the crowd is totally into their rendition of Pharrell Williams' *Happy*. By the time they finish the song, Ivy and Rogue have completely lost all evidence of nerves. In fact, Ivy seems to have stepped into her former role as a cheerleader and is encouraging the crowd to sing along. When the song is over, Rogue and Ivy can barely contain their laughter.

"That was so much fun! I want to do it again!" Ivy tries to drag Rogue back on stage.

Marcus throws an arm around Ivy's waist and pulls her into his lap. "Whoa Sugar, it didn't take long for the bug to bite you. But, do you mind if we get a bite to eat first? The wings here are awesome."

"I could eat some wings. Would you ladies like something to drink?" I offer, pulling out Rogue's chair. "Since my driving tasks are done for a while, I'm going to have a beer."

Rogue wrinkles her nose. "I'm not much of a drinker. Lord knows, Marcus has tried to convert me, but

I don't like it much. I guess I'll have whatever's on tap, but make it light."

I make an involuntary choking sound. "I think I see your problem; most people would have difficulty liking that stuff. It's a little like drinking a side of warm piss with your meal. There's nothing appetizing about that. You know, I can afford to spring for the good stuff," I tease.

Rogue laughs softly at my joke but says, "You know what? I'm just going to play it safe and order a Dr Pepper instead."

Ivy nods. "As long as this isn't going on my bill, I have no such qualms. I'll take a Hefeweizen please."

Rogue's eyes widen. "A what? Did you just order a drink? It sounds like you sneezed."

Ivy laughed. "No, it's a German beer made of wheat. My dad is a beer and wine connoisseur, so he's been boring me with lectures about this stuff long before I could ever try it."

"Is it any good?" Rogue asks curiously.

Ivy shrugs. "It kind of reminds me of homemade bread. You can try some of mine."

"All right, the wings come in teriyaki, mild, medium, hot and 'Don't-Kiss-Anybody-For-a-Week'. What's your pleasure?"

Ivy and Rogue instantly respond, "Hot!"

Marcus stares at them both in surprise. "Are you guys sure? Even smelling their straight-up hot buffalo wings are enough to bring tears to my eyes."

I can tell Ivy is tempted to pat Marcus on the

head. "Yes, I'm sure. I go through about a bottle and a half of Sriracha sauce in a month. My family thinks I'm certifiably nuts."

Rogue high-fives Ivy. "Oh my gosh! I thought I was the only person on the planet who did that. At least it's getting a little more common in the stores now and I don't have to special order it over the Internet."

Marcus looks at the two of them with a slack jaw. "I've got mad respect for the two of you. I can barely eat the green salsa at Taco Bell without sweating."

"You'd be amazed how many small start-up companies there are who specialize in producing barbecue and hot sauces with the word pain in the name. I helped a guy set up a domain name once and did a little marketing research and I was shocked," I interject. "Would you ladies like potato skins or mozzarella sticks with those?"

"Mozzarella sticks," they reply in unison.

Marcus smirks. "Well, at least that simplifies ordering."

After we finished eating, Rogue and Ivy make their way to the stage. Marcus nudges me. "You do realize they are the hottest women in here, right? How do you suppose a couple of guys like us got so lucky?"

"You're the one who looks like a rock star, I have no idea why I'm here."

"I don't know, it seems to me Rogue thinks you're cool. I've never seen her pay attention to anything outside of work or school before and you seem to be front and center in her life. So, I'd say you're making some progress."

Just then, the speakers come to life with the Sister Sledge song, *We Are Family*. The twins are facing each other belting out the song with fantastic finesse and great enthusiasm. The crowd is having a raucous good time. But, they have no way to guess there's a deeper meaning to the words for Ivy and Rogue. So, they're a little confused when in the middle of the song, Rogue gets choked up, sets the mic down and gives Ivy a teary hug. By the end of the song, they are both openly weeping.

By nature, I'm a logical, analytical kind of guy. Emotions are buried deep in me and I don't show them often. As the ladies return to the table, I have to discreetly wipe my tears away before I gather Rogue to my chest.

Ivy taps me on the shoulder. "Tristan, this time, she's having a tough time. But, I don't think she wants my help. I think she needs you. You got it?"

"Yeah, I've got her. Go give your man a cuddle. He's so worried about you that he's about to have an apoplexy."

I drop my arm around Rogue's shoulders in a protective gesture as I escort her through the crowded tables out to a secluded outdoor patio. Surprisingly, it's completely abandoned. I gesture to a small wrought-iron bench. "Shall we sit?"

"Umm, no. I think I need to move. I'm feeling a bit claustrophobic. Do you mind?" Rogue asks anxiously.

"No, I don't mind. I've sat enough today to last a while." I extend my elbow to her in an old-fashioned gesture of gallantry as we exit the patio on to the sidewalk. But, I hesitate. "Give me a second to text

Marcus and let him know we'll be gone for a few minutes."

"Good idea. Let me tell Ivy I'm okay too, although she probably has already figured that out through our weird connection."

After we resume walking I ask her, "Have things really improved or are you just saying that to make me feel better?"

Rogue shrugs eloquently. "It's a moment by moment thing. Sometimes this all seems like it'll be the most epically cool thing to ever happen and it explains most of the weirdness in my life. If I start to think about it too hard, it opens up so many more layers of weird. I can't even fathom all the decisions I'll have to make in the next few weeks and months because of this discovery. I was barely coping with all the chaos in my life before I met all of you and you all have made it infinitely more complicated."

I turn to face her, holding both of her hands in mine. "So, how can I un-complicate it for you?"

"I don't know. I guess you need to be here when it all blows up. I think you've already tried to fix things for me once. It's not that I don't appreciate it; but, I don't even know how to process your help. I mean, I guess today is officially our first date and you've already spent hundreds of dollars to fix my car. Who does that? It kind of stresses me out. What if you start to date me and you decide you can't stand my taste in music or the way I chew my food?"

"I'd like to think I'm not superficial and shallow. If for some reason we decided that we're not right for each other, I'd like you to consider the car repairs as a simple gift. Consider it good karma for all the nice things you've done for other people in the world."

"That's far too generous," Rogue starts to argue.

I try not to let my agitation show. "Look, I don't talk about money very often. But, you need to know that as a percentage of what I'm worth, the cost of me paying for your car repair is about equivalent to you buying me a lotto ticket. I'm not worried about it. I don't expect anything in return and I'd rather not even talk about it again. I did it so you could be safe. It's really that simple. I had no other ulterior motives. If I was trying to be impressive, I could've bought you a car dealership chain, not merely make the necessary repairs to your car."

"Well, your argument might have been on a little firmer moral ground had you not had them completely upgrade my stereo system to the most premium sound system available in the entire store. That's where your argument starts to fall apart. You did not have to get my vehicle equipped with a hands-free mobile system, I could've picked up an inexpensive device at RadioShack which would've probably worked as well."

"True. You could've gotten something economical and sensible, but what fun is that? I have the means to spoil you and I fully intend to. I really haven't taken the time to enjoy the perks of my job. Maybe you've given me a good reason."

"Tristan — I was going to call you by your middle name, but I realize I don't even know it — don't use me as an excuse to be irresponsible. You worked hard for your money. Give it to a good cause — like I don't know… Big Brother/Big Sister or the Ninth Ward in Louisiana. Something … anything … other than me. I'm not a charity case."

I massage my temples. Obviously something is getting lost in translation. It's clear I'm not coded to speak 'woman-speak' well. Give me ones and zeroes and I'm all over it, but this multi-layered emotionally heavy stuff has me talking in circles. I take another run at it.

"Riley. My middle name is Riley, because with a name like Tristan what else would it be? Still, I must be giving the wrong message. I think you are one of the most capable people I've met in a very long time. Your energy and creativity are a sight to behold. I'm in total awe. I'm not doing these things for you because I think you need to be bailed out like some dilapidated charity. I do nice things for you because I like you and it makes my heart happy to see you smile."

"Um, wow," Rogue swallows hard. "There's not a lot of room for misinterpretation there."

"Nope, I thought that was the whole point of talking things through. Should I have left more mystery? I'm never quite sure of the proper balance."

"Don't worry, you're not the only one who's confused. The only thing I am sure of right now is I like you too. Beyond that, it's all pretty much a muddled mess. If you're patient enough to stick around while I figure it all out, more power to you. But, for the record, you do not have to buy me things to make me smile. I think you're a smart and clever guy. Just being around you makes me smile."

"Just to be clear — it's not against the 'Rules of

Dating Rogue' to buy you something nice every once in a while, is it?"

"It depends… are we talking about dinner and movie tickets or shares in Apple?" she challenges with a raised eyebrow.

I chuckle because it hasn't taken her long to figure out my number. "Nice is nice. You don't get to choose your surprises. It's all relative."

"I find that oddly frightening."

"Makes it all the more fun," I answer with a mischievous grin. "Do you know how many women look at me and only see dollar signs? It's discouraging. You're the first person who I've had a real conversation with in as long as I can remember. Most people are too busy calculating what I can do for them. I have to say, it's a totally refreshing change of pace."

Rogue studies me for a few long moments. "How odd. We're at polar opposites of the social spectrum and on the surface we shouldn't have anything in common, but it seems you have even less reason to trust people than I do. It's a sad commentary on modern life, if you ask me."

"I think you're right. I think we have a lot of things in common. As far as my social station in life goes, I think you have forgotten that this is a pretty new thing for me. I'm not far removed from collecting cans to be able to make my rent."

"Are you ever afraid you'll end up back in a bad place?"

"Sometimes, in my deepest nightmares, I am. I

think that's why I still work crazy hours, even though the financial folks who work for me tell me I could retire to some beach somewhere with a frosty drink, complete with an umbrella."

Rogue breaks eye contact with me and looks down at her feet. "I actually have never had the pleasure."

"Really? How long have you lived in Florida?" I ask, incredulous. "I thought it was a rite of passage."

"Me too. When I lived in Vermont, I used to fantasize about what it'd be like to live here. I used to think I would live in a cute little ocean front condo and go to beach parties every weekend. Instead, I live in an apartment that's approximately the size of a crackerjack box which backs up to a dilapidated bowling alley and I share custody of it with cockroaches which have lived several generations longer than I've been alive."

It's all I can do not to growl out loud when I hear about her living situation. "Marcus needs to pay you more. I've seen the quality of your work and you deserve a raise."

"Believe me, he's offered several times. Still, I can't take advantage of our friendship. I need to be treated like every other apprentice in the industry — otherwise I won't ever be respected."

I softly brush a kiss against her forehead. "You are certainly a fan of the road less traveled. How about if I keep you company on your path?"

CHAPTER EIGHT

IVY

IT'S EXTREMELY HARD FOR ME to pay attention to what's going on around me because I'm worried about my sister. It's still bizarre to think of her in those terms. But, for me she really has always existed. I just didn't know she was real.

Marcus taps me on the shoulder and I about jump out of my skin. "It's gonna be all right. I've known Ro for a long time and she's a tough cookie. Tristan will take care of her, I'm sure."

"Oh, I know. She's already feeling better. I wish I didn't upset her so much. I had no idea signing up for a stupid dating site would lead to so much turmoil."

"Wait a second! I'd like to think it's led to a little more than that. I've been called a lot of things in my life, but there's a lot more to me than just turmoil."

I fight the urge to stick my tongue out at him. "Talk about taking what I said out of context ... I meant the sisterly relationship, smart aleck. Although, my presence in your life probably isn't doing any favors for your relationship with Rogue."

"You'd be surprised. Rogue's been trying to match me up with her friends for a while. So, you could consider us the ultimate blind date."

"If you say so. But you have to admit it's got elements straight out of any cheesy daytime soap opera."

"I'm surprised a good girl like you would waste your time watching soap operas. Speaking of wasting time, let's go sing a song. We shouldn't let great karaoke go unsung."

"Sounds like a plan. But, I'm slightly afraid to let you choose the song."

"If you're feeling brave, there's always the option of allowing the karaoke machine to choose the track for you," Marcus challenges.

I sigh dramatically. "Well, after the last song, it's not as if I have a lot of dignity left to preserve. I say let's go for it."

Marcus rubs his hands together in glee. "This ought to be good."

Marcus places his arm around my waist and snugs me up to his side as we walk up to the stage.

Marcus programs the machine to make a random choice for us and when we turn around to face the audience, someone shouts, "What happened to the other one? Did you lose her? I'll be more than happy to take her off your hands."

Marcus laughs. "Thanks for the offer, but it's not necessary. She's my buddy's girlfriend. Only this one's mine."

Another voice from the audience pipes up, "Don't you ever get them mixed up?"

"Nah, not really. They aren't actually much alike when you look closely. In fact, they have completely different personalities."

The first guy says, "It's too bad the first girl had a boyfriend, it would've been fun to have identical twins."

Much to Marcus's credit, he visibly shudders at the comment. "No thanks, I think I'll pass. That's not a fantasy I've ever had."

I about swallow my tongue when I hear the opening notes of the song the karaoke machine has chosen for us. It's the Katy Perry and John Mayer song, *Who You Love*.

In light of the conversation we had, there is a certain degree of irony in the lyrics of this song. However, it is a bit awkward considering that we've just now officially started dating.

On the surface, Marcus is everything my conservative, by-the-numbers dad is likely to hate on sight with his wild hair, piercings and tattoos. But, if my dad can look past all the superfluous differences, I think he'll find they actually have a lot of stuff in common. They are both small business owners who bucked family tradition to forge their own path in the world. My dad comes from a family whose legacy includes several generations of firemen and policemen. Although my dad thinks those are fine professions, they were not ideal matches for him. He preferred to see the world through the much more ordered and precise prism of numbers and accounting rather than adventure and adrenaline.

Marcus and my dad could have some spirited discussions about baseball and the politics around the inclusion of players into the Baseball Hall of Fame. It would be an interesting meeting to say the very least. I can't shake the feeling that it could grow into an amazingly supportive relationship for everyone involved.

As Marcus sings the lyrics of the John Mayer song about finding someone you least expect when you're not really looking, the lyrics hit home for me. In fact, it's appropriate in more ways than I can even imagine. I set out with the hypothesis someone was playing a cruel, extended prank or scam on me only to find a sister I never knew I had and a phenomenal boyfriend who seems almost too good to be true.

I have to stop singing and swallow hard to collect my emotions as the song draws near an end. I know it's far too early for us to be even almost considering tossing the L word around, but it's mentioned repeatedly in the song. It's a stark reminder that our personal lives are not the same as what we often hear sung about in songs or read about books. We're not there yet. There's no guarantee we'll even make it that far.

Marcus finally steps out of his karaoke stage persona long enough to study the expression on my face. He turns to the crowd. "I guess I've learned something today. A random song choice can say everything you'd like to say, but the timing can be all sorts of wrong. So, I hope I didn't scare this one away by inviting her out for karaoke tonight because I hope she decides to stick around."

A woman from the audience yells, "Honey, you should give him another chance. It wasn't his fault the karaoke machine chose that song."

I turn to answer the woman, "I think he worries a bit too much. He would be shocked if he knew what I was actually thinking. I was wishing that we had been dating a little more steadily. I have a long list of songs with lyrics I love. But they don't seem appropriate because we've just officially started dating," I blurt. However, as soon as the information comes flying out of my mouth, I'm immediately embarrassed. This is not the time or place for me to have a public airing of all my deepest dirty laundry.

I thought I was pretty circumspect about all my somewhat-dirty-leaning thoughts. However, it quickly becomes apparent maybe I haven't been when I hear a thought from Rogue intrude my thought process as clearly as if she's standing right next to me, "Careful, it is surprisingly easy to embarrass Marcus. He's more fragile than he looks."

Immediately I gaze out into the audience to see if I can find what has become my own personal Jiminy Cricket. Rogue winks at me when she catches my eye. Marcus grabs my hand so we can give a theatrical bow. Fortunately, I'm getting used to the weird twin phenomenon with Rogue, so I'm not completely thrown off balance. Hopefully, nobody noticed the really strange lapse in concentration this time.

Marcus doesn't let my hand go after the bow and we walk hand in hand back to the table. When we get there, Tristan is already paying the tab. "Hope you guys don't mind, but I think Rogue has had enough for the day. While we were out on our walk, we reserved a couple of hotel rooms up the street."

"Well, this isn't awkward at all …" Marcus says, rubbing the back of his neck.

"Come on Ivy, it's time for us to go freshen up," Rogue declares, pulling me in the direction of the bathroom.

"I don't really ne —" I start to protest.

"I'm pretty sure it's not what she means," Tristan explains with a chuckle.

"Oh," I mumble, embarrassed to be so slow on the uptake. I can't even blame it on the beer. By the time I finished giving samples to Marcus and Rogue, there wasn't even enough left to develop a good buzz.

Therefore, I dutifully follow my sister into the bathroom. She takes a paper towel and dries off the sink before she hops up on the counter and sits down. "So, *Manita,* how do we want to handle this?"

Okay. Nothing like getting right to the crux of the matter. I can't help but feel like this is some sort of test. I'm totally clueless about how I'm supposed to answer the question. If I'm honest and tell her I'm right in the middle of a dicey conversation with Marcus, she might take it to mean I don't want to spend time with her. Yet, that's not exactly true. I'm just not sure which one I should choose.

Rogue examines me with an amused twinkle in her eye. "You know, if you think much harder about this, little blue trails of smoke are going to start to come out of your ears."

I glance up, startled she could read my thought process so easily. But then again, I guess I shouldn't be. She seems to know my thoughts before I actually think them. "I'm sorry, I'm trying to figure out the right thing to do without offending anybody."

"Well, if the guys are offended if we choose to spend time together after we were just reunited, they need to get over themselves and if you're worried about offending me, don't worry about it."

"Really? You wouldn't be upset if I spent the night with Marcus? It seems like we're at a kind of critical point in our relationship. I'd just like to figure out where we're going with things."

"It's not a problem. Really. Did you honestly think I'd have a problem with being spoiled all night by a guy who, by all appearances, seems to worship the ground I walk on? I actually think I'm okay with that. Go have fun with Marcus. Be gentle with him though. He likes to act all street-tough, but he's got a tender heart. Most people don't even realize he's one of the good guys."

After Rogue hops down from the counter, I give her a brief hug. "I'll try to take good care of him. Best friends are hard to find. We'll see you in the morning for breakfast."

As we walk hand-in-hand back into the restaurant, there are four very curious, intent eyes on us. Marcus nudges Tristan. "Uh-oh, they're holding hands. This doesn't look good for us buddy. A marathon of WWE pay-per-view, it is, roomie."

Tristan quietly studies us for a moment. "No, I

think you've jumped to the wrong conclusion. I suspect you and I will be parting ways tonight. I believe I'll be tucking Rogue in tonight."

My mouth drops open in shock. "That's impressive. I have no idea how you did it, but you busted us."

"I hate to break it to you, but you're not all that difficult to read. You either put on ten times more blush than you usually use or you are embarrassed and you can't look Marcus directly in the eye. So, something is up. Given the topic of discussion on the table, it isn't hard to put two and two together."

"Well, I guess it's a good thing I don't have any career aspirations to be a spy or anything, isn't it?"

Tristan nods solemnly. "Yes, the world is probably a safer place."

Rogue playfully punches him on the arm. "You didn't have to agree with her. She was making a rhetorical statement to illustrate her point. You didn't have to rub it in."

"Sorry, I wasn't trying to be rude. I was just agreeing with what seemed like an obvious statement. I didn't mean to offend you."

I have to laugh at his obvious contriteness. It's clear he really wasn't trying to be rude and I really wouldn't make a very good spy. Still, it's nice to have someone come instantly to my defense. I wish she'd been around when I was growing up and the bullies were picking on me at school. It would've been downright handy to have another person on my side —especially someone as spunky as Rogue.

"It's all right. I fully accept where my strengths and weaknesses are. They're not a newsflash to me."

Marcus fidgets a bit before he finally blurts, "Well, are we going to get this show on the road, or what? I suppose Super-Secret-Spy-Guy stays in a much higher-class hotel than I'm used to. I bet you don't have to pay an additional deposit for extra blankets and pillows and you probably can't see through the towels either."

"I should hope not. If we can, we need to get our money back and stay somewhere else."

"Since I'm designated driver tonight, I'll drive your rig over. Text me the name of this swanky palace, okay?"

"Sure, let me give Ivy her key. Everyone's already signed in. So, we'll see you at breakfast." Tristan fishes a key out of his jacket pocket and hands it to me. My eyes widen as I see the name on the key. I'm used to pretty nice travel. Still, I'm not used to the kind of places they feature in travel magazines. This is that kind of place. My fingers are itching for my Leica M7. People think I'm weird for not making the jump to digital. But I like the old-fashioned process of developing my own film and sadly all I have with me is my cell phone. The camera is decent, but it's not the same. I do have my pad and colored pencils. So, that's something at least.

"Sounds good, see you *mañana*," Marcus ushers me out the door. Perhaps I should be worried by the predatory expression on his face, but I have a feeling I can give as good as I can get. He just thinks I'm the uptight shy one. I can be fun and spontaneous — I hope. Okay … I admit, this is way outside my comfort zone.

But, I started this whole adventure because I wanted to do something different, give myself permission to be someone different. This certainly fits the bill. So, I take a deep breath and smile as I tuck my hand into Marcus's back pocket while we stroll down the sidewalk toward Tristan's SUV.

After he unlocks the door, he traps me against the seat. He runs the back of his hand along my cheek, "You are just so beautiful. It takes my breath away."

Something about his compliment strikes me as funny. "Yeah, I look like the spitting image of Rogue. Funny how that works when you're twins," I respond sarcastically.

"At first, I thought I would notice mostly the similarities. But, the longer I hang around the two of you, the less I remember the twin thing—unless you guys have one of your twilight zone episodes. It's not a big deal to me."

I feel like he has knocked all the air from my lungs. "No big deal? How in the world can you say that? Being a twin has the potential to change my whole world — maybe destroy it as I know it. Someone screwed up and tore us apart. How can you say it's not a big deal?" I ask, my voice beginning to sound hysterical.

Marcus cups my face in his hands as he kisses me gently on the lips, "Ivy, relax, Sugar. I didn't mean to suggest the mistakes shouldn't matter to you. They really should, all the way down the line. Everybody who lied should be held accountable for their actions because that's simply wrong. You didn't choose to be adopted and Rogue didn't choose to have the survivor's guilt over being the one left behind. The whole situation is just messed up."

I sniff back my tears and try to wipe them on the sleeve of my sweatshirt so Marcus doesn't realize what a mess I've become. "It really is a tangled ball of ugliness, isn't it? Do you think we'll ever get to the bottom of it all?"

Marcus shrugs and pushes his Ray-Ban sunglasses up to the top of his head. "I don't know."

"Why are you wearing sunglasses anyway? It's November."

He shrugs. "Habit I guess. I started wearing them when I was a kid, so the thugs I was hanging out with couldn't tell I was way younger than Tomás. I just wanted to fit in. I suppose not much has changed over the years."

I reach up and pull them completely off his head and throw the sunglasses behind me on the console. "That's really too bad because you shouldn't hide these gorgeous eyes from anyone." I run my fingertip along his brow line. I cringe when I encounter a barbell in his eyebrow.

"Didn't it hurt? I know that I'm a big baby when it comes to my eyes. I have to psych myself up just to pluck my brows."

"It didn't hurt as much as some. But, it hurt more than some others. Let's put it this way. It's not something I'd want to have done every day. But, that's pretty much true of all my piercings. I'd much rather get a tattoo any day."

"If they hurt so much though, why get them

done at all?" Confusion rings clear in my voice.

Marcus drops his hands to my waist. He's massaging the small of my back as he answers my somewhat random questions. "I don't know, Ivy. It's difficult to answer because it's different for every person. But, I think most people find tattoos a little addicting. For some it's the whole concept of having your entire body as a canvas. For others it's actually the repetitive sting of the needle; still others are attracted to the counter-culture aspect of it all. I guess it's an individual thing and different for everyone."

"Why does it hold such allure for you?" I ask, pointing to the big bandage on his arm from this morning.

"For all the reasons I spelled out — and a couple more I don't know you well enough to share yet."

I nod. "Fair enough. But, I hope you think I know you well enough to do this —"

I pull him closer and kiss him. At first, I'm tentative. But,. tightening his arms and drawing in a harsh breath, I kiss him more assertively. For a minute or two, we exchange progressively spicier kisses until he pulls away.

"I need to take a breather and remember that we're in a strange city. We don't need to be arrested for public indecency. Lucky for you, your sister's boyfriend has arranged a place for us to take this someplace private. Are you still game?"

After the hottest few minutes I can ever remember enjoying in my life, I can only come up with one plausible response, "You bet."

CHAPTER NINE

MARCUS

AS WE ENTER THE LOBBY of the hotel and encounter a floor-to-ceiling waterfall with a built-in aviary I lose my battle not to gawk like a curious seven-year-old. However, as I glance over at Ivy, I realize I'm not the only one dazzled by our surroundings. She has her cell phone out and she's kneeling on one knee like a professional photographer as she tries to capture a particularly colorful macaw.

I run my hand along the rich burl wood railing. "So, this is how the other half lives, huh?"

She stands up and walks in a slow circle taking in her surroundings. "Don't look at me. I'm not in the half that lives like this. This is definitely a first for me."

"Come on, let's go to our room. If the lobby looks like this, can you imagine what our room looks like?" I practically bounce with excitement.

"Well, this is certainly not the Super 8," she comments dryly.

"I know. Isn't it great? It does not suck to have friends that have money and aren't afraid to spend it."

Ivy starts to bite her lip with indecision, but finally she speaks, "Umm, you can tell me to shut up if this isn't any of my business —"

I have to fight my natural tendency to do something radical to break the mood. So, I smother a grin and encourage her to continue. "Go ahead. I don't have very strong privacy filters in my life."

"I know," she grins. "That's true. I've seen your Facebook page. I guess I'm just confused. It looks like your shop is doing really well. Everything looks top-notch and modern. Are things not going okay?'"

Her concern is touching. So, I hasten to assure her, "No, you're right. My shop is actually doing just fine. I just have other obligations to my family and the causes I support like Big Brother/Big Sister and Habitat for Humanity that I dedicate most of my paycheck to. So, I choose not to live very large. Rogue teases me all the time about my decision to live in accommodations which are barely tolerable for a homeless person."

"Is it really that bad?"

"No, not really. I'm kind of taking artistic license in my description. By Florida standards, it's pretty low end considering that I don't have any kids. It's not what you would classify as a swanky bachelor pad, that's for sure."

"Well, I can think of a lot of worse reasons to live in a junky place. I think it's cool that you're taking care of other people. I wish there were more people in the world like you," she says as she grabs my hand and pulls me toward the elevator. "Come on. Let's go see what pure decadence feels like. I have a feeling Tristan was feeling the need to show off a little for Rogue and we may have been the unintended beneficiaries."

I wink at her as I give her a mock salute. "Here's to the accidental perks of double dating. May your sister's relationship with Super-Secret-Spy-Guy live long and prosper."

She playfully swats me on the butt. "You are so bad! That's your best friend you're talking about. You cannot give my sister dating advice based on the quality of perks you're going to get from her boyfriend! That's just wrong."

I draw my brows together for a moment as I think about that. "You know, come to think of it, it has been a really bad strategy. Lawrence Poser had his own nightclubs, but he was a terrible boyfriend. Then there was that Henry guy; he had court-side seats to the Miami Heat and ran a fantasy basketball league. There was only one problem — he carried an iPad everywhere he went and never put it down. You could be having a conversation with him and his eyes never left the screen. It was totally annoying. Rogue never said anything but I don't believe she even had the opportunity to kiss him because I don't think he ever got the iPad out of his face."

Ivy giggles. "You're beginning to see why sites like BrainsRSexy.com exist. It's a strange and scary world of dating out there. What about you? Have you been dating?"

"Well, I've been going on a lot of first and second dates; but, not much beyond that. A lot of women have a very glamorous idea about what it's going to be like to date the owner of a tattoo shop — especially one like mine. They expect that there's going to be a never-ending stream of rock stars and celebrity clients through the shop every day and that after-hours we're going to be constantly partying with these people like we know them personally."

"How shallow can you be?" Ivy huffs indignantly.

"Right? That's what I always thought. But, some of my friends said I should just get over it and settle into the hero worship schtick. It just feels artificial to me. We don't really have all that many celebrity clients and those who do choose my shop are relying on me to keep their information confidential. So, I'm not going to go blabbing about their tattoos so my girlfriend can feel like she's dating somebody important. Does that make any sense?"

Ivy smiles at me as she fixes the collar on my jacket. "It makes perfect sense to me. It's not a very hard concept to understand. I don't even have a tattoo yet, but even I understand that it's a very personal, private thing that everybody processes and shares differently. You probably hold as much confidential information about somebody as a hairdresser or bartender — if not more, because you spend so much time together. If someone can't respect that, they don't need to be in your life. Don't compromise your values in order to be with somebody; that's just stupid."

Until this very moment, I didn't realize how important it was to me that somebody truly understand me and my personal value system. But, as my brain and my heart process her simple declaration, I feel the hardness that's been protecting my heart melt away like a glacier in the tropics.

"Thank you," I murmur against her temple.

She pulls away looking at me quizzically. "Thank you for what? I didn't really do anything."

"Actually, strangely enough you have. From the time we met, you've taken the time to look beneath my appearance and my job to try to find out who I am and what I'm about instead of jumping to conclusions based on the stereotypes. To me, that means the world."

The tips of Ivy's ears turn red and she looks down toward the ground. "It just so happens that I think you're well worth knowing, Mr. Brolen."

Ivy hands me the key to the door. With a snick of the lock, it opens easily. I guess I shouldn't have really been surprised when we step inside and encounter a suite about the size of my entire apartment.

"Wow! Can you imagine what Jessica would say about this? She would have a cow! We could fit two of our dorm rooms in this and still have some room left over, I think." Ivy sits on the bed and runs her fingers over the comforter.

I walk over to the closet and pull out two very lush robes. I turn to Ivy and suggestively wiggle my eyebrows. "Well now, what do you suppose we should do with these?"

Ivy practically sprints over to the side of the bed to get the hotel guide. She rapidly thumbs through it until she finds the hotel map. "Oh my gosh! You're not going to believe this! They have two!"

Her enthusiasm is way over the top, but then again, I suppose mine is too. I've stayed in places that I've considered nice, but they've never approached anything like this. "Okay, I'll bite. They have two what?" I ask with an amused grin.

"Saunas! Can you believe that? They have two saunas. Do we prefer Tropical Paradise or Majestic Rain Forest?"

"I don't know that I have a preference. I've never actually been in a sauna before. So, I'll have to defer to your expertise on this one."

Ivy taps her chin in contemplation. "I suppose saunas would be more popular in Vermont than in Florida, wouldn't they?"

"Yeah, our weather pretty much takes care of the need for saunas around here. All of you out-of-towners think this is the perfect place for a vacation while the locals know the real truth."

"Really, and what would that be?" Ivy asks with crossed arms.

"On our snarkiest of days, we locals call Florida the armpit of Satan."

Ivy scoffs at my characterization of our warm, sunny weather. "Oh, you poor abused man suffering from a few too many ultraviolet rays and the rustling of palm trees. Come talk to me when you've had to dig out from inside your house when your entire front door has been snowed shut—right up to the eaves of your house twelve or thirteen feet high. Then you might have the right to complain about miserable weather. Until then, you'll have to excuse me if I play you the world's smallest violin which is so small that I'll have to use a microscope to play it."

I hold my palms up in a gesture of surrender. "Okay, you win! Obviously I have no reason to complain about Florida weather in comparison to the weather in Vermont. I guess I'd rather deal with hot and sticky than several feet of snow any day."

Ivy gives me a smug grin. "I thought you might see it my way. Not much can compete with winters up north when it comes to weather catastrophes. It's funny, when most people celebrate the first snowfall of the season, whenever we get the first snow, all of us Vermonters are looking at each other saying to ourselves, 'Oh crap. Here we go again. I wonder if it will be July before we're unburied again.' It sort of takes all the joy out of it for us."

"I'm not sure how you do it. I'd go stir crazy for sure. How do you like Florida?"

"To be honest, I miss Vermont more than I thought I would. I miss the hokey stuff like warm PJ's and hot spiced apple cider." Ivy closes her eyes and leans her head back on my chest. "Soup. I miss soup. No one eats a good hearty thick soup in Florida."

"Stop! You're making me hungry!" I protest, rubbing her tummy because she's standing in front of me.

She turns around in my arms. "I have a feeling that very little doesn't make you hungry. Let me guess, when you go home, you still con your granny out of homemade cookies like you did when you were five, don't you?"

I frown at her innocent question. "No, sadly I can't. She died from lung cancer."

Ivy slides the pad of her thumb across my throbbing temple. "I'm so sorry."

"It's not your fault, Sugar. It happened a really long time ago. It still makes me sad though. She was a good person."

"I understand. There's not many folks left in my family either. It's just my parents and me. Think that's why my dad is so set on having the whole family business thing."

"I know I haven't met your dad yet, but I'd be willing to bet he doesn't want his baby girl unhappy. I can tell from the face that you make when you talk about anything to do with business that being an accountant definitely would not make you happy."

Sighing heavily, Ivy rests her forehead against my shoulder. "But what if I have to choose between making myself happy or making my dad happy?"

"I can't help but think that's not the choice here. I think that if your dad knows you at all, he's going to understand that accounting isn't really your gig."

"I hope you're right and it's just that simple. But I have a feeling this thing with Rogue is going to open up a whole new can of worms. So, who knows where this conversation will go. I'm afraid that my relationship with my dad will be forever damaged beyond repair. What if he hates me for finding Rogue and disrupting our little family unit?"

I place my arms around Ivy and pull her close. "Or, what if they think it's the most miraculous thing they could've ever imagined?"

Ivy draws a shaky breath. "That's the other thing that I'm afraid of. What if they meet her and they think she's a better version of me? She's cooler and more street savvy. She's led a far more interesting life than I could ever dream of. It's possible that they could love her even more than they ever loved me."

Marcus kisses my forehead. "Now you sound like a real paranoid sibling. In my experience, that's not how parental love works. Somehow, parents all around the world manage to find something unique and special about each child without sacrificing their love for their other kid. It's amazing how that works."

"I know you think I'm being stupid. But I just don't know how to process all of this. I've never had a sister before and it seems like Rogue is all the things I'm not. She's edgy, fashionable, comfortable in her own skin and popular with people. I can see that it would be much easier to love and accept a person like her."

I grin at her. "I think you'd be really surprised if you heard Rogue's assessment of you. She's worried about not being accepted by your family because you are so much more gentle, refined, cultured and beautiful. She thinks that your sense of humor is hysterically funny and sharp and pointed. She thinks you have a brilliant mind and she's afraid she may not match up to your success."

"Me?" Ivy whispers hoarsely, "What is she talking about? I don't have a tenth of her talent and I can't even muster the courage to have a conversation with my daddy about what I want to be when I grow up. So much for my brilliant mind, huh?"

"Well, I think your mind is pretty brilliant. But I also think it needs a break. So, what's it going to be? The Tropical Paradise room or the Majestic Rain Forest room?"

"Well, I've always had a thing for the movie Fern Gully, so I guess Majestic Rain Forest it is."

"You're kidding! I thought I was the only kid totally obsessed with that movie. I wouldn't let my mom throw away any paper for six months after I watched it. I thought for sure she was going to kill every tree in the forest," I remark, laughing at the memory.

A look of panic crosses Ivy's face. She strides over to her suitcase and dumps it out on the bed. "Oh, please tell me this isn't happening —"

She starts to dig frantically through the piles murmuring a few choice curse-words under her breath. She's not sounding so refined right at the moment.

As things start to fall off the bed, I pick them up and fold them, placing them in a pile. This is triggering my OCD in ways that I can't even explain. Finally, I can't handle it anymore I walk up behind her and envelop her in a hug from behind. "Sugar, tell me what's going on," I coax.

"I should've listened to Jessica and done a stupid checklist, that's what's going on —"

"That doesn't really tell me much."

"I forgot my dang swimming suit. I can't go in the sauna without a swimming suit."

I arch my eyebrow. "Well, actually you can. I definitely wouldn't mind."

Ivy blows out her breath in frustration. "Actually, I would. We don't know each other that well yet. You truly don't need to see me naked. I've got all sorts of battle scars. I've been sick a lot and I've had multiple surgeries it's not a pretty sight. We're going to have to get to know each other a whole lot better before I show you any of that garbage."

"Oh, is that all? That's no big deal. I'll just get you a suit from the gift shop."

"At this time of night?" Ivy asks incredulously.

"Oh it's not a problem if you've made friends with the concierge."

Ivy looks dubious. "How do we make friends with the concierge now? He probably just wants to take a nap."

"I don't think we have to worry about that, Sugar. I think Tristan took care of it so that everybody in this hotel will take care of whatever we need — no matter what the cost."

"I hope he knows he didn't need to do that," Ivy shakes her head in disbelief.

"I think that's part of the reason that the Super-Secret-Spy-Guy likes to do it for us. He knows that we don't expect it from him and that we'd like him either way. So, I think he does it as a way to befuddle Rogue. She does seem uncharacteristically confused by his behavior."

"I agree, Tristan seems really comfortable with Rogue. He probably can't afford to be that open and vulnerable with a lot of people. I suspect most folks try to take advantage of him because of his money."

"Trust me, Rogue won't be one of those people. His money totally freaks her out. I've never seen a woman so resistant to being treated nicely in my whole life. This is going to be fun to watch. So, shall we go talk to the concierge or would you like to rummage through my luggage too?"

Ivy looks over at the destruction on the bed. "Uh oh! Don't tell me that you're one of those neat freaks — "

"Is this going to be a deal breaker?" I rub the back of my neck nervously.

"I don't know," Ivy answers with a small smile. "To be honest, I'm not all that surprised. I've seen your shop. It's totally meticulous. It's so clean and well organized I don't think you've ever had so much as a dust bunny. Frankly, that level of clean intimidates the heck out of me. I don't know if I can live up to that kind of perfection. Since I like you, I'm willing to give it a shot. The question is how long can you put up with me. I'm not a total slob, but compared to you? There's no way I can measure up."

I'm really shocked that she's noticed that much about me. Most people see the crazy hair, the big earrings and the menacing, colorful tattoos and they don't bother to look at anything else. They don't understand that I'm a complex ball of contradictions under the stereotypically bad boy persona.

I may look like the personification of a bad biker boy but I'm really a family guy who's trying to turn my life around from the scared-wanna-be-gangbanger I was at twelve. I was using drugs and alcohol even back then to cover up things I knew I shouldn't be doing. Fortunately, for me, somebody with some brains saw that I had artistic potential and took me under his wing on the condition that I stayed clean and sober.

Lucky for me, I was scared enough that I took Picasso up on his offer. If I hadn't been, who knows where my life would be right now? Yet, being clean and having a career focus hasn't completely quieted the nervous energy that's haunted me since I was a kid. It's always been a struggle for me to focus on the stuff that I'm supposed to pay attention to.

In kindergarten, when we were supposed to be learning our letters, instead of focusing on how to form the letters, I would be sidetracked by how the colors didn't match in the illustrations, if my T-shirt itched or if the class hamster made a noise. It seemed that I could never quite tune into the right frequency. It was really frustrating to be labeled the bad, rambunctious kid in school. I didn't want to be moving constantly. I just didn't know how to calm my mind and body. Eventually, I developed my own little coping mechanisms like mentally counting, hyper organizing and wearing headphones and sunglasses all the time to help limit the outside input. The other kids just thought I was being cool. I was okay with that perception because it helped me hide a lot.

Picasso was pretty much a genius when it came to motivation. The more successful I was in school, the more complex tattooing work he allowed me to do. So, he was able to motivate me to excel in school and move up within his organization at the same time.

Picasso is the reason why I work with kids in the Big Brother/Big Sister program. I want to pay forward the help I was given as a young teenager. If I can save another kid from going down the same path I went down, it'll be totally worth it. Better yet, if I can keep him out of jail so no mother has to go through the pain that my mom went through when Tomás went to jail, that would be even better.

"That's okay. It would be good for me to learn a little bit of flexibility. I can be a little set in my ways. Maybe we can both teach each other a few new tricks."

I can't believe that the whole point of the sauna is to sweat. All this time, I thought that it was something really glamorous, but I can get this working in my backyard. Sure, the wood paneling and the music, foliage, candles and aromatherapy that they've included in the Majestic Rain Forest Room provide a very nice romantic atmosphere. But, in the end it's still a big room where you sweat. Ivy doesn't seem to be having any of these reservations as she sits reading a glossy chick magazine with a plethora of celebrity pictures. She looks up at me, her eyelashes spiky with sweat. "Can you believe they opened up the gift shop for just the two of us? Isn't that wild?"

"It was rather epic to be treated like some sort of celebrity. I could get used to that. I really like your purchase, by the way."

Ivy preens and strikes a few model poses in her red bikini with teeny white polka dots. "Thanks, this definitely doesn't fit within my usual bounds."

I leisurely study her from head to toe. "I don't see why not. You look absolutely gorgeous. You would give any fashion model a run for her money."

Ivy laughs out loud. "Now I know you're just being polite. I've got enough ugly scars on me to make a Rand McNally map jealous. I also know this little scrap of material they cleverly call a bathing suit disguises nothing. So, as much as I appreciate your manners, a fib is still a fib."

I grab a towel and dry myself off as I walk over to her and pull her up to a standing position. I run my fingertip down the scar over her sternum. "I don't find this scar ugly at all. Do you know what it means to me?"

Ivy shakes her head mutely as she searches my face for clues.

"It means you're a born survivor. You're a fighter and stronger than I could ever hope to be. This is tangible proof that you don't give up. Wear it with pride, you earned it. As I understand, few people actually live through what you did, let alone thrive."

"I've never really thought about it like that. I always figured my scars were what made me different and less attractive."

"I can't speak for everyone else, but that's not the way I see you."

"Well, obviously you've never hung around a bunch of junior high school kids."

"I'm sad to say, I was probably one of the kids who would have bullied you back in the day. I was not what you would consider an upstanding citizen."

Ivy strokes my shoulder above my bandage, "That's okay. I think we're all capable of changing. I've done some things I'm not so proud of either."

"I can't imagine you ever being anything but perfect." I kiss her tenderly.

Ivy chuckles softly as she pulls away. "I think you must have me mixed up with some other spoiled suburban Princess, but I'll just leave that to your imagination."

"Ivy, I hate to admit this, but I think I recognize the garlic pizza I ate last week. I don't think I have much more sweat left in me. So what's next?"

Ivy grins mischievously. "It depends. How adventurous are you feeling?"

Well, that's an open-ended question if I've ever heard one. My mind goes in a million different places, so I decide to take a gamble.

"I'm not the kind of guy to play it safe. Give me what you've got," I challenge.

"Did I tell you I like a man with a true sense of adventure? Do you know what I love even more than that?"

I shrug, totally clueless about where she's going with this, but completely intrigued. A few weeks ago, she was calling my bluff about not really being an edgy, bad boy, so I'm very curious where she's headed.

"Well, I love a guy who's willing to trust me implicitly. Especially when you don't know what I've got up my sleeve."

I give her an appreciative once over. "Not to be technical or anything, but from where I'm standing you can't exactly be hiding much in that gorgeous outfit, so I guess I'll just take my chances."

"Oh, you'd be surprised —" Ivy teases as she grabs my hand and leads me out of the sauna. At the last minute, I scoop up our towels.

As she quickly escorts me down a series of short corridors, I ask, "Where are we going?"

Ivy grins. "Trust me?"

"Sure, what do I have to lose?" I reply philosophically.

Ivy giggles. "Okay, I'll remind you that you said that when you hate me. Close your eyes."

I dutifully close my eyes. How bad could this possibly be? The sauna was weird, but it wasn't bad. So, whatever she's got planned can't be all that terrible.

Suddenly, I hear instructions from Ivy, "Hold your breath and jump on three. One. Two. Three. Jump!" She is giggling so hard that she can barely speak. Fortunately, all the years I spent jumping off docks as a kid pays off and the movement is almost instinctual.

I had conveniently forgotten the sensation of being immersed in ice water which is made ten times worse by our recent trip to the sauna. Immediately the breath rushes out of my lungs and my skin feels like it's on fire.

As I break the surface of the water and wipe the chlorinated water out of my eyes. I immediately search around for Ivy.

She is about two feet away treading water like a synchronized swimmer with a wide smile on her face. "Isn't this great? It's my favorite part of using the sauna."

"I'm not sure I classify this as 'so great'. I may be talking like a soprano for a week. You could warn a guy."

"But what fun would that be? I tried to warn you that I'm not quite the angel you think I am."

"Well, the least you could do would be to come over and warm me up."

Ivy appears to contemplate that option but then yells over her shoulder as she takes off, "Swimming laps is a good way to warm up too. I'll meet you at the other end of the pool and give you your reward for being such a good sport."

"I'm good with that, I'll see you on the other side," I shout my reply to her retreating figure.

Ivy is a remarkably fast swimmer. Still, she's no match for me. I was born with freakishly long arms and hands the size of Ping-Pong paddles. It was an interesting challenge to learn to handle the small delicate tattooing equipment. It took me a while to find a brand of tattooing machine to fit my hand comfortably. Sometimes I work on a big back piece for hours and holding the wrong size equipment can cause real pain.

Lounging against the edge of the pool, I wait for her to reach me. When she does, her expression is comical. "How did you do that? I even had a head start! I usually win these things." She tries to catch her breath. "You're right, it is pretty cold in here. Do you want to steam things back up in the sauna?"

I raise an eyebrow at her question.

Ivy blushes as she realizes her statement can be taken in multiple ways.

CHAPTER TEN

ROGUE

WHAT IN THE WORLD AM I doing here? That's my overwhelming thought as I sit in the middle of the bed in a hotel room which probably costs as much as three months' rent where I live. Granted, I live in a dump, but this place is just too excessive. Who lives like this? Oh yeah … Tristan lives like this. So, why is a guy like him with someone like me? Not that there's anything particularly wrong with me — Tristan and I don't really travel in the same circles. I'm the person who usually waits on the people like Tristan at the fancy parties he goes to. In fact, the restaurant I sometimes work at to pick up extra hours just held a catering job for an entrepreneurs' lunch. Tristan would've fit right in there. Unlike most of the catering jobs I work, those people were nice to me, looked me in the eye and asked my name. I actually made decent tips that night.

Tristan went to find some ice for his knee. Apparently, driving all those hours irritated his old injury. I teased him about having the concierge do it for him since we were living the high life. But, he simply blushed and said he doesn't take advantage of people like that and insisted he could get his own ice. He's an interesting mix. He thinks nothing of slapping down his ultra-platinum card and instructing that no expense be spared if any of us need anything, but he insists on doing everything himself even though he tipped the bellman and valet attendant as if he'd used their services.

I didn't bring much with me. But fortunately, I've learned from my many modeling gigs to always stick a basic swimsuit in my suitcase just in case. Tristan said we could buy whatever we needed to make ourselves comfortable. But I don't really want to buy a new wardrobe just to look cute on our date. This isn't Pretty Woman after all. I pick up a ponytail holder and my swimsuit from the suitcase and head to the bathroom to change. I have to laugh out loud when I open the door. I didn't realize bathrooms like this existed outside the pages of magazines. This is ridiculous! One whole wall of the bathroom is occupied by a huge marble tiled shower with frosted glass doors. I walk over and gingerly peek. I'm almost afraid to touch anything. All of this looks nice enough to be in some fancy museum exhibit or something. The inside of the shower looks like a study in decadence. There are two built-in benches and no fewer than six shower heads. There are even stereo speakers in the shower. Slowly, I back out of the shower, uncertain what to think of all this sensory overload.

I turn around and look at the rest of the restroom. There is actually a bidet. I've read about those in magazines. But I've never seen one. On the vanity there's a cornucopia of beauty products which put my own to shame. I pick up a couple of bottles and notice there is both a conditioner to curl your hair and to straighten it. Talk about your full-service hotel.

I close the door and lock it while I quickly change into my bathing suit. As I get back into the bedroom suite and try to find a place to put my suitcase, I find a couple of plush robes with the hotel's insignia on it. I smile to myself because I always assumed they were something people made up for soap operas on television. I didn't realize the robes were a real thing. I feel so spoiled.

I turn the television on and I'm astonished at the sheer number of television channels available. It's not a surprise there are more television channels than I have at home because I only have the smallest cable package available. My budget simply doesn't allow for more. However, I didn't even realize there were this many cable channels available on the planet. Flipping through the premium movie channels, I see almost a hundred. Who knew there were so many? I'm starting to feel like a real backwoods hick. Tristan comes through the door holding the ice bucket and what looks like some sort of pie.

He sets it all down on the dresser and glances at the television set as he comments, "Isn't it ridiculous? A person can only watch one channel at a time. What do you like to watch?"

"I don't have a lot of time to watch TV. You'll probably laugh if I tell you what I watch."

"Oh come on, it can't be any nerdier than what I watch."

"You might change your mind after I tell you. As they say in my marketing class, I'm not the typical demographic for these shows."

"Okay, now you've got me curious —"

I try not to cringe. "I like to watch the Antique Roadshow and the History Detectives on Public Television. Sometimes people get lucky and they discover they have paintings or pottery worth millions of dollars. I think it's really interesting to learn about that kind of stuff."

"I don't find that strange. In fact I think it's totally sexy you have a brain and aren't ashamed to use it. I like those shows too. We can totally geek out together when we watch TV. One of my guilty pleasures is to watch the National Spelling Bee — not exactly nail-biting television, but I watch it every year because I have such admiration for those kids. Spelling was always my weakness."

I can't help but grin from ear to ear. "I thought I was the only one who watched it from start to finish. When I was a freshman in college, my lab partner thought I was absolutely nuts when I turned down a chance to go to a huge party because I wanted to watch the Spelling Bee live."

Tristan walks over to the dresser and picks up the pie. "I hope you don't mind. I ran into the pastry chef when I was looking for ice. He just made a key lime pie; he tried a new recipe and he needs guinea pigs. So, he gave us a big piece. Do you like key lime pie?"

I smirk at him. "Do I live in Florida? Of course I like key lime pie and virtually every other kind of pie."

"Okay, for fun let's make this a game. For every bite we take, we have to say one thing that's true about ourselves and one thing we wish was true."

"Does it have to be true in the present or could it have been true in the past?" I clarify.

"You are such a stickler for the rules. Are you sure you don't have a secret desire to be a lawyer under all that artsy stuff you do?"

"Oh, no thank you!" I protest. "Could you see me in a suit all day? I don't think so. I just needed to be sure I understood what you wanted from me so I don't cheat."

"Rogue, it's no big deal. This is just a fun game for me to get to know you better. No life or death consequences here. For all I know, you could lie your way through the whole game."

"That would be stupid. Then you wouldn't learn anything new about me."

"I wasn't suggesting you actually lie; I was just saying a person could if they wanted to. I would much prefer you tell me some things you'd like me to know about yourself," Tristan responds with a frustrated sigh.

I almost laugh out loud at the look of angst on his face. I hold my hands up in surrender. "Okay, I wasn't trying to be difficult, I promise. I understand now. Fun game. No rules. Silly icebreaker. Social interaction. I think I've got it. I'll try not to over-analyze everything."

"If you took it as a criticism, I didn't mean it that way. I'm fascinated by the way your mind works. I'm almost tempted to have you read all my contracts because you're so quick to think of all the loopholes. It's a handy skill to have in business."

"I'll let you tell Mama Rosa that when you meet

her. It used to drive her crazy when I was growing up. Whenever she laid out a punishment or a new household rule, I was always trying to define all the outer edges. She got used to it, but when she married my stepfather, he interpreted my curiosity and need for precise details as mouthiness and disrespect. I think he hated me at first sight. I was pretty devastated. All my life I had looked forward to having a dad like everyone else, so I wanted it to be like I had seen on television where the stepdad comes in and loves the new daughter like his own. Unfortunately, what I hoped for was so far removed from what actually happened, I didn't know how to react. It became an all-out battleground in our house. My mom was forced to choose sides. To save her marriage, she chose to side with Clive. I'm not sure if I'll ever fully understand how she could pick him. But, I guess being alone for so many years took its toll and she was willing to sacrifice everything."

Tristan puts the pie on the nightstand and sits down on the bed, propping himself up against the headboard. He pulls me up so I'm sitting next to him. He places his arm around my shoulders and murmurs against my temple, "I'm sorry. That was too high of a price to pay."

"I thought so too. So, I quit high school and came to Florida. My relationship with Mama has never been quite the same."

"What about Clive?" Tristan asks, offering me a bite of pie.

"That's the tragic twist. They've been in an on-again off-again thing. I'm not sure if they're even together right now."

"It must have been painful to be essentially thrown away for a new guy after it was just you and your mom for so long."

"You have no idea," I confess wryly. "I felt like my whole world was collapsing."

"I can sympathize. I felt much the same way when my mom took in Elliott. I didn't know whether to consider him my brother or my nephew. It was like the world revolved around him for a while. Still, I was in a better situation than you were. My parents didn't really choose between the two of us, it simply felt that way. They always still loved me; their focus just moved to Elliott for a while because he was in a crisis since his mom died. After I finally got some perspective, I understood the need. But, I was lonely for a while."

"How is your relationship now?" I impulsively ask and then I wish I could take back the question because it feels intrusive.

"It's fine. My parents are split up now, but I still see them both if I go home for a visit. They still don't understand the whole software industry. When my dad reads about the dot.com bust and he's sure everything related to computers and the Internet is going to go belly up at any moment. So, he tells me that anytime I want it, there is a job for me at his construction business. Elliott is a natural at construction. He has absolutely no fear. I stopped by to see my dad the other day when I was in town for business and Elliott was walking along the top of some framing twelve feet off the ground as if it was nothing. He scares the crap out of me, but more power to him."

"That's freaky. Was he at least wearing a safety harness?" I ask with a shudder.

"He's got one. But my dad says he has a heck of a time getting him to wear it."

"Your mom must be thrilled," I remark sarcastically.

"I know. My mom says Elliott gets his hard-headedness from his grandfather. My dad once had to have his fingers surgically reattached because he cut them off in a band saw because he took the guide off so it would cut faster."

"Yikes! Do you have any of these dangerous tendencies?"

"Not unless you count an addiction to coffee, all night chess matches and a little day trading on the stock market."

I narrow my gaze at him and ask, "Enough day trading that you might be standing out in the middle of the street in your underwear if the DOW crashes?"

Tristan laughs out loud at my assertion. "No, I had a CD mature and rather than reinvest it, I took the money out and decided to try my hand at day trading. It turns out I'm pretty good at it. For the most part, I am in the black by a good margin. If I didn't have forty-thousand other things on my agenda, I might actually do more day trading. It's fascinating and good mental exercise."

"I guess I'm just too risk-averse with money. If you've got a talent for the market, I guess you should go for it. I couldn't imagine doing it myself. I would be catatonic if I lost money. I can't even buy a lottery ticket."

"So, I'm guessing Vegas is not your speed?"

"I don't know. I've never been. I don't think I would enjoy it very much. I work too hard for my money to spend it on the mere chance of getting more. The odds don't seem very good."

Tristan chuckles. "See, you and I just keep finding more and more things we have in common. As a computer geek, I don't play the lottery or do Vegas. It doesn't make logical sense to me. All my friends call me a stick in the mud. They think now that I have money, I should just throw it away. I've never quite gotten the logic of that either. Just because I worked hard and developed a product when no one else did, why should I blow my money on some worthless activity?"

"This is just a theory, but did any of these friends by chance want you to blow the money on them?"

Tristan feeds me another bite. "Smart and beautiful. It's my favorite combination. It so happens one of the guys was getting married and couldn't afford a bachelor party. It's funny how a guy who barely spoke to me during college suddenly considered himself my best friend once my software sold."

"So, did you throw him a bachelor party?"

Tristan grins widely. "I sure did. We went bowling and I had it catered by Panda Express."

"Yum! I love Panda Express; the orange chicken is my favorite."

"Mine too. We would've probably had a good

time that night except the guy told all of his buddies I would fly them on a Cessna to Vegas for a night with some private entertainment from some showgirls."

"Well, that's just gross. He deserved to have a bad night for lying to all of his friends. Not to mention that he completely planned to use you."

"I knew his plan all along, which is why I didn't go all out for his party. If he had shown any respect, I might have actually flown him to Vegas like he was expecting — minus the showgirls of course, because that's disgusting. I still gave him what could reasonably be expected for a bachelor party when you're a college student. The food was good and the bowling was fun. I even hired a DJ to play music."

"It sounds like you went above and beyond the call of duty. I'm sorry your friends turned into jerks when you got rich. That kind of sucks. Are you ever allowed to let your guard down?"

"As odd as it seems, I've been more comfortable since meeting you, Ivy and Marcus than I've been around anybody outside of my family."

"That's sweet of you to say —"

"No, it's really true. Do you realize none of you have asked me to fix your computers, phones, or iPads? No one has asked me to spy on any ex-lovers, and no one has asked me for money. I haven't had friends this loyal since I started working on computers. Things have gotten exponentially worse since I started Identity Bank. For some reason, everyone thinks because they once had a class with me or worked with me sometime in the distant past, they should get an automatic discount on my fees.

Of course, I can afford to do that now since I've sold the software program. The point is, I shouldn't have to just because we had a paper route together when we were fourteen. You know what I mean?"

"Wow! That is bold. I can see your direct family members asking for a discount. But … classmates from junior high? That's stretching it a little."

"You'd be surprised," Tristan shakes his head.

"Actually, I'm not. I ran across a friend who I hadn't seen since the fourth grade while I was waiting tables and she wanted me to give her the employee discount because we were such good friends."

"That's flat-out rude."

"Thankfully, I could truthfully tell her I don't work enough hours to earn an employee discount. I'm not sure what I would have told her if I needed to come up with another answer. I was completely at a loss for a socially acceptable reply which wouldn't get me fired."

"You have my complete and utter respect working as a waitress. I could never hack a job like that. The first time someone was rude to me I'd probably either collapse into a heap of self-loathing or lash out at them — neither of which is an acceptable response when you're working with the public."

"I think you're probably underestimating your ability to be charming. After all, you work with the public every day in your job."

"True, but as a general rule my customers respect what I do and don't treat me like dirt for doing my job."

"For the most part, most of my customers are

pretty nice. Every once in a while, I'll get a big jerk. But, at least the place where I'm working now doesn't tolerate them. If I tell management I have a problem with a customer, the customer is asked to leave and I get to keep my dignity. I've worked at other places where they don't support the waitstaff. It's totally a drag."

"I'm glad you have found a good place to work, but I wish you didn't have to work so many hours. Don't your many jobs interfere with your ability to study?"

I arch an eyebrow at him and cross my arms in front of my body. "No 'Dad'. I think I can handle it all by myself, thank you!"

Tristan looks chagrined. "I didn't mean to imply you couldn't handle your own stuff. What I meant to ask is, 'Can I do anything to make it easier for you?' Unfortunately, I made a very clumsy attempt."

I sigh as I feed Tristan a big bite of pie and wipe the corners of his mouth with a napkin. "Tristan do I have to refer you back to the conversation we just had? Remember all the things you liked about our friendship? One of those things was that I don't ask you for money. I don't intend to start asking now. I've said it before and I'll say it again. You are my friend — maybe my boyfriend, you are not my sugar daddy. I won't take advantage of you just because you have money. If I wouldn't ask my boyfriend who works at Kentucky Fried Chicken to do something for me, I wouldn't ask it of you."

Tristan looks at me with wide eyes. "You have a boyfriend who works at KFC?"

"No! I was giving you a hypothetical example. I thought with you being all scientifically inclined, you might appreciate it."

"I most definitely would not appreciate you having another boyfriend."

"Don't worry, I barely have time to date one guy. I would never have time to date two. You're completely in the clear."

"I think that's what started this conversation. I was trying to help you with your lack of time. First of all, I said I like the fact you guys hadn't demanded favors from me. That does not mean I can't offer them of my own free will."

"But, don't you see — if I accept help from you, I'm no better than the leeches who hang on to you only for your money? I don't want to be that woman."

"It's a completely different thing if I offer first."

"I don't want you to ever have to wonder if I like Tristan Macklin for the funny, charming, quirky guy you are or if I'm only after you for the credit cards in your wallet. Do you get that? It's for the health of us. I've been making it for a long time on my own before I met you. I'll continue to figure it out. It'll be a challenge to juggle it all. But I think it'll be worth it."

"You are the definition of stubborn, can I tell you that? But I appreciate what you're doing. I really do. It feels nice to be liked simply because I'm me."

"Take heart Tristan, I like you just fine," I declare as I feed Tristan another bite of key lime pie.

"I like you too, Rogue Betancourt," Tristan says as he swallows.

"Now, was that the truth about yourself or the

thing you'd like to change?" I tease.

"That's very definitely the truth. Right now, if I could change something, I wish I lived closer to you. I don't like the fact that we live three hours apart."

"I don't either. Skyping is nice, but it's not the same as having you in the room with me. Not to be superficial or anything, but you smell great and you're nice to cuddle with. I miss you when you're not around."

"I'll have to do some research into expanding my business. I think Kate can probably take over the original Tampa branch of Identity Bank and I can expand to Gainesville to be closer to you."

"Why would you do that?" I ask, my heart suddenly pounding. "Tonight was like our first official date. How can you even think about moving your whole business? You don't even know me yet."

"Actually, I do know you. I know a lot about you. Ivy came to see me during the first week of July. This is the third week of November. We've talked virtually every night since I located you. Sometimes, we talk for hours. That's more than most people talk when they're actually dating. Sure, it's fun to play a few get-to-know-you games to learn useless trivia, but I've gotten a sense of what makes you tick over these past few months and I like you. Besides, tonight wasn't really our first date, it's more like our third. We've had a coffee date and I took you out for ice cream cones when you got your car fixed. I tried to take you out for lunch, but you insisted you didn't have time."

"The first time at the coffee shop does not count as a date!" I exclaim. "You were on the job delivering life-altering news."

"True. That's why I didn't count it," Tristan agrees.

"Then what are you talking about?" I ask, feeling flustered.

"That's okay. I forgive you for forgetting because your brain was fried from pulling an all-nighter. Remember the time I brought you croissants and hot chocolate before your midterm?"

I flush from embarrassment as I recall, "Oh yeah, that was the day you had the meeting at the airport with the TSA officials and you flew into town. I still can't believe you took a taxi to campus to come see me."

"They changed the schedule on me and bumped my meeting to the afternoon. There was no way I was going to be in the same town as you and not stop by and visit."

"It was a good thing you did too. I still can't believe I set my alarm for nine at night instead of nine in the morning. Had you not paid a visit, I would've slept through my midterm."

"I'm honored to be your multi-service boyfriend. Whenever you need an alarm clock, just let me know," Tristan teases. But, then his expression turns serious. "I don't know about you, but I consider us a couple. Whenever anybody asks me where I'm going or who I'm talking to, I always say, 'My girlfriend'. I'm not interested in dating anyone else."

I crawl to the middle of the bed, so I'm facing Tristan. We are both sitting cross-legged as if we are ready to play a child's game of patty cake. I take his hands in mine. I place my hands on his wrists in an effort to steady myself on the plush bed. I can feel his pulse race under my fingers.

"Tristan, if I am totally honest with myself and you, I have to tell you I don't know if I'm comfortable with the idea that you might move your business to be with me. Don't get me wrong, I like you. I like you a lot, otherwise there's no way I would have carved out the time in my life for you. I just don't have it. But, I've made us a priority because you're so important to me."

Tristan slides his arms from under my hands and interlaces his fingers with mine.

"Moving your business to Gainesville is a huge step. It's the kind of thing that married couples do together. You're absolutely correct, we have grown close over the past few months. Closer than I've been with anybody, even Marcus who is my best friend. I don't think we're at the point in our relationship where you should be making multi-million-dollar decisions. That's completely scary."

"I think all relationships are scary. Just think of it as if I were relocating my job for you. Because, that's essentially what I'm planning to do. I just have to open an office to make it happen."

A loud laugh escapes my lips as I process his logic. "Tristan, do you know how insane you sound? What are you going to tell the bank? 'My college-age girlfriend who works at a tattoo parlor is a little tied up with her classes at Santa Fe Community College, so I'm going to relocate my established business to be closer to her.' I'm sure that'll be a winning pitch."

Tristan smirks. "Well, you never know. My bank likes me a lot right now. They'd pretty much loan me money for any project at the moment. But, if I were pitching this business, I would probably add a few facts about emerging markets, vulnerable seniors, surrounding communities — you know, the usual stuff."

I blanch. "Oh my gosh! You're really serious about this. You're planning to get money from a bank and go forward with this project?"

"I probably will at some point. But, if it makes you feel more at ease I'll wait until we've dated a while longer. I don't think it'll make much difference. But, I want you to feel comfortable about it too."

"This is a colossally huge, gargantuan big deal, you know that right?" I ask, my voice shaky from unshed tears.

"I suppose you could consider it a big deal. Or, it could be something couples do for each other all the time. Couples change jobs pretty routinely."

"Maybe in your world, but not in my world. My friends have a hard time getting their boyfriends to compromise about putting the toilet seat down or sharing the remote control. So, the idea of building a whole new business is incomprehensible."

"It sounds like I'll have to work a little harder to win you over," Tristan teases.

His words hit me hard. They remind me that I must seem like a shrill, paranoid, heartless witch.

"I'm not trying to play hard to get. It's just hard

for me to believe you would be willing to make that kind of sacrifice for me. It'll take me a bit to adjust my mindset, I guess. Please be patient with me."

"Rogue, I'm not going anywhere until you tell me to, okay? I told you from the outset I would be by your side throughout this whole process. I keep my word. I'd like to be your suitor for lack of a better word — but first and foremost — I'm your friend."

Finally, I feel like I can take a breath. I move back over to sit beside Tristan and take the pie from him. I make a big production of taking a large bite. "I guess I owe you a few answers for eating this delicious pie. The first truth is I am profoundly grateful you're my friend. The thing I wish was true about myself is pretty obvious. I wish I was brave enough to follow my heart instead of my brain."

Tristan turns and gives me a devastatingly thorough kiss. I am by no means new to the world of kissing. I was introduced to it at an embarrassingly early age, having matured quite early, but nothing in my experience has ever compared to this. Unlike most guys, Tristan is responding to my reactions, instead of just showing me a menu of moves. Even though he initiated the kiss, he is clearly allowing me to set the pace. There is something empowering about that.

When I thread my fingers through the hair at the nape of his neck and pull him closer, he groans and wraps his arms around my shoulders and deepens the kiss. If I thought the kiss was hot before, this takes it to a whole new level. A surge of desire passes through me. I almost laugh out loud at the unfamiliar sensation. It strikes me as funny that it's been so long since I've dated that my body doesn't even recognize what it feels like to be turned on. I really should get out more often.

Tristan notices my reaction. "What are you smiling about?" he asks with a curious smirk.

I hide my face in embarrassment. "Promise not to laugh?"

Tristan nods and brushes the hair out of my eyes.

"I was thinking how pathetically long it's been since I've been thoroughly kissed and how wonderful it makes me feel. It kind of took me by surprise."

Tristan winks. "Again, I'm happy to oblige anytime you need me. I'm a totally willing volunteer."

CHAPTER ELEVEN

IVY

THE MOOD AT BREAKFAST IS strange. I'm having a hard time reading Rogue. Although she seems happy, she's also pensive and closed off. She doesn't appear to be fighting with Tristan. Their body language seems to indicate everything is fine between them. They are being openly affectionate with each other. In fact, they are being more cutesy than I would've anticipated from either one of them given their personalities. Tristan is currently teasing Rogue like I would've expected from Marcus. Given our surroundings, I'm a bit surprised by their PDAs. I don't know much about Rogue yet, perhaps she's more used to this kind of environment than I am. But the opulence of this place is more than a little intimidating. I'm afraid I'll break something just by breathing on it.

I tried to tell Tristan we could get breakfast at the local Waffle House or something. We didn't have to eat at the hotel. But he insisted eating in the hotel would be the most convenient.

Last night after the sauna, Marcus and I went over

to the convenience store across from the hotel and bought some candy bars and microwave popcorn. We watched Mel Brooks movies most of the night until we crashed. Many people my age don't even know who Mel Brooks is — let alone know the catalog of movies he's done. So, I was shocked when Marcus not only agreed to watch the movie marathon with me but could recite the lines right along with me. It was thrilling to find my movie soul mate. We laughed so hard last night my ribs hurt this morning.

I focus back in on the conversation between Marcus and Tristan.

"I figure I'll bring an office to your neighborhood in Gainesville. It looks like a thriving little business community. Did they redo all the business fronts?"

From my perspective, this seems like a good development for Rogue, so I wonder why I feel a wave of pain from her in response to Tristan's comment.

Marcus nods. "Yeah, the city got some sort of federal grant to refurbish the business district. So, we all got new storefronts. It has really revitalized the area. My shop gets a lot more foot traffic than it used to. I bet your business would do well here. There are a lot of corporations around along with both the Santa Fe Community College and the University of Florida."

"That's definitely a plus; I'm sure the bank would consider it as part of the reason to back me."

I can feel Rogue's anxiety level rise as if it's a physical entity in the room. It's time to investigate what's going on. "Rogue, I need your assistance with something in the restroom please."

"Do you just want to go up to the room?" Rogue offers with a surprised glance.

"Sure, if you haven't checked out yet."

"No, we didn't check out because Tristan wanted to be able to charge breakfast to the room."

"Marcus, I'll be down in a few minutes. Try not to get into too much trouble while I'm gone, okay?"

Much to my shock, Marcus stands up when I stand to leave the table. Rogue grins from ear to ear as she says to Marcus, "Very good, Grasshopper. You have learned your lesson well."

"Rogue, don't discourage him! That was perfect gentlemanly behavior. Women like me eat that kind of thing up." I comment as I brush a thank you kiss across Marcus's surprised lips.

Rogue flashes Marcus a quick smirk. "See, I told you so."

"Yeah, but does her opinion actually count as separate since she's your twin?" Marcus asks.

Tristan kicks Marcus in the shin as he instructs, "Marcus, remember when we talked about your mouth getting away from you. This is one of those times to put a cork in it. Think about it for a minute, you're in a no-win situation — either you criticize your best friend or your girlfriend or both."

Marcus looks at Tristan and stammers, "Um … okay. I'll shut up now."

After Marcus's near-death-experience by compliment, I grab Rogue and practically drag her up the elevator to her room. I thought our room was large, but their room is even bigger. When I comment on it, Rogue tells me the hotel immediately upgraded Tristan's room as soon as they saw the color of his credit card. He tried to tell them he didn't need the executive suite, but they wouldn't listen and insisted he take this suite.

Since I really did have to use the facilities, I about had a heart attack when I saw the bathroom. "Please tell me you spent a couple of hours in this shower at least."

Rogue chuckles. "I did spend an unhealthy amount of time in the shower, I will admit that."

"Oh? Were you showering alone or in pairs?" I tease.

"That's none of your business, Sis. It wouldn't matter anyway since you could fit a whole class of kindergartners in this shower and still have room left over."

"That's not really my scene, but I guess if it works for you —" I tease.

"So, do you want to tell me why we're hiding up here in the room instead of enjoying the breakfast which probably costs as much as a term of college tuition?" Rogue interrupts my banter.

"Oh that … well I'm worried about you," I confess. "You seem stressed out about Tristan moving even though it looks like things are working out between the two of you so I figured maybe you would like to talk about it."

"How do you know that? I didn't even say a word," Rogue asks, then shakes her head as she adds, "Oh never mind it's the twin thing again. I forgot I'll never be able to have another private thought again in my life."

Her words feel like a slap in my face. I wasn't prepared for the sting and I visibly flinch. "I'm sorry, I was just trying to help," I whisper, hoarsely.

Rogue sways as she takes in my expression. "*Manita, lo siento mucho.* I never meant to hurt you. I know you're trying to help. I'm overwhelmed by all of this. It seems like everything is changing in my life and I can't slow down to take a breath. I feel like I'm on a roller coaster which doesn't end. One minute I'm excited about what's happening in our lives and the next minute I'm totally terrified. As if the family drama with us isn't complicated enough, I've got all the stuff with Tristan to worry about."

"I thought things were going really well with him. You guys certainly seem cozy enough," I ask, trying to clarify the situation.

"They are going well. Almost too well. He's too good to be true, if you know what I mean. Don't you think it's strange that he wants to totally relocate his business to be next to me? I mean, we just started dating. Sane people don't do that! I know couples who have been married for years and only see each other on the weekends. For all he knows, he could make a huge move — then get to know me better and decide he hates me. It's bizarre."

"So, let me get this straight. You're having a meltdown because you like Tristan and he's too committed to you? I know it's early and I stayed up really late last night, but I'm not following your logic here."

"Funny. Very funny." Rogue sticks her tongue out

at me. "This is serious stuff. I don't want Tristan to hate me forever if things don't work out. I can be a bit of a hothead and I'm not very cooperative when I'm cornered. I don't know how great I'll be in a relationship. I've never really tested it out. I've been too busy trying to survive on my own. The few times I've tried have been colossal failures. In the few months I've known Tristan, he's already become important enough to me that I don't want to chalk this up as another failure. But, I'm not sure I want him to make the huge commitment to move all the way here. What if I can't make this work? It wouldn't be fair to him. It would cost him thousands and thousands of dollars to start a new business."

"Rogue!" I interrupt her tirade of self-doubt. "Take a breath or you'll pass out and if you pass out, I'll be right behind you. I really want to go back and eat breakfast because I'm hungry. So, breathe."

Rogue takes a deep breath and blows her bangs out of her eyes and then takes a couple more for good measure. "There. Are you happy?"

"Much better. Thank you. Now, Tristan is generous to a fault. But I've also noticed he is very much his own man. That guy doesn't do anything he doesn't want to do, regardless of who tells him to do it. So, if he says he wants to open a business near you, he's put a great deal of thought into it and has planned for every contingency."

"Yeah, but it's so much money —"

"Yes, it's a lot of money. But, it's his money to spend and as I understand it, the man could basically wallpaper every port-a-potty in the state with thousand-dollar bills and still have plenty of money left over to build skyscrapers galore. What's more, he's probably got plans in his head for more cutting-edge computer programs we can't even begin to imagine which will make him a thousand times richer. So, until he tells you to be worried about money, I wouldn't worry about it."

"I don't want him to think I'm asking him to be reckless. He shouldn't be making sacrifices just for me."

I sit down on the lushly appointed bed with Rogue. "You know, I don't think he sees it that way. I think you are giving him something he's never had in his life."

"What can I possibly give him? The man has everything!" Rogue argues.

"Before you, he did not have everything. You've given him a center or a port in the rough sea of his life. I think for all his outward success, Tristan was a very lonely man before he found you. I suspect you are the one person he feels truly safe with. He can't buy love and security. Only you can give that to him," I reason.

"Oh, Ivy it's so scary. If I'm honest with myself, I can admit this feels totally different. I want to trust the connection we have with each other and just go with it. But, things are moving so fast, my head is spinning."

"Not that I'm an expert or anything, but I'm told the feeling is called being in love."

"Enough of me being on the hot seat. How about you and Marcus?"

I guess I should have anticipated her question and been prepared with a coherent answer. However, I've been so focused on trying to unravel her frazzled emotional state, I've given little thought to my own tumultuous thoughts.

"Well, you were right. There's a lot more to Marcus than he shows the public. But, I'm having a great time discovering the real man underneath all the layers of social armor he puts on."

"I hope you're able to look past some of the mistakes he made growing up because they helped forge him into the amazingly strong human being he is now. But, I don't think they should taint your opinion of him."

"Oh, you mean his involvement with the street gang and his drug and alcohol use?"

"Wow!" Rogue exclaims. "When you said you were discovering Marcus's layers, I had no idea he'd be this forthcoming with you. I guess you guys are getting close. We were friends for years before he told me any of that stuff."

I shrug. "I don't know. In a weird way, it almost felt like he was giving me reasons why he didn't deserve me. I think he was surprised to hear it didn't matter much to me. I just told him we all make mistakes and have things we would do differently under different circumstances."

Rogue gives me a hug. "It looks like Tristan is not the only one who's found his port. Marcus has needed this so much in his life. I'm so glad he's found you. He's such a good guy and no one can seem to look past his rough exterior and his goofy mannerisms to see his true heart. I am so glad you've taken the time to see the real Marcus."

I don't know why, but having Rogue's explicit endorsement of our relationship brings tears to my eyes. I haven't known Marcus for years like Rogue, but it's very clear from watching the two of them together, they have a very special friendship. I don't want to intrude on it in any way.

"Thank you Rogue. I'll do my best to take care of him. He's pretty special."

"Thanks for talking me out of my panic attack. Shall we go down and eat some breakfast before the guys eat it all? I should warn you Marcus eats enough food to feed three professional linebackers in the NFL. So, if you want anything to eat in your relationship, don't leave food laying around."

"Duly noted. Thanks for the warning."

As we pull into the driveway of the little ranch style house with the faux stucco finish, my heart is racing. My pulse is beating so hard, I can feel it pounding at my temples. Vaguely, I hear Marcus muttering in my ear, "Breathe Sugar. You'll trigger an asthma attack if you don't. Follow me. Breathe in through your nose and out through your mouth; slowly in and out. There you go. That's much better."

Once again, Marcus's calming ways allow me to collect myself and calm my breathing before it gets to be a crisis situation. Once I've gathered myself and given myself an albuterol treatment, Marcus asks Rogue and me if we're ready to go in.

As I sneak a glance, it is clear Rogue is as panicked

as I am.

Tristan rubs the back of Rogue's hand and says, "I know this is hard, Baby — but, you won't know any answers until you do this. You and Ivy can't move forward with your lives until you settle the past."

"What if this is all a huge mistake?" Rogue asks in a shaky voice.

"What if it's not?" Tristan replies quietly. "You guys will never know until you talk to Rosa. Marcus and I will be right here."

"I know. You'll never know how much I love you for that," Rogue says as she presses a kiss on his cheek. The two of them go up to the front door while Marcus and I wait in the car. Since we didn't know what the story really is, we thought it might be too much of a shock for her to see the two of us together at her front door. So, Rogue and Tristan elected to try to ascertain her story first and break the news to her softly before presenting the visual of us together as twins.

I'm at a complete loss of what to do with myself in the SUV. It seems artificial to try to have a conversation with Marcus. Yet, if I don't talk, the silence is completely deafening. Marcus wears an old pocket watch that belonged to his grandfather and I found out this morning that it still requires hand winding. It was quite a sight to watch him handle such a delicate task with his large hands. It was a weirdly domestic scene this morning as we were packing and he was winding his watch as we were watching *Good Morning America*. I had this weird vision of what our life might look like in the future trying to get ready for work and getting kids ready for school while catching a glimpse of the news and weather on TV as we head out the door. Right now, his pocket watch is ticking like it's attached to a megaphone. The sound echoing through the SUV is reminding me of every second Rogue and Tristan are gone. My brain can't stop coming up with bizarre scenarios. What if she says she never had twins and I'm not related to Rogue? What if she admits that I am hers but claims she never wanted me and doesn't want me now? What if she never consented to the adoption at all and I was stolen from the hospital?

Marcus senses my discomfort. He flips on the ignition and pulls down a DVD screen from the roof panel of the SUV. As the Netflix panel comes up, he searches for *Robin Hood, Men in Tights*.

As the movie credits start to come up, I can't help but laugh at his strategy. "Thank you. It is impossible to be upset when this movie is playing."

"That's my plan, Sugar. We can't change the outcome in there, so there's no need to stress about it."

"I know, but it's so hard not to worry."

"What does your weird, twin Spidey sense tell you?"

"She doesn't seem overly stressed out. So, it must be going well. At least I hope that's what it means. Maybe Tristan is doing a great job of keeping her calm. I don't know."

"I'm sure it will be fine, Ivy. Who wouldn't want to meet someone like you?"

"This is all such a giant mess. I almost wish I could put the genie back in the bottle."

"Well, I don't. Because if it hadn't been for this 'giant mess' as you call it, you and I would have never met. And I'm just not okay with that outcome."

"You're right, I wouldn't be okay with that either. I wish we could have the good stuff but avoid the pain."

"That's the whole secret of life right there in a nutshell, isn't it? I wish I could make this easier for you. But, unfortunately I think this is something you and Ro will have to get through the best you can."

Just then there's a knock at the window of the SUV. Marcus and I were so involved in our conversation, we didn't even hear Tristan approach.

"They're ready for you," he announces with a grim expression on his face.

I study him carefully. "What's wrong?"

"It's a little volatile in there. It could go either way. This is so hard on Rogue. She's trying to be so tough. But, I can tell she's pretty shattered inside."

"Do you think someone could get hurt?" Marcus asks gruffly, as he pulls me closer, placing his arm around my waist protectively.

"Only emotionally," Tristan answers cryptically.

"I guess we better hurry and get in there. I hate to leave her alone." My stomach lurches with fear.

As we open the door, it's immediately clear where Rogue and I get our hair as an older lady with straight dark brown hair shot through with silver strands answers the door.

When she sees me she exclaims, *"Hay Dios mio!* You are real. The nurses told me you died. I tried to argue with them, but they told me you were too sick to live. They told me to go home and raise my living daughter and to be thankful I still had one."

I gasp. I can't imagine how shocking this must be for her. I can feel my fingers tremble as they touch my lips.

"I'm sorry *Bebita,* I need to sit. This is quite a shock. For twenty-two years I've prayed for your soul. Now you're here in front of me. I do not know what to think. It is obvious you are my *bebita.*"

"Yes, please sit," I quickly pull out a wooden kitchen chair and helping her into it. "I'm sorry, but my high school Spanish is rusty. Could you please translate *bebita?*"

"Oh no! You have no knowledge of the language of your people? How sad. *Bebita* means my baby girl. You must know I've never forgotten you. They told me you passed into the arms of the angels. I never knew what to believe because in my heart I felt I should know if you were gone, but I always felt your spirit around me. Then, when Rogue felt her mysterious pains, one of the priests at my church said it was your ghost haunting us and suggested your presence in our life made Rogue evil somehow. After that, I stopped telling people about it because I didn't want them to think Rogue was possessed by the devil."

After I hear the explanation that I've been waiting to hear for months, I feel surprisingly numb. I thought this explanation would answer all my questions. But, instead it's raised so many more. Why would they tell Rosa I'd passed away when I was, in fact, very much alive?

If she did visit me in the NICU, wouldn't she have been able to tell I wasn't doing well but I was holding my own? Wouldn't the nurses have been able to figure out she was a loving and caring mother? What about my pediatrician? Wouldn't he be aware I didn't die? Why hadn't he told my mom the good news? The sheer number of questions is mind blowing.

"Mama, why didn't you tell me I was a twin? It would've made things in my life so much easier to understand."

Rosa wipes away tears as she hugs Rogue. "There was no way to tell you without opening Pandora's Box. I had no answers about why she died and you lived. It was easier to pretend she never existed. Then, when I ordered your birth certificate for your school records and they had written only one baby, it seemed like God had spoken. I took it as a sign to mean I was only meant to have one baby from God."

"So, you have nothing to remind you of me?" I ask, my heart strangely shattered at the thought.

"No, *bebita*, only in my mind and heart," Rosa replies regretfully.

"That's sad. It's kind of like I really did vanish from the planet."

"What happened to you after I left the hospital?" Rosa asks as she blows her nose on a Kleenex Tristan quietly hands her.

"I'm only able to tell you what I was told, of course. But, from what I understand, I spent about six months in the hospital recovering from a blood clot they had to surgically remove, so I could gain weight and adjust to medication. I was lucky it did not travel to my heart or to my brain. For a long time I took blood thinners to ensure I did not get another blood clot. I also had to take doses of surfactant to make sure my lungs matured."

"Were you immediately adopted?"

"I was. A very nice teacher named Lenore Montclair and her husband, Roger Montclair, who is an accountant, adopted me and provided a very nice home for me."

Rosa's face turns pale and she takes a quick drink of water.

Apparently, I am not the only person to notice Rosa's odd reaction. "Mama, are you okay?" asks Rogue with alarm in her voice.

Tristan rushes over with a cool washcloth and places it on Rosa's forehead. "It's all right ma'am, this is a stressful situation for everyone. Take your time."

For a couple of moments, Rosa just sits there with the rag on her forehead. I'm not sure what I should be doing or saying. Marcus steps up behind me and puts his arms around my waist as we stand there silently watching the situation unfold. A lone tear trickles down the fine lines in Rosa's face. It's one of the most heartbreaking sights I've ever seen.

After several more beats of silence, Rogue prompts, "Mama, are you okay. Do we need to get help?"

"I'm fine. I'm just trying to figure out what to say. This all happened so very long ago. But, it's not all my story to tell. *Bebita*, you really need to talk to the woman you call your *madre*. She will be able to give you answers I cannot."

"Mama!" Rogue barks with frustration. "Why can't you just tell us? We drove all the way up here and we're standing right in front of you. Clearly, you know more than you're telling us."

"Because I want you to hear the story told from a place of joy, not pain. Right now, my heart is broken into a million pieces and I cannot be fair to the people who raised Ivy. You deserve to hear both sides."

"Speaking of hearing from all sides, where was daddy during all this? Why didn't he check with the hospital to make sure Ivy was okay or did he even care?"

"Rogue Medea Cisneros Betancourt!" Rosa chides. "Of course your father cared. He cared very much. He even went to one of those medical supply stores and bought one of those special machines for listening to the baby's heartbeat. He would listen to each of your heartbeats every day. He wrote them down and kept track of them in a tiny notebook he carried with him. If there was more than a few beats difference, he would be calling the doctor asking for advice."

"If that's true, where has he been my whole life?" Rogue demands, her voice cracking with emotion.

"I have absolutely no idea. Don't you think I want to know too? I was alone most of your childhood. There were times we could have definitely used some help. All I know is one day, he said he was working on a priority project and he never came home."

My eyes narrow. "Didn't you call the police?"

Rosa bristles. "Of course I called the police. But, they told me he was an adult and free to leave home if he wished. They said he probably wasn't ready to be a father. So, they refused to even try to look for him."

"That's it?" Rogue asks incredulously.

Rosa closes her eyes as she relives painful memories. "Well, I asked all of his friends and family if they knew where he was and they said no. I made flyers and hung them in the neighborhood. I didn't have money for a private investigator and there was no social media back then and even if there were, I didn't even have money for a computer."

"I forget how far technology has come in the last few years. I can't imagine how frustrating it would've been for no one to believe you. You must've been heartbroken," I reply.

"I was. Isaac Roguen was the absolute love of my life. I'll never get over him."

"I was named after him?" Rogue asks in an astonished whisper. "I didn't know. This is the first time I've ever heard you say his name. All these years, I thought you hated him."

"Rogue, I could never hate him. He was my heart. He gave you life. You, and now Ivy, look just like his sister Selena. He would be so proud of you."

"Mama, I don't even know what to think about all this. It's like everything in my childhood is completely turned upside down and backwards. First, I thought I was an only child and it turns out I have a sister. Then, I thought my dad was some deadbeat who you hated with the very fiber of your soul, but he turns out to be the love of your life. You did marry Clive because you loved him, right?"

Rosa looks very uncomfortable. "At the time I thought I did, but I think I was more in love with the idea of being in love and so terribly lonely that I was willing to fall for anything. I'm so sorry I fell for his stupid lies and deceit."

"Oh Mama, what did he do —" Rogue asks, skepticism and fear clear in her voice.

"Nothing a million guys before him and after him haven't tried to do. He saw an opportunity to trade me in for a younger model and took it. He tried to take some of my money too, but your dad taught me how to protect myself from that kind of stuff. The bank tipped me off. So, I hope Clive is happy with the bimbo whose smarts are smaller than her shoe size."

"I'm sorry that happened to you mom. As you know, I was never his biggest fan. So, I can't say it was a huge loss," Rogue comments bitterly.

"You know what, Rogue? Neither can I," Rosa responds laughing.

I am so focused on my conversation with Rosa and Rogue that I miss the change in body language from Tristan. So far, aside from helping Rosa earlier, he's been a silent observer to our family drama. However, he is now walking over to Rosa with purpose.

He kneels down in front of her and takes a tissue out of his pocket and hands it to her so she can wipe her tears. After she tucks the tissue into her bra strap, Tristan takes one of her hands and covers it with his.

"Mrs. Betancourt, I don't want to make you any false promises, but finding people is what I do for a living. Would you like me to look for your first husband?"

"How much would you charge me for the help? I'm retired from the school district and my pension is not much."

"I wouldn't charge anything for my help, ma'am."

"Young man, I wasn't born yesterday. Nobody does anything for free. What are you trying to pull?"

Tristan chuckles. "You sound a lot like your daughter, ma'am. She asks me the same thing all the time. I could give you a long and complicated answer, but the short answer is that I'm falling in love with your daughter. Since you're important to Rogue, you're important to me too."

A stunned silence has fallen over the kitchen. I don't think anyone expected Tristan to announce his feelings quite so publicly especially in front of someone he just met today. I glance over at Rogue. Her nostrils are flared as if she can't quite get enough oxygen in her lungs.

Rosa is watching her reaction with some amusement. "*Mi hija*, what's wrong? Is he not suitable? Should I be chasing him out of here with your grandfather's shotgun? Do you fear you cannot grow to love him?"

"No Mama, none of that's true. He's very suitable. He's one of the nicest, most generous men I've ever met. But, it's all happening so fast. What if none of this is real? What if I wake up and it's all a dream?"

"*Si*, it is very real," Rosa confirms, reaching out

to grasp my hand and then Rogue's. "I can now touch both of my daughters — something I only dreamed of. If God can bring my daughter back from the dead, he can help your heart find love, even if you don't believe it's possible."

Rogue buries her face in Rosa's neck and sobs, "Oh, Mama, I want to be brave enough to believe."

"Then you must. Your heart will give you no choice."

Chapter Twelve

Tristan

Watching Rogue lose it in her mom's arms because of my ill-timed words was one of the most difficult things I've watched in a while. The intellectual side of me argues that her reaction isn't entirely due to my statement but because of the stress of the day as a whole. But, let's face it; I didn't help matters much. Sometimes I have the social graces of a sewer rat.

As the women disappear into the kitchen, Marcus lays a hand on my shoulder and remarks, "Believe it or not, this really isn't as bad as it looks. Rogue is kinda like one of those old-fashioned pressure cookers. You never know what's simmering under the surface. Everything can look fine until she needs to let off some pressure. It looks scary, but it can be done without harming anybody. She's been stewing about this day for weeks. She's been running every horror movie she's ever seen through her head. At one point, she was so worried she almost had herself convinced some weird religious cult had abducted Ivy from the hospital where they were born."

"I wish she would've told me she was so worried; I could've shown her some of that stuff couldn't happen. Maybe I could've lessened her stress level."

Marcus chuckles. "Here's one thing I've learned in five years of being Rogue's best friend. She'll worry about what she decides to stress out over. There isn't any rhyme or reason to her choice and there isn't anything you can do to change her mind."

Thinking I must have misunderstood him, I ask, "Really? She doesn't seem scattered."

"Oh no. I'm the scattered one in the relationship. Rogue is extremely focused. It's just that she can get mired down in the negative aspects of a problem. It's like she always expects the worst outcomes."

"Now that I understand a bit more of her background, I can understand where she's coming from. I'm not sure if I would view the world any differently if I were in her shoes."

"So, I guess your challenge will be to change the glasses through which she sees the world and establish your own special identity in her heart."

"Marcus, who knew you were such a poet? I like that concept 'identity of the heart'. I'm definitely a very different person when I'm with her. She brings out things in me I've never shown another person."

"It's weird isn't it? It's like they're magicians, hypnotists or something and can convince us to reveal things about ourselves we don't tell any other living soul. Ivy has been more effective in getting me to open up than any of those paid shrinks I had to go to. It's too bad she doesn't want to go into counseling or drug and alcohol treatment. She's got the touch for sure."

"You've probably noticed Rogue is effective at getting me to say things I don't intend to say out loud. After all, it was my clumsy attempt to reassure Rosa which sent her crying into the kitchen."

"I think you're shouldering too much blame. Rogue learned lots of new, upsetting things today. I don't think the fact that you admitted you have an epic crush on her is the cause of her falling apart. Speaking of that, do you think you'll actually be able to find Isaac Roguen? The story sounds intentionally vague. I wonder what Mama Rosa is actually hiding."

"I thought so too. But just because her story is vague doesn't mean she wasn't the victim of a crime. I can't believe the police department didn't even care enough to file a basic police report. You can't always assume someone willingly walked away from their family. You should at least do some sort of investigating. So, I'll start with the family unit. If we can't get DNA off some old clothes or belongings, I can always use the ladies' DNA. It will take longer to trace the parental line and exclude theirs. But, it can be done. However, I think I'd like to start by interviewing all of Isaac's former friends and colleagues to see if anyone recognizes him hanging around."

"I wonder if Rogue has a picture of him?"

"I doubt it. The way Rogue was raised, her dad was akin to the personification of evil in her eyes and I don't know if she felt she could or should be looking for her dad. I doubt if Rosa made the adoption open, given her mysterious clues today."

"Those were strange and off-the-wall, that's for sure. I don't know what to make of them."

"I don't know if we'll have any answers until we meet with Lenore and Roger. Even then, they might not be forthcoming. I have a hunch we may not get straight answers from everyone until we get everyone into the same room together and talk it all out."

"I have a feeling there are more than a few secrets somewhere in the story. Now, Ivy and Rogue will have to decide whether they really want to know all the secrets. It may be better if they don't know each and every secret. Anyway, I can't make that judgment call for them because it's not my life. They have to live with the decision and whatever fallout happens. But, there is no right and wrong decision. There is potential collateral damage from every choice we make."

Marcus makes a sound of frustration. "I frickin' hate that this is so complicated and painful for everyone involved. Do you think you will actually find this Isaac guy for Rosa, or were you just trying to make Rogue feel better?"

"Unless he's in the witness protection program, I think I stand a good chance of finding him. I've got a lot of experience skip tracing. When you combine it with my ability to track down identity fraud and comb through forensic accounting, there isn't much people can hide from me unless they go completely off the grid. These days, it's next-to-impossible to go one hundred percent off grid without a completely concerted effort to do so. You pretty much have to dedicate your life to avoid leaving a digital footprint and when you do that, your behavior is so aberrant it gets you noticed. So, it's not a great way to hide."

Marcus smirks at me. "So the short answer to that is yes, you can find him?"

I nod and I smile for the first time in a couple of hours. "Yes. I think I can find him with relative ease."

Marcus gives me a casual shrug as he remarks, "I don't know why you didn't just say so to begin with. Some of us are just simple tattoo artists and not Super-Secret-Spy-Guys."

"Actually, I did say that. I just used Super-Secret-Spy-Guy words," I quip.

Rogue and Ivy are holding hands as they come out of the kitchen. Rosa is walking slightly behind them with her arms resting on their shoulders. Rosa nudges Rogue forward. Rogue walks toward me and gives me a warm hug before she says, "Look, I'm sorry I had a meltdown earlier. I've been really stressed out. What you said was incredibly sweet. I wasn't really angry about that. It was more about life in general."

I softly kiss her temple as I murmur, "It's all right. I couldn't have picked worse timing if I'd tried. I'm sorry for upsetting you."

"Tristan, would it be all right with you if we have a slight change in plans?" Rogue asks.

"Sure, what did you have in mind?" I respond curious to hear what they cooked up in the other room.

"It's clear that we won't get all of our answers here. We discovered Ivy's parents only live about a half an hour away, just outside of Barton. We would like to go visit them for Thanksgiving. They are visiting a friend out of town until tomorrow, so it would add a day to our trip. Will an extra day be an issue?"

"No, that's not a problem for me. What about your classes?"

"One of Ivy's classes has already been canceled. I won't miss much in mine because it's the day after vacation."

"I've got the shop closed for the whole week because they're updating the heating and air system," Marcus adds.

I pull out my phone. "Okay, let me find a hotel. Do you want to stay in town or closer to the Monclairs'?"

"Young man, there will be no hotel. You are in Mama Rosa's neighborhood now. You will not sleep in a stranger's bed."

"Mama, you may not approve of our relationships —" Rogue tries to warn.

"*Mi Amor*, I may be old, but I am not too old to understand these boys are your *dilectos*. I've been lonely a long time, but I still remember what that means."

"*Dilecto!*" Rogue sputters. "Really Mama? Don't you think calling him my beloved is going a bit far?"

Rosa just holds Rogue's gaze. Finally, Rogue sighs. "You're right Mama. There isn't a better term. Beloved about sums it up because I really do cherish him and hold him in great esteem."

From the adoring gazes Marcus and Ivy are exchanging, I guess they don't have a problem with the term *dilecto* either.

I wipe the sweat from my brow as I move another box for Rosa. It's clear to me — no one has been in this attic for a couple of decades. The layers of dust are thick and undisturbed. However, for some reason she's decided she trusts me to help her retrieve some old pictures of Isaac.

Marcus is accompanying Rogue and Ivy to the store. Rogue has decided Ivy needs a lesson in proper Latina cooking. So, they plan to make tamales for dinner.

I've been left behind to help try to rebuild the past. Finally, beneath several boxes of miscellaneous Christmas decorations I spot a box of leather-bound books which look promising. My grandmother had some similar to these which were photo albums. I remember helping her painstakingly glue little white corner anchors for pictures against special acid-free black photo paper.

As I open up one of the heavy leather-bound books, I see a handsome man smiling up at me. There's not much doubt that this is Rogue's father. It's something about the defiant stance and the quirk of the eyebrow. The wide smile and lanky build are familiar too.

"Your husband was quite a handsome man. He looks like he could've walked off a studio lot."

"Yes, I always thought so too. I always teased him about being Mr. Hollywood. He thought that was a very funny joke because he was very shy. He would rather build things with his hands than be noticed in a crowded room."

I study the picture some more. "With these movie star looks he must've found it difficult. I'm sure he got attention everywhere he went."

"*Si*, but he much preferred if people paid

attention to me."

"How did you meet Isaac?"

"Oh, my Isaac was a very big hero. I had just moved here from Arizona. I wasn't used to driving in the snow and putting on tire chains. Apparently, I didn't get the chain attached correctly. So, as I was driving, it came loose and got caught somewhere on my car. It caused my car to slide out of control and crash into another car partially flipping me over. I've never been so frightened in my whole life. Isaac was in a car a few vehicles back. He saw me hanging upside down and scared for my life. He did not wait for the paramedics to come. He had a pocketknife in his car so, he cut the seatbelt in my car and got me down. After we gave our statements to the police, Isaac asked me out for hot apple cider. I did not know what cider was. I had never had it before. Yet, I was more than happy to try it because it meant I would spend more time with my dashing knight in shining armor who had rescued me. As they say, the rest was history — until he disappeared."

"Rosa, you've heard nothing from him in twenty-two years?"

Rosa sadly shakes her head. "*Nada.*"

"Have any of his family members?"

"Nobody that I know of. But, most of them don't talk to me anymore because they think I told Isaac to leave. I did not, but they don't believe me when I tell them we were not fighting."

"What about his coworkers?" I ask trying to narrow the list of possibilities.

"Isaac said he couldn't tell me about his job. He said he had important things to do and people to meet. I always thought it was very strange considering he worked for a moving company. I understand people relied on him. But, I didn't understand the need to keep it all secret. He had a side business repairing go-carts and helping parents of Boy Scouts build go-cart engines, but those didn't seem very personal either."

Thoughts are whirling around my brain at a million miles an hour. But I don't feel comfortable sharing them with Rosa at this point until I do more research. None of the scenarios I am thinking about will make her feel particularly comfortable. Quite frankly, none of them really explain why he couldn't eventually be with his family either. Any way you slice it and dice it, it's a big mystery.

"Rosa, you don't by any chance have some old insurance paperwork which would have his driver's license and his Social Security number on it, would you?"

"*Sí*, I keep it all in a file in the safe," Rosa replies. "Would you like to see it?"

"Yes ma'am," I reply. "It would make my job much easier."

CHAPTER THIRTEEN

MARCUS

I'M NOT SURE I'D BE dealing with all the random things being thrown in Ivy's direction half as well as she is if I were her. But, I can tell from her body language that it's catching up with her. She looks exhausted. It's no surprise. We were up most of the night watching silly, goofy movies together. It's been forever since I've been able to totally be myself in front of somebody. I thought I was the only person alive who knew all the words to every Mel Brooks movie ever made. I was completely blown away when she could match me line for line.

Mama Rosa already knows me from the times I've been here with Rogue, so she's used to my antics. I actually think she likes me despite my rough appearance.

I notice her struggling with some garbage cans full of corn husks. I take them from her and carry them to the curb. As we walk back to the house together, I comment, "Mama Rosa, I think Ivy's had a long day. Do you mind if I steal her away from all the excitement and insist she get some rest?"

Rosa gives me a long hard look. I try hard not to squirm under her examination — I feel a bit like I've been sent to the principal's office. "You know, I always wondered why you did not marry my beautiful daughter. You clearly care for her a great deal. But, now it's obvious. You were just saving space in your heart so you could fall in love with my other beautiful daughter."

Sometimes, I curse my blond hair and fair complexion. This is one of those times. I'm sure she can read every thought which crosses my mind as I try to formulate the right words. I'm not even sure what those would be. True to form, my mouth engages slightly before my brain.

"Mama Rosa, you know I have loved Rogue for a very long time. But, I'm not in love with her. I never have been. My feelings for Ivy are very different. We haven't really put a label to them yet, but let's say I could see us coming to visit you with some kids, a dog and the whole nine yards."

"That's beautiful Marcus," Mama Rosa embraces me. "Have you told my *bebita*?"

"I've made hints, but I don't think I've said it as clearly as I've told you."

"Perhaps you should. A woman likes to hear she's loved and adored. It does a heart good."

"I'll try to remember that, Mama Rosa. Have a good night."

Rosa made us a makeshift bed in her office with an air mattress on the floor. Sitting on the air mattress I'm propped up against the wall with Ivy situated between my legs. Ivy is sorting through a pile of pictures Tristan had made for her. Mostly, they are of her father. However, there are few of her parents together. Right now, she is holding one in her hand which depicts her dad standing behind her mom while her mom is several months pregnant. Isaac has his hand lovingly placed on Rosa's abdomen. You can clearly see the pride and affection in his eyes.

Ivy turns to me with tears streaming down her face. "Marcus, what happened to their love story? Why is this our last family portrait? I don't understand. I don't think I'll ever understand."

I pull her against my chest and rest my chin on her head as I gently rock her. "I don't know, Sugar. I just don't know. I wish I did."

I shift positions so I can cradle her in my lap. It's a little awkward because we're sitting on the air mattress, but she doesn't seem to care. I put some soft pop music on my iPhone and rub her back until she relaxes against my chest.

At last, she gives a deep shuddering sigh and her eyes drift shut, her long lashes spiked with tears. I continue to gently stroke her back and shoulders, enjoying the feel of her soft skin under my fingers. She has the long, lean lines of an athlete. I wonder if she played basketball in high school. But, then I remember that she hurt her ankle playing soccer. She doesn't look like the quintessential jock I remember from my days in high school; she looks far too fragile. But, I'm learning that there's a lot more to Ivy Love Montclair than you can see on the surface.

When she starts to delicately snore, I try to maneuver us into a prone position. However, I inadvertently knock over the stack of family pictures. I wonder if my mom has a similar hidden stash of pictures of the guy who sometimes pretends to be my dad.

I carefully move the pictures to a nearby chair and scoot us down on the air mattress. I spin her against me and pull the sleeping bags up over us. I don't know if it's just me and the weird way my brain operates but the whole time I'm struggling to zip the sleeping bags together so we could use them as one big bag, I can't help but think it's a pretty accurate metaphor for how our lives have become enmeshed and intertwined in such a complex and sometimes uncomfortable way. All the pieces are supposed to work together, but sometimes it's not an exact match. As I'm waxing philosophical about zipping up sleeping bags, I have to poke fun at myself for being so stupidly melodramatic. In the grand scheme of things, I'm not inventing world peace or anything, I'm just making the bed.

After we get comfortable in bed, the overhead heater turns on and blows a gust of hot air through the room. This causes one of the pictures to flutter off of the chair and fall a few inches from my face.

Seeing Ivy so torn up over the absence of her father makes me wonder what I'm missing in my relationship with my dad. I guess if I think about it hard enough, I can come up with a few positive memories. Even then I'm not sure if those memories are of my dad or of Tomás.

I vaguely remember going to some baseball

games and eating peanuts and drinking Coke. I remember my dad putting jalapeño peppers on my hotdog; making me eat it and laughing hysterically as I threw up until I cried. To this day I can barely stomach spicy food.

I also have memories of my dad making a huge deal over holidays like Christmas and sometimes birthdays. I remember being confused. He would be gone for months and sometimes years at a time and then suddenly swoop in with armloads of presents as if a new bike or computer would suddenly fix everything. I never knew what to do with those feelings. I was always super excited to get the new toy or game, but I remember being incredibly angry because he would pop in and out of our lives and pretend everything was normal.

Tomás Senior would always promise to do better and call more often. He would complain about my mom all the time and tell me he couldn't stand to live with her because she was too needy and clingy. Clingy is completely the opposite of how I see Anna Lucille Brolen. In my eyes she was always a pillar of strength despite seeing her world collapse around her.

By the time my brother got involved with the gang and became addicted to drugs and alcohol, and ended up in jail, my dad was nowhere to be found. We had all sort of become used to it by then and expected him to be the way he was. When my dad announced about four years ago, he was going to divorce my mom so he could marry a coworker, no one was particularly surprised or sorry about his decision. In fact, one of my mom's coworkers threw her a "happy divorce party".

If I'm ever lucky enough to be a dad, I don't want

to be the kind of dad nobody misses.

I decided to drive today because if I don't do something with my nervous energy, I might go a little nuts. I think I might be even more on edge than Ivy and Rogue if that's even possible. Since it's not physically possible for me to pace while I'm in a moving vehicle, driving is the next best thing. The navigation equipment in the Escalade is sweet. So, I'm not worried about getting lost. In order to not lose focus on my driving, I'm about to turn up the music on my phone so I can tune out the animated conversation coming from the back seat. But, it seems something exciting is happening.

Everyone is hunched over Tristan's laptop. Apparently, they've made some sort of discovery about Isaac, but Tristan is trying to temper their excitement until he can run some more paperwork through the official channels of his office to double check the authenticity of the match.

"I know you can't tell me officially, but you've been doing this a while, Tristan. What does your gut tell you? Do you think this is our dad?"

"Rogue, it's hard to tell from a few Facebook pictures and a LinkedIn profile. He does look similar and the demographics look like a good match, but it could be a weird coincidence. I don't want you to get your hopes up. Please let me make some calls to the office when they come in. We'll check the IP address and some other stuff and try to make a definitive match. This is too important not to get right."

"How far does he live from Rosa? Does he have

other kids? Is he married?" Ivy asks, spewing questions like a fire hose.

"Ivy, it might be easier for him to answer your questions if you ask them one at a time," I tease.

Tristan scrubs his hand down his face as he admits, "I wish I had more answers, but I don't know much more than you guys do at this point. Reading between the lines in this profile, I'd say he's probably a retired law enforcement officer of some sort. It looks like he teaches criminal justice at a community college out in Denver. Beyond that I can't tell much. He's careful about his social media. He's been far more judicious than most people. His digital footprint is tiny. There is not much here for me to track down publicly. That would be consistent with how Rosa described his personality, but we have no explanation as to why he ended up on the West Coast or why he would abandon his family."

"What do we do now?" Ivy sounds sad and defeated.

"I'm sure Super-Secret-Spy-Guy has more tricks up his sleeve, he just needs a little more time to make it happen. So, I guess we'll have to wait to see what he comes up with," I say with a shrug. "In the meantime, I guess I get to meet your parents and see how much they hate my tattoos. I'll even take out most of my body jewelry to make it easier. I try not to wear my glow-in-the-dark ear gauges when I meet parents for the first time. I save those for when the parents have already fallen deeply in love with me. Ask Rogue. Her mom thinks my skull earrings are the funniest thing she's ever seen because the eye sockets glow red."

"I'm sure Tristan is fully capable. I just don't want to wait. Since we've started down this road, I simply want the journey to be over. Intrigue sounds fun when you're reading about someone else's life — but when it's in your own life, it is not so amusing. By the way, don't feel like you need to change yourself for my parents. If they can't accept you for who you are, that's their problem not yours."

"Are you listening to yourself *Manita*?" Rogue asks Ivy quietly. "If they can accept Marcus with his tattoos and piercings, I'm sure they can accept that you don't want to be an accountant."

"I don't know, Rogue. My dad has been planning for me to go into business with him for so long. I don't want to let him down. They've made so many sacrifices for me, it just doesn't seem fair for me to want to go my own way."

"I think it's not only fair, I think parents expect it," Rogue responds.

Ivy laughs softly. "That's easy for you to say. Mama Rosa is laid-back and easy-going compared to my traditional suburban parents. You haven't met Lenore and Roger yet. They might have a little culture shock when they find out I want to pursue something humanities-based rather than business."

"Speaking of meeting your parents, isn't this your exit?" I ask as I hit the blinker.

"Oh my gosh, it is! The drive went so quickly. I can't believe it." Ivy exclaims. "I still haven't figured out exactly how I'm going to explain all of this."

Her reaction is so panicked I pull into a gas

station parking lot off the freeway so we can all talk. I turn to Ivy with a teasing grin. "Well, it's pretty simple — you and Rogue could stand next to each other and no words would be necessary," I suggest, only partly kidding.

"Marcus Taylor Brolen! We want to give her parents good news, not a heart attack," Rogue chides. "Show some sensitivity here."

"Well, she was looking for a way so she didn't have to explain it. I was just trying to be helpful."

"For what it's worth, I got the impression from Rosa that perhaps one of your parents already knows Rosa or Isaac. I could be wrong, but I don't think I am," Tristan suggests, studying his notes. "Unfortunately, without more information I can't figure out for certain which one. However, I think it might be Rosa."

"It would make sense because both our moms worked in kindergarten classrooms in Vermont," Ivy adds.

"Wouldn't it be bizarre if Mama Rosa was a classroom aide for your mom?" Rogue asks in a hushed voice. "I didn't expect us to have grown up so close together. It's weird we never ran into each other before."

"I just got goosebumps and I'm not sure they're the good kind," Ivy answers. "Mama Rosa didn't talk like she ever planned to give either one of us up for adoption. So, how did my mom end up with me? If they knew each other —"

"— and that raises the spooky quotient on our mystery to off the charts," Rogue finishes Ivy's sentence with a visceral shudder.

"Let's not get ahead of ourselves," Tristan cautions. "This is all conjecture. We don't know if any of this is true. The real story could be completely different and make a lot more sense. Let's wait until we hear their side of the story before we jump to any wild conclusions, okay?"

"Tristan, I understand where you're coming from, I really do. But Ivy and I can't help but think about the options. It's all we've done since we've been introduced. It doesn't matter how much I tell myself not to worry and obsess over it, it's still constantly in the back of my mind. If it's been in the back of my mind since you found me in August, I cannot imagine what it's been like for Ivy to know she's been adopted her whole life. She's probably been looking for her parents on some level ever since she knew what it was to be adopted."

Ivy nods. "It's true. Although I love my parents fiercely, there has always been a connection missing. For as long as I can remember, I've searched in random places for anyone who looked like me."

"I'd say you found her," I quip under my breath.

Ivy snorts, choking on the drink of water she just swallowed. Rogue hits her on the back. "You are so bad! Don't you take anything seriously?" Ivy asks when she can breathe again.

"Not much. What would be the point? The serious stuff still sucks, but other people aren't having fun. I like my way better."

Pulling his notepad out, Tristan clears his throat. "Did your parents tell you anything about your birth family?"

"No, actually, it was weird. They made no secret of the fact I was adopted, but any time I asked them about my family, they shut me down. The only story I know is about my funny birth certificate."

"Well, I guess you'll probably find out a lot more today. Don't worry. I'll be right by your side," I assure her, lightly squeezing her hand.

"I don't know Marc, given your current mood, Ivy may or may not find it a soothing thought," she jokes.

"Point taken, maybe you should pretend Super-Secret-Spy-Guy is your boyfriend," I suggest.

"No thank you!" Ivy responds at the same time as Rogue declares, "No, I don't think so! Spy-Guy is mine."

It is difficult for me not to fidget like a five-year-old as we are standing on an immaculately clean front porch waiting for someone to answer the door. "Why don't you use your key?" I ask curiously.

Ivy shrugs. "It's easier this way because my dad likes to reset the security code and he sometimes forgets to include my identity in the exclusions. I've had the crap scared out of me a few too many times to fully trust it."

Abruptly, the front door flies open and an older gentleman with curly gray hair and twinkling blue eyes scoops Ivy up into a large bear-hug.

"Love Bug! I didn't know you were coming. You should've called me. Are you having boy problems?"

Ivy giggles. "Daddy! No! As a matter of fact,

everything is going very well in the guy department, thank you very much. I did text Mom, by the way. Don't you two ever talk?"

Mr. Montclair peeks around Ivy to see me standing there. "Who is this cowering behind you?"

As I step forward to shake his hand, the porch light spotlights my vibrant new work. "No hiding here, sir. I was waiting for you and Ivy to say your hellos before I introduce myself. My name is Marcus Brolen. I'm the new guy in your daughter's life. She's an amazing young woman."

Her dad thoroughly examines me from head to toe before muttering to Ivy, "Are you sure you don't have boy problems? Because I could make you have some if you want me to —"

"Daddy — Don't. You. Dare! See this smile on my face? It means I'm good and happy. Marcus takes great care of me. Even my weird random asthma attacks don't even faze him. He had a grandma who had emphysema; breathing treatments and nebulizers are nothing new to him."

"But you look tired, Love Bug," he insists.

"I am tired, Daddy. But, that's not Marcus's fault. He tries to encourage me to sleep but you know how stress gets to me."

Mr. Montclair gives me the stink eye.

"Ivy Love Montclair! I do not believe we gave you permission to live with anybody except for that lovely little Jessica girl. She was raised by good people."

Ivy practically stamps her foot. In a stronger tone

than I've ever heard her use, she addresses her dad, "Oh for Pete's sake! Dad! Listen. At the moment, Marcus and I literally live hours apart. Our hot dates are over the computer. Not much sordid going on there, trust me. Even when we are together, Marcus is a complete gentleman."

Mr. Montclair glances over at me skeptically. "He doesn't look like a gentleman."

"That's what I'm trying to explain to you. He is more of a gentleman than anyone I've ever dated."

"Even the exchange student?" her dad asks with surprise in his voice.

"Especially the exchange student," Ivy insists.

"Huh … he came with such good references too."

"Just do me a favor and give Marcus a chance. I think you two will actually have a lot in common."

"So, if you're not here because of boy problems, why are you here looking like you haven't slept in a month?"

"Do you mind if we come in?" I ask, wiping my feet on the mat. "This will take a bit."

"Oh certainly, I got involved in the conversation and forgot the basics. Of course you can come in. Lenore would never send you away without a meal — especially this time of year. I think there's a turkey about ready to come out of the oven in about a half an hour. Make yourself comfortable."

Ivy scoots past her dad and kisses him on the cheek as she passes by. "Thank you, Daddy. I've missed you. Where's Mom?"

"Well, you know her. She's probably setting up some table-scape with leaves and bark and acorns and stuff. She goes all out this time of year. You know, it's not like I don't appreciate it, but sometimes a good paper plate is all you need."

"Daddy, you know she misses doing all the arts and crafts with the kiddos. She has to get her craft fix somehow. So, she binges on Pinterest on all the holidays. I'll go get her because I need to talk to you guys."

Mr. Montclair appears alarmed. "Is everything all right at that university you picked? I told you that you should've gone to school a little closer to home. Tampa is too far away."

Ivy just sighs. "Dad, just wait a minute and let me get Mom so I can explain."

Ivy leaves the room and suddenly the silence is deafening. I look around the living room to see if I can figure out a safe topic of discussion. Fortunately, it appears we both root for the same sports teams so perhaps we can avoid being mortal sports enemies.

"It's so odd to face the season without Lebron James being part of the Heat," I comment haltingly, hoping that I've ventured onto safe ground.

Mr. Montclair shrugs philosophically. "Basketball survived before him; it'll survive now. But, he was fun to watch. Do you like any other sports besides hoops?"

"I used to watch a lot of baseball with my grandfather. He got me into collecting cards when I was little and turned me into a huge baseball fan."

He regards me with more interest now as he scoots forward in his seat. "Got any favorites?"

"Well, I have to root for my hometown favorite Jeff Keppinger from the Tampa Rays. It's just a waste that he broke his foot in the dugout. He was having an amazing season."

Mr. Montclair scoffs. "Players these days … they don't even know the meaning of a true athlete. They break their toe and the whole world ends. Look at people like Lou Gehrig who played with a debilitating disease for years before anybody even noticed. Now, there's an athlete for you."

"I don't disagree with you. Lou Gehrig was a heck of a player. What he went through makes today's athletes seem like lightweights."

I notice movement in the corner of my eye. I remember the impromptu lesson on manners I received from Rogue and Super-Secret-Spy-Guy, so I stand up. The radiant grin of appreciation on Ivy's face is enough to make me want to ask them to leave the room so I can do it all again just to see her smile.

Mrs. Montclair walks up and shakes my hand. "Hello, I'm Lenore. Nice to meet you. I'm the mom. This is Roger. He's the dad. He's also a sports fanatic who will talk your ear off if you're not careful." She notices my tattoo and comments to Ivy, "Oh my! Did you see this dear? Have you told him about your dragonfly collection?"

Ivy flushes slightly. "No, it hasn't really come up yet. We've been busy dealing with some complicated issues back at home."

Lenore blanches slightly. "Are those big city college professors giving you a hard time? I worry about you. I wondered if you were ready for life in a big town. Your dad could make a few phone calls. He knows some pretty important people."

"Mom stop, please. This has nothing to do with my college life or my love life — or at least not in the way you think. It's more personal than that. What I came to talk to you about is going to impact our whole family."

I glance over at Roger Montclair who looks like he's about to blow a gasket. He turns to me and roars, "How dare you hurt my daughter and then come in here pretending to be her boyfriend! If you only knew a fraction of what she's gone through in her life you wouldn't even think this was remotely funny."

"Daddy!" Ivy yells back, "For once and for all, listen!" Ivy paces back and forth between her parents. "Look at me," she commands, twirling slowly in a circle. "I am fine. In fact, thanks to Marcus, I am better than fine. He has kept me happy and relatively calm during what's been a totally crazy, completely topsy-turvy time in my life. I have known him since August. Obviously, he has not hurt me in any way. So, can we put away all the stereotypes and pre-judgments and talk about what we really need to talk about?"

From the stunned look on her mom's face, this is not usual behavior from Ivy. Lenore reaches out and pats Ivy on the hand. "Whatever you need, dear."

I flash her a surreptitious thumbs-up. When she sees it, she takes a deep breath and starts over, "I'm sorry for sounding harsh, but there's no easy way to bring this up other than to simply start. So, I apologize in advance if this is difficult. I want you both to know I love you very much and that will never change."

I watch as Ivy takes a deep drink of her bottled water. I walk over to her purse and fish out her inhaler in case she needs it. She swallows hard and gives me a grateful smile. "I think I'm good Marcus, thanks though."

A frown creases Roger's brow. "Is this bad news?"

Ivy expels the breath she's been holding. "I hope not Daddy, I really do."

"Well, Love Bug, I think it's time for you to quit stalling and just spit it out."

"Do you guys remember anyone named Rosa Marie Betancourt or Isaac Roguen?" Ivy asks quietly, with a hint of trepidation in her voice.

Lenore's eyes go wide with shock when she hears the names. Roger rushes to his wife's side. She looks up at him. "Do you think she knows the whole story?"

CHAPTER FOURTEEN

ROGUE

I'M STARTING TO HAVE A new sense of appreciation for Ivy. It really is different when you're on this end of things. My hands are sweaty, and my heart is pounding so hard I'm pretty sure my blouse is about to come unfastened.

I must've tried on four outfits this morning before I decided this one was appropriately toned down enough to meet Mr. and Mrs. Montclair. I don't dress particularly sexy, but my clothes tend to be avant garde with lots of rips, tears, pins and unusual stitching. It's not the type of thing you'd find at Saks Fifth Avenue.

Tristan is still on the computer and he's currently Skype-ing with members of his team back at the office trying to track down leads on my dad. I know I should be more appreciative of his efforts but, right now I'd like to kick Tristan's computer a few inches up his colon to get him to put it away so he can just hold me. I've graduated from just sweaty palms to actually trembling.

Marcus and Ivy have been in there a long time. I

don't know what's going on in there but whatever is happening is making Ivy hellaciously angry. I can feel sparks flying off her psychic energy like a welding machine.

I hate that I can't go in there and help her right now. I can feel her reacting physically to whatever they are saying to her. Something big must've just happened because I just felt the energy crescendo and then wane.

Suddenly, I hear Ivy's voice in my head, *Get ready … it's tense in here but we need to do this. It's just as I predicted. They are being very odd.* I have to say it, as cool as it is, it still weirds me out that she could talk to me in my brain.

Yeah? It's no picnic for me either.

Private thoughts would be nice.

So would winning the lottery, but it's not ever likely to happen.

You're so funny, I forgot to laugh.

Time to get serious here. I don't know what will happen once you guys come inside. I've never seen my mom become quite so distraught.

Remember, we've had a few months to get used to this, your parents haven't. This came out of the blue for them.

You're right. You'll still love me at the end of all this, right? I have a feeling it might not be pretty.

Manita, I specialize in gritty and tough, remember? I've got your back.

Tristan touches my shoulder and I startle, almost spilling my Dr. Pepper all over.

"Are you done having a conversation with your sister?"

"How did you know that's what I was doing?" I ask, a little embarrassed to be caught.

"Don't worry, it's probably not obvious to anyone but me. You just get this intense expression of concentration on your face and you stare off into space for a minute."

"Gah! That's embarrassing," I admit, blushing.

"So, what's the verdict? Do they want us in there?"

I'm still half a beat behind the conversation because I'm concentrating on what he just said about my appearance when I talk to Ivy during our episodes of 'twin talking'.

"Well, in or out?" he prompts.

"Oh ... um ... I guess we're supposed to go in," I respond, sounding scattered.

"Rogue, are you okay with this? You know you don't have to go in if you don't want to," Tristan assures me as he tries to warm up my hands.

"No, it's not that. Ivy really needs our help. Everything got overwhelming there for a second. But I'll be fine."

As Tristan helps me from his vehicle, he gives me a long, comforting embrace. "I'm here if you need me; just say the word."

I smile through my tears as I brush a light kiss across his lips. "I know. It's one of the reasons I know I'll be just fine."

Ivy meets us out on the front porch. She's slipped off her shoes and I notice Marcus has given her his favorite sweatshirt. What concerns me is that her eyes are rimmed in red and she's obviously been crying.

"I'm sorry Rogue, I don't know any other way to do this. We'll just have to show them and let the chips fall where they will. I guess we'll deal with the aftermath later. There's just no gentle way to say, 'Hey, did you know your daughter has a mysterious twin sister?' I've tried to prepare them the best I can, but I still think it'll be a huge shock to them."

"It's okay *Manita*. We didn't cause this mess, remember? We were just innocent bystanders who got caught up in the drama."

Marcus steps up and cuddles Ivy from behind. "Besides, you two are too cute for them to stay mad at for too long. I'm sure once they get over the shock, it'll be just fine."

Tristan holds the screen door open for us as Ivy and I hold hands. Those few feet into the sunken den seem like some of the longest I've ever walked. When you consider my history, that's saying quite a lot. I've been known to use my thumb to get around if I was short on bus fare. Movies and television shows make it seem like it's a glamorous way to travel, but what it really translates to is a lot of walking on hot asphalt with the sun beating down on you. Still, in some ways, walking into this lushly appointed house is more frightening. Yet, I can feel the presence of the men in our lives, just a few inches behind us, ready to be called on if needed. The feeling of rock-solid support is more powerful than my fear.

Ivy carefully maneuvers us to a love seat and much to my astonishment, we are able to smoothly sit down without falling on our faces. I can feel every pair of eyes in the room scrutinizing me.

After what seems like a decade of silence, Roger finally speaks, his voice choked with emotion, "So the rumors were true."

"Are you sure this is wise, Roger? She could be out to get us," Lenore cautions, twisting a Kleenex in her hands.

Roger runs his fingers through his hair making his curls even more haphazard. "Lenore, look at them. They're obviously bonded; they are sisters in every sense of the word. The story will come out eventually. They are adults and we can't shelter Ivy Love any longer."

My stomach clinches at the warning tone implicit in his words. I frantically try to remember all the different scenarios we put together with Tristan and mentally try to put the puzzle pieces together with Lenore's words and determine if anything fits. But, every scene I come up with in my head is more frightening than the last.

Do not pass out on me! Ivy directs me sternly via our private line of communication. I need you here with me.

I'll try — but, to be honest my vision is getting a little gray at the edges. I don't know how much longer I can hold on.

Suddenly, Ivy yells, "Marcus, she's going down. Do your breathing trick."

Tristan grabs the gift bag in which we brought wine and pulls the wine out and hands it to a very startled Roger. He tosses the bag to Marcus.

Marcus kneels in front of me. "Ro, come on, focus!" He puts the bag in front of my face. "Now, just follow me. In through your nose and out through your mouth. No. Slow it down. Just like me. Breathe when I breathe. Nice deep breaths. Good girl. In and out. In and out. In and out. Very nice. Feeling any better?" Marcus asks.

I'm so intent on following Marcus's breathing pattern that I'm a little surprised by his question. I do a brief self-assessment and decide my head is feeling much clearer and my vision isn't fuzzy anymore. I nod. "Yes, I'm feeling much better. Thank you."

"Good, I'm going to let your guy here help you. He's looking territorial enough to tear me apart limb by limb."

"Don't be silly. Tristan would never hurt you," I insist.

"Oh yeah? Are you sure? He's looking a little possessive to me," Marcus teases.

Tristan raises an eyebrow. "If you're done harassing my woman, I'd like to check and see what made her almost pass out to begin with."

"I appreciate the concern, but I'm fine now. Really. I just got a little emotionally overwhelmed by the situation and I was too nervous to eat much today. I think it all just piled up on me," I explain. I turn to Roger and say, "Please continue with your story."

He looks very concerned. "Are you sure? I don't want to make things worse."

"I'm fine," I declare. "Getting it all out in the

open will help. I've been letting my imagination get the better of me."

Lenore pins Ivy with a knowing glance. "That sounds just like someone else we know."

Roger turns to Lenore. "What do you think?"

Lenore blows her nose delicately and shrugs. "I suppose there's no harm. We were just following the advice of the adoption lawyer. If we don't tell the girls, it's obvious we'll just be causing them pain."

"Okay. But, Lenore — if I'm going to tell the story, I'm going to tell the whole story. Even the parts which don't make us sounds so glamorous."

"If you think you must, Roger. But, please remember we were much younger then and very naïve. We fell in love in high school and wanted nothing more than to be parents. As Ivy knows, Roger faced terrible pressure from his family to carry on the family tradition of being police officers and firefighters. He simply had no interest in that type of physical job. He much prefers the mental challenge of dealing with numbers and concrete evidence. We wanted kids right away so we started trying as soon as we got married. But, year after year nothing happened."

Roger tenderly pats his wife's shoulder, but it's clear — this trip down memory lane is hard on him as well.

Lenore dabs her eyes with a tissue and continues, "I had just finished grad school and gotten my teaching certificate, so we didn't have any money for any infertility testing or treatments. Then, one of my aunts died leaving me a small inheritance. We were able to use the money to consult an adoption attorney. He said he'd never seen a couple with as much childcare experience as the two of us and he assured us we should have no trouble finding a couple that would choose us. It was excruciatingly painful for me to work around a bunch of kindergarten teachers with all those adorably cute kids in my classroom knowing I might not ever get to be a mom."

Lenore sobs into Roger's shoulder before collecting herself and resuming her story.

"To make matters worse, there was a teacher's aide in my school district whose name was Rosa Betancourt. Since all the kids had trouble with her last name, everyone always called her Mama Rosa. That particular year she was actually going to be a mom. I had met her once or twice at teacher training, but didn't know her well. She always seemed exceptionally sweet, but there were some strange rumors going around about her husband. Some people thought he was a member of the Mafia. Other people thought he might sell drugs for the Mexican drug cartel. Whatever the truth was, the perception remained that she might be in danger."

At this point, Lenore pauses and looks to Roger for reassurance. He nods almost imperceptibly. So, she takes a large gulp of coffee from the steaming mug she had brought in earlier and sets it back on the tray. I can't help but notice that her hands must be trembling as much as mine. She breathes deeply and resumes speaking. "We briefly thought about asking her if she was interested in giving up her baby for adoption since her world was in such chaos. But it quickly became apparent that she and her husband both wanted the baby. So we were put on a more traditional waiting list. We looked into other avenues through our private attorney, but even though the choices were there, they were so far out of our price range we couldn't even seriously consider them."

Roger seemingly decides that Lenore has endured enough of the burden, so he picks up the storytelling, looking directly at Ivy.

"After waiting months and months for any results through the public agency, the private adoption attorney called us and said he had a rather dicey situation on his hands. He explained that you were in the hospital needing urgent medical care. It was strongly implied your mother had simply thrown up her hands and walked away when she found out how much your NICU bill would be. But, not a single nurse on the hospital staff would tell us one iota about your birth mom."

"It's a strange thing about dads in the hospital. When you hang around long enough. They start treating you like you're part of the woodwork. You become rather invisible. So, one day after we were waiting for you to come back from a series of complex tests on your lungs, I noticed a bunch of paperwork about you lying around. Well, by that time I had become a bit of an armchair medical sleuth. I used to write down all the terms the doctors would use and then I would go home and research them at the local library. So, I was doing my routine scour of your most recent records when I came across some paperwork I didn't recognize."

Roger turns to me and looks me in the eyes. "I didn't know what I was reading about at the time. But, in retrospect, it was clearly about you. It was just a brief mention about another female infant. There weren't any details. Just initials. We hadn't been told anything about Ivy's birth mom and there were no hints you were part of a multiple birth. So, I just thought it was a filing error. The only thing which gave me any pause at all was later when the senior nurse saw the file, she completely berated the nursing student for allowing the information to be placed in the file. I'll never forget what she told her, 'Don't you realize you could've jeopardized everything? No one is supposed to know anything!' Of course, I couldn't ask any questions because I wasn't supposed to be snooping in the files to begin with nor was I supposed to be eavesdropping on personnel issues with the nursing staff. I just kept my concerns to myself."

Tristan is sitting on the edge of an ottoman with his notepad and pen. "You said there was a lawyer involved, what role did he play in this?"

A look of alarm crosses Lenore's face as she looks at Roger.

"Mom, I'm sure enough time has passed that even if you did inadvertently do something wrong, nothing would be done about it. Rogue and I are adults now. Nobody can take me away from you," Ivy assures her.

Roger scrubs his hand down his face and wearily answers, "I promised that I'd tell you the whole story — even the unflattering parts. Well, it looked like everything was going just fine with the adoption. Our lawyer had everything handled and Ivy was getting better every day. One day, the nursing supervisor came to me and told me they had a problem employee who had been let go. He was threatening to go to the media with an exposé on hospital practices. The nurse said he was planning to name us specifically and that it might tie up Ivy's adoption in legal proceedings for years."

"Oh how terrible! Mom must've been fit to be tied," Ivy murmurs sympathetically.

"She probably would've been if I would've actually told her. But, she was so worried and focused on getting you better, I didn't want to add to that. So, I took out a collateral loan on the business and authorized our attorney to offer the employee some incentive to keep his opinions about the hospital to himself. Then, the attorney put the adoption on the fast track, citing Ivy's delicate medical situation."

"Did you ever have any idea about the identity of Ivy's birth parents?" Tristan asks, jotting notes down.

"No, we were completely fine with the idea of open adoption. But, we were told that because of Ivy's medical challenges, the birth parents were not interested in ever being involved in her life. We decided if that's the kind of people they were, we wouldn't encourage contact. Ivy didn't need negative influences in her life."

"It appears there were more half-truths going on in this story than a daytime soap opera," comments Marcus.

"Lenore? Do you want to know who my mom is?" I ask carefully, not wanting to cause her any more pain.

Lenore blinks away tears as she studies me. "Honey, I think I already know. I can't believe I didn't see it all those years with Ivy. You both have her eyes, her laugh and her famous dimples. Did you stay with Mama

Rosa or were you adopted as well?"

"I didn't even know I was a twin until Ivy found me," I explain. "It was just Mama and I for years until I moved to Florida."

An expression of comprehension crosses Roger's face. "Ah, so you go to school with Ivy Love? Are you an accounting major too?"

"Oh, not quite sir," I answer quickly. "I live about three hours from Ivy. Right now, I'm attending art classes at Santa Fe Community College until I can see if I can get enough scholarships to transfer to the University of Florida. I'm also studying to be a tattoo artist at Marcus's shop, Ink'd Deep."

"Isn't she great, Daddy? Look at the amazing tattoo she just gave Marcus."

Marcus walks over and shows Roger his tattoo. I know him well enough to know Marcus flexed his muscle just a tiny bit. I hold my breath as Roger examines my work. I'm not sure why I hold his opinion in such high esteem, but for some reason his approval is important to me.

"Impressive. Very impressive. I always wish I had the artistic ability Ivy has. Math has its uses, but people are rarely impressed by addition and subtraction," Roger compliments.

"I've seen some of Ivy's drawings, she could give me a run for my money. Hers are downright amazing. She should consider a career in the fine arts," I remark, trying to sound casual.

"Well, I suppose it's up to her. I don't want to be

like my family and try to push her into a career she doesn't want. If it were up to my family, I'd be wearing a firefighter's uniform. We all know what a disaster that would be since I can barely climb a flight of stairs."

"What about your plans, Daddy? You know — 'Montclair and Montclair'?"

"Love Bug, I made those plans to motivate you to strive to do well, not to trap you into a life you don't want. Go find what makes you happy. Go find your bliss. Life is too short to be sad."

Ivy hops off the love seat and launches herself into Roger's arms. "Oh Thank you Daddy, I love you so much!"

You are my hero! I so totally owe you!

Don't mention it. After all, that's what sisters are for.

I love you too, Manita.

Lenore looks at Tristan quizzically and asks, "What's going on?"

Tristan chuckles lightly. "Welcome to the wonderful world of 'twin-dom'. They are having one of their private conversations that only they can hear. Marcus and I are used to it now. We barely notice anymore, but it takes a bit of adjustment. It's quite remarkable to see."

"Roger, do you suppose she was having conversations with Rogue the whole time she was growing up and we didn't know it? I feel so bad for separating them," Lenore laments.

"Ma'am, it appears you and your husband didn't

know what was happening. Rosa had been told Ivy had passed on and didn't survive. Until Ivy showed up on her doorstep, Mama Rosa had no idea she still had two daughters either," Marcus explains.

Lenore pales to a ghostly shade of white. "How horrible! I can't even imagine a pain so deep. She must think we're awful human beings. I bet she thinks we stole her child."

"I don't really know what Mama thinks. We tried to ask her, but she wouldn't answer. She just said we would have to get the story from you. I think she might have some misunderstandings about what happened. I think the only people who know what happened might be the uppity ups at the hospital and maybe your lawyer," Marcus adds.

"Whatever happened to your dad? Was he really some big-time drug dealer?" asks Roger.

"Roger Montclair! Where are your manners?" chides Lenore.

"I'm sorry if I was rude, but doesn't everybody want to know?" inquires Roger.

Marcus laughs out loud. "I would've so asked that question if I were in his shoes. Unfortunately, Roger, we don't know the answer yet."

"Hey! I don't think my mom would've been in love with a leader of the drug cartel. He could have disappeared for other perfectly legitimate reasons. If the guy we think might be my dad turns out to be authentic, it looks like he may have had a career in law enforcement," I protest.

"I'm working on tracking all that down. It'll probably just be a couple more days. It's clear that someone was underhanded in all this. It'll just be a matter of determining who. Clearly, both you and Mama Rosa were somehow tragically duped. I think the key to solving all this will be determining who had the most to gain," Tristan replies.

"I can tell you that we were told the adoption would be one fee and by the time it was all said and done, it was substantially more."

Lenore narrows her eyes at her husband and remarks, "So much more, in fact, that Mr. CPA over here won't even fess up to the amount."

"It just wouldn't be helpful for you to know, dear," Roger responds as he squeezes his wife's knee affectionately. "In the end, what's a few hundred extra tax returns every year when I have a perfect family now? I feel stupid for being taken advantage of, and I am sorry the girls were separated for so long. Yet, I will never be sorry I made sacrifices for my beautiful daughter."

Observing the sweet conversation is enough to bring tears to my eyes. I wonder if my dad feels that way about me. Those pictures I saw seem to show he was excited we were coming. Every conversation I've had about family issues in the last six months has taught me not to make assumptions about what I think is happening without knowing all the facts because I'll likely be wrong.

I'm hoping that the same is true about my father. I hope to God the rumors about him are not true. Yet, I can't seem to get the nagging thought out of my brain that my mom thought she had great character judgment about Clive too and she was dead wrong. So, what if she has a pattern of choosing colossal losers and my dad was merely the first?

CHAPTER FIFTEEN

IVY

IT'S SURREAL TO BE BACK in my childhood room. I know I've only been gone for a little over two-and-a-half years, but it seems like a lifetime ago. Seriously? Did I really put a Justin Bieber poster on my wall? I'm almost embarrassed to let Rogue see my room. She's so cool and sophisticated compared to me. I feel like I should do a cursory sweep for Bratz dolls or something.

Rogue peeks her head around the corner and her eyes widen as she takes in her surroundings.

"Wow! This is rad. I would've given anything for a room like this when I was a teenager. Is that surround sound on your TV?"

"I used it to practice my cheerleading routines. Dad wanted to make sure I heard my cues even if I was hanging upside down," I admit, painfully blushing.

Rogue walks into my closet which backs up to a private bathroom. She spins in a small circle as she slowly studies the room. "Don't you have any clothes at school?"

I giggle. "Yes, I have clothes at school. According to Jessica, I should be assigned my own dorm room just for my clothes."

"Then why is this closet stuffed to the gills with clothes too? Shouldn't one of them have at least a few empty spaces in it?"

I wave my hand dismissively. "Most of those don't even fit me anymore since I put on the freshman fifteen. But, you'll have to talk to the Guardian of the Closet, the Queen of Television Shopping, Mrs. Lenore Montclair. She's in charge of all the shopping stuff, I can't stand it; I'd rather not ever try on clothes if it were up to me."

Rogue sighs dramatically. "Boy, I wish I had a fairy god-shopper. It must be nice."

"Be careful what you wish for, my mom might actually hear you and your closet will look like this."

"That would definitely not be pretty considering my whole apartment could probably fit into your bedroom. When I was growing up, I used to help my mom pay bills by cleaning houses a lot like this. I used to pretend I lived a whole other life where I was a princess living in a perfect world. I guess I never knew how close to reality my fantasies really were."

"I don't know, I think the open, easy-going relationship you have with your mom is pretty much the stuff of fantasies too."

Manita, did you forget — she's your mom too? she telegraphs.

I jump when her words hit my consciousness.

I smile shyly as I project back, *I guess I did. It's very strange having two moms now*

Just when I think my life can't get any stranger, it does. I guess I should have been more specific when I said I wanted to break out of my bubble and expand my horizons. This is beyond anything I ever dreamed of. We are on a freaking private plane.

"Can you believe this?" I mouth to Marcus.

"No. I'd like to think of something appropriately smart-alecky to say here, but I've got nothin'. This is awesome. Were you able to reach all of your professors?"

"Yes, they were remarkably flexible. I just told them I had a family issue and I asked for any homework. I don't have any exams scheduled since it's right after Christmas break. Therefore, they were all willing to work with me. I have some reading to do."

"I'm sorry we couldn't schedule this trip during Christmas break, but the Body Art Trade Show was amazing — even if Marcus is still pouting neither one of us caved about getting tats yet," Rogue says, poking fun at Marcus.

"That's all right — the conclusive DNA didn't come back until two days ago anyway," Tristan interjects. "It was a fun way to get our mind off things."

Marcus laughs out loud, "Did you really need a genetic test with these guys?"

"Me? Not a chance. However, Isaac may be harder to convince. You have to hit some men over the head with a two by four before they can see what's right in front of them. A DNA test can cut through a lot of B.S."

Rogue turns to me as if we weren't interrupted by the side conversation. "Anyway, my professors were pretty good too. I have to do a portrait of someone in charcoal or pastels. Hey, Ivy if I do one of you, do you think they'll believe it's not a self-portrait?"

"They probably will if I take a picture of you drawing her," Tristan suggests.

"Would you please? That would make a cool photograph I might want to turn into a painting later."

"… and I could photograph you painting the picture of you painting my picture. We could blow their minds."

"That sounds like a phenomenal plan. Let's do it," Rogue agrees with a laugh.

"Does Mr. Roguen know we're coming?" Marcus asks, returning to the other conversation as he pops open the little fridge next to his seat and pulls out a Dr. Pepper for Rogue and a Sprite for me.

"He's aware we're coming, or more precisely he's aware I'm coming — you guys may be more of a shock," Tristan replies with a crooked grin.

Rogue gasps. "Exactly why does he think you're coming?"

"If I were to venture a guess, I'd say he thinks it's related to a case he worked on."

I throw my hands up in the air as I exclaim, "Oh great! That's just what this situation needs — one more person telling a lie."

"Actually, strictly speaking, I didn't actually lie to him," Tristan responds defensively.

"What exactly did you say to him?" Rogue asks skeptically.

"Nothing like you're accusing me of," Tristan responds. "I merely told him my name, the name of my business, and the type of cases I usually specialize in. Any conclusions he drew were entirely his own. It's not like I could go into the whole story over the phone."

Rogue visibly relaxes. "I never thought about that. There is no real roadmap on the right way to handle this mess. I'm sorry I tried to second-guess you. It'll be awkward as heck no matter how we do it. Even if we plan every syllable of every word. It probably won't go to script," she concedes.

"I know it's probably because I'm really tired, but my overwhelming thought is even if we wrote a script about all this, no one would ever believe it. What's happened to us over the past few months is far too crazy even for a Hollywood script. We couldn't write a script crazy enough to cover what's been happening to us. If you think about it, we're too nuts for Hollywood," I quip, cracking myself up.

Rogue grins at me. "You know, you're probably right. They'd probably tell us to tone it down because nobody lives through something this totally off-the-wall and crazy."

"I've got a creative writing class this term. Should I write about our adventures just to see if anybody believes it?" I suggest with a smirk.

"It would be fun if we went to the same school

wouldn't it?" Rogue suggests wistfully.

"Unfortunately, I haven't decided what I'm going to do about school yet. If I follow my heart, it means I'll have to practically start over. Most of my coursework has been in stuff I can't stand. I can't see building a career based on what I've been doing. So, you probably don't want to wait around for me. I might be in school forever," I complain, dejectedly.

Rogue actually chokes on her pop as she laughs. "Ivy, does it look like I'm on the fast track to you? I've been taking a class or two a term since I was seventeen. Sometimes I get lucky and can take three classes. But I've had terms where I haven't been able to take any because I've had to move or something. Life happens. We just have to do our best to figure it out. At this point, I figure I'll be doing well if I finish college before I have kids and they graduate from college."

"If your scores were so great, why don't you get some financial aid?" I ask, curious as to why my very talented sister doesn't have more support.

"Well, after Mama got together with Clive, financial stuff got really weird. He got stingy with money and took over her finances and didn't want to let anybody know what was going on. If I applied for financial aid, I would've been considered a dependent and she would have had to ask him for information. I didn't know until this last visit that she finally kicked him to the curb. If I had known he didn't have control over her life anymore, I might've done things differently."

Tristan drapes his arm around Rogue's shoulders and he gently cuddles her to his side as he murmurs against her temple. "I wish I would've known you sooner. You didn't deserve to be put in such a difficult spot."

"They should make an exception for students like you. I still think you should have declared yourself as emancipated," Marcus argues. It's clear this is not the first time they have had this discussion.

Rogue shakes her head as she explains, "I couldn't do that to Mama Rosa. My beef wasn't with her. It was with Clive. Filing for emancipation would have been like disowning her. It would've crushed her. So, I'll do it my way until I turn twenty-four. Hopefully, by then I'll be making some serious money doing tattoos and it won't make a difference anyway."

"Heck yeah, you'll be making serious money doing tattoos," Marcus declares. "I'll be like your walking billboard. You'll have the busiest chair in the shop. My sign will say Ink'd Deep — tattoos by Rogue Betancourt (Oh yeah, a guy named Marcus Brolen works here too)."

Rogue throws a crumpled up napkin at Marcus as she scoffs. "Yeah right! Like that would ever happen! As I recall, they made you the youngest owner of Ink'd Deep for a good reason. It's because you're crazy talented and super smart."

Marcus shrugs. "I never said I wasn't Ro. I just think you can surpass me in no time flat."

I smack Marcus on the thigh as I ask, "I know I've asked this before, but are you sure you're not in love with my sister? You say the nicest things to her."

Marcus turns in his seat and gives me a bone melting kiss. As he pulls away, he says, "Yes, I am one hundred percent certain I am not in love with your sister.

I say nice things to Sadie too. I'm not in love with my sister either. My relationship with Rogue is as platonic as it gets."

I relax a bit after his reassurance. He's so supportive of her it's difficult to remember sometimes that they are simply friends.

Manita, I promise it would be like kissing my brother. So gross I can't even imagine. I am beyond thrilled for you guys. But there's no chemistry between us. There never has been.

I blush as her reassurance pushes its way into my thoughts. I'm embarrassed my insecurities took me to a place where she's even had to try to make me feel better.

"I'm sorry guys, it's been a long day and sometimes I let my wild imagination get away from me," I utter out loud.

"Sugar, you wouldn't be the first person to misinterpret my relationship with your sister. It's confusing to a lot of people that we can just be friends. I guess it's pretty unusual. I'm attracted to only one person on this plane and it's you. In fact, you can ask Ro; I haven't even mentioned any other women since I met you."

"Well … there was that one woman with the obnoxious perfume who tried to completely disrobe so you could do a tattoo on her wrist —" Rogue teases.

"Rogue Medea Cisneros Betancourt! You are so *not* helping!" protests Marcus. "You know I had nothing to do with that shop bunny. I tried to pass her off to you, but she wasn't having anything to do with you."

Rogue shrugs. "Can I help it she didn't think I

knew how to draw a smiley face with a party hat? She wouldn't even let me show her my sketchbook."

"Seriously? Do women treat your place like it's a club or something?" I ask.

"Definitely. But, it's not only women. We've got our fair share of men. I've got guys wanting things from Jade too. She gets so irked because she just wants to be treated like every other artist in the shop not like some dressed up Barbie doll. She's a phenomenal artist who does amazing portrait work."

"Rogue, how come you're not apprenticing with her? Wouldn't it be helpful to learn from another woman in the business?" I ask, as the seatbelt sign flashes.

Rogue shifts in her chair taking her legs off of Tristan's lap. "I hope to get a rotation with her at some point, but she already has two other apprentices working with her and her time is limited. But she said she'd work with me if she got some free time."

"Jade is all kinds of cool. I hope that works out. You should work with as many tattoo artists as you can so you learn several styles because everybody does it differently and everybody's got tricks of the trade they don't always share with everyone else, but they'll usually share them with their apprentice. It can save you a lot of time and make you more effective," Marcus comments.

I look out the window and realize we're about to approach an airport. I look up at Marcus and Tristan with total astonishment. "Oh my gosh! You guys are amazing. Somehow you managed to distract us through the whole flight. I have no idea how we got here so fast. Usually, I have to take medication to make me calm enough to fly and even then, I'm usually queasy the whole time. This was no different from sitting around in our living room shooting the breeze. The only thing missing was my dad yelling vile things at the referees during the games and my mom telling him he'll scar me for life."

Tristan grins at me. He holds his hands out like he's holding an imaginary pen and paper, "Okay, I got it. Ivy's new and improved belated Christmas wish list: One private plane for everyone. Check."

"Tristan Riley Macklin! Don't even think about it," Rogue warns.

Tristan's bottom lip slides out like a toddler's. "But new planes are so much fun —"

Rogue sighs and rolls her eyes. "I can see that it's time once again for Real Life 101." She points to Tristan. "You are a multi-kajillion-billionaire. You need a plane." She then points to us. "Ivy and I are college students. We need gift certificates to the bookstore, printer paper and quarters for the washer and dryer. Notice the difference?"

"I dunno, I could use a few other things too. Like a lifetime pass to Starbucks, a professional proofreader, a masseuse on call —"

"Ivy! We do not take advantage of our friends, even the rich ones," Rogue chastises.

"Newsflash, Sis — we're riding in a private plane on a mission to go find *our* dad. Besides, Tristan was asking for wish lists. I was merely complying with his request."

Tristan nods. "Ivy's right, you know. I have been asking you a hundred different ways since we've met how

I can help you and you haven't given me an answer until this very moment."

"That's because it's not your responsibility to make all my wishes come true. This isn't some Disney movie. This is modern day life. I'm supposed to take care of myself. That's how the real world works. There aren't any knights in shining armor anymore," Rogue argues.

Tristan picks up her hand and kisses the back of it in an old-fashioned move of gallantry. Rogue blushes but makes no other comment.

"I think every guy has a bit of knight in shining armor buried somewhere inside of him. It's just that some of us wear our identity a little closer to the surface. I acted this way long before I ever had money. I remember pulling slivers out of Megan Mahoney's finger when I was about seven and putting a *Garfield* Band-Aid on it. I'll never forget how good it felt to make her tears go away. I was hooked on being a good guy for life. My Band-Aids have gotten bigger since I have money now, but the concept remains — I like being a good guy. I *want* to be a good guy for you."

Rogue looks skeptical. "But still Tristan … planes?"

"I was kidding, mostly. If it didn't take so long to get through security, it might be worth having one at your beck and call so you can come to see me anytime you get a whim."

"Tristan, I have a vague idea about how much jet fuel costs. It's very unlikely I'd ever just come see you on a whim. It would be the definition of wasteful."

Tristan sighs. "You know, I am not only focused

on me. I work on one Habitat for Humanity project a month and I often donate the plane and pilot for their use."

"That's very kind of you to donate money to them. I'm sure they can use it," I comment.

"I don't think you understand. I *help* Habitat for Humanity on projects. I give them money as well, but I actually enjoy building houses most of all."

"Why do you take the time to help build houses when it would be so much easier for you to hand over a big check and get your name in all the papers?" I ask.

"Well, since my goal has never been to get splashy news coverage, I'm not too worried about it, I guess. I do it to honor Francine. She and Elliot were about to move into a new Habitat House when she died. So, I figure if volunteers were kind enough to build her a home, I ought to carry her legacy forward and help build for someone else, just like I know she would have done."

Rogue scrubs a tear out of her eye with her sweatshirt sleeve. "Darn it, you got me. Can I help you the next time?"

The plane touches down and hops slightly. This is the first indication I've had all trip that Rogue may be as nervous as me. She digs her nails into Tristan's arm as she shrieks.

"Rogue, Baby —"

"What?" she snaps, still gripping his arm so hard I'm afraid it may start to bleed.

"We're safe and sound now. We're taxiing to the gate."

"Why didn't you say something?" Rogue grumbles.

Tristan shrugs easily. "I tried, but you don't seem to be in a listening mood."

It turns out having a sister can provide hours of fascinating entertainment.

CHAPTER SIXTEEN

TRISTAN

DESPITE MY ADAMANT ASSERTIONS THAT I haven't skirted any ethical lines, I know I'm edging pretty darn close on this one. The boundaries of my job are generally clear. There are usually good guys, bad guys, heroes and villains. Usually it's relatively easy to tell who's who in each case — but absolutely nothing has gone to script in this case. I've never seen anything like it and neither has anyone who's been helping me with it. Given the personal nature of this case, I haven't told very many people what I'm looking into, but I did bring in a former Secret Service agent and a long-retired FBI agent. Between the two of them, they had a combined thirty-seven years on the force and they'd never seen a case as complex as this.

I'm trying not to let my anxiety show because Rogue is already strung as tight as a violin string. Sometimes, I'm a little jealous of Marcus's relationship with Rogue, but right now, I'm just grateful for it because he's doing a masterful job of keeping the ladies calm.

I'm not entirely sure where we're going, but based

on the Google map description of Piedra, Colorado, I rented a Jeep Cherokee. As we hit a particularly rough patch in the road, I'm glad I made that choice. The Weminuche Wilderness area is every bit the driving challenge I expected it to be.

"Sorry," I say as I steer around a mud puddle.

"Man! You were supposed to drive through it! I thought that's what these rigs were for," Marcus protests.

"It's all right, you can play in the mud after we talk to the grown-ups," Ivy teases.

"Can we really?" Marcus asks excitedly.

"Be careful how much you encourage him, otherwise he'll be bugging us to leave every ten minutes like an impatient nine-year-old with ants in his pants," Rogue cautions.

"I'm aware. I had to use bribery to get him away from a vintage Pac-man machine at the grocery store the other day," confesses Ivy.

"Hey, in my defense, you don't run across those things every day. It turns out, I still have my touch at Pac-Man."

"I'm not complaining. It just creates some scheduling challenges, that's all," Ivy responds.

"See, isn't it great? She loves me anyway!" Marcus boasts.

"I really kinda do," Ivy admits in a startled voice. "I can't imagine my life without you in it. You were amazing with my dad. I can't believe you helped him set up a fantasy football league on Facebook. That's too funny to me. I hoped you guys might be able to find common ground, but you went out of your way to help them feel comfortable with you. I appreciate that."

"Ivy, it was no big deal. It was fun hanging out with Roger. He can be prickly at first. But, if I had a daughter as beautiful as you, I'd be a little overprotective too. I'm the living nightmare of most dads. I'm the poster child for who you don't want your child to bring home for dinner. But, much to your parents' credit, they got over me pretty quickly. So, kudos to them. I figured they'd be cool because they raised such an amazing daughter."

Rogue fishes an ice cube out of her drink and lobs it at Marcus's head. "Here's a public service announcement from your BFF. You're a doofus."

"What? What did I do?" Marcus asks as he picks the ice out of his hair.

Rogue looks at me and rolls her eyes. "Guys are so clueless!" She turns awkwardly in her seat and looks back at her best friend. "Marcus, in case you missed it my sister told you she loves you."

"Oh, yeah, I know. Isn't it awesome? Somebody I love finally loves me back. I kind of wish I was a songwriter, a poet, or something so I could write about it."

After about thirty seconds of stunned silence, both women dissolve into peals of laughter.

I glance up in the rearview mirror and notice Marcus is looking completely befuddled. "Now what did I do?" he asks me, meeting my gaze.

"Did you happen to actually tell Ivy that you love her too?" I ask, hazarding a guess based on the ladies' reaction to his odd pronouncement.

"Well no, I guess not — not in so many words, at least. I sort of figured she knew."

"I think that it's one of the major things a woman likes to hear spelled out in a relationship. It's rather important," I advise.

Marcus rakes his hand through his hair making it stick out even further. "Geez Ivy, why didn't you say something? I would've told you a long time ago if I had known it was so important to you."

"It's all right Marcus —" Ivy interjects.

"If I haven't made it clear how I feel, then it's not okay. I really thought you knew everything changed for me from the moment you came into my life. I've always been a restless searcher, flitting from one spot to another — never able to keep my focus for long. But you've captivated my mind, body and soul. It's as if I can finally completely relax and be me — the real me. I don't have to hide parts of myself from you because you understand that sometimes I won't be able to pull it all together, but somehow you seem like you're okay with it all."

Ivy gives Marcus a watery grin. "Of course I'm okay with you. If I wasn't, I would be the world's biggest hypocrite. How can I criticize you for not having it all together when some days, I think your love is the only glue that keeps *me* together?"

Rogue is trying to wipe away tears before anyone notices. I hand her a napkin from my jacket pocket.

"When I first met you, everything in my life was up in the air, not just my relationship with Rogue. The whole reason I went on this dating website adventure was because I was trying to find a new definition of who I was because I wasn't happy with the person I was projecting to the world because I knew it wasn't who I authentically am. I was pretending to be a happy little business major when the one thing I knew for certain was that I hated nearly every single business class I took. The only time I was ever happy was when I was creating things with my hands," Ivy confesses.

"Your work is spectacular, I hope you know," Marcus murmurs.

"You gave me the confidence to stick up for my right to be an artist. I don't think I would've done it if it hadn't been for your encouragement. You give me the courage to push my boundaries and explore new horizons. Every day with you is a new adventure. You don't see me as a simple, fragile, broken woman, you see me as your partner. I can't express how much you mean to me. I always dreamed I would find a guy like you, but I didn't believe it would happen. I love you because you are willing to live life in full color with exclamation points and take me along for the ride."

Marcus shifts as well as he can considering he's wearing a seatbelt and pulls Ivy close for a kiss. A few moments later, I hear him declare in a low, reverent voice, "What a ride it's going to be. I can't wait!"

Hopefully, this is the last time we'll have to play the game of musical chairs with mysterious visits to unsuspecting family members' front doors. For this visit, I decided the best strategy would be to leave everyone else in the car while I explain the preliminary circumstances to Mr. Roguen and get the lay of the land. I don't just have butterflies in my stomach for this one. I have a freaking flock of seagulls in there. I cannot even imagine how nervous Rogue and Ivy are. Rogue is very invested in getting all the answers as soon as she can. I try to caution her and discourage her from expecting too much. She's been waiting her entire lifetime for this moment. I understand — I remember the wait to find the answers on Francine's paperwork seemed like it took forever and a day. I checked the mailbox seven or eight times every day in case I missed something.

Just as I'm about to use the knocker again, the door opens. Isaac Roguen hasn't changed a lot in the years which have passed. He's older of course, but he's still quite fit and doesn't look almost fifty.

He narrows his gaze at me. "You lost?"

"No sir, I believe we have a meeting in about ten minutes," I offer.

Mr. Roguen's eyes widen as he exclaims, "You came clear out here for a meeting during the holidays? You do know we have Internet service out here, right? We could have Skyped like the rest of the planet."

I chuckle. "I realize that, sir. I consulted on a fiber-optic job for this quadrant. But, I have something really important to talk to you about and I figured you might appreciate the personal touch."

"Well, get out of the cold then. It's icy enough to freeze off a bear's unmentionables out there." He motions me to sit down at a big breakfast bar. He nods to a coffee maker and asks, "Want some coffee?"

"Sure, I'd appreciate a cup."

"Cream and sugar?" he asks while handing me the mug

"Black works fine, thanks."

Isaacs smirks with a very familiar grin and says, "You're a man after my own heart. I could never stand that fussy stuff. If you're going to drink coffee, just drink the darn coffee."

"Amen to that!" I give him a mock toast with my mug.

He levels a serious stare at me. "Okay, the time for bull crap is over. What brings you to the middle of nowhere during Christmas break? You don't even have any skis with you. So, what's the deal?"

"Well, sir. This is rather difficult to explain. There are many complex layers and I'm not sure how they all fit together yet. Perhaps you'll be able to shed some light on that for us —" I haltingly explain. I hate how disjointed I sound. Heck, I think I probably sounded more professional when I started the business at fifteen than I do now. How pathetic is that?

Mr. Roguen looks very frustrated. Finally, he says, "Son, I specialize in complicated. I had a whole career unraveling what most people considered unsolvable. If I can do that, I can help you get to the bottom of whatever is bothering you. So, start at the beginning please."

"I believe I told you I own a business in Florida which helps people solve identity fraud. It's called Identity Bank. I'm gifted with computers and I've owned the business since I was a teenager. A student at my alma mater came to me with concerns which appeared while she was using an online dating service. It appeared someone had commandeered her profile and was pretending to be her. Yet, the men who had met this other person said the other person appeared to look just like Ivy and didn't seem to be doing anything nefarious."

"It sounds like a sophisticated cat-fishing job to me."

"That was my first thought as well. So, I went to this woman's place of work and investigated. What I found shocked me. Everything in this case went against type. If I expected the case to go one way, it went entirely the opposite direction. It's been one surprise after another."

"So, was it a cat-fishing ring? You know, they've gotten more sophisticated and they're using multiple partners to cover up their tracks now."

"Oddly, it wasn't a case of cat-fishing at all. It was a computer vulnerability at the online dating service complicated by a classic example of the twin's weird ability to communicate telepathically."

Isaac chokes on his coffee as it goes down the wrong pipe.

I strike him sharply between the shoulder blades to help dislodge the liquid. When he recovers, I ask, "Are you all right, sir?"

"No son. I don't know that I'll ever truly be all right," he responds with a haunted look on his face.

"Sir?" I ask, uncertain what to do next.

"It's nothing you did. It still sneaks up on me sometimes. You would think I'd be over it by now. It's been over two decades but, every once in a while, it still gets me."

If I needed any more confirmation other than what my team found for me, I just got it in spades.

"I lost my wife and my twins. They never even made it through childbirth," he explains, gruffly.

"Well, sir that's actually why I'm here today," I reply as gently as I can. There are only so many ways you can completely shift someone's life paradigm.

"If you're here about the life insurance money I accepted, I'm sorry I never got you the death certificates. I tried repeatedly to get them from the hospital. They ran me around in circles. Since I was deep undercover, it wasn't like I could give them hell over it. By the time I finally got out, I was in no shape to cope with the administrative nightmare of trying to sort out the death of my wife and daughters. I went through a deep depression and I barely knew my own name."

"Mr. Roguen, look at me and listen to me carefully. I'm not here to collect any money. I don't represent an insurance company, the hospital or any governmental agency. I'm here because your daughter, Ivy Love Montclair got a little freaked out because someone else was using her dating profile. That someone else turned out to be your other daughter, Rogue Medea Cisneros Betancourt."

"What? How do I know this isn't all one big scam?" he demands, but his hands are shaking as he puts his coffee cup to his lips.

"I was suspicious too. That's why I ordered DNA tests. Ivy and Rogue are indeed identical twins and the biological daughters of Rosa Marie Cisneros Betancourt and Isaac Randall Roguen."

"I didn't give a sample; how did you do the test?"

"Ms. Betancourt had your old shaving kit and she gave it to me. The lab was able to extract some epithelial cells and blood."

"Rosa? My Rosie is alive too? How can this be?" he asks, shock coloring his tone. "The hospital called my handler and said she went into early labor and died before they could save the babies. I never even got to say goodbye."

I put my hand on his shoulder to help steady him as he walks over to the couch. "You're sure she's not dead?" he confirms, his eyes gleaming with unshed tears.

I nod my head. "Yes, she definitely is not dead. I had tamales with her and the twins over Thanksgiving. She is a wonderful woman."

"You mean you've seen my babies?" Isaac asks in a shaky voice. "I know Ivy hired you, but you've seen her since?"

"Yes sir. I see them quite often since I've taken a personal interest in this case," I cautiously reply.

"Just how personal is your interest?" he shrewdly asks. "I took a personal interest in someone once and I married her. It was the smartest thing I ever did."

I smile as I respond, "I'm not sure Rogue and I are quite ready to book the church yet, but I'll admit I'm thinking along those lines. I *am* rather fond of your daughter."

Isaac shakes his head in disbelief. "I can't believe my Rosie named the girl after me and I didn't even know she was alive. Some law enforcement expert I am —"

"I wouldn't be too hard on yourself, sir. You didn't have any reason to believe someone lied to you. Who does that? It's cruel. I think you've been punished long enough. Would you like to meet your daughters?"

"My babies are here? In Piedra? Why didn't you say something?" Isaac holds his hand over his heart.

"I thought it might be better if I explained a little of the background before springing them on you since I didn't know exactly what I was walking into. I had a duty to protect them too. Although, it appears you were a victim as well."

"Heck yes, I was a victim!" Isaac declares vehemently. "By the time I'm done, heads will roll all over Vermont. I'll deal with that later though, right now all I want to do is see my babies."

"I understand, I'll go get them from the Jeep," I respond as I zip my jacket.

"You left two women alone in the freezing temperatures in the middle of the woods? Macklin, I had you pegged as a better professional."

"I didn't realize that you did any research about me. As it turns out, Rogue is a tough cookie in her own right and Ivy brought along her boyfriend who looks pretty tough, although I suspect Rogue could still wipe the floor with him."

"Son, when you're in my line of work, you don't just talk to anybody who calls you up. Of course, I did a full background on you. But, I'm familiar with your work. I saw you at a LEO Conference a few years back. You were the keynote speaker about security on mobile devices. You're an extraordinarily smart young man."

"Thank you, sir. I try to work with what God gave me. Let me go get the ladies. I should tell you they're a little nervous — they don't quite know what to expect from this meeting."

"Well, that makes three of us," Isaac quips.

When I return to the Jeep, both women look sick with anxiety. Rogue can barely stand to look at me. I hold out my hand so that she can make the awkward climb out of the sport utility vehicle. When she makes it to the uneven snowy ground, I take advantage of the excuse to hold her close for a moment. I gather her into a loose embrace and kiss her gently.

She looks up at me with pleading eyes. "How terrible is the news?"

"I guess it depends on your perspective," I answer, dropping a kiss on her forehead.

"Oh my gosh! It must be awful," Ivy whispers harshly as she walks up behind Rogue gripping Marcus's hand tightly.

"No, I didn't mean to scare you. The news is actually great for you guys. It's been rough on your dad for the last couple of decades. It turns out he was lied to just like everyone else. He was told all of you died, including Rosa."

"No wonder he never went back to Mama!" Rogue breathes in a tortured gasp. "He must've been totally destroyed."

Ivy's brows draw together in concentration.

"Wouldn't he have figured it all out at the funeral when there was no one to bury?"

"Apparently, he was deep undercover and didn't find out about the 'deaths' right away. There was just enough subterfuge and fuzziness to make it all seem plausible. Later, when he tried to get death certificates, I guess he got nothing but the runaround, but because he was operating undercover, he couldn't make an issue of it."

Marcus shakes his head in disbelief as he comments, "Either this is the strangest case of unrelated coincidences or a massive case of fraud." He turns to me and asks, "Super-Secret-Spy-Guy, how do you go about figuring out which it is?"

I pop my neck and knuckles — a bad habit I acquired when I was in elementary school and still revert to when I need to stall and collect my thoughts. "I guess I would have to meticulously rebuild every file and document every single conversation. I don't even know if it would be possible since a lot of the personnel involved would have retired and perhaps passed away by now."

Rogue nods slowly. "I'm not even sure it would be worth it because the damage has been done. Mama's life has been destroyed. All the hopes and dreams she had when she married dad ended the day he vanished and never came back. As close as Ivy and I are now, we'll never know what it would've been like to be raised as sisters."

Ivy nods, "Rogue is right. We've all lost so much."

"You can begin to make new memories," Marcus

suggests. "Your dad is waiting on the other side of that door and he's probably ready to tear it down. I know I would be."

Ivy briefly hugs Marcus before grabbing Rogue's hand and pulling her toward the front door. "Marcus has a point. It won't do us any good to dwell on what could have been. Because we can't relive the past. Let's go meet our father."

Rogue blinks away tears. "Here's hoping Padre Pop's every bit as awesome as I made him out to be in my imagination."

Ivy stops dead in her tracks as she whispers, in a barely audible voice, "What did you call your imaginary dad?"

Rogue looks away from Ivy and then gazes down at the ground as she confesses, "Okay, you have to cut me some slack here — I was really little when I made this up — but I used to call him Padre Pop."

Ivy appears stunned as she exclaims, "No *freakin'* way! I used to call my imaginary family Padre Pop and Madre Mop."

Rogue raises an eyebrow at Ivy. "Dare I ask what my name was in this little scenario?"

Ivy sticks her tongue out at Rogue. "That was a no-brainer. Your name was Kelly. Just like Barbie's sister. Aren't all sisters named Kelly?"

Rogue laughs out loud. "That's funny since I had absolutely nothing in common with Barbie or her little family. But, that is spooky about our imaginary families. These days nothing about the way our brains work surprises me. Still, I think we should let Isaac take the lead on what he wants to be called."

I knock on the door, but I barely get one percussion in before the door opens wide. I wish I'd thought to film this reunion. The total look of adoration on Mr. Roguen's face is absolutely priceless. I know Mama Rosa would have loved to see this.

"Oh my! You girls look just like your mother. You are beautiful. I don't know why I was thinking that you would still be children. Clearly that's not the case. You are lovely young women. My Rosie must be so proud of you."

He tentatively reaches out to shake their hands, but Ivy is the first to break the ice and envelops him in a warm hug. "It's so nice to meet you. It's funny, I was just thinking how much Rogue looks like you. You both have the same wonderful smile and twinkle in your eye."

Isaac does a bit of a double-take. "I guess that means you must be Ivy."

When Ivy nods, Isaac continues, "So, doesn't it stand to reason that you look like me too?"

Ivy's light laughter fills the air. "I suppose you're right. As odd as it may seem, I forget Rogue and I are mirror images of each other because we're so different. She seems so much prettier and more sophisticated than I am. I forget people see us as being the same."

"Well, from this proud *padre's* point of view, you are both gorgeous, stunning women."

Rogue has been standing back observing the interaction, but finally she speaks up, "I'm sorry, what did you say?"

Mr. Roguen looks contrite. "I apologize. I was presumptuous; perhaps it's too soon to refer to myself as a *padre*. You may call me whatever you wish."

I can feel Rogue start to tremble in my arms as she stands in front of me. I subtly place my arms around her waist from behind to let her know I'm here for support if she needs me.

"I think you've misunderstood my question," Rogue clarifies as she wipes away a tear with her thumb. "I've been waiting my whole life for someone to really call dad. When Ivy and I were little, we both had imaginary families and independently of each other, we both christened the father figures in our families as Padre Pop. I find an amazing amount of irony there."

Isaac digs a cotton handkerchief from his back pocket and wipes tears from his eyes. "Some people might call it irony; other people might call it a miracle. There's nothing more in this whole world I ever wanted more than to be your *padre*."

Isaac holds his arms out wide as he collects both of his daughters in what is sure to be a lifetime of group hugs.

Chapter Seventeen

Marcus

THIS IS A VERY ODD situation for me to be in. I'm part of the circle, yet strangely I feel very excluded. Usually, I make it a point to be the center of the action. Though, in this situation, it would be inappropriate for me to intrude. So, that's how I've found myself sitting quietly holding Ivy in my arms in the lushly appointed oversized leather seats of Tristan's private plane headed back to the East Coast. Ivy and Rogue are busy filling Isaac in on as much of their childhoods as they can remember. It's been quite amusing to discover how many similar experiences they've had despite their different upbringings — from the names of their hamsters to their best friends growing up. They even have the same taste in mundane things like the type of toothpaste they use.

Once Isaac determined Mama Rosa was alive and well, he expressed an interest in seeing her face to face. Although Rogue is more cautious, Ivy, ever the romantic, is completely in favor of the idea. I'm not sure which side I come down on. I have a hunch Mama Rosa still has feelings for Isaac, but I also think she may also be more than a little ticked off he's been gone all these years. If I'm right, this could be an interesting reunion.

Tristan generously offered Isaac a ride back with us on the plane. Tristan and Isaac are developing some sort of law enforcement bond. This is fascinating to me as well because I know Tristan is some sort of highly paid consultant, but as far as I know, he doesn't have any law enforcement training. Yet, Isaac has accepted him as if he's one of his own police brothers. Come to think of it, I'm not exactly sure what Isaac does. He's very mysterious — it's easy to see how all those rumors got started about his past.

I realize I've lost complete track of the conversation when Ivy pokes me in the chest, and points to Isaac's calf, "Marcus! You will never believe this in a million years! It's just too freaky!"

I snap to attention as I look down at Isaac's calf. "That's freakin' amazing —" I marvel as I examine it.

"You'll have to excuse me, I'm lost," replies Isaac as he looks at all of us with an expression of befuddlement.

"It's okay, Padre. This is going to take a little explanation," Rogue says as she takes a drink of Dr. Pepper.

Ivy nods in agreement as she adds, "… and an open mind."

"Marcus is my supervisor at his tattoo shop, Ink'd Deep. As part of my apprenticeship, he had me do a cover tattoo for him in which he gave me complete artistic freedom. He told me a meaningful story from his childhood, and I came up with the tattoo you see on his arm," Rogue explains.

Ivy picks up her drawing pad and shows Isaac her tattoo design and continues the explanation, "As Tristan and I were driving to the tattoo shop, I drew this as an idea for a tattoo before I ever set foot inside their shop. I might even get it if I ever get brave enough."

It takes Isaac a few moments to compose his emotions and he has to swallow a couple times before he can speak. His words are rough with emotion when they finally emerge, "Since I could never bury you girls and your mother, this tattoo was my way of saying goodbye." He traces his finger around the black and gray dragonfly with the script. 'True love comes with a price. Always be prepared'. "It was my way to remind myself to never be caught away from someone I loved ever again. I've never forgiven myself for leaving Rosie alone while she was pregnant. That decision has haunted me every day of my life."

At the end of his impassioned speech, tears are streaming down everyone's face — mine included. The one flight attendant on the plane discreetly hands a box of tissue to Tristan who takes one and passes the box around to the rest of us.

Rogue untangles herself from Tristan's lap and goes over to kiss Isaac on the cheek. "Padre, I'm so sorry you were robbed of your family. It seems so unfair. But you can forgive yourself now. We are all alive and well. You could not have predicted what would happen. No sane person could. So, we'll all just have to move forward from here."

"It's true, Padre. We have to build our lives from this day forward."

"Isaac, come on … sit. You're going to wear a hole in your shoes. I never thought I'd meet somebody who paces more than me. It's going to be fine, I swear. I've been through several of these sessions already. I seem to be the one waiting out here most of the time. Tristan and Rogue are great at explaining things."

"They're good together, aren't they?"

I nod. "Yeah, I'm really happy she found somebody. She deserves it more than anybody I've ever met."

"Rogue tells me you guys have been friends for years. Why didn't you end up dating her?"

I shrug. "I don't know. Rogue has always been more like my little sister. She is truly my best friend."

"I take it you feel differently about Ivy?"

"Yes, sir. I know it sounds weird because they're identical twins, but my feelings for Ivy in no way resemble what I feel for Rogue. In fact, unless they're having one of their spooky twin moments I rarely think of them as identical twins. I love Ivy very much."

"Spooky twin moments?" Isaac asks, seeking clarification.

"It's something you'd have to witness to understand, but it's along the lines of the dragonfly tattoos and the nickname they had for you as a child."

"I'm sorry if I overstep my bounds here, I haven't

been a dad for very long and I know she's already got one, but Ivy said she'd like to change her major to something to do with the arts. Are you going to be able to support her with both of you being artists?"

"It's quite all right, sir. It's a valid question. I choose to live below my means at the moment because I've been helping to support my family and some charities I care deeply about. When the time comes to step up for Ivy, I'll be more than capable. Ink'd Deep does quite well."

"With all due respect, why the heck aren't you paying Rogue enough that she doesn't have to scramble to do fourteen jobs to be able to go to school?" Isaac probes.

I laugh out loud at his question. "Isaac, believe me I've tried to pay your daughter more, but she has a stubborn streak a mile and a half wide."

"She gets that from her mother," he quips.

"Rogue has gotten it into her mind she doesn't want to take advantage of our friendship. She won't allow me to do anything more for her than she perceives would be done for any other apprentice. It was difficult to persuade her to take any wage at all, let alone a decent one."

"So, you're saying if I want to help out my daughters, I'm going to need to be crafty?"

"Like a Secret Service agent," I respond.

Isaac grins. "That I can do."

My phone chimes and when I check the inbox, it's a message from Ivy.

"She says Mama Rosa is in a bit of shock but wants to see you," I report to Isaac, filtering out the goofy emoticons.

"Maybe I should've just left well enough alone. What if I cause her terrible pain?" Isaac asks, panic coloring his voice.

"Isaac, the last time I was here, she spent several minutes showing me pictures of you and waxing poetically about your love story. I'd guess that missing you forever would be much more painful than the momentary shock of finding out you're still alive."

"Really? She still talked about me after all these years?" Isaac pushes.

"Yes, she did, quite openly and affectionately. If I had to guess, I'd say she still carries a torch for you."

"Well, I'm not a man opposed to praying for miracles. But I feel like I have had more than my fair share already. My wife and my daughters are alive and well. I hesitate to ask for more."

"I'm not sure you actually have to ask for this one. I think it just is. I don't think she ever fell out of love with you."

"I hope you're right, son. I know I never fell out of love with her."

"Well, let's go see the love of your life, then," I instruct as I sling my arm around his shoulder and escort him to the front door.

We don't even make it all the way to the front door before Mama Rosa swings it open and runs out at a dead sprint and lands directly in Isaac's arms. He swings her around in a big circle. She is sobbing as she whispers, "Isaac, *mi cariño*" into his neck. "Is it really true? Is my heart finally back?"

I sit down on an Adirondack chair on the porch and I pull Ivy down on my lap. Together we watch the joyful reunion.

"Yes, Rosie, it really is me," he responds laughing as she rains kisses all over his face.

"You're about twenty-three years too late for dinner. The enchiladas are cold," she scolds, tearfully. "Where have you been?"

"Rosie, they told me all of you had died when you went into premature labor. When I could get loose from my job, I went back to the old house and there was not a trace of us there, so I had no reason to believe otherwise. I was so devastated I nearly lost everything. I wanted to follow you all into the grave. The only thing that saved me was my job," Isaac admits, his voice cracking with emotion.

"Someone called and told me you died too. Yet, I never believed them. I knew I would feel it in my heart if you died. Still you never told me what was so important about your job with a moving company. All those years and I never understood —"

"You couldn't understand my job because I couldn't tell you what my job actually was. I had a job similar to what Tristan here does except I did it for a now-defunct government agency. We were in charge of tracking the flow of cash and collateral in and out of the drug cartels.

"When I saved you from the car accident, I was

actually deep undercover and shouldn't have even intervened. Yet, I couldn't let you suffer so I had to break cover and rescue you. But, I was not allowed to tell you who I was, what agency I worked for, or even that I knew how to use a computer."

"Even after we got married? I was no security threat to you. I was born in Arizona. Just because I speak Spanish doesn't mean I'm not an American."

"Rosa, it wasn't about that. All agents, regardless of who they're married to or even if they aren't married, were not allowed to discuss their jobs. It's for operational safety. If we were to open up about our jobs, it would make both you and us potential kidnapping targets. Believe me, there were many times I wanted to tell you what I was doing, but I was just keeping you safe. I was so devastated when they called me in on the last operation and I was away from you while you were pregnant. I will never forgive myself as long as I live."

Rosa frowns at him. "Well, trust me, it wasn't a popular call with me either. But, if I would've known all the facts, I would've probably understood better. It hurt thinking that you were abandoning me to help move somebody's couch and ottoman."

"Oh, Rosa I have missed you so much. I've especially missed your wonderful offbeat sense of humor. You'll be happy to know I'm retired from the agency which no longer exists. There will be no more clandestine missions. I am free to be at your beck and call. I'll even take those dancing classes you wanted me to take back in the day."

"What makes you think you have license to waltz

in here and pick up right where you left off?" Rosa demands, with her hands on her hips. "After all, you've been gone for more than two decades, a woman has the prerogative to move on, you know."

"Of course you do, but you didn't," Isaac states confidently. "I have about a hundred lipstick prints on my face to tell me that. Even if you did change your mind, I would spend the rest of my life trying to change it back because I've never, ever fallen out of love with you, Rosa Roguen."

"You never let me go by that name before," Rosa comments with surprise.

"It was for your own safety. But, now Rogue or Marcus can tattoo it on your forehead if you choose."

"You're so silly! But, I was thinking about a nice pretty dragonfly like Rogue made on Marcus. I thought it would look really nice on my shoulder. I just have to work up the nerve. Needles are not my favorite thing."

"It must be a family thing," I murmur into Ivy's ear.

Ivy giggles softly. "Hush, you're going to ruin a sweet family moment."

"What? You don't have a tattoo. Rogue doesn't have a tattoo. Your mom doesn't have a tattoo. The only person brave enough to get a tattoo is your dad. I'm merely saying I sense a pattern here, that's all."

Rogue hears me from across the yard with her bionic-like hearing. "Hey! I didn't say I was afraid of needles. I'm simply delaying my tattoo work until I'm done with the modeling gigs, remember?"

"You're going on modeling gigs?" asks Isaac with alarm. "Do you know how many of our cases had to do with girls going on those jobs? People advertise for false modeling jobs all the time. I'm not saying you're not pretty enough to be a model, but very few of those listings are actually legitimate. You could be putting yourself in real danger."

"Padre Pop, I'm careful to screen clients carefully before I meet anyone, and I always meet clients in a public place. I'm very cautious. I know how to tell the difference between the scumbags and the real clients."

"I've heard that line from the majority of families I interview. Most of the victims were confident they could tell the good guys from the bad guys." Isaac looks at Rogue and then over at Ivy. "Please, you girls are so beautiful and so young. You need to be especially vigilant. I know you found each other because of a dating site. As a dad, I'm worried about that too."

Ivy and Rogue glance at each other as Rogue comments, "Okay, Padre Pop, I don't think it will be a problem. I don't think Ivy and I will be needing any dating services any time soon anyway."

CHAPTER EIGHTEEN

ROGUE

As soon as I walk in the door, Jade tosses a pile of mail in my direction. "I was telling Marcus the other day that he needs to put in mailboxes and charge a fee. First it was all the tattoo artists and then the photographers who always seem to tag along with them, and now it's all you guys too. At least you don't ask me to text you and let you know you've gotten a letter. There's one chick who worked here five years ago who still wants me to text her every time she gets a piece of junk mail. Hasn't she ever heard of going to the post office and getting a forwarding address?"

"Weird. I don't even do that to my mama," I comment as I rifle through the mail.

"I think it's funny you and Iris are getting the same mail. Do the companies automatically send two letters when you're twins?"

"Ivy," I correct absentmindedly. "Her name is Ivy and as far as I know, there's no tendency for companies to send out matching mail, although I haven't officially been a twin long enough to figure that out for sure."

Jade shrugs. "It must be a coincidence you guys both got the same letter from The RCBR Trust."

"Yeah, it's probably one of those financial aid scams, because it's not from one of the scholarships I applied for."

I open the ivory parchment paper envelope. It certainly doesn't feel like typical junk mail. It's the kind of material they use in wedding invitations and diplomas.

"How is this even possible?" I mumble under my breath as I read the letter to myself.

"How is *what* possible?" Jade probes impatiently. "How am I supposed to properly gossip if you don't tell me what's going on?"

I read it again just to make sure I'm not hallucinating. "This says I've been awarded a scholarship to the college, university or program of my choice to advance my higher education renewable each year until I graduate contingent upon me making demonstrative progress toward my degree."

"What? That's totally amazing! That's like the answer to your prayers!" Jade announces as she dances wildly and high-fives the other people in the shop.

"Wait! Stop!" I instruct sharply. "Don't you all think it's incredibly strange? I never applied for this scholarship, gift, endowment or whatever the heck you want to call it. I don't even know who this 'RCBR Endowment for Higher Education' is. They could be nothing more than a few hackers posing as a huge scholarship company to try to get my personal information — or they could be the front for some criminal enterprise. All I know is I never applied for any grant from this place and I'll bet you dimes to dollars Ivy didn't either. Something smells more than a little fishy here."

"But, what if it's real?" Jade pushes back. "Wouldn't it be the coolest thing ever? It would be like those people at the ball games who have nothing to lose and launch a ball from behind the three-point line. Maybe this is your ultimate three-point basket."

I start growling deep in my throat as I try to smile at Jade. "It's possible, but very, very, *very* unlikely. I strongly suspect my mysterious beneficiary lives a few hours away and has an odd fascination with all things chess and the *National Spelling Bee*."

Jade's eyebrows shoot to her hairline. "You think Tristan, the guy who still takes a peanut butter and jelly sandwich to work and mows his own grass suddenly got a wild hair up his butt and started handing out cash? You *have* met the man, right?"

I smile as she recounts Tristan's quirky behaviors. "Mmm hmm," I nod. "He also recycles his grocery bags as garbage bags, but he wouldn't think twice of paying for my tuition, Ivy's tuition and probably the tuition of everybody I care about if I would let him."

Jade looks a tad gobsmacked. "Really? I wish I could find a guy like that."

I shrug as I continue, "It's a good thing I love the man because right now, I'm ticked at him. We've talked about this several times. I don't want him doing things like this for me."

Marcus looks up from the massive back piece he's been working on and makes an observation, "Are you sure Super-Secret-Spy-Guy doesn't view this as one more example of doing something nice for you. When you're used to dealing with multimillion-dollar corporations and stock deals worth billions of dollars, is a few thousand dollars a year in tuition money really much of an expense?"

"Gee thanks Marcus, I don't know if I feel better or worse," I respond.

"I'm sorry Ro, I'm just trying to make you feel better. Tristan is working hard to make your world a happier place. Don't you think you should at least hear the guy out before you decide he's guilty and send him to the hanging gallows?"

Deep down, I know Marcus is right. Tristan has never been the kind to indiscriminately throw around his money just to show me he can. If he's ever spent large sums of money on me, it's been for a specific purpose to relieve some urgent need in my life. He has, for the most part, honored his pledge to treat me like a regular girlfriend. His one notable exception was to help me throw a block party in my neighborhood on New Year's Day. My poor local Panda Express franchise didn't quite know how to handle an order that large. Needless to say, Tristan and I are their new favorite customers because I think he probably single-handedly quadrupled their quarterly profits. But, I'm not sure my neighborhood will ever quite be the same.

After the proprietor of the old bowling alley saw how many children had moved into the area, he looked into ways to refurbish his property and reopen the bowling alley with a new video game center attached. I'm relatively sure Tristan is involved with financing his endeavor as well. I guess one of his first computer jobs when he was a kid was to help a guy fix his computerized scoring system at a bowling alley. Instead of paying them in cash, the guy let Tristan and his family hang out at the bowling alley which explains why he completely wiped the floor with me. It's a good thing we were not playing strip bowling because I would've been playing stark naked in absolutely no time.

I call over my shoulder to my boss as I stick my mail in my purse, I gather up Ivy's as well so I can read it to her over the phone, "Marcus, I'm sorry to do this to you since I just got here, but I need to deal with this real quick."

Marcus gives me a crooked grin. "Go on Ro. Fix your little lover's spat. I know I won't be able to get any work out of you until you do. Your first client doesn't come in for a couple hours anyway. The filing can wait until you sort out your personal drama."

I blow him a raspberry before I respond, "That's easy for you to say, you and Ivy hardly ever fight over anything. But, in the event you ever do fight, I've got you covered."

Marcus scoffs. "Yeah right! — like you'd ever side with me against your sister. The two of you even have a secret language. If we're ever in a fight, I'm toast."

I chuckle. "Good point. Yeah, you're probably toast. I'll be right back, this shouldn't take too long."

"Have you forgotten that sometimes I'm on the

other end of those phone calls between you and Ivy?" he asks incredulously. "So, I'll tell you what. If you're still on the phone when I lock up, I'll tap you on the shoulder and let you know we're going," he quips good-naturedly.

"Hardy-har-har," I snort as I pretend to laugh. "Seriously, I have a bunch of stuff to do around here, so I'll make this quick."

I sit on what I consider to be my special bench in the coffee shop down the street from Ink'd Deep as I dial Ivy's number. She picks up on the second ring, but she sounds winded. "What are you doing, *Manita*?"

"Oh, I'm just moving some clay for my pottery class. That crap is heavy! I wish Marcus was around. I could use some of his muscles right about now. Why are you calling? I thought you had to design the chest piece with all the cherry blossoms and Japanese characters for the breast cancer survivor today."

"I do," I respond. "But, you got some mail at Ink'd. I thought you might want to know what it says."

"Oh crap! Is it bad news?" Ivy asks, trepidation clear in her voice even through the scratchy connection of my cell phone.

"Not as far as I know; I didn't get bad news from this place. Suspicious news, but not bad news."

"Now you're freaking me out. What are you talking about?"

"Would you like me to read you the letter?" I ask, fishing around in my purse for it, though I suspect it will probably say exactly the same thing mine says.

I giggle as a sarcastic thought hits my head as hard as if Ivy was standing right next to me.

Of course I want you to read it, Duh! It's not like I can open the envelope with my psychic twin brain. What are you waiting for?

Into the phone I say, "All right, all right, hold your horses. I'm on it."

I unfold the letter and speed read it. Just as I suspected, hers is almost identical to mine. They have her identifying information and her birth date correct, so they didn't mix up our identities.

I take a deep breath as I prepare to read it out loud, but then I change my mind. "You know what, Ivy? I'm going to take a picture of this and send it to you so you can see the whole thing. But basically, I got an identical letter. The details are specifically addressed to each one of us with the proper information so they didn't get us mixed up or anything. It essentially says we've both been awarded scholarships to any college or university that we want to go to — and it's renewable until we finish as long as we're making progress toward our goals."

After a moment of stunned silence, Ivy asks, "We got scholarships? From where? I haven't applied for any new scholarships. In fact, I just met with my advisor. The University of South Florida doesn't really have the type of major I need on the Tampa campus. It looks like I'll have to transfer to one of their satellite campuses. I haven't even begun to process all the stuff I was told. My meeting was earlier this week, there's no way even the most dedicated advisor or financial aid people could get me a scholarship so quickly."

I sigh deeply. "I was afraid you would say that. I have a feeling my sometimes too awesome boyfriend has struck again. It doesn't seem to matter how many times I explain to him he doesn't need to spend extravagant amounts of money on me, he can't seem to help himself."

"You know, I don't think this is him. He's been striving to be just a typical, average, everyday boyfriend. He even called me up to see if his idea for your birthday present would be within the 'rules'."

"Well … was it?" I ask, curious about Tristan's plans. He's been secretive and it's driving me crazy.

"Sorry sis, I'm not spilling the beans. But, I can tell you Padre Pop is coming next week. He and Tristan have some business thing they're doing with computers and then we're going up to Gainesville. I thought it would be cool if we all had dinner for your birthday or something."

"It's your birthday too, silly," I tease.

"I know, but I always forget. So much has changed in the last few months. I feel like I've become a whole new person. I finally decided I'm going to celebrate both birthdays. I am a little of the new Ivy and still a lot of the old Ivy, so I guess it's appropriate I celebrate being born on two days."

"I guess part of me was born on your birthday too. When you breathed on your own, I officially became your *manita*. So, whenever you get annoyed with the big sister part of me, you can ban me from your birthday parties."

Ivy laughs, "Since you can invade my brain, I'm not sure how effective it would be. I guess I better get back to slinging this clay around. This sculpture won't make itself."

"Goodbye *Manita*. I'll talk to you later."

Before I can lose my nerve, I call Tristan. "Hey, did you forget to tell me something important?" I ask after he greets me.

He chuckles. "Let me guess, Ivy sent you a 'twin-gram' about Isaac's visit? It's darn near impossible to plan a surprise around you two."

I have to choke back a laugh at his matter-of-fact acceptance of our unconventional communication skills. "No, this time, I actually found out compliments of AT&T. Ivy and I actually own cell phones and we occasionally use them. But, that's not what I'm talking about. I'm talking about something which could run you a couple hundred thousand dollars in the long run."

"Rogue, you need to back up because I have no idea what you're talking about," Tristan asserts. "The only big money deal I've got going on right now won't cost me anything, unless, of course there's a design flaw, which there's not. Still, I stand to make several million from the deal. I'm not set to spend more at this point. We launch in a few weeks, but all the groundwork has already been done."

I let out a huge growl of frustration. "Tristan, I know you think it's just stupid, but I've got a real hang-up about relying on people for what I should be able to provide for myself. Now that I know the whole story with my dad, it makes my issues seem even more ludicrous — but they are what they are. I learned very early I can't trust people to be there when they say they're going to be.

That's why I can't let you do this whole scholarship thing. I can't get used to you stepping in to rescue me all the time. Maybe someday you won't be there when I need you."

"Shoot, this is one of those times I hate living so far away from you and now I'm on the stupid cell phone instead of a video call. I've got a meeting with a client in precisely twelve minutes… you know what?… Screw it. You're more important."

"Tristan don't blow it off —"

"Rogue, it's fine. Let's start with the easy stuff. First, I have no idea what you're talking about. I had nothing to do with any scholarship. I've been so busy I haven't even had a chance to set up a scholarship at the University of South Florida, let alone anywhere else and even if I had set it up, I wouldn't be responsible for choosing the recipients — that would be a conflict of interest."

"Wow! Just wow. If you didn't do it, who did?" I ask in total disbelief.

"I might be able to help you answer that question if I had any inkling of what you're talking about," Tristan replies, sounding confused.

"Well, Ivy and I were just awarded full scholarships to any college we want to go to. It's bizarre because we didn't actually apply for them. Given your past record of extreme generosity, I figured you were behind it."

"This time, I can plead total innocence. I have no idea what's going on. Although, I do find it interesting that you're somehow interpreting this as bad news. Do you realize this means you could go to any college you want to based on the strength of its art program, not the thickness of your wallet? It also means you and Ivy can go to school together anywhere you choose."

His simple statements stop my mental protests right in their tracks. I guess I was so busy trying to convict Tristan of extreme niceness that I hadn't stopped to consider what impact the scholarships could have on our lives.

"Tristan, I need to go," I respond in a shaky voice. "There's too much to think about right now. Besides, I have to figure out how to make someone's terrible mastectomy scars look like a celebration of survival. I can't let my thoughts wander to my personal problems today, because in comparison, I have none."

"Okay, what time do you think you'll be off tonight?"

"The janitorial crew said they're waxing the floor tonight, so we have to be out of there at five o'clock."

"I'll talk to you then, have a good day, love you," Tristan says, but before I can answer him, my piece-o-garbage phone dies in my hand.

What a day! All I want to do is climb into a bath with a good book. Doing tats is hard on your body. Marcus sometimes moves like an old man. It's one of the reasons he is such a stickler for making sure we have all the best equipment which can be adjusted for not only our height, but be adjusted for the size of our clients too. It's a good thing for me. I ended up giving a special request tattoo today on a guy who must have been six-foot-four. Marcus does all the police and firefighter memorial tattoos for free. Usually, he or Jade cover them. But Liam apparently noticed me doing my homework for my Life Drawing class the other day when Jade did a portrait of their dog on his girlfriend. So, he wanted me to do his buddy's fire boots on his upper shoulder. I was totally unnerved, but Marcus reminded me I'd have a reference photo and that he'd be right there to check my work each step along the way. Liam wanted it all grey scale except for a hint of an American flag. Grey scale, I could do; I'd been drawing with charcoals forever. In the end, everyone was thrilled. He gave me a tip which would have twice covered the cost of the actual tattoo.

My arms are so sore, I can barely lift them over my head to remove my shirt. But, mentally, I'm even more fried.

I spent the morning trying to make sense of what cannot make sense and attempting to find a path to beauty in the ravages of pain. Tattooing directly on scar tissue can be tricky at best, but Jaynelle wanted me to hide as many of her scars as possible. In her words, she wanted to "forget the killers were ever on her chest." The process of designing it was sobering and enlightening. I guess in the grand scheme of things, I could have far worse problems than an upgraded stereo system and a boyfriend who thinks Tuesday afternoons are cause enough to buy extravagant presents.

I think of Liam who rode to work with a coworker and ended up having to drive Oliver's truck home to his wife and daughter when a roof gave way on a routine house fire during clean-up operations. The danger was supposed to have passed. You just never know what's around the corner.

I test the tub water with my toe as I try the whole bath thing again. Perfect. I'm good to go. Of course the button of my shirt gets stuck in my hair as I struggle to pull it over my head. I'm still jammed in this half on and off position when I hear my front door open.

"What in the h—! It's against landlord/tenant law for you to barge in here like that, you know!" I yell angrily as I try to take refuge in my bedroom.

I hear Tristan's deep chuckle as he quips, "One would hope you wouldn't go just anywhere dressed like that."

I whirl on him, forgetting my arm is stuck. "Tristan? O.M.G! You really are *here*! But why? Aren't you getting ready to out-launch Microsoft? Shouldn't you be at some big meeting?"

Tristan drops his bag and walks over and drops a hot kiss on my lips before he helps untangle my hair from the button on my shirt. "I was needed here. So, I came," he responds matter-of-factly.

I shake my head as if to clear an aspiration from my field of vision. I'm still not sure he's not a creation of my overtired imagination. But, as he kisses me again, it's very clear he is a hundred percent live, a flesh and blood very hot creature and he's standing right in my living room. Wearily, I sigh. "Do I even want to know how you got here? I just talked to you before lunch."

"Yeah, I wouldn't ask too many questions if I were you. It would probably offend your budget-conscious sensitivities."

"Tristan Riley Macklin, you are a crazy man. Who blows off a software launch for his girlfriend who's had a bad day at work?" I ask rhetorically. I start to pick up random things around my house because I totally wasn't expecting company but I flinch as my shoulder starts to spasm.

"Oh crap!" I scream as I run up the hallway to the bathroom to turn off the tub right before the water spills over the edge.

Tristan follows me into the bathroom to evaluate the seriousness of the emergency. When he sees the candles and the book I had placed next to the tub, he comments. "Obviously, you had some mega-plans before I interrupted you. But, to answer your question, I didn't simply blow off the product launch, that's why I hire a team of, highly qualified, better compensated than most, professionals. They're paid to pick up the pieces of the stuff that I can't manage or choose not to manage."

I smirk a bit at his answer as I respond, "As if there's anything you would choose not to personally manage in your business. That's just not your style," I tease.

"I guess I deserve that. But, things are changing. You've changed me. Your well-being is more important than a deal. If you ever need me, I'll be here. No excuses. That's the meaning of true love. It's not about the places I can take you to or the things I can buy you. Although those are nice little perks, they're not what our relationship is about."

"That's nice in theory but it seems like we're always talking about money. It's like this monster between us which will never go away. You'll forever have more of it than you can ever spend in this lifetime and I'll never be able to keep up."

"Rogue, it's never been about that for me. If I hadn't gotten exceptionally lucky or my ideas had been any earlier or later in the evolution of computer technology, you'd be waving goodbye every morning as I put on my polo shirt to work at some big computer technology warehouse. I'd probably be running some technical service department somewhere. I'm really nothing special, Rogue. I'm just incredibly fortunate."

I start to say something, but he immediately continues, "I wasn't anything special *until I met you*. You take the time to see me. You know that there is more to me than my wallet and my brain. The reason you know this is because you've taken the time to actually ask me what's going on in my life every day. Even if it's just sending me stupid cat memes, you always check in. I don't know if it's because I was always the 'responsible one' or if it was because my parents were going through their own turmoil, but for the first time in my life, I feel truly cared for. So, while you might not bring a large bank account to the relationship, you bring so much more. The love you bring to us is priceless."

I don't know what has taken me so long, but it's finally like a light bulb is flashing above my head. All the arguments from Ivy, Marcus, and even Jade, coalesce in my brain.

I bow my head to the floor and walk over to the shelter of Tristan's arms. He immediately envelops me in a hug. "I'm sorry Tristan. I didn't get it. I didn't see how important I am to this relationship too. When I was little, my mom and I struggled a lot. Sometimes, we didn't have enough to make it all the way through the month. I didn't realize how much those early days affected my whole life. In those days everything was reduced to how much it was going to cost. If I was hungry and had a glass of milk, my mama would say, 'Have water, that *leche* costs thirteen cents.' If I went out to pizza with friends, my mom would comment, 'Don't eat too much, I don't have enough money for bigger school clothes.' Don't get me wrong, my mom never intended those remarks to be at all cruel. She was trying the best she possibly could. But the message I received was every thing in life boils down to dollars and cents, relationships included."

"It's strange how we internalize the messages from our parents differently than they ever intended them to be sent."

"I guess I was afraid if I couldn't contribute as much money as you do, you would think I don't love you as much as you love me."

"Nothing could be further from the truth. I completely and fully respect the fact that it's a complete miracle my product became the dominant choice in its niche market. There are thousands — if not tens of thousands of competitors out there. It could've just as easily been one of them. So, it would be really stupid for me to claim because I happen to have a substantial amount of money for the first time in my life, somehow I'm more qualified to love you. Talk about ridiculous. If anything, like you pointed out — it makes me less qualified to love you because I'm prone to be distracted by the business. Being a small business owner is hard work. I am more fortunate than most because I can afford to delegate my tasks."

"Show off," I mumble disgruntledly. "I wish I could delegate some of my homework."

"I can get you some help," Tristan offers magnanimously, but with a teasing glint in his eye.

"No, it's all right. I'm pretty sure stuff like that is considered cheating. I don't want to be kicked out of college before I even have a chance to graduate."

"Okay, but don't let it be said I didn't offer," Tristan quips. "Go finish your bath and I'll see what I can do about some dinner."

"That sounds phenomenal. I'm starving and exhausted. So, if you hear snoring coming from the general vicinity of the bathroom, it means I fell asleep in the tub. Today has been grueling. So, it's a distinct possibility."

"I could play your lifeguard just to make sure you're completely safe," Tristan suggests.

"As much as I appreciate the offer, I think I'd appreciate dinner more. But, I might take a rain check on the coed bathing at some point."

I was wrong. I don't stand a chance of falling asleep in the tub right now. My brain is too busy trying to process everything that's happened today. The possibilities are simply mind-boggling. I finally give up any pretense of relaxing in the tub. I throw on some flannel PJs and join Tristan in the kitchen. Marcus thinks my flannel pajamas are hysterical. No one — and I mean no one in Florida actually wears flannel pajamas except me. But, it's a throwback to Vermont I can't seem to give up; I guess I still miss my mom and my home. Consequently, I have been known to sleep in my flannel PJs with two fans on me.

When Tristan sees me, he smiles and remarks, "Interesting fashion choice for Florida, I can't say I've seen it done before."

I shrug as I throw my hair up in a sloppy bun. "I guess I like to be comfortable."

Tristan grins as he pulls off his jacket and his tie, "I do too — but I didn't want to take the time to change clothes before I came." He throws his shoes and socks over on my shoe pile and sits down on my dilapidated polka dotted seventies-style beanbag chair. "I love furniture like this. It's too bad that when we become grown-ups, it's no longer socially acceptable for us to have furniture which squishes into different shapes or a miniature basketball hoop in the house — because that kind of stuff is plain good stress relief."

"So why don't you? It's not like you don't have enough money to buy yourself everything in the entire furniture store or have everything custom designed. You work hard. Just design the living space you want to live in and the heck with everybody else."

"You could deal with having an old-school arcade in the living room?" Tristan jests.

"May I remind you Marcus is my best friend? Arcades are not a new concept for me. If you don't put a keg in the middle of the room, it's a notch above his design plan. Although I doubt he'd be brave enough to do it."

"Yeah, I think he's all talk. I don't think he'd ever do that. I could absolutely see him building an elaborate hot wheels display with his kids someday, but I don't think he is quite the party boy he presents himself to be," Tristan remarks as he dishes me up some fragrant New York style pizza.

Sometimes, I have to admit there are some perks to dating a filthy rich guy. This is one of them. He not only can seem to read my mind and figure out my secret food cravings, but he can magically make even the most obscure food appear out of thin air. As an upper East coaster, I've been known to be picky about the way I eat my pizza. So, usually I avoid it altogether just to avoid all the hassle and disappointment. One day, I mentioned casually in passing how much I missed really good New York style pizza and the next day, Tristan had some delivered for lunch. I had been searching for such a delicacy without much success since I transplanted myself to Florida.

As I stuff my face with pizza, I ask with a smirk, "I wonder if Marcus would be disappointed if he knew how few people are actually buying his bad boy act?"

"I think he knows we're on to him by now and since he met Ivy, he seems to care a lot less about what everyone else thinks about him."

As I gather up the remains of our dinner and throw it all in the trash. I join Tristan on the beanbag chair, collapsing into his lap. "I can sympathize with his paradigm shift. Everything I thought I knew about relationships has completely changed since I fell in love with you. I've discovered love doesn't have to be destructive and scary. It's not about grabbing and keeping control, it's about surrendering your heart and trusting someone will be there to catch it. So, I have decided to throw out my rulebook and start with a clean slate."

"So, does that mean I have free reign for your birthday?" Tristan asks eagerly.

"Yes, Tristan, I trust you. You may spoil me rotten. Just try not to give me a heart attack in the process, okay?" I tease as I kiss him lightly.

Chapter Nineteen

Ivy

"MARCUS, WHAT WERE WE THINKING? This has disaster written all over it. We don't even know the whole story yet. What if they all hate each other?" I fret as I stack French bread and spaghetti noodles on Marcus's counter.

Given all the warnings he provided about his apartment, I expected him to live in a real hovel, not a relatively average apartment which looks like the interior designer got lost somewhere in the mid-eighties. The pink and blue backsplash is an interesting touch you don't see every day anymore.

"Ivy, the pieces of the story we do know seem to point to the fact that everybody and their dog was completely lied to in this situation. As hard as it is to believe, Super-Secret-Spy-Guy hasn't found any evidence any of your family or Rogue's family did anything wrong. If you'll pardon my French, the whole thing was just one big giant cluster-eff where everyone got royally screwed."

"Okay, umm … that's putting it bluntly —" I

remark, unable to completely disguise the laugh in my voice.

"Well, come on, you've got to admit it's true. The only people not hurt in this were the people who got away with the money. So, there's no reason not to bring the two halves of your family together and make it whole. It's not like you and Rogue won't be hanging out on a regular basis, right?"

"No, that's kind of what we're hoping for. We're trying to get permission from the RCBR Endowment for the two of us to go to the same school. I think we've decided we're both transferring to the University of Florida for the start of fall term. Rogue doesn't want to leave Ink'd Deep. For some reason, she is under the mistaken impression she might not be promoted if she is under another artist. She still thinks only you see her talent. I told her she'd still be amazing regardless of who teaches her. But, she doesn't believe me. What do I know, I'm only the 'little' twin sister?"

"I love both you guys, but you are by far and away my favorite. You know that, right?"

Marcus always knows how to calm my nerves. It doesn't matter where we're at, or what we're doing. He always knows the perfect words to say. "That does help — more than you can imagine. Even if things go down the drain, I know I've got one person in my corner tonight."

"Sugar, I think you're going to have far more. You're going to end up with multiple families who love you and call to make sure everything's okay. It will probably drive you nuts after a while."

"Still, that's a lot different from everyone meeting face-to-face. Rosa didn't seem too happy when I mentioned my mom and dad's name."

"That's exactly why I think this is a good idea. When everyone is in the same room, we can talk about what really happened instead of what people think might've happened. It'll give everyone a chance to look at the facts objectively and figure out what happened once and for all. There'll be no room for misinterpretation and no weird games of 'telephone' where the facts get all distorted as each person retells it."

I sigh warily as I slowly nod my head. "Okay, but if there's a resulting bloodbath, don't say I didn't warn you."

Marcus kisses me tenderly. "Ivy, it'll be fine. Everyone involved loves you or your sister. It would be silly not to get this all sorted out. It will be less painful for everyone involved in the long run. You don't want Lenore and Roger thinking Isaac is a drug dealer your whole life, do you?"

"I'm a little frightened to consider what else we might find out about ourselves. It seems the more questions we ask, the more controversial facts we dig up from the past. It's quite frustrating."

"Tell me about it. Tristan tells me it's been that way ever since you walked through his doors. Everything he expected to happen in the case of your mixed-up identities didn't and things have been mind-bendingly complex ever since."

"I don't know about you, but I'm ready for some peace in our lives."

My mom and dad are the first to arrive. I can tell it's going to be an extremely tense night when my mom starts gushing over my table settings. In honor of our Italian night Marcus had gone to the local discount party store and purchased a red and white checkered vinyl tablecloth and some red paper napkins, along with some long white taper candles. This was the extent of my table-scaping, apart from a couple baskets for the French bread, but you would've thought I'd rubbed elbows with Martha Stewart. I know it's my mom's way of dealing with her nervous energy. I do the same thing — so between the two of us, we probably sound a bit like Alvin and the Chipmunks.

I hear the distinct squeak of Marcus's front door. As my birth parents stroll in holding hands, I brace myself for what might be an ugly showdown. Yet, on one level, it still makes my heart happy to see Padre Pop with Mama Rosa. He immediately took a sabbatical from his teaching position for a term until he could settle his personal life. They still have much to work out, but it appears to be a positive start.

When Mama Rosa sees my mom, her body tenses, but she at least aims for polite. "*Buenas Noches*, Ms. Lenore. You're looking well. I can't believe how many years it's been."

My mom looks confused for a moment as if she wasn't quite expecting politeness. "Good evening to you too, you are as beautiful as ever. It's clear why the girls are so beautiful."

"Mama?" questions Rogue as she and Tristan

round the corner with their hands full of presents. "Ivy didn't mention you were coming. I thought Padre was flying in from Denver."

Rosa shrugs. "We are, how do you say it these days? 'Exploring our boundaries.' I don't know how it'll work out, but it's nice."

"Please tell me he's not really a drug dealer," my mom declares, her voice rich with accusation.

"A drug dealer?" Isaac asks incredulously. "Why would I play for the other side?"

"I don't think Ms. Montclair really means to offend, *mi cariño*," Mama Rosa interjects, patting Padre Pop on the arm. "Don't you remember how vicious the rumor mill could be in the teacher's lounge?"

Isaac shakes his head and mutters, "Still Rosie … I almost lost you and the girls fighting that filth and now she thinks I'm one of them?" He turns and looks directly at my mom and asks, "I took our taxes to your husband for Pete's sake. How crooked could I be?"

My dad pops into the conversation. I jump when I hear his deep baritone voice, "That's right, you did. You were one of the only clients I ever had who didn't take a beating when Silicon Valley nearly went belly up. I still don't know how you did it with all your tech investments. I'd love to know your secret. Lenore, he's a very straight shooter. I've never seen such organized records in my life. He even knew when his interest collected interest."

Padre smiles when he sees my dad. "I see nothing has changed; you're still trying to get stock tips from me. Like I told you all those years ago, I just pay attention to the little stuff. Twitter has made it even easier now."

Tristan's mouth drops open in shock. "You have a Twitter account? We looked for days."

"I can be hard to track when I need to be. Let's just say ABirdyToldMeSo3," he says with a sly grin.

Tristan hits his forehead as if he suddenly has a colossal migraine. "Isaac, I hate to tell you this, but we have a massive conflict of interest."

Padre looks stymied for a moment, then a look of recognition crosses his face. "Nerds4theWinFL?"

Tristan nods, but he looks very somber.

"Oh no, not Elliot's Center!" Rogue says softly, clearly distressed. I look at Marcus and my parents, but we're all lost.

"How do you keep beating me in every round?" Padre Pop grouses.

"I am willing to bid the whole job pro-bono," answers Tristan.

"Even the support staff?" Padre Pop whistles softly through his teeth. "Can't match you there. I have to hire temps for mine since I'm pretty much retired."

"Any reason you can't sub-contract on my bid? I read your bid synopsis online. You've got some ideas in yours that are superior to mine. I'd like to see the project be optimal."

Padre gets a twinkle in his eye. "I guess, if you're going to start stamping your name on building projects — you want them to be as top notch as possible," he teases.

"I do want it to be top of the line, but not because my name is going on it, but because my sister's and nephew's names are. It means the world to my mom. When Elliot came to us, he didn't have the skills to cope with the grief of losing his mom. My mom was doing the best she could, but knew little about depression in children and how to help him cope with the sudden death of his mom. Programs like the one we bid on should help."

"I'm definitely on board then. I always thought the project was too big for one contractor," Padre announces.

"Great! We've settled all the business stuff, so let's go eat something. I'm starving," suggests Marcus.

"You're always starving," reply all the women simultaneously.

"What?" Marcus protests innocently. "I'm a growing boy."

I shake my head in amusement. "Well, you're growing something, that's for sure."

As everyone laughs in good humor, I wonder why I was so worried. It seems that everyone is getting along spectacularly well. Rogue is talking to the two moms about college courses and the dads seem to be bonding over the woes of their 401(k) plans.

I step into the kitchen to grab some more garlic bread and when I emerge, Marcus has produced a big birthday cake with a photograph Tristan snapped a few weeks ago when we were all in California. Rogue and I were riding as many of the rides as possible at Disneyland. In this particular shot, she's trying to make me dizzy on the teacup ride. The only problem is she underestimated my capacity to spin. She didn't know I spent many years as a flyer on the cheerleading team and nothing much fazes me. In freeze-frame, Tristan had caught the look of pure joy as she delighted in trying to make us tumble like Weeble-Wobble toys.

Big tears roll down my face when I see the beautiful cake and the symbolism represented there. My heart is so full. I feel like it could burst. For the first time in my life I feel like I completely belong. I have a place in Rogue's life, with Mama Rosa and Padre Pop. Much to my surprise, my dad doesn't seem to have an issue with my new family or with Marcus. In fact, he seems to treat Marcus as if he's the son he never had.

Just as I'm set to bask in the pleasure of the day, I see the mutinous set of my mom's jaw, and I know this won't be good. I know from experience, my mom is ready to erupt. My mom turns to Rosa. "She may have found you, but this changes nothing. She's still my daughter. You apparently never wanted her or you would've looked for her a long time ago."

Instantly, two sensations hit my body. First, I have an overwhelming desire to vaporize myself from the planet and secondly, I suddenly feel the need to urgently throw up.

"Lenore!" my dad chastises in a raised voice I've rarely heard him use. "That was cruel and uncalled for. This is hard for all of us."

"My wife couldn't look for our daughter because we were told she was dead. Do you understand that? *Dead.* I almost killed myself when I found out. Do you know what it's like? Did you pay off the hospital so you could have one of my beautiful daughters without having to go through me? Maybe it was you who spread all the rumors about me at school to make it look like I couldn't be a good *padre*," Isaac responds angrily to the accusation.

"Enough, all of you!" Marcus directs. "Super-Secret-Spy-Guy, here has done a ton of research on everyone here. Do you want to know what he's found?"

The room descends into stunned silence at Marcus's forceful presence. Usually, he projects the image of a 13-year-old on summer vacation at a beach resort, ready to catch the next wave.

"Tristan found two families who were ready to love both of you with open arms. He found two families who were ready to make great sacrifices to make their dreams of the perfect family come true. He discovered two families who had faced unimaginable tragedies. But, do you know what else he found? He found two families who were the victims of some incredible hoax through no wrongdoing of their own. You guys can continue to throw barbs at each other if it makes you feel better, but the only people you're hurting are your daughters."

My mom diverts her gaze from Mama Rosa and fiddles with the silverware.

"You didn't find any evidence they paid the hospital an extra fee to cover up an illegal adoption?" Padre Pop asks Tristan.

"No sir, everything I've found points to the fact they thought the adoption was legal and above board. They did pay an additional fee, but they thought it was to get rid of a troublemaker who would impede the progress of the adoption. That person was listed as a problem employee of the hospital. They had no way of knowing about the full implications of the employee's testimony."

"What about the lawyer?" he presses.

"Unfortunately, we'll never know. He and his wife were killed in an experimental plane crash in the mid-nineties. She was his legal secretary. He had no other office staff. His records have long since been destroyed."

"Are you saying we have no way to find out what really happened?" Mama Rosa asks, a deep frown marring her usually sunny expression.

"I suspect there was some malfeasance somewhere in the upper management of the hospital, but I have no way to prove it at this point. There have been too many administration changes and a change of ownership at least once and perhaps twice."

I walk around the table until I am standing between the two moms. I am incredibly moved when Marcus moves to stand behind me. It isn't a grand, flamboyant gesture; but rather one of quiet support.

I place a hand on each of my mom's shoulders. "What you guys ultimately decide to do against the hospitals, doctors or agencies involved with my adoption isn't up to me, but I want you to know I consider you both to be my mom. I wouldn't have the identity I have without you."

I hug Lenore from behind and say, "Without you, I probably wouldn't be a complete book-a-holic and be nuts about arts and crafts. It was you who read to me for hours on end as I recovered from surgery and taught me a million and one hundred and one things to do with popsicle sticks and how to decoupage everything on the planet. What we have is special and I'm not giving it up for anybody."

My mom wilts a little in her chair. "Oh Ivy Love, I'm so relieved. I've lived in fear of this day since the day I first saw you in the NICU with all those wires and tubes attached to you. You are such a beautiful little fighter, but your skin was so transparent, I could practically see your heartbeat. I guess I always knew I would have to share you one day. I just didn't know it would be with people as perfect as Rosa, Isaac and Rogue."

"Mom, Rogue isn't as perfect as you think she is. Do you know she burps like a trucker?" I tease.

"*Sí*, it is true. I tried to teach my daughter manners, but she always forgets. You did a much better job with the one you raised, I think. It does not seem she considers herself to be one of the boys," Mama Rosa comments shaking her head in dismay. "Rogue's too much like her Padre."

I laugh as I say to Rosa, "Hmm, it sounds like I have some skill building to do. By the way Mama Rosa, I plan to keep you and Padre Pop in my life too. You bring such an easy, casual joy to life and you made me feel so welcome — not to mention that my Spanish and my cooking skills have vastly improved under your influence."

My mom looks hurt and crestfallen at the same time as she mutters loud enough for us to hear, "So, that's it then, huh? You find a more interesting hipper version of a mom and I'm just out?"

"Lenore, that's not what she said and you know it. Your words are making her feel bad. You understand, right?" Rogue gently chastises my mom as she brushes a hand across her shoulder in a comforting gesture.

My mom glances over at me with alarm, "I'm sorry Love Bug. This is very difficult. I feel like you're not really ours anymore."

"It's okay, Mom, I'm not going anywhere. It'll be a challenge for us all for a little while, while we redefine family."

Rogue nods in agreement as she looks at my mom. "Mrs. Montclair, I hope you don't mind, but I'd like to spend some time with your family too. Ivy has shown me a bunch of the stuff she made and I'd like to learn how to do that."

Turning to my dad she asks, "Would you mind helping me set up some accounting software on my computer? After I finish my apprenticeship, I'll be responsible for managing my own station at the shop and I'll need a way to track expenses and inventory. I want to make sure I have it set up right from the very beginning. With all due respect to Marcus's artistic talent, computers and accounting aren't his thing. I'd be happy to pay you for your time, of course."

"Don't be ridiculous!" my dad responds. "I couldn't charge you for that kind of advice any more than I could charge Ivy. We can set up a Team Viewer session or you can just bring your computer to Vermont the next time you come to see your mom."

My mom stands up and I give her a big hug and whisper in her ear, "I love you, Mom. It'll be different, but not worse. I promise. Are we going to be okay?"

My mom gives me a watery smile and nods as she gathers Rogue into our embrace and asks, "So, what do you want to make first? I have this cute idea for Easter baskets…"

CHAPTER TWENTY

TRISTAN

I CAN'T BELIEVE IT'S SUMMER break already. So much has changed in the last few months that it's hard for me to comprehend it all. Since their huge blowout birthday party in February, Ivy and Rogue have both transferred to the University of Florida with their new scholarships. Even though they could've gone anywhere, they both decided to stay close to Ink'd Deep. Rogue feels like she owes it to Marcus for giving her a chance when no one else would. Eventually, Rogue got used to the idea of me opening my business in Gainesville so I can be near her.

Isaac and Rosa did the stereotypical retiree thing and moved to Florida. Isaac has been working for me as a consultant on the childhood grief center and several other projects.

Just as I'm about to head out the door, Isaac pokes his head in the door. "Did you make sure you have your passports? The TSA is getting really picky about those these days."

"Yes Dad," I reply, trying to keep the sarcasm out

of my voice. "It's not like I don't travel a hundred days a year or anything."

"*You* travel a lot, but Rogue doesn't and you guys aren't traveling on your deluxe puddle jumper," he cautions. "You guys will have to travel like common folk."

"Isaac, I appreciate your concern — but I've got it handled. I've got checklists for my checklists. I've been planning this trip pretty much since my first conversation with Rogue."

Isaac nods thoughtfully. "Hmm, so it was like that for you too, huh? I was a goner for my Rosie even though she was hanging upside down the first time I saw her. If my supervisors knew all I did to get her out of the so-called Jalopy she called a car, my career would've probably been over before it even started."

"How did you know it was the real thing and not the adrenaline of the moment taking over?" I ask, interested in his perspective.

"I guess at first, I didn't know the difference. I suppose no one really does. But, as time wore on, it didn't seem to matter what we were doing I just wanted to be in her presence."

I flash Isaac a shy grin, "I'm relieved to find out it's not just me. The other day, she was studying for finals and I was coding a big project and I felt better knowing she was sitting in the same room with me. We weren't even doing anything particularly 'couple-like' — it was simply comforting to have her there. I thought I might be going nuts."

"I totally understand what you mean. There would be lazy Sunday afternoons when Rosie would be doing nothing but puttering around in her garden while I was doing yard work. We wouldn't be doing anything amazing or earth-shattering, but her presence would calm me and allow me to focus better. The other day, I was working on a case and I noticed it's still true. As soon as she sat down to do a crossword puzzle, my mind settled right down."

"Women are pretty miraculous, I'll grant you that."

"Has your 'miracle' figured out what you're up to yet?"

"As far as I know, she doesn't have a clue. But, Rogue is so smart I wouldn't bet on it."

"You better hurry or Marcus won't able to keep her distracted much longer."

"Okay, I'll see you in a few days."

Rogue squirms in my arms as she protests, "Despite what you've seen in virtually every music video and romantic comedy ever written, this isn't romantic. It's embarrassing! Somebody will think you're kidnapping me."

"I've got it handled, Rogue." I set her gently in her seat and brush a kiss against her temple. "No one will think badly of you, I promise. I've thought of everything."

"Really?" she asks haughtily. "Was the blindfold required equipment for your plan or just a fun little bonus?"

I chuckle. "Oh, I'd say it's pretty much required at this point, I want to keep you as clueless as possible."

"You know, I could call your mother, Tristan Riley Macklin," she threatens menacingly as she crosses her arms and sticks her bottom lip out in a pretty little pout.

"Just so you know, your threat is not as effective with me as it is with Marcus because, as much as she likes you, my mom would side with me on this one."

"Can I tell you how much it sucks that you're totally not afraid of me?"

Just then a slightly garbled voice comes over the intercom system and instructs the flight attendants to close the cabin doors so the plane can take off to Paris.

Rogue turns her face toward mine and her jaw drops open in shock. "You seriously did this?"

"Yes, I seriously did," I answer, with a wide teasing grin. "Happy belated birthday. You told me you were too busy with school to go on vacation during the school year. Just think of this as your birthday present a few months late."

I carefully remove the blindfold and she blinks to adjust to the light. "How in the world did you get me all the way through the airport without me knowing a thing?"

I blush. "Umm … high-level negotiations with the TSA? … and a few well-placed signs."

"Well-placed signs?" Rogue repeats to herself as she looks down and pulls off a piece of paper I taped to her jacket.

She takes a moment to read it to herself. She looks up at me with confusion on her face and then rereads it. By the time she looks up again I'm down on one knee.

Someone from a few rows back yells, "What does it say? I couldn't get close enough to read it!"

Rogue clears her throat as she reads, "Shh! Be very quiet. I'm going to ask my girlfriend to marry me. She doesn't know we're going to Paris. Don't ruin the surprise, please."

When Rogue sees the square cut diamond I picked out for her, her eyes widen and she starts to laugh softly. "Tristan, I can't believe you, the ultimate plan maker, would do something so risky. There were thousands of people in the airport. Any one of them could've blown your surprise."

I shrug philosophically. "It was a gamble I was willing to take. I figured enough people were romantics at heart to play along. I was right, everyone did — including the airline personnel and the TSA. I was able to quietly board you onto the plane so I could ask you, Rogue Medea Cisneros Betancourt, a very important question."

Rogue's eyes tear up as she gasps. When she gasps, the people in the first four rows behind us collectively let out a gasp as well. For a perpetually shy guy who hates to be the center of attention, this is a worst-case scenario for me. My mouth feels like I've been sucking on cotton balls.

"Rogue, the day I set out to find you, I had no idea it would be the best treasure hunt I've ever gone on.

I love you so much. I can't imagine my life without you in it. Would you please do me the honor of becoming my wife?" I ask, holding the ring out, waiting to place it on her finger.

After the longest five seconds of my life, Rogue extends a shaking hand toward me with her fingers spread apart so I can place the ring on it. She nods mutely as tears stream down her face.

"We didn't hear what you said, honey," a voice echoes from the back of the plane.

"Yes! I said yes!" Rogue responds loudly as she throws her arms around my neck and kisses me soundly. "Tristan Macklin, I can't wait to be your wife. Our love snuck up on me when I was least expecting it. It's the best thing ever to happen to me — and that's saying a lot since a lot of great things have happened this year. Yet, loving you has anchored me so I could deal with all the other chaos in my life. I never expected to find someone like you, but I'm so glad I did. I love you."

The flight attendant stands up and makes an announcement over the intercom, "In celebration of his upcoming nuptials, Mr. Macklin has generously provided a free drink ticket to all passengers over the age of twenty-one on the plane if you would like one."

With her simple pronouncement, I became the most popular person on the plane. In a sense, I knew it was coming because I authorized it. However, I thought they would do it compliments of the airline not specifically name me. I hate it when I get singled out for my acts of generosity. I don't do it for the acclaim. I do it because I like to make people smile or make their lives easier.

Rogue takes notice of the uneasy expression on my face and merely smirks. "If you plan to be so nice to people, you're going to need to learn to graciously accept peoples' thanks. The two kind of go hand-in-hand."

I unbutton the collar of my shirt and fold up the cuffs. "Well, to be honest I was hoping to fly a little under the radar on this one."

Rogue grins at me. "I hate to break it to you, but you're a pretty famous kabillionaire since you've got two very successful computer programs out there. People are calling you the next Bill Gates or Steve Jobs. I have a feeling not much of what you do will fly under the radar anymore."

"I hate to break it to you — *you're* going to be the wife of a relatively famous kabillionaire," I tease. "That'll be interesting for you and Ivy. You two can pull some interesting tricks on the paparazzi."

"You really think there'll be paparazzi around?"

"It's entirely possible. They seem to have an unnatural fascination with my state of bachelorhood. If they get wind something has changed, they'll probably send a gaggle of reporters to try to figure out what happened and it won't be pretty."

"That's bogus. It's none of their business. I don't get into their love life. Why should they get into mine?"

"A perfectly legitimate question no one seems to know the answer to," I reply as I snuggle her into my side the best I can in airline seats. Even the first-class seats are not ideal for cuddling.

As we finally step off the plane, I comment, "I always forget how long that flight is. Even with first-class seats, it's a pain in your neck and back and legs."

"Okay, I agree. It was a very long flight, but for a novice like me, it was also cool to be treated like a movie star. I've eaten in restaurants which didn't have a wine selection that nice. Quite frankly, I was a little intimidated. You didn't tell me you speak fluent French."

I roll my shoulder nonchalantly. "I'm not so fluent, it just sounds that way. I had an international student for a roommate in college and he was more comfortable speaking French than English. I was lucky because it came to me pretty easily. The ability comes in handy on international collaborations."

Rogue looks around as we climb into the limousine to go to the hotel and says, "Tristan, I don't know if I will ever get used to this. It's like something out of a movie. I feel like I'm living someone else's life."

"I know the feeling. I still feel that way when I get up in the morning."

Standing on the marble steps of the Louvre, Rogue looks down at her casual sundress skeptically, and asks, "Are you sure this is appropriate? It seems rather mundane for a place like this. I feel like I should be wearing church clothes and pearls or something."

I point to my own khaki shorts and T-shirt. "Trust me, you'll be sweating by the time you're done. It's very warm inside. Are your batteries charged on your camera?"

Rogue nods and pulls me toward the end of the longest line. I shake my head, place my arm around her waist and escort her to a side entrance by the food court. Her eyes widen as I pull tickets from my wallet.

"Where did you get those?" she probes.

"Oh, I've had these for a while," I answer vaguely.

"How long is a while?" she asks suspiciously.

"A few months," I answer evasively.

"Why would you get me tickets to go to Paris back then? You barely knew me," she stammers.

"I don't know if I can totally explain this to you because my actions will seem totally irrational, but they make sense to me. I guess you have to live in the weird bubble I've been living in to completely understand it. You were the first person in over two years to have a normal conversation with me. You didn't grill me about my net worth or how to break into the gaming world. When you found out I had money, you didn't even try to spend a single dime of it on yourself. In fact, when I offered, you came up with a ton of excuses why you should be last on the list."

"Of course I shouldn't have been on the list. You were a stranger," Rogue protests.

I gather her up into a loose embrace. "I found your actions so remarkable that I wanted to move you to the top of the list. If it had been my choice, we would have just traveled to Paris on a random Tuesday, but you were stubborn and insistent about your rules that I could not be extraordinarily nice to you. So instead, I set up The Identity of the Heart Foundation and implemented all the suggestions you gave me that day and added an afternoon art program for junior high school kids because I figured Ivy would like that too."

For a moment, it's eerily quiet and the only noise present is the ambient noise from the traffic and the surrounding crowd. I know how Rogue feels about me spending money without advance notice. I wonder if I've taken it several steps too far this time. Her expression is almost too blank to read.

Finally, the corner of her mouth quirks up. "Well, I guess it's a good thing for you that I changed the rules on extravagant gift giving because this certainly qualifies."

I've been to the Louvre many times but I've never seen it through the eyes of a true art lover. Most of the time when I bring business colleagues to see this Paris treasure, they stick to the tried-and-true tourist hot spots like the Mona Lisa, Venus de Milo or The Glass Pyramid. After stopping by the gift shop to buy some art supplies, Rogue is content to sit and sketch. She marvels over each and every thing we encounter. It doesn't matter whether it was a small pencil drawing from Leonardo da Vinci to a huge multistory fresco, she is mesmerized. She is especially tickled when we cross paths with a little girl who's mimicking all the marble statues in what seems to be an indoor statute garden of all the greats. I know there is a formal name for this room, but that's what it reminds me of. Rogue is sketching a mile a minute and muttering to herself, "What I wouldn't give for my watercolors right about now."

When the girl finally gets tired and leaves, Rogue turns and laments, "I think the jet lag is catching up with me too. I'm exhausted. There is no way we can see everything. I'm so sad because this is like taking a walk through my art history book."

"Rogue, there's no reason we can't come back any time you want, remember? I told you a long time ago you don't have to save these trips for special occasions. Any random Tuesday will work."

Rogue's eyes light up. "Does it actually have to be on a Tuesday?"

"All you have to do is let me know when we're going," I answer with a grin as I tuck her drawing tablet under my arm and escort her back to the limousine.

CHAPTER TWENTY-ONE

MARCUS

"I SEND YOU ON VACATION and you come back all engaged? What's up with that? He didn't ask my permission," I say with mock outrage. "Way to steal my thunder —"

"Are you serious?" Rogue asks as she whips her head around to look at me and pulls her hand back from where she's displaying her rock to Jade.

"Are you sure you'll be able to balance your tattooing machine with that added boulder on your finger?" I ask drily.

"Oh quiet you! You know I give tats with my right hand anyway. Besides, Tristan thought of that. He got me a solid gold band to wear when I'm working. This is just for show," Rogue responds as she tilts her hand to demonstrate how the ring catches the light.

"Of course he did, because he's Super-Secret-Spy-Guy. He thinks of every contingency," I mutter under my breath.

"If you're done making fun of my fiancé, tell me about what you've got planned for my sister," she prompts impatiently.

"I don't know if I should tell you. You and Ivy communicate way too much for my comfort level."

Rogue makes a gesture of locking her lips shut and throwing away the key. "Mum's the word, I promise. I won't even send a mental hint, I swear."

"I'm sorry I didn't get a chance to include you in my surprise. Remember when I had to go back to my old neighborhood a couple of months ago when my uncle died? Well, there's a silversmith who works there. He was working on this and it was perfect for Ivy, even though it's unconventional for a wedding set, it just screamed her name. Cameron is designing the wedding band part of it now."

As I open the little bamboo box to expose the ring, her gasp of awe tells me everything I need to know. I can only hope Ivy's reaction is as positive.

"Marcus, you got her a dragonfly! Look at the tiny amethysts and diamonds in the wings. Did you know those are our birthstones?"

I grin like a kid at recess. "Who do you think requested they be added, Ro?"

"You're just a big sentimental marshmallow who likes to dress in motorcycle gear, aren't you?" she teases, but I notice she's wiping away a tear when she thinks I'm not looking.

"Shh … I don't want any of my customers to think I'm a softy," I caution.

Rogue giggles. "Marcus, I think you were busted a really long time ago. You tape every postcard you get from Sadie on your station. I think people have figured out by now you're not very bad-ass."

"I can be when I want to be," I argue petulantly.

"You can be what?" asks Ivy as she drops her backpack on the counter.

I distract her with a kiss as I slip the ring back into my pocket.

"I was telling your handsome boyfriend he's a nice guy. For some reason he seems to find the concept objectionable," Rogue replies.

"He is very nice," agrees Ivy.

Okay enough of this. It's clearly time to change the subject. "What are you doing here so early? I thought you were teaching the Arts 4 Tots class at the Park and Rec District today."

"I was, but then they had a small chlorine leak at the pool and sent us all home," she explains with a shrug.

"Are you okay?" I ask, as all the worst-case scenarios play out in my mind. "No asthma attack?"

Ivy laughs softly. "Oh, I'm fine. It was really nothing, but they didn't want to cause mass hysteria."

"Still, you were never in any real danger?" I push.

"No, not really. They had a paramedic there the whole time."

I walk over to the entrance of the break room and grab our duffel bags. "Say your tearful goodbyes and all that jazz, we have an epic vacation calling our name."

Ivy stands in front of me with her arms crossed, "I don't suppose you're going to tell me where we're going. How am I supposed to know if I packed the right stuff?"

"Actually, I've decided it's kind of fun to keep you in the dark. But, no worries. I've got you covered. Mama Rosa and Rogue have assured me they've taken care of every possible need."

"Well, aren't you clever?" Ivy suggests sarcastically.

Not rising to the bait, I answer with an easy grin, "Why thank you. I do try."

Ivy walks over to the light table where Rogue is working on a complex stencil of a back piece designed to look like a stained-glass window in a church. "Wow! That's amazing! The happiness rolling off of you is so contagious, it's practically coming out of your pores. If I wasn't so blissfully content in my own relationship, I might be a little jealous. Congratulations!" she exclaims as she gives her twin a careful side hug so she doesn't shake the light table.

"Thanks, he totally took me by surprise," Rogue admits.

I snicker quietly, but apparently not quietly enough as Rogue turns to me and asks, "What?" with a question in her eyes and her hands on her hips.

"I just don't know how you could possibly be surprised, that's all," I explain. "It's clear Super-Secret-Spy-Guy has been head over heels with you ever since he stood up to me when I tried to get in your face on the day we met."

"Okay guys, enough dissecting my love life. Go on vacation, or something —" Rogue demands as she sticks her drawing pencil behind her ear and shoos us out the door.

"Explain to me again how you can work on the same sculpture for hours or an oil painting for weeks, but you've asked me four times in the last twenty minutes when we'll get there," I tease as Ivy's about to jump out of her seat trying to figure out where we're headed.

"All right, now you're just being mean." She flops back in the seat of the Mustang. We would've taken the bike except we brought too much junk to make the trip comfortably. I couldn't really tell her she didn't need to bring all that stuff without spilling the beans about where we're going.

"It's totally different when I'm working on a piece. I have a vision in my head where I want it to go, so I vaguely have an idea how long it'll take me to get there — unless of course I completely change my mind in the middle. But this is completely different. I have no idea where you're taking me. We could be going to Nova Scotia for all I know."

"I seriously doubt it. Didn't we already establish a while back that I totally despise the cold? Why would I willingly go anywhere near it on vacation?"

"Okay, you have a good point. Which brings me to the other question; why are we actually going anywhere? I figured after you worked so hard while Rogue was gone, you'd just want to sleep for a week and watch a little wrestling, basketball and football.”

“Well, I suppose I could've — but hanging out at home would've defeated the purpose of having you all to myself. I have very intrusive friends and family members who don't know the meaning of 'alone time'. I plan to take advantage of every moment with you. I think you'll decide what we're planning to do this weekend is far more fun than couch surfing could ever be.”

“Stop with the torture!” Ivy exclaims with a laugh. “You know my imagination is going in a million different directions. You're adventurous enough that we could be doing anything.”

“Ivy, I did try to warn you I like to color outside the lines. I can guarantee you, very few of our dates will ever just include a nice sedate dinner and the movies.”

“May women everywhere rejoice! Dinner and a movie is actually a pretty complicated date if you've never actually gone out with the person before. You've got to decide how much violence and lustiness you'll accept while sitting next to someone you don't know. If they disagree with the movie choice or if they're handsy, it just makes matters more awkward. The worst sin of all is to have a guy who has absolutely no conversational skills. Then, you're stuck next to him for a good three to five hours. Trust me, I've been known to alphabetize my craft room on dates like this. Here's a piece of helpful dating advice from women everywhere — just say no to first dates where we sit around and stare at each other all day,” she finishes in a rush of breath, before she takes a long sip of her Sprite.

“That's all very solid advice.” I hand her what's

left of the Doritos. "Still, I must not be making things very clear."

Her brow wrinkles in confusion, "What do you mean?"

"I was just thinking, if I could wave a magic wand, I'd never have to go on another first date again in my life," I confess.

"Aww, you're so sweet. You must be taking lessons from Tristan. Rogue tells me about all the perfect stuff he says to her. I swear, the man's talents are wasted programming computers. He should be writing dialogue for romantic comedies or greeting cards. Welcome to the sappy side," she chortles as she winks and starts to read her Kindle again.

I want to kick myself for my impromptu statement. Actually, I want to beat myself over the top of the head with a stupid stick. My mom always told me being the class clown would come back to haunt me. I always laughed it off, feeling invincible. But now, I don't feel so invincible. I feel old, creepy and vulnerable. I am at a stage in my life now where I want to be taken stone cold serious but no one except for Ivy can see beyond the goofy affable, living-my-life-on-the-edge kind of guy and even she seems to be missing my true intent here.

Ivy looks up at me through her thick lashes, "Are you okay, Marcus? Your internal peace seems to be fading."

I decide maybe the car isn't the best place to have this kind of discussion, so I mentally shake it off as I remark, "You know how I get when I'm hungry, but luckily this is our exit."

Abruptly, Ivy sits up straight in the seat and stares out the window. When she sees the large billboard she squeals with delight, "Please tell me we're going to Ripley's Believe It or Not!"

All of her earlier fatigue seems to have dissipated and she's practically vibrating with excitement. Her happiness is infectious and helps to chase away my earlier bad mood. "If I would have known something so simple would have brought you this much joy, we would've come a long time ago."

"I know it's stupid. But, the hospital I stayed at when I was younger had one of those big Ripley's Believe It or Not! books in every pediatric room. I used to study all the obscure pictures and think how fun it would be to be noticed for something. Wouldn't it be ironic if they found something unusual about Rogue and I and we were listed on some weird Discovery Channel program? I guess those programs are kind of like the modern-day Ripley's Believe It or Not!"

I raise an eyebrow in surprise. "I guess if you say so."

"It's true! Between Ripley's Believe It or Not!, The Guinness World Records and Madame Tussaud's Wax Museum, I was one really weird kid. I used to drive my mom crazy. I would hoard all the ketchup and sugar packets from my meals because I was sure I would set some world record and be listed in one of those books. She was forever trying to throw away my 'world-famous' collection and my dad was always sneaking in more. The nurses must've thought our family was the pilot for some twisted sitcom."

"I don't know, your family seems pretty All-American and enviable to me. Maybe it should've been on T.V." I respond.

Ivy fidgets in her seat before she haltingly explains, "I guess it's time for me to explain a few skeletons in my closet since you've so eloquently explained all of yours."

"Don't feel like you have to just because I did. It's entirely up to you. Everyones got a past. Lord knows, I'm in no position to judge anyone else's," I say as I reach out and grab her hand and give it a reassuring squeeze.

"No, I want to share my story. I think it's important for you to understand where I've come from," she explains with a sad smile. "Please understand that I'm not the same internally tortured, angsty teenage girl anymore either — although, I still have a tendency to care a little too much about what people think of me."

I point to myself. "Hello Pot, meet Kettle. I think it happens to all of us. Don't beat yourself up about it too much."

"That's easy for you to say because you don't know all the stuff I put my parents through. There was a time in my life during late junior high and early high school where I decided I didn't want to be a 'patient' anymore; I stopped all my treatments and I didn't tell anybody. I stopped my blood thinners and asthma medication without tapering down first. The results could have been potentially fatal. Fortunately, they weren't, but it was touch and go for a while. My parents were nervous wrecks and the whole thing took an awful toll on my parents' marriage."

I reach out to grasp her hand for support. "I'm sorry," I whisper.

She wipes away a tear. "It was so stupid. In the ultimate twist of fate, my move almost cost me my spot on the cheerleading squad and the soccer league. My desperate antics to become part of mainstream society almost marginalized the athlete I really was. Talk about one of my all-time idiotic moves."

"How are you feeling about things now?" I ask.

"Well, I finally came to grips with the fact that I'm not totally normal and I won't ever be. Even the doctors can't agree on what might eventually happen to me. Some have gone as far as to suggest that I may need a lung transplant. Other doctors say I won't need any surgical intervention at all."

"Look on the bright side, it's not like the medical profession has been a reliable source of information in your case up to this point, so maybe the ones who are suggesting you need a lung transplant have no idea what they are talking about either," I suggest, not entirely tongue-in-cheek.

"I know, right?" Ivy replies with a grin. "I used to spend hours obsessing over this stuff as a teenager. It's my own fault my parents watch me like a hawk. For a long time, I didn't give them any reason to trust that I could take care of myself, because I didn't. I thought if I ignored my asthma, I could pretend it wasn't there. Unfortunately, that's not the way it works."

"But, you take better care of yourself now?"

"Much. I take all my medication and go to the doctor like I am supposed to now. I've come to the conclusion asthma is not the only reason I'll never be considered totally normal, so I might as well just roll with it," she quips with a wink.

"Hey! I resemble that weirdness remember? We quote Mel Brooks movies together like Jeopardy champions. I already mentioned several times that I think you're beautiful inside and out. I wouldn't change anything about you," I declare emphatically as I lace my fingers through hers and pull her hand up to my lips and kiss the back of her hand.

The tips of Ivy's ears grow red as she stammers, "Even after all these months, I still can't believe a guy like you feels that way about me, a gawky college student who can't seem to find my way in the world. It's baffling — the way love works. For the record, I wouldn't change anything about you either. It's a weird concept to wrap your brain around because I wish there hadn't been so much pain and suffering in your background. But, maybe in a weird way, it had to be there to make you the man you are today. If you hadn't made every single step you made in your past, our paths would not have crossed."

"I suspect my mom could've done without my jaunt into juvenile delinquency, but other than that, I agree with you. My grandma used to have a saying, 'We are where we came from.' I suspect she meant it in terms of being proud of my heritage, but I think she also meant I needed to own the decisions I made in the past. If it hadn't been for the rough patch in my life, I wouldn't have become a tattoo artist and I wouldn't have met your sister — which means I wouldn't have met you. So, I guess it all works out in the end."

I turn off the ignition and walk around the car to open her door. As she unfolds her long graceful legs from the tight confines of my 1970 candy apple red Mustang, I consider what a natural look it is for her. I've been eyeing a nice sweet little '65. Maybe, just maybe, I need a second commuter car to share with my soon-to-be wife. Even on a casual day like today, Ivy looks stunning in a pair of crisp white shorts and a yellow tank top.

"Why are you staring at me?" Ivy asks, self-consciously, looking around.

"I'm thinking about how amazingly lucky I am," I answer, resisting the urge to bare my soul in the middle of the parking lot.

"From where I'm standing, I'm pretty lucky too," Ivy responds, pressing a kiss against the side of my neck as she weaves an arm around my waist and practically skips toward the entrance's graceful stone steps.

It's fascinating to watch Ivy divide up our lunch while she's chatting excitedly about our adventures at the museum. She's not even paying attention to what she's doing, yet she is able to flawlessly order for me and then divide up our lunches so we could take advantage of the specials without hassling the waitstaff. It cracks me up when she puts extra ice and lemon in my Pepsi. That's such an obscure thing to know about me, yet she does. She even hunted down a packet of relish so she could make me her version of fry sauce. She steals the tomatoes off my burger and donates the pickles from hers and places them on mine.

"Are you done rearranging lunch?" I tease.

She looks around the table as if realizing for the first time how elaborate her rituals have become. "Sorry, I guess we should have paid the three dollars extra for a custom burger. It seems stupid — especially when you consider we're ideal matches for each other. We balance each other out perfectly. I like tomatoes, you like pickles. You like the hamburger buns, I like the fries. You like pizza crust, I don't care for it much. It all works out. We're like the perfect yin-yang. Rogue and Tristan are that way too. Rogue only likes dark meat and I guess Tristan prefers white meat. It's all kind of perfect that we all found each other."

I reach into my jacket pocket. My fingers closing around the little wooden box. I take a deep breath and try to focus. I couldn't have been handed a better opening line if I had scripted it myself. I take a calming breath and then two and then three.

"Ivy, you're right. I can't think of anything more perfect. I've had that opinion of you since you almost passed out in my arms the first day we met. I know it didn't seem very romantic to you, but to me it meant the world. You trusted me to help you that day. I felt about ten feet tall for a week afterward."

"That's really funny. I had the opposite reaction. I was weak, helpless and embarrassed. After you helped me, I felt as if you not only kept me upright, you helped keep my world from spinning off its axis. I remember feeling sad because I thought Rogue already had dibs on you."

I smile at the memory of the conversation we had. Even though it was slightly less than a year ago, in some ways, it seems like it was a whole other lifetime ago. Everything seems so different now.

"It's weird that this whole adventure between us started because you thought someone was pretending to be you and you originally went on the site because you wanted to find who you really were."

Ivy nods and murmurs, "To think I almost didn't go see Tristan that day —"

I swallow hard. "In reality, I think you actually helped me find out who I really am. You gave me permission to stop pretending to be everyone's favorite 'bad-ass-dude' and just be me. With you, I can be the guy who would just as soon build picnic tables in his backyard with a troubled kid from the neighborhood than go out with a bunch of random women to keep up appearances. I always hated the club scene, and as a recovering addict, it was never particularly healthy for me."

"Marcus, I'm sorry you felt like you couldn't be real with people," Ivy offers sympathetically.

"Don't get me wrong, it's not like Rogue didn't try to call me on my superficial behavior. She did. But, it wasn't until you nailed me with your dead-on personality reading that I realized I'd rather be the person you described than the person I was pretending to be."

"Haven't you been that person all along, underneath all your social armor?" Ivy asks me.

"That's what's so crazy about it," I admit. "Everyone around me seems to realize that. I was the last person to know. What I adore the most about you is that you love all sides of me. You recognize there'll always be a messed up little boy inside me who may never be able to leave his dysfunctional past completely behind and you recognize the hard-working professional I am now trying to be; to make up for who I used to be. But, most importantly you see the kind of man I want to be. Miraculously, you seem to be in love with all of me."

Ivy wipes a tear from her cheek as I hold the bamboo box in my suddenly shaking hand and drop to one knee. Several thoughts hit me at once. *This is symbolic on so many levels. Super-Secret-Spy-Guy manages to pull off a surprise proposal on a trip to Paris with a flawless diamond. We're on the junkie outdoor patio of a burger joint in hot, sweaty Florida, next to the dumpster — complete with an orchestra of flies — I'm such a freakin' romantic.*

I try to bring my thoughts back into focus so I can continue, "I can't promise I'll ever be the kind of perfect guy Tristan is for Rogue. I can promise you this, Ivy Love Montclair, I love you with every cell of my being. Please marry me so we can keep being perfect together." *There, that didn't sound half bad. It sounded almost as good as what I rehearsed in the shower this morning.*

Ivy doesn't wait for me to put the ring on her finger she grabs the box from my hand and starts to jump up and down. through tears, "Oh My Gosh! Yes! Of course I'll marry you. You are perfect for me. Do you see this ring? I'd be crazy to say no to a guy who understands me well enough to give me this ring. Do you see this ring?" she asks again as she takes it out of the box to examine it more closely. Her joy is absolutely effervescent.

I can't hide my grin. "Yes, I see the ring. It'd be hard not to — because I helped design it."

"No way!" Ivy exclaims as I ease the ring onto her ring finger. She tilts it in the sun so the stones catch the light. "It's absolutely gorgeous! Did you know amethyst stones are supposed to promote meditation and clairvoyance and diamonds are for purity and love? They are also the birthstones for February and April, you've got both of my birthday celebrations covered too."

"Umm, that was kind of my plan —" I try to interject.

"I can't believe I get to have a dragonfly for my wedding ring. I never had a chance to show you my collection of dragonflies when we were at my parents' house or you would better understand what this means to me. I started drawing and painting dragonflies when I was two and a half. It's like I've always had some deep spiritual connection to them."

"That's amazing. I just wanted to do something for you as unique as our love. A friend of mine made your ring for us. He's still working on the wedding band."

Ivy's eyes widen, "You mean there's more to it than this? Oh wow! I love this so much, I can't imagine anything more."

"Well, you know me. I'm the master of coloring outside the lines —"

Ivy takes me by the hand and walks around the side of the restaurant and pushes me up against the brick wall. She stands on her tip-toes and begins a series of blindingly hot kisses.

As I groan and clutch her waist, she whispers, "This coloring thing is a funny business, I used to be all fussy about boundaries, but then I met this really cool guy who just became my fiancé and he's taught me that sometimes it's fun to do things way outside your comfort zone."

Epilogue

Isaac

"Rosie, can you believe we're here in Paris at Christmastime, in front of the Eiffel tower? What strange turns our lives have taken." I re-wrap her scarf. I've gotten a little spoiled by the weather in Florida. It's more like Denver here, although it's raining and not snowing — but, Rosa wanted to get out of the limousine and see the Eiffel tower up close. I tried to tell Tristan we didn't need such a fancy ride. Still, he insisted we treat this trip like a second honeymoon and splurge a little.

"No, I can't believe it. I still have to pinch myself every morning when I wake up next to you. Officially, you weren't even alive until we got the paperwork a couple weeks ago. Do you know how it broke my heart to have to go to court and have you declared dead? I waited years for you to come back. I even postponed the declaration for three years beyond when I could've filed because I was sure you couldn't possibly be gone. But I needed insurance money for Rogue; I had no choice."

"Rosie, I don't question a single choice you made.

Neither of us had any idea it would turn out this way, but it's a miracle from God that our girls are safe and you still love me."

"Our girls are such a miracle. Especially Ivy. I can't comprehend she grew up only miles from our home. If I'd only had money to put Rogue into dance classes, they would've probably gone to dance competitions together. I feel so guilty."

"Do not feel bad, my love," I murmur as I shelter her under my arm. "Did I tell you what Tristan uncovered?"

"No, did he find more?" she asks with alarm in her voice.

"Unfortunately, yes. The fraud goes even deeper than we expected. We weren't the only victims. We were likely just the most unusual ones. Do you remember when you decided not to have an ultrasound at your regular doctor's office because of my dad's connections at the military base?"

"We were so poor back then we were trying to save money wherever we could." Rosa smiles affectionately as she reminisces, "I remember. I baked a lot of bread and tortillas. I even learned how to sew and I made hand-made dresses for the girls."

"Tristan suspects it never made it into the file that you were expecting twins. Do you remember the person who led the hospital tours? Betty White?"

A look of recognition passes over Rosie's face. "Oh yes! I remember now. I thought it was funny because she had a famous name. I'm a huge *Mary Tyler Moore* fan and I remembered Betty White from the show."

"Not surprisingly, it was not her real name. Her real name was Pryscila Northlend. She was the Vice President of Customer Affairs for a chain of hospitals in the Northeast for fifteen years. She worked with a ring of corrupt adoption attorneys to funnel babies into the black market of adoption. More often than not, the parents who adopted the babies didn't know any different."

"I don't understand. What was in it for attorneys like ours?" Rosa asks, puzzled.

"That was the other piece of the shakedown. Aside from extremely high attorney fees, it appears there was almost always some glitch with the adoption. In our case, they threw in the story about the disgruntled hospital employee and Roger bought it hook, line and sinker. Apparently, it was a ruse they used a lot. Another one was unexpected hospital bills. In retrospect, it appears they pulled that one on the Montclair family too. They were billing your insurance for both girls and they were billing the Montclairs' for Ivy."

"That's disgraceful!" Rosa exclaims.

"There was seemingly no end to their greed because they were claiming the insurance was not paying for Ivy's bills and they were billing Roger privately without telling Lenore. He was afraid if he told Lenore what was happening, they would tell her what was going on with the employee he paid off. This was a pattern we saw over and over again. Sometimes, they would claim the birth mom wanted to keep the baby or they would say the birth father had come back and asserted his rights. One of the most egregious strategies was to claim the babies were drug-addicted and needed expensive treatments to be able to go home. Of course, in the vast majority of cases, the babies were perfectly healthy and being kept at the hospital — basically for ransom."

Rosa turns pale. "Ivy told me she was at the hospital for nearly six months. That's an awfully long time for a little baby to be at the hospital. Do you think they held her hostage?"

"I don't know, *mi cariño*, most of the participants who were caught have served their time in jail. The others like Ms. Northlend are dead or in nursing homes. She has a severe case of Alzheimer's and has to have twenty-four-hour care."

"Well, I guess we had a little help from a higher power," comments Rosa.

"My thoughts traveled in a similar direction," I admit. "I think the only thing we can do now is move forward. The girls are back in our lives and we can't move the clock backwards or recover memories we didn't have a chance to make. If we continue to fight, we will just become bitter."

"Very true, *mi cariño*. Besides, I have two very important weddings to prepare for," she replies, gawking around at the postcard-type scenery around us. It has stopped sprinkling for the moment, but people are still carrying brightly colored umbrellas.

Rosie is so busy watching all the bustling tourists and Parisians, she hasn't noticed that I've taken my glove off and have something on my pinky finger. I pull the ring off my finger and hide it in my palm as I kneel in front of her. This is much more difficult than it was nearly thirty years ago when I did it the first time.

The whispers of people around us causes Rosie to turn her attention back to me. The look of astonishment on her face is priceless. "Isaac Roguen, what in the world are you doing? You'll catch a terrible cold. The ground is soaking wet!"

"Come now Rosie, has it really been so long that you don't remember what it's like for a man to profess his undying love and to ask his beloved for her hand in marriage?" I ask with a teasing lilt in my voice. "Come to think of it, you didn't think I was serious the first time I asked you either."

"Speaking of forgetting, you silly man, did you forget I'm already married to you?"

"Well, that's up for debate. It's complicated since you had me declared dead and you remarried someone else. To address any questions about the matter, I would like to say to the world despite all the things which happened between us, I would happily marry you all over again, Rosa Marie Cisneros Betancourt Roguen. I never stopped loving you for a millisecond of time. Rosie Roguen, will you marry me?"

"Isaac Randall Roguen, before I go any further, please get off the ground," Rosa instructs with a teary smile.

After she helps me to my feet, we walk over to a wrought iron bench and sit down. She faces me and takes my hands into hers. "Isaac, my heart, I never stopped thinking of you as my husband, even when I was married to Clive. It's probably why our marriage didn't work. Well — that and the fact that he's a moron," Rosie quips.

I laugh out loud at Rosa's sense of humor. I've missed it so much. She doesn't ever seem to plan her jokes in advance. They just seem to flow naturally from her genuinely funny outlook on life.

"But, in the beginning of our relationship, Clive vaguely reminded me of the way you used to make me feel. He would leave notes in my lunchbox and have flowers delivered to me at work. For the first time in a long time, I remembered what it was like to be in love. I realize now that I was never in love with Clive, I was in love with the feeling of being in love. I could never fall in love with Clive or anyone else because I never fell out of love with you," she confesses.

"I hear you saying you still love me and I still love you. Does that mean you'll marry me?" I clarify.

"*Si*, you silly, sweet man. I will marry you. I don't know when since we'll be busy with the girls' weddings right around the corner."

"Would you like to get married right now, in Paris?" I ask after I've kissed her thoroughly. I can't believe how much I've missed the simple act of kissing my wife. "I don't know about you, but I have been away from you for far too long. I am ready to pick up the pieces of our life again and be your husband as it should've been all along. We had such dreams for our lives when we were young, perhaps it's time to live them now."

"Isaac, I don't understand. How is it even possible?" Rosie exclaims, with hope and fear warring in her eyes.

"Well, it turns out the young man I work for is very resourceful," I respond, gathering Rosa in a loose embrace and fiddling with her long hair. "All you need to do is show up at room 207 at six o'clock tonight and everyone will take care of everything you need," I explain. This is going to be interesting for sure. I hope my future son-in-law knows what he's doing.

EPILOGUE

ROSA

BEFORE I KNOCK ON THE hotel door, I look down at what I'm wearing and shake my head in dismay. No self-respecting woman wants to get married wearing purple rain boots with poodles carrying umbrellas and an orange and purple striped scarf. What was that crazy husband of mine thinking? Who gets married on the same day they get asked? I guess the good side is I don't have to worry about stressing over losing twenty pounds before I get married. But there are many things to worry about. Do we even know a minister who speaks English or Spanish? We're in France, after all.

Even as I am mid-knock, Rogue answers the door. My daughter fibbed to me! I talked to her no more than two hours ago and she made it sound like she was getting ready to go to bed because she had a long day planned at the tattoo shop. As I step into the hotel room, I discover she's not the only one when Ivy comes out of the bathroom carrying a dress which looks very much like the wedding dress I wore for my first wedding.

"How in the world did you girls pull this off?" I demand as I pull them into a tight hug.

As soon as Rogue can breathe again, she laughs lightly. "As it turns out, it's a handy thing to have a guy who likes to fly to Paris on random Tuesdays fall in love with you. What's even better is when he doesn't mind flying in a bunch of your friends and family members too. Happy wedding day, Mama!"

"You weren't kidding when you said that boy was the nicest man you've ever met. Your heart has chosen well."

I look around the room and notice some other people. I recognize Rogue's coworker Jade. But, I'm not sure about the little redhead. It is nice to have another normal-sized person in this land of the giants.

When she sees me studying her trying to figure out who she is, she steps forward and extends her hand for me to shake. "Hello, my name is Jessica Walker, I'm Ivy's roommate from college. I'm also the granddaughter of your minister today. You might want to hold on tight, Grandpa can tend to go off script a bit if the spirit moves him," she adds with a grin.

For some reason, this strikes me as funny and I start to laugh so hard tears stream down my face.

"Are you all right, Mama Rosa?" Ivy asks as she hangs my dress and veil in the corner of the room.

"I'm fine," I gasp, between giggles. "There is no script for this crazy life of ours. Your grandpa sounds like he will fit right in with this bunch. If you think about it, everybody in the ceremony was supposedly dead at one point or another. So, if you want to call this 'The

Incredible Wedding' I suppose you could, even without considering the fact that we're having it the same day I got asked."

"There is no doubt my grandpa Walter will fit into your clan. He was struck by lightning while digging up potatoes from his yard in the middle of a rainstorm. The doctors declared him dead, but he woke up on the way to the morgue."

"That's a story almost as strange as ours. You're right, I think he'll probably fit in just fine."

Jade steps forward. "Come on, I'm your one-woman makeover team. Let's go get you beautified for your big day."

Since my own *madre* passed away years ago, in a strange twist of fate, my own daughters are escorting me down the aisle to marry the man I never thought I'd see alive again.

They leave me at the end of the aisle to be tended to by Jessica who is standing in as one of the bridesmaids. It is very easy to understand why she is one of Ivy's best friends because she is a bright spot of laughter and sharp wit. She is exactly the comic relief I need to steady my nerves on a day like today. I know it seems odd for me to be nervous about marrying the person I've been married to for over a quarter of a century. Still, it all seems very new to me.

The first time we got married, we said our vows in the small courtyard by the courthouse where I was going to school. It seems like such a mundane, stupid reason now. We were struggling to make ends meet while I was a student. When they changed the way they calculated grants, it seemed I might get more financial aid if we were married. We went shopping for a wedding dress at a thrift store and got food with our best friends at a grocery store deli and headed over to the courthouse. There was enough of a break in the weather we were able to do a small ceremony with the judge and the file clerk outside in the little courtyard area. It was very sweet. It was almost as if we were having a real glamorous wedding.

When I see the expression on Isaac's face, I wonder if he's having the same thoughts. Watching our daughters walk up the beautifully appointed aisle with perfect synchronization and grace in a historic building with massive paintings on the walls and ceilings like a fancy museum is surreal. I am filled with pride. Our daughters are beautiful women inside and out. All three men are up at the front of the small church wearing identical expressions of complete awe and adoration.

I'm so caught up in the moment of watching Tristan and Marcus admire my beautiful daughters, I'm taken by surprise when we reach the front of the church. Jessica whispers to me as she straightens out my train, "Look at the expression on your husband's face, Mrs. R. He still thinks you're as beautiful as the day you met. Someday, I want someone to look at me that way. Go marry the man who holds your heart."

"It is so true. Isaac Roguen has owned my heart since the day he found me hanging upside down on the side of the road. Nothing much has changed in all these years, he still rights my world yet makes my heart flip when he walks into a room," I answer softly as the two ministers get situated at the front of the church.

The one I presume to be Jessica's grandfather steps forward and fiddles with his lapel mic. "Hello? Hello? Umm hello, I am Walter Walker. I'm the American minister. There are two pastors here today just to make sure we're all legal-eagle since Mr. And Mrs. Roguen are getting married in fancy-schmancy 'Pay-ri'. I can't say I've ever been called on to remarry a couple who've never actually divorced, but I guess there's a first time for everything."

Jessica rolls her eyes as she addresses her grandfather, "Grandpa, they might appreciate a little less commentary and a little more tradition."

Pastor Walker looks up at Jessica, as if he's startled by her presence. "Oh hi Buttercup! You look very pretty today. You may have a point." He clears his throat and turns to the wedding party and says, "Dearly beloved, we are here today to remarry two people who should've never been separated. It is clear they are still very much in love. I have officiated many weddings throughout my thirty-three years as a minister and I have a sense for these things. I think this marriage is meant for eternity. Do you all agree?"

Everyone in the sanctuary nods solemnly except for Marcus who declares quite heartily, "Heck yes!"

Everyone including the French officiant laughs at his outburst.

"Since you all have done this before and you know all the technicalities, I'm gonna skip to the good stuff." He turns to the twins and asks, "Technically, I guess I need to ask this, and it's just a guess here — based on the huge grins on your faces — I'm going to assume you ladies are the ones giving your parents away and you approve of this wedding?"

In perfect unison, the twins respond, "Yes, we do."

"I figured as much, but I have to go by the book. Now that we've gotten that out of the way, shall we continue?"

I reflexively nod as I grip Isaac's hand. I had forgotten how emotional this simple ceremony can be.

"Isaac please look at your beautiful bride as you commit to these vows."

Isaac takes both of my hands in his and smiles down at me. I have a moment of déjà vu as I remember the same expression on his face from our last wedding. He may be older, but he is still the most handsome man I've ever seen in my whole life.

"Isaac Randall Roguen, do you take — I apologize in advance if I get this wrong; it's a very long name — Rosa Marie Cisneros Betancourt, to be your wife? Do you promise to love, honor, cherish and protect her, forsaking all others and holding only to her forevermore?"

Isaac is a man who plays his cards very close to his vest. I rarely see him publicly display emotions. Yet, a tear escapes and trickles down his cheek before Tristan silently hands him a handkerchief. He clears his throat and discreetly wipes his face before stoically saying, "I do."

The rare show of emotion is almost my complete undoing. Fortunately, Rogue notices my distress and slips me a folded Kleenex. I delicately wipe my nose and wait for Pastor Walker to continue.

The pastor turns to me and says, "That's a very handsome man you have there; would you please look at him while you commit to these vows?"

"Rosa Marie Cisneros Betancourt, do you take Isaac Randall Roguen, to be your husband? Do you promise to love, honor, cherish and protect him, forsaking all others and holding only to him forevermore?"

"Absolutely, I do."

"I suspect you all have rings to exchange," the pastor states looking at Isaac expectantly.

Panicked, I glance over at Ivy and Rogue. After a couple of seconds, Ivy gives me a thumbs up. Tristan fishes a box out of his pocket and hands it to Rogue who hands it to me.

"I'm sure these two have a few words to say to each other. If not, I can make up a few appropriate ones."

"Geez Grandpa, this is their wedding day, not improv night at the Eagles Lodge!" Jessica mutters under her breath.

Isaac quietly coughs and announces, "I have something I'd like to say."

"By all means son, the floor is yours." Pastor Walker says as he hands Isaac the microphone.

Isaac takes my left hand and places the ring on it but doesn't let me see it. However, he doesn't need to. It may have been twenty-two years, but my heart has never forgotten the feel of my ring. I have no idea how he has managed to accomplish this miracle. I had to sell every bit of jewelry I owned including this ring when Rogue had to have her appendix taken out. If I hadn't done it, we would have lost our house to foreclosure. The medical bills were simply too high. It absolutely broke my heart. I cried for months afterwards — just as I am bawling openly today.

Although he's typically one for observing formalities — especially in church, Isaac gathers me into a gentle embrace and whispers, "This is not a day for sorrow, it is a day for new beginnings, my sweet Rosie."

"How in the world?" I start to ask.

"Our soon-to-be son-in-law is an incredibly smart man," Isaac explains.

"He is and he loves our daughter very much," I agree.

I look over to Tristan and mouth, "Thank you" as I try to collect myself and discreetly blow my nose on the tissue Rogue gave me earlier.

Isaac takes my hand again. "The first time I was married to you, I got to be by your side for four years, seven months, twelve days and nine hours. I made a tragic error and messed it up. I almost lost everything that was ever important to me. We used to have a ritual. Every time you would take the ring off to do the dishes, mop the floor or help me build furniture, I would place the ring on your finger as if it were the very first time. I know you thought it was a silly little game. Yet, to me it meant the world. It was my way of showing you I fell in love with you each and every day. Rosie, I want you to know when you look at this ring, it's not a sign of all the days we've missed, it's a sign of all the days I've fallen in love with you over and over. I never gave up on our love even when we were apart because my heart always belonged to you."

Isaac adjusts the ring on my finger and kisses it like he's done a thousand times before. "Rosa Marie Cisneros Betancourt Roguen, please take this ring as a sign of my love and commitment. I will love you in good times and in bad and I will never again forsake you."

I nod mutely with tears streaming down my face. "Of course, I have never truly loved anyone else," I manage to croak through my tears.

Ivy hands me a bottle of water and some tissue. "It's all right Mama, take a minute. We could all use a second. Your love story packs quite a punch."

When I can breathe without sobbing, I retrieve the ring from the box Rogue handed me. By now, I think I'm emotionally prepared for what I see. Yet, it's still difficult to see Isaac's ring nestled in the velvet. I can see the inscription that reads, "My life, my heart". With trembling hands I place the ring on Isaac's strong masculine hand.

"Even when I had to try to pick up the pieces of my life and move on when the world told me you were dead, there was a piece of my heart which always felt your presence. I don't think it was any coincidence I always called you my heart in Spanish. For that's what you've always been to me — as vital as my heartbeat. Without you in my life, I felt as if I had no identity or purpose.

You were literally my counterbalance. The person in all the world who perfectly balances me. When you were gone, I felt like a mere shell of myself. Now that you're back, my true identity of the heart has returned. I hope you don't mind, but I never plan for us to be separate again. It was just too painful."

"I don't plan to go anywhere, Rosie. You're stuck with me," Isaac responds.

"In that case, Isaac Randall Roguen, please take this ring as a symbol of my love and faithfulness. It is a symbol that my love has no beginning or end and will be there always."

"I can't tell you how good it feels to have this ring on my finger again Rosie. I never thought I'd see our family back together again," Isaac says as he studies the ring.

Pastor Walker clears his throat from pent-up emotion as he declares, "I think I know when to wrap things up." He turns to the other officiant and asks, "How did I do Pastor Laurent? Did I hit all the necessary highlights?"

The French pastor smiles kindly, nods vigorously and responds, "*Oui, très bien.*"

"Well, I guess my job here is done, by the power vested in me as a minister in the state of Florida, New Jersey and Kentucky, I now pronounce you husband and wife. Isaac, you may now kiss Rosa." Pastor Walker instructs as he starts to turn away. "Oh, and if that wasn't official enough the French government also says you're married. Try not to get unmarried this time, okay?"

Isaac chuckles as he gathers me in his arms and

kisses me very thoroughly. After a minute or so I hear Marcus mumble, "Maybe we should give them some privacy…"

"I think they might appreciate that. After all, they have quite a bit of time to make up for," remarks Tristan as he escorts the wedding party out the door. As they're leaving, I hear Rogue tell Tristan, "You know, I wouldn't mind if our next trip to Paris ended a little something like this and I don't think I mind random Tuesdays anymore —"

The End (for now)

You can continue to follow the adventures of Rogue and Ivy and all their friends in Sheltered Hearts (A Hidden Hearts Novel #2)

Note from the Author

Dear Reader,

Thanks for giving my book a read. If you liked reading about people who are not so stereotypical, then I've got good news…

…there's more.

The spotlight suits Jessica Walker.

Jessica feels like she's always waiting in the wings for love. She finds a dog as pathetic as she feels. Dogs are great at unconditional love. They never judge you for your past.

She names her Hope. Is the dog a sign of things to come?

You'll love how she meets Mitch and the twists that lead to them trying for a new future.

If you love sweet romance with a hint of mystery, *Sheltered Hearts* is for you.

Get it now in paperback, in ebook format or read it through Kindle Unlimited for free.

~Mary

Because love matters, differences don't.

ACKNOWLEDGEMENTS

This book was an absolute labor of love for me. It's deep and complex, just like life. None of the relationships are simple and they are ever-changing.

There is no simple, one-size-fits-all definition of family. Sometimes, your family is who you're born to. Sometimes, your family is who you're adopted by. Sometimes, your friends become your family. For some of us, it's a lucky combination of all three.

I was asked what I thought would be the central message of this book. As an author, I always hesitate to answer that question because I think reading is a very personal experience and what each reader takes from a book may be very different for everyone.

Having said that, here's what I hope to convey. Even though you may think you know someone's story, you don't really know their story until you've sat down and had a conversation with them (or several). That is true whether you're trying to understand someone's family history, employment history or their health issues.

In my career as a Disability Advocate, people often ask me, "Which is the most challenging disability?" My answer is always—without a single doubt: an invisible disability. Conditions like Asperger's syndrome, sensory integration dysfunction, obsessive-compulsive disorder, diabetes, fibromyalgia or lupus can radically impact the way you interact with the world, yet to the outside world you appear absolutely normal. This is a hard concept for people to understand. When I drive my big power chair around, people instinctively understand I might need some help. But, if a person with sensory integration disorder is having difficulty in the checkout line of a busy grocery store, it's far more difficult to explain. But just because it's hard to explain doesn't mean the struggle isn't present.

Awareness is the key. I've made it my mission to include characters of all types in my books whether you can see the differences or not. I want to make my characters more true to life. I hope you'll support my endeavor and tell your friends and family about my books. Additionally, if this book spoke to you, please take the time to leave a review.

As a writer, I spend a lot of time working on each project by myself. But this book was a little different. I've had some great outside help from my friends who generously volunteered their time to make sure it was the best it could possibly be even when I sprung a surprise deadline on everyone. I'm going to name some people, if you've helped with this book and I've forgotten you, I deeply apologize and cite extreme fatigue as my excuse.

First, I want to think Cindy McPhetridge for being so enthusiastic about my crazy idea when I first ran it past you several months ago. Thank you for our crazy plot building session at Block 15 in Corvallis. It is my firm belief that every restaurant should have tables that resemble chalkboards and provide multicolored chalk just for fun.

There aren't enough thanks on the planet for my proofreading/beta reading team of Christine DuVal, Ruth Hawes, Heather Truett, Annie Angelich and Laurie Reber.

I also appreciate the tireless efforts of Michelle Elliott-Storer, Heather Lange-Wilson, Rachel Bostwick and Antonia Trujillo. You all work incredibly hard to get the word out about my books. Your efforts don't go unnoticed.

I'd be remiss if I did not thank my husband and my sons for their incredible patience through this process. Being the spouse and child of a writer is an incredibly thankless job. We tend to function in a constant state of sleep deprivation and do things like forget to cook for weeks at a time when were in the middle of a project. Thank you so much for being my biggest fans despite all of this. I couldn't do this without you in my corner. I love you all.

Resources

Here are some links to some resources that you might find helpful. This is not meant to be an exhaustive list and inclusion on this list is not meant to be an endorsement of any particular website over another.

Habitat for Humanity (http://www.habitat.org)

A nonprofit Christian organization that supports providing decent affordable housing across the globe using donated resources and volunteer labor. In the US, recipient households secure low rate financing to help pay for their Habitat for Humanity homes. Habitat for Humanity also runs Re-Stores to repurpose building supplies from remodeling projects.

Adoption.com (http://www.Adoption.com)

This is a website that examines adoption from all perspectives. It gives resources if you are pregnant and looking to give up a child for adoption as well as having resources for prospective adoptive parents. Additionally, there is a registry for people who are seeking their relatives who have been separated through the process of adoption. These resources are listed by state and specialty.

Sensory Processing Disorder Foundation (http://spdfoundation.net/about-sensory-processing-disorder/spdadults) This is a very comprehensive site about sensory processing disorder. It specifically addresses how sensory processing disorder presents in adults. It includes several personal stories and some helpful tips for coping with symptoms as well as ways to talk to medical professionals and employers.

Obsessive-Compulsive Disorder Help Guide (http://www.helpguide.org/articles/anxiety/obsessive-compulsive-disorder-ocd.htm)

This is a site dedicated to providing resources to people with obsessive-compulsive disorder including a checklist to help you talk to your doctor. It also includes some coping techniques and a screening guide.

Asthma Resources from the American Lung Association (http://www.lung.org/associations/charters/midland-states/program-information/asthma/caare/resources.html)

This site lists medical and educational resources for the most recent treatments for asthma and other related lung conditions in children and adults.

Big Brother/Big Sister Organization (http://www.bbbs.org/)

A nonprofit organization that seeks to serve at risk youth by matching them with community mentors to do recreational and educational activities. This site will allow you to find a program within your community and volunteer.

Americans for the Arts (http://www.americansforthearts.org)

A nonprofit organization that promotes free art education in public school. This site has lots of good information for teachers and community organizations.

About the Author

I HAVE BEEN LUCKY enough to live my own version of a romance novel. I married the guy who kissed me at summer camp. He told me on the night we met that he was going to marry me and be the father of my children.

Eventually, I stopped giggling when he said it, and we've been married for over thirty years. We have two children. The oldest is a Doctor of Osteopathy. He is across the United States completing his residency, but when he's done, he is going to come back to Oregon and practice Family Medicine. Our youngest son is now tackling high school and where he is an honor student. He is interested in becoming an EMT.

I write full time now. I have published more than thirty books and have several more underway. I volunteer my time to a variety of causes. I have worked as a Civil Rights Attorney and diversity advocate. I spent several years working for various social service agencies before becoming an attorney.

In my spare time, I love to cook, decorate cakes and of

course, I obsessively, compulsively read.

I would be honored if you would take a few moments out of your busy day to check out my website,

MaryCrawfordAuthor.com. While you're there, you can sign up for my newsletter and get a free book. I will be announcing my upcoming books and giving sneak peeks as well as sponsoring giveaways and giving you information about other interesting events.

If you have questions or comments, please E-mail me at Mary@MaryCrawfordAuthor.com or find me on the following social networks:

Facebook: www.facebook.com/authormarycrawford

Website: MaryCrawfordAuthor.com

Twitter: www.twitter.com/MaryCrawfordAut